I0635793

Capscovil and their authors support several non-profit
organisations.
For further information please visit:

www.capscovil.com

Acknowledgements

Heartfelt gratitude goes to Niall Sellar for translating and Helen Veitch for editing. Both have done another exceptional job, continuing to be indispensable partners for Capscovil.

About the Author

Stephan Schwarz was born in the north of Germany. When he is not writing crime novels featuring his lead characters Felix Büschelberger and Emilio Perfondo, he is travelling around the globe in connection with his day job.

He currently lives with his wife in a small town just outside of Munich.

Connect with the author: http://about.me/schwarzstephan

STEPHAN SCHWARZ

ELECTRIFIED

Translated by NIALL SELLAR

A CAPSCOVIL BOOK | GLONN | GERMANY

Original edition „Krötenmord" published by Capscovil Verlag, Glonn,
Germany, December 2011

*

First International English Edition
Perfect Paperback
Copyright © Capscovil Verlag, 2012
Published by Capscovil Verlag, Glonn, Germany, September 2012
ISBN Print 978-3-942358-22-4

Design: Capscovil Verlag, Glonn, Germany
Editor: Helen Veitch
Printed by: Lightning Source
Capscovil® is a registered trademark of Britta Muzyk

Additional electronic editions are available for various reading devices
and platforms.

www.capscovil.com

Attention: Organizations and Corporations

For information on exclusive editions or special offers for sales
promotions, premiums or fund-raising, please write to:

projects@capscovil.com

"Whenever you find yourself on the side of the majority, it is time to pause and reflect."

— Mark Twain (1835-1910) —

Chapter 1

A steady drizzle was beating down through the beam of the head-lights as Felix Büschelberger parked his car on the empty road. He sighed. The rain would soak him through again and it wasn't exactly an especially warm evening to start with. Then his gaze fell upon his two companions. They were also staring out into the darkness. Only their faces weren't lined with doubt; they displayed the sort of keen anticipation that is common in all people who truly believe in what they are doing.

Just then the lights on the car behind him went off and two more of his companions emerged. Both were wearing reflective orange jackets and carrying little blue plastic buckets. Felix allowed himself a smile at last: This was no ordinary night – tonight, he didn't have to solve any murders; he was here to cheat death with his four friends. Tonight, on this stretch of road halfway between Langenhain and Eppstein, there would be no crime.

The five of them spread out along the road and began to shine their torches up and down. There was a toad-crossing here. Pitted against their heavily motorized adversaries, the amphibians had little chance of reaching the lakes on the other side, where their mating spots lay. Felix picked up his first toad of the evening, a male that clung immediately to his middle finger. Astonishing how these little creatures reacted to movement of any kind.

They didn't notice when they crawled past a stationary female, but the slightest movement in the grass would send them into a tizzy. He slipped the toad off his finger and placed it in the bucket. Afterwards they would count and catalogue them, before releasing them once more.

Felix picked up another toad, a female this time, piggybacked by two males. She croaked several times in quick succession before being transferred to the bucket. He had often wondered what these animals were trying to tell him. In the glow of his torchlight, he could see it was going to be a good haul and remembered how his group had managed to save over 3,000 toads during the migration period two years ago.

There had even been a little article in the local paper, alongside a photo of everyone who'd helped, taken at some party or another. Naturally, it hadn't taken long for the report to find its way into the police station where Felix worked, earning him the nickname "Chief Inspector Frog." It had been pointless trying to explain to his colleagues that it wasn't frogs they saved, but toads. That would only have added fuel to the fire. A week later, a giant inflatable frog had appeared in his office. It was just sitting there in the corner one morning when he came in to work, and had given everyone a good chuckle.

Felix had left it at that and the frog was still there to this day. His colleagues had never understood why he continued to devote so much of precious free time to these creatures each spring, but the truth was he enjoyed it. It felt right, and all those who helped were idealists. Since his job involved dealing with violent criminals on a daily basis, these people were important for his mental stability.

Petra, for example, who was picking up toads next to him, was a marketing manager for a big Frankfurt company. Once they had bumped into each other at the mall and he had barely recognized her in her Gucci trouser suit, all made up and clad in ridiculously expensive designer shoes. Right now she wasn't wearing any make-up at all, just faded jeans and a baggy jumper under her protective jacket, with both hands deep inside a bucket full off toads. Idealists, people who still believed in something – yes, that was how he'd ended up with this group, and the reason he'd stayed.

The atmosphere was lively, in spite of the weather. As usual, they were competing to see who could find the biggest she-toad with the most males on her back, and, as usual, Petra was sure to win. She seemed to know exactly where to look. The first buckets had already been taken over to the other side, complete with their crawling contents. Things were going well with the second batch too, when suddenly Petra cried: "Four on one, I win!"

Her laughter was still ringing out in the night air as Felix and the others came over to look. A four-leaf clover– their technical term for this arrangement - was rare, and they all wanted to see it for themselves; besides, it came as a welcome little break. They

8

stood closely together, goofing around and looking at the tangle of toads under the light of Petra's torch. No-one heard the heavy vehicle approaching at high speed from Langenhain.

It wasn't until it was barely seconds away that they eventually took notice of the dark BMW 5 series suddenly careering round the bend, blinding them with its xenon headlights. It veered off the road, heading straight for them. Felix threw himself on Petra and managed to get her to safety. The others also responded just in time. But still the car caught two of their buckets and sent them high into the air, before disappearing seconds later in the direction of Eppstein.

Peace descended once more over the darkened road, and for what seemed like an age, no-one said a word. Then Petra began to groan. Jochen, the group's founder, cursed loudly and unleashed a volley of expletives.

Felix thought only of the smell of Petra's hair as his memory transported him back to an evening two years before. She had made him a pretty clear offer but, as a recent divorcé, he had felt disinclined to accept.

He forced himself to return to the present, and dragged himself up. Then he helped Petra to her feet and asked if anyone had been hurt. All of them responded in the negative, though their oaths and obscenities were testament to the anger they felt.

"Couldn't you have shot at the tires?" asked Eric, the youngest of the group.

"I think you watch too many American action movies," Felix replied. He couldn't help laughing though, as he imagined himself valiantly firing his gun in the wake of the fleeing car. "Besides, it would be illegal. Did anyone manage to get the registration number? I could only read F-MS and even then I'm not so sure."

But no-one had seen anything. One of the buckets lay destroyed about fifty feet away; the second had vanished completely. Unsurprisingly, none of the toads had survived the accident.

The atmosphere was heavy. They collected toads for a further half hour, and then set off back towards Frankfurt. As they went their separate ways, Felix promised to investigate the driver of the BMW the next morning.

Back at home, he took a hot shower. He loved the feeling of warm water running down his body. But the whole time all he could think of was Petra. He could still perceive the scent of her hair, and the memory of lying on top of her made him feel aroused. Sitting down in the living room he poured himself a glass of the red wine he had opened the previous evening. It was dark red and dry with a berry flavor: just the way he liked it.

But where on earth was Django? He looked around. Django was his grey tomcat; adopted a few years back during the Alex M. murder. There had been no next of kin and the animal shelter had wanted to put their latest four-legged acquisition down. Who would want to take home a cat that was missing an ear and that wasn't exactly the cutest in the first place!

The inspector couldn't bear the thought of the tom meeting his maker this way and since then, the two of them had formed a bizarre team. Django seemed to sense when his human cohabitant needed a quiet, sympathetic ear.

In return for this service, all he demanded was to be allowed to come and go at liberty – and that his food bowl be filled on his return. Otherwise, Felix could bring home whomever he pleased. They all met with Django's approval, usually expressed in the latter's total disregard for the visitor in question.

On this particular evening, however, his sixth sense appeared to have deserted him. Felix would have to talk to himself if he wanted someone to listen. Sighing softly, he was just about to pour himself another glass of wine when a stray cat paw scratched against the living room window and demanded entry.

"There you are, my friend. I thought you'd forgotten about me."

The animal disappeared into the kitchen where his feeding dish awaited. Felix stayed in the living room. There was no point giving him the hurry-up; Django would come when he was good and ready. Indeed, just a little later he hopped onto the living room table and settled down in his favorite corner. His ear was pricked in anticipation and he was looking at Felix as if to say: "Come on, tell me all about it."

His tail dangled over the edge of the table and moved in time to Felix's account.

"You were nearly orphaned today, though everything worked out OK in the end. The only thing is I can't think of anything but Petra since it happened. And that, I suspect, is a problem." Felix was aware how muddled he sounded. He looked the cat in the eye. "You think I'm babbling, don't you?"

Django blinked and yawned, then had a good stretch.

"OK, understood. I'll call her tomorrow and then we'll see what happens." Felix emptied his glass and released the animal back into the night. Then he turned out the lights.

The inspector entered the office at quarter past eight and greeted his colleagues, who were already in the midst of their early morning tea ritual. Emilio was on spiced black tea at the moment – Syrian style today, with a hint of cinnamon and cardamom; Frauke, like the inspector, had a preference for green tea; and Arno only drank East Frisian tea, which his mother would send him specially from Aurich. Arno didn't even trust the blends in the tea shops here in Frankfurt.

Frauke handed Felix his cup. "I've made sundew tea for us today!"

He smiled at her and couldn't help thinking about the strange reputation enjoyed by his team. He didn't know of any other unit that consisted solely of tea drinkers. Java consumption might have been high elsewhere; here it was practically non-existent.

"Before we discuss our brief for today, I'd like you to check a registration number for me," the inspector turned to Arno. "It's a black or dark blue BMW 5 Series, partial registration F-MS."

"That's odd. We got a call twenty minutes ago about a male corpse that has been found in a vehicle at the east port. A black 530d, registration number F-NS 609. Looks like suicide at first glance. Police and forensics are on-site already; the case will probably be assigned to us."

Felix looked at Frauke, who had surprised him with this information, and felt a tingling sensation. Could it be true? He wasn't even sure he'd made the number plate out properly.

The telephone rang. He answered. "Murder squad, fourth district, Chief Inspector Büschelberger."

It was the DA, Cando. "Good morning. I hope the tea break's over because I have work for you. You've heard about the dead man at the east port? I want your team to take the case; all other units are conducting on-going investigations. Good luck." Cando hung up without waiting for a response.

Felix looked at his colleagues. "Frauke was right as usual, we're on. So, Emilio and I will head out there. Arno, use the registration number to find out what you can about the owner. Check if there's a license plate with MS while you're at it. And you, Frauke, you take care of the admin side of things. We'll meet here when we get back."

Emilio had the keys in his hands already and was reaching for his jacket; Felix meanwhile drained the contents of his mug, burning his mouth in the process. Still swearing under his breath, he climbed into the black Focus, a Lazio FC sticker adorning its trunk. Though it was against regulations, the inspector tolerated it because Emilio was reliability personified. If need be he would work through the night and on weekends, even though he was the only one who was still married.

This Ford Focus was the second reason the unit was viewed as rather special. The Mayoress of Frankfurt, a Green, had purchased ten electric vehicles of this make and required volunteers to test their suitability for public service functions. Felix was the first and only policeman to have ordered an EV for his unit – but ultimately even Emilio, the Italian car friend, had grown to appreciate the zippy number.

The car hummed softly as they shot out from the courtyard. Emilio always drove as if he was on the racetrack at Monza. During the journey Felix smiled as he recalled the discussions concerning the benefits of an EV. His colleague had harbored reservations about its acceleration performance. After all, the Focus offered five full-sized passenger seats and a high load capacity. Would it be fast enough for them?

It was an argument their test drives had countered with ease. An EV had a better acceleration ratio than many cars with internal combustion engines. Besides, even Emilio had to admit that high speed car chases occurred only very rarely. In truth, it was the discussion surrounding the car's range which had proved the more problematic.

In rough conditions, such as driving through rush hour on a cold winter's day, the Focus should still be able to do 100 miles fully charged, since the braking force was converted back into energy, recuperating the battery. Emilio had once managed a trip of 110 miles non-stop, but always with a careful eye on the special visuals in the instrument cluster. The telematic system calculated the possible extra range he could go beyond the next charging station, and this was represented as little blue butterflies on the dashboard. Charging the Focus normally took just under four hours if connected to a 240V charging station.

A statistical evaluation of all company and state owned vehicles had revealed that police patrol cars covered an average of 60 miles per day. This meant that it would be risky if they had to go on a longer trip and needed to use every feature the car was offering; both Felix and the Mayoress were well aware of it. With the trial, they hoped to find out how much the use of flashing blue lights and sirens drained the battery and thus affected the vehicle's range.

The Focus was equipped with a telematic system featuring an 8-inch display which together with the instrument cluster made Emilio feel like he was sitting in a sci-fi command center. Its GPS system offered a special feature to calculate the most economical route. And the system could also be remotely controlled to pre-program charging, or to switch on the HVAC prior to setting off. It had become second nature for Emilio to connect the Focus to the charging station as soon as he got back to headquarters.

An added advantage of the EV, the one that had finally convinced the Italian, was its handling. As the batteries were located on the underside of the vehicle, its center of gravity was very low, allowing Emilio to take each bend as though driving a Ferrari. The final point in favor of this zippy electric speedster was the result of the crash test: it had shown the car to be just as safe as comparable vehicles with conventional internal combustion engines. Moreover, the car's power supply was deactivated as soon as the airbag was released – so there was no chance of passengers or passers-by being electrocuted.

They reached the east port in record time.

"Come by plane, did you?" asked Chief Constable Müller, as they came screeching to a halt in front of him.

Felix liked Müller. Always calm, he had seen it all before and collected a wealth of experience during his thirty years in the force, which he made available to anyone who wished to draw on it.

The inspector gave him a friendly tap on the shoulder. "You've seen how Emilio drives; one of these days, we will take off. But he must have made a pact with some saint or another – no accidents yet, despite his kamikaze style. So, what have you got for me?"

Emilio rolled his eyes, growling audibly as he followed the pair to the site where the body had been found. Sometimes the joke just wasn't funny.

"The corpse is male, thirty-nine years old. He was in the driver's seat; exhaust fumes entered the cabin through a tube. Thanks to the driver's license we've already managed to make a positive ID: the deceased is a Dr. Uwe Kaptain, registered as living here in Frankfurt at 16 Beethovenstraße. He was discovered at nine minutes past seven this morning by a jogger, who then tried to resuscitate him. However, he very quickly realized it was pointless. Those are the bare facts. But if you ask me, I have a strange feeling about this. I don't think it was suicide, though I couldn't tell you exactly why."

A red and white ribbon cordoned off a wide area around the site. Felix saw the forensics team working around the BMW, trying to secure the evidence. At the helm was Dr. Kevin Dour, the best man possible for the job. He was a pathologist with a second doctorate in philosophy, and enjoyed a very good reputation among experts. In tricky cases, his opinion was sought nationwide – even though he was known to be extremely moody.

With the inevitable cigarette sandwiched between his lips, he was busying himself with something in the car grille. Felix couldn't remember ever having seen Dr. Dour without a cigarette. He even smoked during autopsies. In fact, he had probably been born with one of those things in his mouth.

Both men respected one another and were on friendly terms. As well as Dr. Dour's team, there were also three police officers present, one of whom was currently speaking with a man in running gear.

"Felix, check this out!" called out the pathologist.

"Be there in a sec," he replied and turned towards Emilio. "Take a statement from the jogger so he can go home. But get him to stop by tomorrow so we can take his fingerprints and run a comparison. If he wants, the police can drive him." He pointed the two officers standing around looking bored.

Emilio nodded. Felix silently took everything in once more. First impressions of the site were important; he needed to take it slow. After all, it could also have been the crime scene.

This was his only chance. If he slipped up here, he might overlook an important clue. It was his first partner who had taught him that and, as so often before, he had been right. Felix still met the now-retired Chief Inspector Ludwig Ruebens from time to time. They would discuss Felix's current cases over a few bottles of beer; although these opportunities were becoming increasingly rarely these days.

In the background the inspector saw the Frankfurt skyline – or Mainhattan, as it was often called. The river Main ran along it, all cold and grey. Given the vehicle's position, the driver must have been looking at the skyline as the fumes filled his lungs. Night-time, the city in lights: a spectacular view for sure.

Otherwise there was nothing out of the ordinary and so Felix went over to see the pathologist, who, to his amazement, was grinning broadly. Dr. Dour was a fitting name: he wasn't a man with a particularly well-developed sense of humor. Right now he was leaning against the grille, lighting another cigarette.

"I was starting to think that you weren't interested in my discovery." He displayed his wolfish grin once more, before stepping to one side and pointing to the lower part of the grille. "An interesting mascot, very rare I'd say."

Felix realized immediately what Dr. Dour was referring to. The toad wedged into the middle of the grille was indeed a bizarre sight. It seemed that the driver from the previous evening had been found.

"I knew this would please our Frog Prince," the pathologist smiled.

"Chief Inspector Frog, I'll have you know. Besides, it looks more like a common toad to me," Felix replied.

"Exactly. A member of the Bufo bufo genus. An unusual cause of death at any rate. I've never seen our local amphibians jump so high as to get caught in mid-flight. You know as well as I do that the majority die on the road – and not because they've been hit either. The high air pressure generated by the cars as they speed over them causes their innards to burst. The French developed a weapon in the mid-eighties that operated on a similar principle. They used sound waves to provoke internal bleeding in their enemies. But I digress. Anyway, I've no idea how our little friend made it up here." Dr. Dour glanced at the dead toad.

"That I can tell you. I was out with my environmental group yesterday evening. We were almost run down by this car; the driver wiped out two of the buckets we'd been using to collect toads. One of them must have been catapulted into the air, landing here. We've been trying to identify the driver. Guess I don't need to anymore."

The inspector scratched his head. Dour whistled through his teeth.

"Well, just be careful that they don't try and pin a motive on you!" Then he smiled, revealing his nicotine stained teeth. "But all joking aside, the man's been dead for at least five hours and I can't believe he died through carbon monoxide poisoning. His face is the wrong color – it just doesn't seem grey enough. Of course I won't know anything for sure until after the post-mortem. You know the procedure."

"Müller doesn't think it was suicide either," said Felix.

"Then you've got a lot of work to do. You'd better leave me in peace!" With these words, Dr. Dour turned to his team: "Are you ready?"

"If you want to see the body again before we take it away, now's the time," he said, focusing on Felix once more.

They went around to the other side of the car, where a white sheet covered the deceased. For the inspector, seen like this, death always had something unreal, almost peaceful about it. He associated the color white with innocence. Dr. Dour lifted back the sheet.

The victim lay there as if asleep, his face appeared relaxed. Uwe Kaptain was wearing a beige polo neck sweater, blue jeans from Joop and light-brown, expensive-looking branded shoes. As Felix circled the victim he saw the label Salvatore Ferragamo woven into the soles. Italian handmade, he realized, not without a hint of jealousy.

He had often dreamed about such expensive but comfortable shoes. However, given the places his work took him, it didn't seem worthwhile investing a lot of money in footwear. Nothing else was particularly noteworthy. Overall, the victim seemed very refined and must surely have turned a few heads in his lifetime. An avenue they ought to pursue, Felix thought to himself.

"Can you tell me anything more?" He looked at the pathologist, who gave a reluctant shake of the head.

"Not for the moment; you've already heard what I think. So can we take him down to the lab?"

"Sure, he's all yours."

The inspector himself, however, was in no great hurry to learn what was required to coax secrets from the dead. Kevin Dour signaled for the employees of the funeral home to take away the deceased before the pair was joined by Emilio.

"Our witness's name is Matthias Grüntal; he lives close by, at 13 Holzgasse. He runs along the banks of the Main twice a week and found the victim this morning, slumped over the steering wheel. Our man opened the doors to pull the body out and then tried to resuscitate him. Although it was soon clear that nothing could be done for Kaptain, he continued to check for vital signs before finally giving up, switching off the engine and notifying us by cell phone at seven fifteen. All in all, he seems to have coped pretty well with the incident. He even noticed that the BMW's heating was still on. Why he switched off the engine he can no longer say. He's going to stop by the office in the next few days to clear up any questions and make a formal statement."

"But you smell a rat?" Felix asked, having surmised from his colleague's tone that something wasn't quite right.

"I've questioned a lot of people who've found dead bodies, but very few were so laid-back about it. I don't like it. We need to take a closer look at this Grüntal," Emilio growled.

"Good, then do it. But for now let's go to Uwe Kaptain's address and see what we can find out." Felix headed to the car.

From the outside, 16 Beethovenstraße appeared thoroughly unspectacular, just a regular residential building with twenty-four tenants. No-one would ever have suspected that one of them could own such expensive clothes as the victim.

When pressing the buzzer next to Kaptain's name provoked no response, Felix began to push them all until an elderly female voice came on the line: "Yes?"

"Good morning, Mrs. Schumm," he replied, glancing briefly at the plaque. "My name is Chief Inspector Felix Büschelberger and I'd like to speak with you for a moment if that's possible."

The buzzer sounded and they went in. The fact that she lived exactly opposite the victim's flat was a happy coincidence in Felix's eyes. The door was slightly ajar and a pair of blue eyes regarded them vigilantly: "Could I see your ID please?"

"Of course!" They showed their ID cards and after a lengthy examination, Mrs. Schumm let them enter the apartment.

"You can never be too careful."

The two officers could only nod in agreement. Felix noticed straightaway how fresh everything smelt. Often apartments gave off a strange odor, particularly those belonging to elderly people. There was no trace of that here. He surveyed the woman with her full lips and snow-white hair worn long and loose, and guessed she was about seventy-five. She had been very pretty once, that much was clear.

"Please excuse us for disturbing you, but this morning we found your neighbor, Uwe Kaptain, dead at the east port. We wanted to see if he had any relatives – and if we could take a look at his flat," said Felix.

A mixture of curiosity and horror was reflected in the blue eyes that surveyed him.

"Oh, how awful, poor Dr. Kaptain! Isn't that dreadful!"

"You know that he was a doctor? Can you tell us any more about him?" he asked.

"I need to sit down first. I've just made a cup of tea if you'd like one. Then I can tell you what I know, which isn't a lot. He was always such a friendly neighbor, sometimes he even helped take my shopping upstairs," she mumbled.

The two inspectors followed the woman into the kitchen and sat down at the table, where a steaming pot of red fruit tea awaited. Next to one of the cups, which Mrs. Schumm had already filled with tea, was the review section of the Frankfurter Allgemeine Zeitung. The room seemed very clean and tidy. Felix and Emilio gratefully accepted their mugs, exchanging a brief smile in the process. All this tallied with their reputation as a tea-drinking unit.

The hot tea seemed to soothe the old lady. "What is it you'd like to know?" she asked, turning towards them.

"Did Mr. Kaptain have a family or did he live alone? Where did he work? What was he like? These are the questions we always try to answer first," Felix replied.

Mrs. Schumm was just about to say something when Emilio interrupted.

His pride and joy was his Galaxy Tab, which he used to take down statements, before transferring them wirelessly to his office computer. Both devices belonged to him. Emilio, the technology fetishist, had become so infuriated with his out-of-date office computer that he had appeared one day with a new PC. This had, admittedly, caused a few problems with the IT department, but since Emilio was technically their superior, the issue had soon been resolved.

"Oh, aren't you well equipped! I don't have any idea about this sort of thing – is that a kind of Dictaphone?" Mrs. Schumm eyed the gadget with interest.

"It could almost be, couldn't it? But no, it's a Tablet PC; the keyboard's operated by a touch-sensitive screen. I use it to take notes; then we don't have to type anything up back in the office. It saves a lot of work. With the right kind of software, these devices can even record conversations and convert them into text

19

documents; things could get pretty interesting then." Emilio was falling into raptures.

"Today I'm going to try something new by transferring the document directly to our Cloud server so that my colleagues at headquarters can access your statement immediately."

"Sorry, who's well endowed? I didn't understand a word of that!" The old lady gave him a confused look.

"Please excuse me. Sometimes my enthusiasm for technology runs away with me," he replied.

"Never mind; I'm quite used to it with my grandson. He's always talking like that and when I don't understand something, he just rolls his eyes. But I'd like to know more."

"OK," Emilio said, after glancing sideways at Felix. "I'd be happy to explain. Cloud technology is the development and sharing of resources via the internet and other networks. If that all sounds a little complicated, then imagine you want a cup of tea in your living room. You've brewed it and taken it through. But then you realize you've left the sugar in the kitchen. So you have to get up and traipse back inside, which takes both time and energy."

Mrs. Schumm smiled. "Believe me inspector: that happens quite a lot!"

"Now you see, that's exactly how the old network system worked. Everything had a fixed place. You needed to know where something was and then put it back there after you'd finished, so that others could find it. The Cloud is different. The name denotes a vast space where individual users no longer have to know exactly where things are located physically. Nevertheless, they are still able to share everything with one another. That's because of special software tools, which arrange everything in the mist of the Cloud and make it available to lots of different people. In your case it would mean having a serving hatch. That would be the Cloud in which your sugar was kept. You'd be able to take a little sugar out of the bowl and your grandson there in the kitchen could do exactly the same. You'd both be sharing the sugar, even though you were in separate rooms. Thanks to the Cloud, different people can share, consult or adapt various programs, documents and reports simultaneously when they're online."

"Well, thank you, I actually understood that! So, everything you write down can be read immediately by your colleagues?" the victim's neighbor asked.

"Exactly. As soon as I've compiled the report, irrespective of where my colleagues are, they can access it and use the information to catch criminals. Crime happens in real time; now we can fight it in real time too!" Emilio's eyes sparkled.

"Since when have we been in the Cloud?" Felix asked in amazement.

"I sent you, Frauke and Arno an email the day before yesterday with your user accounts and log-in details. As soon as you activate them, you'll have access to all the data stored in the Cloud. You can even log in using your iPhone. I'm always saying we need to update our methods so we don't lose any time."

Felix placed his hand on Emilio's shoulder and stopped him before he became completely absorbed in his favorite topic. "So, Mrs. Schumm, what can you tell us?"

"Well, Mr. Kaptain lived here alone, but I think he had been married. I'm sure he told me that once. He was a Doctor of Chemistry in some lab or other and worked very long hours. He is – or was – always friendly; I never saw him angry or upset. No, I have to say that his whole manner was very refined. I can't quite believe he's gone. How did he die?"

"It looks like suicide," came Felix's response.

"No, I don't believe it; no, certainly not! He was always so cheerful… No, inspector, I'm afraid you must be mistaken."

The certainty in her voice made Felix sit up and take notice.

"Naturally, our investigation into the cause of death is still ongoing. Can you tell me anything about the people he mixed with?"

"No, I never came across any visitors; I seldom heard anything either. But the walls here are thick and contrary to what you might have heard about single old ladies, I am not particularly nosy. Live and let live: that's my motto, and it's always served me well," Mrs. Schumm said.

Felix was beginning to like this lady more and more.

"Who owns the apartments here? – and is there someone who might have a second key?"

"Yes, but didn't you find the key on Mr. Kaptain?" the old lady asked.

"We did, but it needs to go to forensics first. We can't just take it like that."

"I see. There was me thinking some stranger was going about with the key to our building!" The relief in her voice was audible. "The building belongs to HL incorporated; it stands for Heavenly Living. That's almost certainly the brainchild of some young marketeer, but this really is a nice place to live. Unfortunately, I don't think our janitor, Mr. Rosen, has a key to Dr. Kaptain's apartment."

"And where can we find this Mr. Rosen?"

"He's on vacation at the moment. In emergencies, tenants are supposed to contact administration directly," Mrs. Schumm replied.

"Call the locksmith," Felix turned towards his colleague, who immediately reached for his cell and gave the address.

"They'll be here in about ten minutes."

Felix looked at his watch. "Are there any other people who knew Mr. Kaptain?"

"The Schmidts and Mrs. Wenzel – they all live on this floor. They'll be at work though. I don't know if anyone else knew him, sorry."

Felix nodded. "That's fine. Let's wait until we find out if it was suicide, then we'll question the others." He stood up. "We'll wait downstairs for the locksmith. Many thanks for the tea."

As the door closed behind them, Emilio said appreciatively: "Che cosa una bella signora."

"Yes, she's a very attractive woman; I thought so too."

They waited exactly eleven minutes for the locksmith. The job was done in seven seconds flat.

"It wasn't locked, only pulled shut," the tradesman said and turned to leave.

Felix followed him with his gaze, and wondered, not for the first time, how many of these locksmiths moonlighted as burglars. It was amazing how quickly they overcame any obstacles.

"That's strange; maybe our man left in a hurry."

The chief inspector couldn't help but agree with his partner, particularly after an initial look at the décor. Money was clearly no object here; whoever lived here had exquisite taste. You didn't leave a flat like this exposed.

The floors were parquet-covered, while art prints hung from the wall in every room. The wallpaper was pastel-colored: pea green in the hall, warm ochre in the living room; the kitchen a light blue and the bedroom a deep shade of red. All in all, the apartment seemed very tastefully arranged, and nothing like a typical bachelor pad.

When Felix thought of his own flat, the difference was all too plain. Here, everything was clean and tidy; a bouquet of flowers even adorned the living room table.

Meanwhile, the detectives put on gloves so they didn't leave behind any unwanted traces. In truth, they shouldn't have been there at all. But three separate people had now cast doubt upon a verdict of suicide, and for Felix that was reason enough to be a little "creative with the rules," as Emilio would have put it. They began to take a closer look around the living room, but found nothing resembling a suicide note. The chief inspector was just inspecting the answer machine when his partner called out. "Hey, you've got to take a look at this!"

Felix found him in the bathroom; there was a lace-up, all-in-one men's leather suit hanging from the shower cubicle. On a table next to it lay not only a leather mask with zip-up holes for the eyes and mouth but also a leather detergent - biodegradable and, as the packet stressed, non-harmful to humans.

The chief inspector whistled through his teeth. "So Kaptain wasn't just friendly. From time to time, it seems, he liked to play a little rough."

Emilio shook his head. "I'll never understand what these men see in it. I think it's perverse!"

"Perhaps more people than you think enjoy this sort of thing. That's what I've heard anyway."

The Italian threw his boss a questioning look but said nothing more on the matter. Since they didn't find anything else of note, they left and headed back to the office.

Chapter 2

Back at the station, Emilio parked the Focus in its dedicated space and plugged in the charging cable. The charging station registered that it was indeed a car that had been connected, and activated the electric circuit. This safety measure ensured a current was generated only when there was contact to a vehicle and it also protected the charging station against misuse – people who touched or fiddled around with it were not placed in unnecessary danger.

"Did you know that we could charge the Focus much faster if the technology was in the charging station itself rather than the car? If there was a direct current, the car could be charged in a quarter of the time!"

The inspector gazed at the vehicle thoughtfully before locking it. "You really should have been an engineer with your interest in all the new technology."

Felix was silent for a moment. Then he posed the question he knew his colleague was about to answer, regardless of whether he asked or not: "So why doesn't the charging station supply direct current, if it would save us so much time?"

His partner grinned. "Because DC electricity is more dangerous. It's harder to transport over longer distances and would mean a massive increase in safety precautions."

"So, that's the reason! Let's go inside then, techno nerd; we have a case to solve." Felix couldn't help but smile to himself.

As an Italian, Emilio set great store by his cultivated, refined appearance; he hated being called a nerd. Those were computer geeks with thick horn-rimmed specs, totally unfashionable people who sat in front of a screen all day and had no idea about the real world.

They were met in the corridor by Arno. "The BMW is registered as a company car, belonging to Dr. Heinrich Zimmer Consultancy Ltd. According to their website, they deal in waste analysis and offer advice on refuse disposal to a number of different companies in the chemical industry. Their reputation is pretty good, it seems; there's a photo of our former science minister on their

24

homepage. Our victim appears to have fronted their lab. And there are 300 registered vehicles in Frankfurt with the partial number plate F-MS, seven of which are dark BMWs."

"Good work," Felix nodded to him. "We'll pay the company a visit this afternoon. And you can call off your vehicle search; we've found our missing BMW."

All three of them went into the meeting room where Frauke was already seated. There was an empty file and stacks of loose paper on the table in front of her, and a blank whiteboard itching to be used.

"There you are. The lab's just told me that the photos from the site will be ready this afternoon. Dr. Dour thinks he'll have the initial analysis completed by early tomorrow morning and said we should kindly leave him in peace until then."

"Charming as ever... Though he was in a strangely good mood at the east port earlier; he even tried to make a couple of jokes," Felix commented.

"So, let's summarize what we know so far. This morning Mr. Grüntal finds the dead man while out jogging and notifies the police. It looks like suicide, but three people immediately voice their doubts. Chief Constable Müller has a strange feeling and Dr. Dour doesn't like it either. The deceased's neighbor also questions whether Dr. Kaptain would take his own life. There was no suicide note either in the victim's car or his flat, which, by the way, is still unlocked. We need to see to that as soon as we get the key from forensics. In addition, we know that the BMW was travelling at high speed yesterday evening between Langenhain and Eppstein, and almost knocked me and members of my group down while we were out collecting toads."

Turning towards Arno, he added: "That's why I wanted you to check that license plate."

Despite the gravity of the situation, Felix could see a smile spreading across each of their faces. And when Emilio whispered something about a "Frog Prince," all three of them burst into laughter.

Not even Felix could stifle a grin. "Very well then, if it's so amusing, I suggest we dub the investigation Toadkill."

That cracked the whole team up, but no-one contradicted him.

"Right, we'll pay Kaptain's company a visit at two and see what we can find. In the meantime, let's make sure we don't concentrate all our resources on this case – at least not until the cause of death has been confirmed."

With that, the meeting was over. Felix sat down at his desk and thought about the previous evening. Once again Petra's face appeared before him, along with the lingering memory of her smell. Just then the phone rang.

"Chief Inspector Felix Büschelberger."

"You're not so easy to find! Nobody wanted to give me your number so I had to fib a little. I told them you were my illegitimate half-brother and that I had very important news for you." There was giggling at the other end.

"Petra," was all the inspector could say before falling speechless. But he basked in her laughter. Hearing her voice felt so good; his heart skipped a beat.

"Just wanted to say thanks for yesterday evening! Not sure I would have been so quick to react. Did you find anything?" she asked.

"Yes, well, we now know who the driver was…"

She interrupted him. "And have you arrested him? I hope you're not being all soft on him."

"No, he's dead actually!" he replied.

"What? You killed him?" Petra was horrified.

"For God's sake, no. What on earth do you people think of us? First Eric wants me to shoot at the car's tires, now you think I've murdered the driver. No, it looks like suicide, but we're still conducting our inquiries."

"Listen, I'm sorry," she said. "I was really calling to invite you out for an Italian, to say thanks. Do you know the Da Claudia on Brettenstraße?"

"Only by name. I've heard you have to book pretty far in advance to get a table," he replied.

Petra giggled again. "Or be good friends with the owner. We take a lot of clients there. How does tomorrow at eight sound?"

"Wonderful!" Felix responded immediately – a little too quickly, he thought.

"Great! Then see you tomorrow evening. I'm looking forward to it."

With that, she hung up. Her last words echoed in Felix's mind, leaving him unable to concentrate on his work for the rest of the day.

After lunch, Emilio came to see him in his office. "Should we go and check out Kaptain's company then?"

"No, take Frauke with you and keep your ears open. Arno can do a little internet research to trace possible next of kin. I have something else to take care of. See you tomorrow morning."

With that he hurried from the office, failing to register the look of surprise that had settled over his partner's face.

Felix was first in the next morning, and boiled the kettle so that the others could make their tea. Within ten minutes, they had all arrived and spread out across the table. Frauke and Emilio reported on their visit to the lab where, until two days before, Uwe Kaptain had still worked.

Basically everyone there was still in shock and unable to come up with any sort of explanation. However, they had only been able to speak to the PA, as the company owner, Heinrich Zimmer, was unavailable – sick in bed, according to his assistant.

Apparently no-one could say why Dr. Kaptain had committed suicide. As far as people knew, he'd been a man without enemies; nor had there been anything unusual about his recent behavior. Dr. Heinrich Zimmer Consultancy Ltd. had existed for eighteen years and was financially strong. In short, there had been no breakthrough at the victim's place of work.

Arno had managed to trace the ex-wife. She now lived in Wuppertal, having remarried; her name was Sophie Harris. Dialing her number had only yielded a recorded message.

"Very well," said Felix, "then we'll have to sit tight for the time being. Arno, could you get in touch with our colleagues from Wuppertal? They need to find Mrs. Harris so we can begin questioning her. You and Frauke keep on searching for other family members.

Emilio can summarize what we know so far and compile an initial report. I'm meeting Dr. Dour at ten. Let's see what he can tell us."

"And what about Kaptain's trip to Eppstein the day before yesterday? Who's going to look into that?" Frauke asked.

"We'll leave that be for now, at least until we've determined the cause of death."

The chief inspector arrived punctually at the forensics lab and found Dr. Dour in the main autopsy room, a cigarette between his lips as he pored over various printouts.

"So, what have you got for me, oh Grand Master of Death?" Felix joked.

Kevin Dour looked at him pensively. "What I can say beyond any certainty is that Uwe Kaptain did not die of carbon monoxide poisoning. Although he ought to have, if he committed suicide. The blood tests returned rather strange results; I don't know what to make of them yet."

"So it was murder," Felix stated.

"Very probably, unless you've ever come across someone who poisoned themselves – because that's what happened here – then got into the car and connected the exhaust pipe? To be doubly sure, so to speak? I don't think so somehow, but I need to run a further analysis. Otherwise, I can tell you that our man had sexual intercourse two days prior to his death and had consumed red wine immediately before dying. An initial examination suggests the victim was in good health."

Felix didn't want to know what kind of examination you had to perform in order to find out if someone had had sex before they died.

"You'll call me as soon as you know anything?" he turned to leave.

"Of course, but you've forgotten something," the pathologist said.

Felix stood still and looked back. "I'm not sure what you mean."

Kevin grinned. "Mr. Bufo, naturally! He died of internal injuries, caused by a brutal external forceful impact. His spine was shattered, like most of his other bones, and he wanted sex."

Only now did the inspector see the handkerchief covering the body on the extra table. He could hardly keep a straight face as he shook his head. "Just be careful; if this gets out, you'll be known as Dr. Toad!"

"We do things thoroughly here," Kevin Dour smiled and turned back to his printouts, the signal for Felix to take his leave.

In the meeting room, the first photos had been hung on the wall and the word "Toadkill" had been scrawled in big green letters on the whiteboard.

Next to it, somebody had invoked their inner artist and drawn a picture of a frog. Felix suspected Emilio, but was unable to stifle a little grin. It was good that they'd all managed to keep a sense of humor – despite the often-trying circumstances in which they worked.

Briefly he outlined the results of the autopsy, before sending Emilio and Frauke back to the victim's flat to take another look around and lock the door. Arno was to learn as much as he could about Uwe Kaptain. Felix himself remained in the meeting room for a long time thereafter, trying to take the various images in; his thoughts, however, had already turned to the coming evening.

He arrived at the restaurant at eight o'clock sharp. Petra appeared five minutes later and greeted him with a kiss on the cheek. Arms linked, they made their way inside. The owner received Petra warmly, before personally leading them to a small table that hadn't been visible at first. Bathed in soft light, the restaurant, with its wooden décor and timeworn furnishings, exuded an old-school Italian charm.

"Nice restaurant, it really does feel like we're in southern Europe," he said appreciatively.

"I'm glad you approve of my choice."

After a quick glance at the menu, which had been promptly brought to them by the waiter, Felix realized that this was a top-end Italian place. Emilio had taught him as much; he always said: "A proper Italian is one that doesn't serve pizza."

Petra ordered antipasti misti, then spaghetti with black truffles and scampi in a tomato-garlic sauce to finish. At her insistence,

Felix also had the truffles following his carpaccio, and ended with scaloppine.

"To my savior!" she made a toast in his honor.

"Come on: you'd have managed just fine without me. You seem like a woman who knows how to take care of herself."

A smile was her only response. He tasted the wine, a special recommendation from the house chef, a Turriga from 1998.

"That is some fine wine! I was familiar with the name, but I'd never tried it before. It's from Sicily," said Felix.

"Oh, a connoisseur," Petra teased.

"Actually, yes. My ex-wife and I developed something of a weakness for red wine. We even went on two wine tours through Tuscany and Umbria."

"Ah, yes: your ex-wife... Are you still in touch with her?" She sounded completely indifferent.

He shook his head. "Once in a blue moon. It's better that way."

"Why, did you have a fight or something?" she asked, her curiosity barely disguised.

"No. She's just changed, that's all," Felix sighed.

"Most men don't cope very well with change, I know. But I thought you'd be more open-minded," Petra taunted.

"I am, I am," he countered. "But it's better if I don't have much contact with her, otherwise my colleagues would make even more fun of me."

"Why? Has she gone soft in the head or something?" Her interest seemed to be growing.

"No, it's just that she's undertaken a new... professional venture."

Silence from Petra.

"She is now – how can I put this? – she's a kind of event manager."

"Event manager?"

"Yes, that's how she describes herself. She's a dominatrix; and runs the Dark Dungeon here in Frankfurt," came the hesitant response.

Petra almost snorted into her wineglass. "A dominatrix? You know that's actually pretty cool."

Her gaze was increasingly attentive as it fell upon Felix. "And while you were married, did the two of you engage in role-play of any kind? Were you her slave?" Her eyes began to sparkle: "I mean you always carry a pair of handcuffs, don't you?"

Just then the waiter brought the primi piatti and with that, the chief inspector was saved, although one look at his companion was enough to tell him that this was by no means the end of the matter. Still, for now he could concentrate on his truffles; and the rest of the evening was delightfully spent.

When they had finished, Petra asked for his number and settled the bill. As they said goodbye in front of the Da Claudia, she kissed Felix once more on the cheek, ensuring him a sleepless – but not dreamless – night.

Chapter 3

Gratefully Felix registered that no-one commented on his appearance the next morning. Not that he was tired; in fact, he felt decidedly sprightly.

"A Mr. Grüntal called yesterday evening to ask if it was OK to come by at two and make a formal statement," Arno informed him.

"Yes, Emilio can take care of that. We need to keep searching for next of kin. Have you found anything yet?"

"Not much. His parents are dead and he doesn't have any siblings," Arno replied.

"What about his ex-wife? Have we made contact with her?"

A shake of the head.

"I'll call Wuppertal and see what's going on," said Felix. Just then his cell beeped. He reached over and saw that it was a text from Petra.

"You still owe me an answer. I WILL get it out of you!! Hope you have a good day, P."

Deep in thought, he was somewhat surprised to find Dr. Dour in the room when he next looked up.

"Good morning dream features, I said!"

"Hello Kevin," Felix replied. "What have you got for us?"

"Murder!" came the response, the pathologist neglecting to register Frauke's critical glance at his cigarette.

"Well, don't keep me in suspense," the chief inspector prompted.

"As I said yesterday, I found some strange substances in the victim's bloodstream. I had to do a GC-MS test to identify them. The results yielded benzodiazepines in almost pure form mixed with chloral hydrate. Enough to put an elephant to sleep; for a human, an absolutely lethal dose. Normally these agents are broken down very quickly and can no longer be traced. However, it seems our victim suffered from allergies and took antihistamines, which caused them to remain in the system for longer – luckily for us!"

"So he couldn't have taken the drugs himself and then climbed into his car?" Felix asked.

"You haven't been listening to me, have you?" Dr. Dour knitted his brow, as he always did when he became angry. "With the amount he had in his blood, there's no way he'd have been able to drive. He must have consumed the mix in the port somewhere. Have we found a glass or a phial anywhere? Somebody probably spiked his red wine. No, no, I'm absolutely convinced it was murder. There's no doubt in my mind. You can't get this drug as pure as this over the counter. So, you're looking for someone with not only knowledge of the substance but access to it. That ought to reduce the number of possible suspects."

"The victim worked in a lab. Would they be able to get hold of it?" Frauke asked.

"It's certainly possible. A chemist would have the knowledge and the access. That sounds like a good lead. But that's your job – mine's just about done," the pathologist said.

"What do you mean? What else is missing?" Felix asked.

In response, Dr. Dour advanced towards the whiteboard and placed another photo next to that of the victim. It showed the head of the dead toad. "Like I said, we do things thoroughly here."

With these words he was gone, but his laughter could be heard all the way down the corridor.

The four police officers looked at each other in astonishment.

"Blimey, he's in a good mood. I've never seen him so happy." Arno's remark drew agreement from all sides.

"Okay folks. Now we are officially conducting a murder investigation. The first thing we need to do is inform the DA; I'll take care of that. Then it's straight to Uwe Kaptain's work to see if we can establish a motive. Let's make sure we turn his apartment upside down as well. Arno, Frauke, you head out there now; Emilio and I will check his office. We'll meet back here at five to compare notes." With that, the chief inspector ended the meeting.

An hour later, Emilio and Felix were in the parking lot at Dr. Heinrich Zimmer Consultancy Ltd. It was the first time Felix had been here, and though he had seen plenty of glass palaces in his time, he was still impressed. The foyer was lined with reflective columns, supporting a large glass roof overhead. Mirrored windows adorning the façade prevented passers-by from gazing inside.

The interior was bathed in marble and chrome, with two pretty blondes in their late-twenties sitting behind the large reception counter. Everything was exquisite. Someone here was clearly intent on impressing visitors, and the inspector was forced to acknowledge they'd succeeded.

Out of the corner of his eye he noticed one of the blondes immediately reaching for the phone.

"Our arrival's being announced," he said.

"Seems like it!" Emilio agreed.

"Good afternoon, Inspector. I've let Dr. Zimmer's office know you're here. Someone will be with you in a moment. I see you've brought another colleague along with you today." The receptionist gave Emilio her best smile.

"Chief Inspector Büschelberger," Felix displayed his ID. "Thank you for relaying our arrival. It was actually Dr. Zimmer we were hoping to see. He's no longer ill, is he?"

"No, he's in today – he's still in shock about Dr. Kaptain's suicide though. He told us to let him know as soon as you were here." Her smile was beamed at Felix this time.

"Thanks; we'll wait here." He looked around the lobby, finding nothing that stood out.

The two detectives sat down among a set of black leather chairs and waited. After five minutes, Emilio gestured towards another blonde who was just leaving the elevator and heading straight for them. "The Big Boss's secretary."

"Appearances are obviously very important in this company," whispered the inspector.

The woman was perhaps in her early thirties, and wore a dark-blue suit with matching high heels. Yet the most striking thing about her was her blonde hair, which was longer than the length of her skirt.

"Good afternoon, gentlemen! My name is Anita Peisker, Dr. Zimmer's PA; he's asked me to take you to him. He's currently in a meeting but will see you in five minutes. If you'd be so kind as to follow me."

They were taken to a meeting room on the first floor and left to wait on their own. The room was dominated by a large oval mahogany table and twelve heavy leather chairs. All walls were wood-paneled; a video display unit had been built into the middle of one of them, along with a giant screen. From the ceiling hung a beamer, which could project images directly onto the screen. On the table were drinks bottles, a pot of coffee and a plate of fresh pastries.

"Please help yourself, gentlemen." Dr. Zimmer entered the room, likewise elegantly clad in a charcoal-grey suit, white shirt and tasteful tie. He had an air of authority about him, underscored by his arrogant manner. Although polite, his body language betrayed the fact that he resented the detectives' presence. He sat down opposite them.

"I still can't believe Dr. Kaptain is no longer with us. And to think it was suicide… How can I be of service to you?"

Felix leaned back and waited before answering. He knew that silence was the best way to unsettle people who were this self-assured. And it worked. Dr. Zimmer looked from one detective to the other, visibly surprised not to have received an answer.

"It wasn't suicide, Dr. Zimmer. It was murder. We are now leading a murder enquiry."

Chief Inspector Büschelberger noted with some satisfaction how the color had disappeared from the face of his audience. He didn't like him, or people of his kind.

"Murder? Are you sure? I don't believe it!" The head of the company had jumped to his feet and was clearly struggling to compose himself. "I'm sorry, gentlemen, but I find that even harder to believe than your suicide theory."

He sat down once more and poured himself a coffee. When he next looked at the chief inspector, he had regained his self-control. A shame, Felix thought to himself: he would have enjoyed unsettling this puffed-up little idiot some more. But then his professionalism got the better of him and he refocused on the case.

"Well, it's a fact. We're absolutely certain that Dr. Kaptain was poisoned; and that the suicide was staged in order to distract from the murder."

"He was poisoned? But that's unbelievable." Dr. Zimmer appeared extremely agitated now.

"Exactly. It was… wait a moment, please." Felix began to leaf through his notes, which contained all sorts of information, though nothing to do with his cases. It was a trick he'd learned watching Columbo – and found highly effective.

He turned towards Emilio and winked. The latter looked down at his tablet and said: "It was a mixture of benzodiazepine and chloral hydrate that killed him."

"But you can find those substances in any sleeping pill. Surely that doesn't rule out suicide?" countered Dr. Zimmer, still somewhat agitated.

Chief Inspector Büschelberger looked at him with interest. "That's very true. However, based on the concentration found in his bloodstream, our pathologist has ruled out the possibility that the victim swallowed the concoction himself before getting into his car and starting the engine. Moreover, the mix was far purer than normally found in sleeping pills. To administer this sort of dose, you would either need to be a pharmacist or have direct access to the substances in question."

Felix paused again.

"Is it possible to get hold of such chemicals in your lab?" he asked, completely relaxed.

"Are you trying to imply that someone here was involved in Dr. Kaptain's death? That is simply unbelievable." Dr. Zimmer was becoming more and more anxious.

"It is our job to pursue all lines of enquiry!"

The chief inspector endeavored to adopt a more matter-of-fact tone. "So, tell me again, is it possible to get hold of these chemicals in your lab?"

Dr. Zimmer took a little time to respond, before countering, with equal neutrality: "We don't use chloral hydrate or benzodiazepine in this company, so they couldn't have come from here, no. But I suppose as a chemical firm we could in theory order any substance, or be involved in its partial manufacture."

"And which of your employees could place such an order, in theory of course?"

"Any lab-worker could submit a request, as long as it didn't exceed an order value of 500 euros. Purchasing would then process it and the product would be made available to us within twenty-four hours," the company chief replied.

Felix nodded thoughtfully and glanced over at Emilio, who was eagerly noting it all down. "Good," he said, "I think that'll be all for now."

Dr. Zimmer threw him a questioning look. "For now? What do you mean? For the life of me I wouldn't know what else to tell you."

"It's possible that further questions will arise during the course of our investigation. If that happens, we'll be in touch."

The company owner nodded briefly and showed them out. In front of the elevator the chief inspector paused unexpectedly before turning to face him once more.

"There is one more thing, before I forget. I'd like to see where Dr. Kaptain worked."

"Very well. My secretary will escort you. Wait here, please." With these words, Dr. Zimmer disappeared.

Soon enough both detectives were being led by Anita Peisker to the victim's office. Felix found himself gazing at her slender legs for longer than professional necessity would normally have allowed. He looked over towards his partner, and saw him grinning broadly. The inspector's wandering eye hadn't gone unnoticed.

According to Emilio, you were only a real man if you were happily married. He'd tried many times to convince his colleagues of this philosophical stance, and, in fact, contrary to every cliché he'd ever heard about Italian men, Felix had never once seen him stare at a woman for longer than was polite – or make obvious sexual innuendo.

Suddenly the chief inspector felt a twinge of jealousy, though his prevailing sentiment was one of loneliness. Only when they reached the office was he finally delivered from these thoughts.

It was a modern office with eight desks and lab benches separated from one another by partitions each measuring around four feet. One corner was completely isolated from the rest of the room by a glass wall; it housed the victim's desk. Felix took a closer look, but wasn't struck by anything in particular; only that everything was very tidy – and not a single personal photo to be seen.

There was a sterilized, uninhabited feel to it all. Neither papers nor files lay on the desk, although these filled an entire shelf on the back wall. Felix noticed his partner gazing wistfully at the victim's computer. Clearly a high-end model, it consisted of a 27 inch monitor with LED backlighting, an optical HandShoe mouse and wireless keyboard, as well as a concealed docking station that contained a built-in laptop.

Turning to the secretary, Emilio pointed towards the microphone in front of the PC. "Does that mean your company uses voice recognition software to control its computers?"

"Management lets us decide ourselves whether we want to work with this software or not. Most of the younger employees use it; and for the upper management it's regarded as something of a pre-requisite. But in practice, the software's only really used for dictations and text files. Apparently Dr. Kaptain also used it for menu navigation in Excel and PowerPoint. He was a real technophile and something of a trailblazer in this regard. It's through role models like him that our company aims to foster technical innovation!" Ms. Peisker replied.

"Wow, just imagine…"

Felix waved his hand dismissively, managing to nip the inevitable lecture on technology in the bud. "What had Dr. Kaptain been working on most recently?" He turned towards Anita Peisker, who had continued to observe them from the doorway.

"Dr. Kaptain was responsible for various projects. We advise several companies on regulations concerning the disposal of toxic industrial waste. Dr. Kaptain is – sorry, was – in charge of Class III and IV hazardous waste, that is to say, extremely dangerous and toxic materials. You know, the Seveso poisoning, things like that."

The detectives nodded, the same thought going through their minds.

"He was also responsible for developing new markets in Africa and Asia," Anita Peisker added.

"And what does that entail exactly?" Felix's interest grew visibly.

"Well, there are currently a number of chemical companies being established in the so-called emerging markets. If these companies want to export goods to Europe, then there are certain norms and regulations that need to be observed during production. Only then are they allowed to sell to the EU or the US. It's our job to support clients as they integrate these norms into their individual process steps," the secretary said.

"OK, understood. I think we've taken up enough of your time for one day."

She smiled. "But Chief Inspector, we've all been truly shaken by Mr. Kaptain's death. We'll do whatever we can to help."

Felix smiled back. "I'll hold you to that."

He could still detect the scent of her perfume as he climbed into the Focus; on the spur of the moment, he decided to reply to Petra's text.

"Some secrets are more interesting when they remain hidden. Thanks for yesterday evening, F."

Back at the station, they found a note from Frauke saying that she and Arno had gone to the victim's apartment with forensics, but that they still hoped to be back in time for the meeting at five.

The chief inspector looked at his watch. It was time for a little lunch. "Fancy coming round the corner with me to Conny's?" That was the station's snack bar of choice.

Only Emilio steadfastly refused to eat there; as a gourmet, he thought it was beneath his dignity. "Mamma mia! I will never understand how you can eat such crap. It's so uncivilized!"

At which point he grimaced and shot back into his office, where his wife's packed lunch awaited him. Felix grinned and went off for his midday ration of curried sausage and fries with mayo and ketchup.

After lunch, he stopped by his partner's office. Emilio was in the middle of printing out his reports to distribute among the group.

"If you guys actually used the accounts I'd set up for you in the Cloud, then I could save myself all this work; we'd not only be consistently up-to-date on the status of each investigation but technically superior to the criminals," Felix's Italian colleague growled.

"Yes, you're right. Why don't you provide us with a little introduction on how best to use them at some point?"

Emilio nodded, not entirely convinced by his colleague's sudden desire to acquaint himself with the new technology.

"So, what's your feeling on Dr. Zimmer and crew?" Felix asked.

"I thought the good doctor became flustered a little too quickly when we asked about a possible connection between the chemicals and his company. Other than that, he just seemed pretty arrogant, though I suppose that could've been a defense mechanism. By the way, I nearly cracked up when you started behaving like Columbo's long-lost brother again."

"Yes, well, astonishingly it always seems to work. Right! We need to keep going on this one. Let's just see what happens."

They were interrupted by a knock on the door, and a young colleague from uniform poked his head in.

"Sorry to disturb, there's a Mr. Grüntal waiting for you in room four."

Emilio nodded and headed for the door.

"Have you managed to get hold of Sophie Harris?" Felix was on the telephone to Wuppertal.

"No, according to a neighbor, she's away with her husband and won't be back until the beginning of next week. We've left a message asking her to contact us."

Thoughtfully Felix stared out of the window. There was nothing to be seen except the grey concrete wall of the house opposite. It was precisely this monotony, however, that had always helped him to concentrate.

What leads did they have? Which were good and which could they ignore for the time being? Not that you could afford to neglect a lead, but, as his old friend and first partner had always said: "Don't let yourself get bogged down. Think it through and concentrate your resources; that way success will be just around the corner."

He sighed. Sometimes he missed those deep and meaningfuls with Ruebens, but he didn't have any reason to complain. His team was a good unit and regarded as one of the more harmonious within the force. Felix turned to his administrative duties; they were necessary, of course, but he hated them all the same. Contrary to the image his friends and acquaintances had about the job, being an investigator sometimes involved more paperwork than action.

At half past four, Frauke came by his office. "We're finished with the initial examination. Should we meet at five as planned?" she asked.

Her boss nodded. Shortly before five, he entered the meeting room, boiled the kettle and waited for the rest of the team. Once they were all sat down with their mugs of hot tea, Emilio began to distribute the latest reports. Felix saw that Mr. Grüntal's statement was already among them, and gave his colleague an appreciative pat on the shoulder.

"You're a real Ferrari when it comes to writing reports. Shame your superiors are clueless when it comes to new technology. They're probably still at the typing stage. Incidentally, I've arranged for Emilio to explain the benefits of Cloud technology to us, so we don't lose any more time on this."

"Sorry, but we still haven't finished our report from today," Arno murmured, looking towards Frauke for assistance.

"That wasn't a dig at you. It's absolutely fine." Chief Inspector Büschelberger skimmed the report on Mr. Grüntal, but it didn't contain any new information. The witness had had nothing to add.

"So, Emilio, what do your instincts tell you?"

"I don't know. He seems a little detached to me, almost too composed. As if he's had a lot of dealings with us in the past, if you know what I mean."

"Good, then we'll run his name through the computer. And what about the apartment? Did you find anything?"

Frauke glanced at her notes. "No sign of violence or a struggle. Though forensics did find prints on the cylinder lock. Seems like someone gained access to the apartment without a key."

"That was us, two days ago. Anything else?" Felix dealt with the topic briskly and no-one said another word about it.

"It appears our victim had a taste for S&M. Hence the leather suit in the bathroom. There were sperm traces in the bedroom and on the living room couch."

"Our boss says that loads of men are into that sort of thing," Emilio interrupted.

"That's interesting. Do you think he's trying to tell us something?" Frauke fluttered mischievously in Felix's direction.

"Perhaps he leads a double life." As usual, Arno's comment was so deadpan it was impossible to say whether he was joking or not.

"Precisely, I have a dark secret!" The chief inspector threw his hands over his face theatrically. His "confession" had caused a spontaneous ripple of laughter, and though tickled himself, he signaled for Frauke to continue.

"Otherwise, nothing of note. No real letters, no messages on the answering machine. Everything appears normal. We found a few bottles of red wine in the kitchen, which we took back to the lab in order to run a comparison. But there were no used glasses in the sink or dishwasher."

"What about photo albums? There were no pictures or anything else in his office; did you find any in the apartment?"

"No," Arno interjected, "there were none there either."

"Good point. That's pretty strange. The whole apartment was so tastefully and comfortably arranged, but photos – an absolute no-show."

Frauke rubbed her index finger against the tip of her nose, a tic that manifested itself only when she was concentrating very hard. "It doesn't tally with the rest of the apartment," she said.

"Another little mystery, then. One of Uwe Kaptain's foibles perhaps. Maybe he wasn't so keen on his appearance?" Arno looked around the room.

"No. He was wearing pretty expensive designer clothing when he was found. Someone like that is sure to be vain and a little in love with themselves. We should take a closer look to see if there are any traces of picture frames or nails on the walls." Felix made a mental note of this additional line of enquiry.

"You mean that someone could've made off with something from the flat?" Frauke looked at him, wide-eyed.

"It's certainly possible."

Meanwhile, he was annoyed at himself for having gained un-authorized access to the flat with Emilio and potentially eliminating other traces. How were they to know now if they or someone else had left the prints on the door?

"Very well, let's go over what we know: Uwe Kaptain was murdered. With a chemical that is difficult to obtain in its pure form. We still know nothing about the motive or where the murder took place. It's important that we establish the crime scene quickly. Can we rule out the apartment? Probably. Nevertheless, I think we should still question the victim's immediate neighbors. And we need to know where he was headed the evening I was out collecting toads with…"

He was interrupted by sniggering. "OK, OK – but we still need to find out where he was going. Who saw him last, and where?"

Felix looked at his watch. "It's now quarter past six. If we manage to call the neighbors and arrange meetings for tomorrow or the next day at the latest, then we can call it a night."

Arno was happy to volunteer for the task at hand.

Chapter 4

Felix came home to find Django waiting in the hall, so he went into the kitchen and placed his tomcat's food in front of him. Then he made himself a sandwich and opened a bottle of Primitivo di Manduria.

He sat brooding in the living room, but was unable to concentrate on the case. The whole time he was thinking about Petra, wondering whether he should call. Just then his thoughts were interrupted by the sound of his cell phone.

"Hi Felix, I just wanted to ask what you were doing tonight?" As usual, Petra's voice was lively and cheerful.

"Nothing much, just drinking red wine and thinking things over."

"You know that drinking alone is the first step towards alcoholism?" she said.

"You're probably right, but I think I have it under control."

"Are you sure?" her voice revealed just how much she enjoyed teasing him. "Should I stop by and keep you company? That would be my good deed for the day. You can take the girl out of the Girl Scouts…"

"That'd be great." He couldn't think of anything else to say. Taken completely unawares, he was annoyed that he'd reacted so listlessly.

"Good, then tell me your address and I'll be on my way."

That done, Petra said goodbye with the words: "See you shortly, and make sure you leave me some wine, otherwise I'll have to think of another good deed to perform." Then with a giggle, she hung up.

Anxiously Felix looked round the living room. Was it tidy enough to have her over? Did he have anything to offer – and why, oh why, had he said yes straightaway?

"Damn, I've been out of the game too long."

Django looked at him in agreement, and seemed to say: "Just join me on my nocturnal rounds! I'll show you how to impress the ladies."

Felix looked at his watch and thought out loud: "It'll take Petra twenty minutes to get here. I can still head to the Greek taverna round the corner and pick up some olives and salad."

Quickly he hurried out the door, almost forgetting his keys in the process. He forced himself to calm down and was back shortly before she arrived. The next few minutes he spent debating with Django whether he wouldn't be happier outside tonight; but his feline flat-mate was in no mood to leave. In fact he seemed completely bored by the whole thing, a sign, to the inspector's mind, of his barely concealed curiosity.

The doorbell gave him a start. After taking a deep breath to compose himself, he went to answer. Petra was wearing black dress-pants, the flares of which just exposed the toe of her brown suede pumps. Setting off the pants was a white Spanish-style blouse. In her hand she held a flaxen-colored rose, which she subsequently presented to Felix. She gave him a kiss on both cheeks, and was well inside the flat before she finally took a good look round.

"Somehow I imagined the apartment of a hard-nosed cop a little differently – less tidy, at any rate; colder. But it's really nice here. Or maybe you've just been cleaning frantically?" Petra's eyes twinkled mischievously.

"No, I always try to keep things tidy. You never know, right?"

He showed her to the living room, before disappearing briefly into the kitchen for a vase and the bottle of red. To his astonishment Django was purring away on Petra's lap when he returned.

"He's never done that before. You must have made a good impression – or did you promise him something?"

She laughed. "Well, I always keep a few mice and some bacon in my bag."

He looked at her blankly.

"Bacon for the men, mice for their cats. You have to come prepared!" she said.

Felix couldn't help bursting into laughter and Petra soon joined in. His nerves had vanished by the time they chinked glasses.

"Are you hungry? I got something from the Greek taverna specially."

"What a gentleman! That'd be great, I haven't eaten yet."

Felix brought out the seafood and Greek salads, which he'd arranged on separate plates. In the meantime, Petra had made herself comfortable on the couch and was stroking Django's fur, the tom now sprawled on his back across her stomach, enjoying every minute.

He turned to face his owner, his ear twitching as if to say: "Hey dude, you can get lost now, I've got everything under control here."

More than anything Felix would've liked to switch places. Was he jealous perhaps? Of course he wasn't; he was just at it again, ascribing human qualities to Django, projecting his own view of the world onto his pet.

Petra beamed at him. "Oh, the perfect host. Lots of female visitors, eh?"

"No, not really. To be honest, you're the first in quite some time."

She fell silent and they began to eat, Django not moving a muscle. While Felix was cleaning up, Petra lifted the tom onto her stomach and lay, with knees bent, on her back. Her head was resting against the arm. "You know you can join me if you like. I only bite when men want me to."

Felix sat down on the couch, while Petra stretched her legs out and put her feet on his lap. All of a sudden he felt very aroused.

"If you want, you can give me a foot massage."

He needed no second invitation and began to massage her feet, first gently and then increasing the pressure. She kept her eyes closed and smiled. Felix would've frozen the moment forever in time – if he had only known how.

"Tell me about your day." Petra opened her eyes and looked straight at him.

He told her everything that had happened so far, before weighing up various strategies and outlining his further plans. His guest listened to him in silence.

When he was finished, she said: "I've heard of Dr. Zimmer Consultancy Ltd. Apparently they almost went bankrupt a few years ago, then suddenly they were making big money again within twelve months. I don't know how. But there are rumors about a silent partner in the Middle East or somewhere like that. I can ask around if you like."

"That'd be great. We haven't come across anything like that in our research."

"Every industry has its insider knowledge. I mean, you don't go proclaiming everything you know to the whole world, do you? And besides, who likes to be seen helping the police?" Petra teased.

Felix was silent. He knew just how right she was with her final remark. Even crime victims themselves often concealed important details from the police out of a misguided sense of solidarity.

Petra yawned. "I'm getting pretty sleepy. Tomorrow's going to be a stressful day. I should probably go."

"Well, if you think so, then maybe you're right," he stammered.

She smiled. "Or maybe I should stay?"

"Oh, I'm not sure…" His stammer became worse.

"You see. As long as you're not sure, then I'm not sure either!"

While she put her shoes on, Felix admonished himself for being so cowardly and searched in her eyes for something resembling anger or confrontation. But all he could see was a deep-seated smile. She kissed him on both cheeks by the door and ventured out into the evening air.

Then she turned to face him once more. "Do you know, you're the only man who's ever given me the brush off? Good night and sweet dreams." With that, she blew him a kiss and disappeared from sight.

Utterly confused and with his mind still racing, Felix remained in the open door for five minutes before returning to the living room.

"Say Django, why are women so hard to understand?"

But Django wasn't about to comfort him either. He seemed to be sulking because Felix hadn't managed to keep hold of his personal stroking service. What a failure! The tom advanced towards the veranda door with great dignity and insisted on being let out. With a heavy heart, his owner released him into the night, finished off the bottle of wine and sank into an uneasy sleep.

On the drive to the office Felix's thoughts were on Petra, and her alone. He was like a schoolboy in love for the first time, despairing of feelings he feared would remain forever unrequited. Shaking his head, he swore to be more direct next time they met. There was no point denying it anymore: he was in love.

His cell beeped, an SMS. But his attempts to retrieve it hastily from his jacket made him jerk the wheel, and very nearly caused an accident. The driver behind him blew his horn and gestured wildly with his arms. With one hand raised in apology, the chief inspector was finally able to wrest the cell from his inside pocket.

"Will be about thirty minutes late. Had to take Nina to the doctor. Frauke."

Shit. Felix was disappointed it wasn't from Petra, even if he wasn't entirely sure what he'd expected. So they'd have to wait for their colleague, but that was fine. Nina had just turned three and spent the days at Frauke's parents'.

Frauke's husband had been jealous of her job and colleagues and had felt obliged to look elsewhere for affection. So now she was raising their daughter alone.

Arriving at the station seven minutes later, the chief inspector shouted to Emilio in passing that their morning get-together would be delayed, and disappeared into his office.

"I spent the whole night dreaming about you. Felix." It'd cost him a lot of effort to finally push the "send" button. But afterwards, he felt suddenly released.

The response came just as he was about to leave.

"I hope they were nice dreams!"

"They certainly were. Not to say intense!"

"Intense or erotic? Or maybe intensely erotic?"

He could just imagine Petra's mischievous grin.

"They were pretty hot, more than just erotic!!"

Barely two minutes later, his phone rang. "I want to hear about your hot dreams!"

"And you will, but not now, not over the phone. Can I see you again tonight? I think Django misses you."

"How could I say no to that? Unfortunately I need to go to Berlin for three days. An important client is a little nervous and needs reassurance. I have to leave in an hour, but I'd love to continue this evening."

"Pity, but that's OK. When should I call?" Felix hoped the disappointment in his voice wasn't too obvious.

"It'll be easier if I call you from the hotel, then my company will foot the bill. I'm not sure how late it'll be though. Say hello to Django for me."

Felix didn't get the chance to respond, but he felt good, and was extremely excited about talking to her. Yes, sending the text had been the right move.

As soon as their colleague had arrived at the station they gathered in the meeting room. Felix waved her away as she tried to apologize.

"Listen, Frauke, everyone understands you're in a difficult situation." He placed an arm around her shoulders and gave her a quick squeeze. "So, back to the Kaptain case. Arno, did you manage to get hold of the neighbors?"

Arno nodded: he had arranged meetings with all of them between seven and eight that evening.

"Good, then let's see what we can get out of Uwe Kaptain's immediate circle. I've been wondering whether he was visiting someone from the company the night he was killed, his boss, for example, or a woman. If one of his colleagues lives near Eppstein, then we could be onto something. Arno, see what you can find. Emilio, you check out Mr. Grüntal; Frauke and I are going back to the apartment. Oh, and one more thing: try and get your hands on Kaptain's bank statements and phone bills. Any questions, suggestions?" Felix gazed around the room.

"Yeah, we've been overlooking something," Frauke replied.

"What do you mean?" He scrutinized her with his gaze.

"How did the perpetrator flee the scene; are there any witnesses or traces?"

The chief inspector wanted to kick himself; both Arno and Emilio stood staring at the floor in embarrassment.

"You're absolutely right: we should've thought of that a lot sooner. Let's look into that immediately. Emilio, go and speak with the central taxi office. Then check for any bus services at that time."

Everybody stood up, and Frauke set off for the victim's apartment with her senior officer in tow. They searched the flat again

49

thoroughly but still found nothing new or unusual. Felix noticed that Kaptain's leather mask and suit were missing from the bathroom; probably the lab was examining them that very moment. No new messages had been left on the answering machine, and any mail was just advertising.

A brochure from a little wine dealership near Frankfurt attracted his attention. As a wine connoisseur, he noted the name and address out of personal interest. Meanwhile the search for photos drew a blank once more. There were no nails or holes in the walls either; nor the outline of any subsequently removed picture frames.

"What do you think, Frauke? What does this apartment tell you? After all, they say that every apartment tells you something about its inhabitant."

"Above all, I see someone who's invested a lot of money but also has good taste. It's not showy or pretentious; rather, well-ordered and quietly elegant. If I didn't know the victim was divorced, I'd assume a woman had had a hand in it. But there's no indication that anyone else lives here," she said.

Her boss agreed.

They met Mrs. Schumm in the stairwell.

"Good morning, Inspector, did you want to speak with me?"

Felix shook his head.

"I still can't believe that that nice Dr. Kaptain was murdered, it's very sad. Since I found out, I've been rather frightened and have taken to bolting my door during the day. These are troubled times, inspector, troubled times," the old lady complained.

"You're quite right: it's always best to be on your guard. Would you be so kind as to call if anything else about Mrs. Kaptain occurs to you?"

Mrs. Schumm promised she would, and then closed the door behind her.

After dropping Frauke at headquarters, Felix experienced a moment of sudden inspiration. He drove on to Münchener Straße, home to the department of financial crime. Upon arrival, he parked the EV in a regular space (there was no charging station here) and went directly to his former colleague Hans Werners, who he'd studied with at police training college.

Hans had been set on the financial crimes department from the start and there was little he didn't know. His problem was that he often lacked the necessary evidence to secure a conviction. Years ago, they would go for a beer in the evening and discuss whether ultimately they weren't just tilting at windmills, like Don Quixote before them; but these days they didn't see too much of each other.

"Hello Hans," he greeted his old friend, the latter's face hidden behind a mountain of files.

"Hi Felix, or should I say Chief Inspector Büschelberger?" Despite his years of service Hans was still a mere inspector; he had ruffled a few too many feathers in his time.

"Oh, cut it out. Anyway, from what I've heard, you're next in line," Felix grinned.

"As long as some banker or CEO doesn't complain that my investigations are damaging their reputation," Hans smiled. He was still an optimist.

"Good to see you - take a seat. I'll get you a cup of tea, or have you finally come to your senses?"

Chief Inspector Büschelberger shook his head and observed Hans as he boiled the kettle and added a teabag to the cup. Spending most of his active service behind a desk had resulted in the beginnings of a paunch, and his short blond hair was now streaked with grey. In contrast to Felix himself, his suit was an elegant cut.

Tea in hand, he casually leaned back and looked his old friend straight in the eye. "What do you know about Dr. Heinrich Zimmer Consultancy Ltd.?"

"Right now Heinrich Zimmer Ltd. is seen as something of an exemplary company, one that is both expanding and hiring. It seems the owner has contacts in the city council. You know how companies involved in environmental protection can currently do no wrong; well the politicians want a piece too. I haven't heard anything specific, but I do know that they were in a bit of a jam financially three or four years ago," Hans recited from memory.

"That matches my information. It was only a query, anyway."

"If you want to investigate them, you'll need some pretty solid evidence. Like I said, Dr. Zimmer has contacts," Hans warned his old colleague.

Felix nodded. "I'll be careful. It's nothing concrete just now. One of their top employees has just been murdered."

"I'll let you know if I hear anything."

While he drained his mug, Felix thought about what his colleague had said. "Tell me something, Hans, why do you go around dressed like that? Are you trying to find yourself a wife or something?" He couldn't withhold it any longer – everyone from the finance department was always dressed as if they were bankers or stockbrokers themselves.

"Disguise is everything. You know how people never divulge everything to us. But go like this to a bar where all the idiots from finance drink and they'll accept you as one of their own right away."

"That's exactly what someone else said to me last night. Right then, see you soon and thanks for all the info."

"Felix?" Hans's voice called him back.

"Yes?"

"Regarding your case, I just thought of a quote by someone, Rousseau I think: 'Behind every great fortune lies a great crime.' Maybe the motive was financial in some way. The longer I spend in this job, the more I realize that money is ultimately behind almost everything."

Felix nodded. "Maybe you should spend some time with Kevin Dour; he studied philosophy. The two of you would make a good team."

"Oh, piss off back to your corpses and frogs and leave us decent hard-working coppers in peace!" Hans droned ironically.

"Sure. We should go for a drink sometime. See you!"

The chief inspector disappeared, smiling at the scurrilous remarks his former colleague was still making. On his way back he stopped off at Conny's, bumping into Arno and Frauke.

After lunch, Felix dialed for Dr. Dour.

"Is there any chance of us finding traces of other cars at the east port, or have you got something already?"

The reply sounded more animal than human. "Felix, are you nuts? I mean, you were there. There's nothing but concrete slabs within an initial radius of two to three miles, and then constant traffic thereafter. How are we supposed to find anything? I'm not a magician."

"Of course, you're right. I just thought the perpetrator must have fled the scene somehow," Felix apologized.

"Yes, well, I'm afraid I can't help you there. Was that all? I'm pretty busy right now!"

"Anything that might interest me?"

"Not unless you're a medical expert; which I suspect you aren't. A lovesick sixteen-year-old tried to hang herself using a pair of tights, only to think better of it halfway through. She struggled for a long time, but in the end she lost. If you ask me, people are pretty stupid."

"And you've ruled out a third party?"

"Yes, Chief Inspector, nothing for you to do here, unless you work in the cleaning industry now too," the pathologist snapped.

"Sorry, I'm not sure I understand." Felix noted that Kevin Dour was living up to his surname today.

"You must have heard that people who hang themselves throw up, only the rope – or in this case, the tights – prevents them. So anyway, our colleagues from uniform had a new recruit with them, who wanted to prove himself. He cut the girl loose, stood in front of her and copped the whole load. That was a little too much for him. I'm sure you can imagine what happened next. And now, goodbye!"

The chief inspector knew his colleague's sense of humor only too well. Life was tough and you had to be pretty thick-skinned to cope with a job that brought you face to face with the dark side of the human condition on a daily basis. There was also no point asking about the examination on the evidence taken from Kaptain's apartment. He would be informed as soon as the findings were in. In that regard, the pathologist was completely reliable.

The team met again at four. Felix turned to Emilio, who was distributing his latest printouts. "So what did find you out?"

"First, Mr. Grüntal. He has several previous convictions, both for similar offences. At seventeen, he stood trial at a juvenile court for common assault; and was later found guilty of GBH following an armed robbery. He's been out on probation now for twelve months."

His boss whistled through his teeth. "You've clearly got a good nose for this sort of thing, but does that make our witness a suspect? Poisoning isn't part of his MO. Besides if he had done it, he wouldn't have been stupid enough to call us and then appear as a witness."

Emilio agreed. "I'd still like to bring him in for more questioning."

"OK, what else did you learn?"

"The central taxi office still hasn't got back to me; the drivers in question aren't back on duty until later this evening. Dispatch will notify them, and then they'll contact us directly. There are two bus lines that go near the crime site, the 237 and the 301, but there's no service between one and five in the morning. I've also been in touch with Telekom and the bank. They'll send us the documents as soon as the DA puts in a formal request."

"Good, I'll talk to Cando."

The chief inspector then invited Arno to say his piece.

"So, Dr. Zimmer lives close by in Frankfurt Harheim. His PA is based in Darmstadt, Mathildenhöhe, also a prime location. I haven't been able to check the others out yet but I'll send a request to the company's HR department."

"Then our investigation is slowly beginning to take shape. Nothing new from our end, except for the fact that there really do appear to be no photos in the apartment. I also paid a visit to the financial crimes department to see what they could tell me about Zimmer Ltd. The truth is that the company's never been implicated before. However, I have discovered that things were looking a bit grim financially a few years back, and then all of a sudden some money reappeared. No-one's sure where it came from. On top of this, the company seems to have some pretty good contacts on the political side. So we should get ready for the inevitable call or two from upstairs."

A general groan resounded.

"If that's all for now, then I'll go straight to Cando and join Arno later to interview the neighbors. Emilio, you take the evening off. You're still married and I want to make sure it stays that way. And you, Frauke, go home and take care of Nina."

Felix paid no heed to the pair's objections.

When the doorbell sounded, the Schmidts, whose apartment was considerably smaller than that of Uwe Kaptain, were already expecting the two officers.

"What can you tell us about your neighbor, the people he mixed with and the man himself?" Felix asked the questions while his colleague jotted everything down.

In contrast to Emilio, Arno had stuck with the good old-fashioned notepad – though he was a rapid scribe.

"Mr. Kaptain was always extremely polite, but he never seemed particularly interested in making friends. One time we had a kind of party for everyone in our block and he was the only person not there. He just didn't want to come," recounted Mr. Schmidt.

"And very tidy, he was that too. He always cleaned the stairwell and basement, unlike some of the shirkers in this house."

Mr. Schmidt gave his wife a surly look.

"It's true though," she defended her statement, before adding: "But he wasn't completely kosher either if you get what I mean."

"No," Felix admitted honestly, "I don't get what you mean."

"Well, he never had a single female visitor. If you did see him, it was always with young men, and generally after ten pm."

"You and your suspicions; he seemed perfectly normal to me."

Mrs. Schmidt's interruption had triggered an argument; meanwhile, Felix threw a glance at Arno, who just stood there helplessly rolling his eyes.

"Good, I think we've heard everything we need to. If anything else occurs to you, please don't hesitate to call." With that, Felix handed them his card, and the inspectors took their leave.

As the door clicked shut behind them, they could hear that the Schmidts' squabbling had only just begun.

"Sometimes I wonder why people bother to stay together when they've got nothing left to say to each other," Felix muttered as he rang Mrs. Wenzel's door.

"To keep us in a job." Arno's dry response drew only a shake of the head from the chief inspector.

Mrs. Wenzel made a far more favorable impression than the Schmidts. She couldn't tell them anything new, but all of a sudden she mentioned something that made Felix sit up and take notice.

"You know, I was amazed at how early Mr. Kaptain was up and about the day he died. I have to leave the house at five every morning; that's when I heard the noises coming from his apartment. No-one's ever up at that time apart from me."

"And you're quite sure that you heard noises coming from Mr. Kaptain's apartment on Monday morning?" Felix fixed his eyes on Mrs. Wenzel.

"Absolutely positive. Why, is that important?"

Felix glanced at Arno meaningfully. "We just didn't know he was up so early that day."

He didn't see any point in telling Mrs. Wenzel that the person she'd heard was probably Kaptain's killer, turning over the flat in the hours following the murder.

"Could you tell me what kind of noises you heard? And please try to be as exact as possible."

"It sounded like someone was pulling a drawer out pretty vigorously. Then when I reached the bottom floor it seemed as if something had fallen to the ground. I remember thinking to myself: Mr. Kaptain's very noisy today."

"And you didn't notice anything else?"

The woman shook her head.

Outside the door, Chief Inspector Büschelberger whistled through his teeth. "Looks like we've got a firm lead. We need to get the boys from forensics back out here. They should check the main door for signs of a break-in; and see whether any of the drawers inside the apartment have been damaged – in case one really did fall out."

As Arno didn't want to go home either, the two of them waited for forensics.

There were signs that the main door had been opened by force, while a drawer in the living room cupboard had clearly been damaged in the far right-hand corner. Felix looked inside the drawer. A few manuals for technical equipment purchased by Kaptain, nothing besides.

"Not a lot here for such a big drawer."

Felix nodded. "But that doesn't necessarily mean anything's missing. Come on, I think that's enough for one day."

They were the last to leave the apartment, oblivious to the curious glances of the neighbors.

An indignant tomcat awaited him when Felix finally arrived home.

"Yes, I'm sorry: you'll get something to eat right away."

He prepared Django's food, adding half a tin of tuna to improve the taste.

"There you are. I hope you can forgive me."

The tom pounced on the food like a tiger, before heading out on his nocturnal rounds. Just as he was thinking about what to eat himself, Felix's phone rang.

"Yes."

"If you're in a bad mood, I'm hanging up right now."

"No, Petra, I'm not in a bad mood, it's been a long day that's all. I'm just back this moment wondering what to eat, and thought maybe it was the emergency office saying something else had happened. But I'm very glad it's you."

"OK, then, you're forgiven. I've just had a hot shower and am now lying on the bed completely naked."

He could hear her giggling, and felt a faint stirring inside.

"Petra, you're torturing me here."

Laughter at the other end. "Why? What's up?"

Felix could well imagine her putting on her most innocent face.

"I just wish I could be there with you right now."

"I see, and there I was thinking you were a gentleman. What could a gentleman possibly want from a naked woman in a hotel room?"

"Well, I…" he began to stammer again.

Her laughter saved him from further embarrassment.

"Felix, don't take everything I say so seriously. I'm just winding you up."

"I'd rather you stripped me down." Even he was surprised by his spontaneous response.

"Let's talk about that the next time we see each other. I know what I'd do to you now if you were here."

"What?"

She laughed again. "No, I'm not going to make it that easy for you. I'll leave it to your imagination; then maybe the reality will surprise you even more."

"I can hardly wait," he breathed into the receiver.

"I know, but what was it again? Some secrets are more interesting when they remain hidden. I think you were right, you know. So, sleep well – and sweet dreams. If you dream of me, then I want to hear all about it. Bye, Felix."

"Wait a minute!" He couldn't bear the thought that Petra was about to hang up.

"What is it?"

"I just wanted to hear your voice again; it's so nice talking to you."

"Finally, you reveal your true feelings. I like talking to you too, but I need to be up early in the morning. So don't be angry if I have to hang up."

"OK, I understand. Then good night – and I will dream of you. I promise."

She blew him a kiss over the phone, and then the line went dead.

Before he went to sleep, Felix spent a long time thinking about Petra; everything else he might've said, and what their future together might be like. He had completely forgotten how hungry he was.

Chapter 5

As sure as death and taxes, Felix overslept the next morning. He jumped cursing into the bathroom, only to discover that Django had presented him with a conciliatory gift of a mouse lying sprawled across the shower mat.

Meanwhile the shower also seemed to have developed a life of its own, and was completely refusing to maintain the desired temperature. After putting some food and water out for the tom, Felix hurried to the office. The rest of the team were already waiting in the meeting room.

"Sorry, I slept in." The chief inspector could hear his stomach rumbling. "Anything to eat around here? I might keel over otherwise."

"I was at Mama's yesterday – she gave me something for you. Might not taste too good at breakfast, but I can get it for you if you like."

He nodded. Emilio's mother had all but adopted him. The two men knew each other from school and when Emilio had threatened to go off the rails, Felix had helped him get his life back on track; hence Emilio's decision to join the force. The chief inspector slurped his Lung Ching tea as he waited for his care package. As he polished off the cold cannelloni, he thought about how drastically his life needed to change. In the meantime, Arno relayed their findings.

When he'd finished, Felix said: "I think we've reached a critical stage in our investigation. We know that after Kaptain's death someone broke into his apartment, most likely the killer. That brings us decisively closer to establishing a motive. We need to know what the perpetrator was looking for and whether he found it. And we need to know where the murder took place. Arno, you and Emilio get yourselves down to Kaptain's office again and see if you can get a print-out of all company employee addresses. If they don't play ball, we'll issue them with a court order. Frauke, you take care of the written stuff and get the DA's authorization to access the victim's bank account and phone records. Try exerting a little pressure when you drop the warrants off so they're quick about it. I need more facts. We still don't have a clear idea of what happened here, and it's beginning to frustrate me."

As they left the room, Emilio took his boss to one side.

"Are you alright? You seem a little agitated – and somehow I don't think it's because of the case. You've dealt with much trickier problems in the past and kept a cool head."

Felix smiled at his colleague. "Just haven't been sleeping too well recently, that's all."

His partner surveyed him silently. "OK, fine – you know you can talk to me anytime if you need. And by the way, Mama wanted to know when you're next coming round for dinner. It's been a long time."

A smile spread across Felix's features: Signora Perfondo would never stop trying to mother him. "Tell her I'll definitely stop by in the next two weeks. And maybe I won't be alone."

"I'm sure she'll be pleased. So long as you know you'd better not come alone now, otherwise there'll be a pretty severe cross-examination," Emilio said.

"I know." Felix marched towards his office with a smile. Yes, he would try and persuade Petra to join him.

There was a note on his desk: "Mrs. Harris has been in touch. Call her on 00254 87756890."

As the ringtone sounded, Felix wondered where the dialing code was for.

"Hotel Kenyan Beach Resort, what can we do for you?"

"I'd like to speak to Mrs. Harris, please."

"One moment please, we will connect you."

Shortly afterwards he heard a breathless female voice. "Yes, hello, Harris here."

"Good morning, my name is Felix Büschelberger and I'm a chief inspector with the Frankfurt police." He didn't want to tell her straightaway that he was from murder squad; he didn't like making people nervous for no good reason.

"My neighbors told me that the police wanted to speak to me. What's happened?"

"I'm very sorry to have to tell you that your ex-husband's been murdered."

The silence at the other end of the line lasted longer than expected.

"Well, I'm sorry to hear that, but I've had no contact with him since our divorce; I can't say I'm too surprised – given the company he keeps."

"Would you care to elaborate?" Felix was curious.

"Did you know the reason we got divorced wasn't another woman? My ex-husband realized all of a sudden that he preferred men. I would've been able to compete with another woman – but with these boys he picks up on the streets? Well, how could I?"

Despite the distance, he could clearly perceive the bitterness in her voice. "I've no intention of ruining the rest of your holiday; you're back soon anyway, aren't you? Therefore I must ask you to come and see me as soon as you return – even if you and the victim haven't been in contact for a long time. I need your help here in Frankfurt."

"Of course, if you need me. Wednesday would be fine."

"Good. See you on Wednesday then; about twelve o'clock would be fine." Felix gave the address and was just about to hang up.

"Is it OK if I bring my husband? I don't want to face my past alone."

"Certainly!"

Felix heard a sigh of relief and then leaned back in his chair. That was an interesting revelation: according to his ex-wife, Uwe Kaptain had a thing for hustlers. So Mrs. Schmidt's suspicions from the night before had been well-founded. He reminded himself that you couldn't just disregard a statement because you didn't like the source. But was it relevant to the case? He guessed they'd find out eventually, and dialed the number for forensics.

"Hi Kevin. Do you have anything for me?"

"Did I not say I'd call you if I did? Can't you people just leave me alone for once? I wanted to stop by this afternoon, since most of the tests are complete. But just for your information, we've found different hair samples: all from men, according to the DNA

61

tests. Nothing in the trunk. That means the body was probably transported in the back seat, where we found the deceased's hair. The sperm traces in Kaptain's apartment are from three different men, one of them the victim himself. No telling how old they are, though. We're still running a comparison with the hair samples from the car. So, see you later."

Once again he was forced to acknowledge that Dr. Dour really did do things thoroughly; what's more, he always seemed to know the difference between what was - and what wasn't - important.

His thoughts turned to Petra: he decided to send her an SMS. "How I long to be the breeze, gently brushing against you."

The response came instantly. "Very romantic for this time in the morning?!?"

"I dreamed of you, as promised."

";-)))" was all he got in return.

Felix was surprised by how quickly Petra could make him feel all confused again.

"I'm looking forward to our next phone call. Tonight?"

"Yes, please."

He didn't get much else done before the lunch break, just sat there dreaming quietly.

After lunch, Felix called Chief Inspector Sulzner, a colleague from vice squad.

"Hello Kurt. We're in the middle of a murder enquiry and it seems our victim was involved with some of the boys from the street. Have you heard anything?"

"No, there haven't been any clients murdered for over ten years now. It's much more common that they murder the hustlers. I'm sure you know that better than I do. Still, I'll ask around."

"Thanks. I'll send you some photos of the victim, though I'm afraid they're only of the corpse. Circulate them among your people and see if he was a known client. Anything you can find would be a great help," said the head of the murder squad.

"Have you not made a positive ID? I mean, why aren't there any photos?" Kurt Sulzner asked.

That was what Felix liked about him: he was always on the ball. "No, we have, but there are no photos in his apartment. I'll send everything over to you right away. Thanks."

He was beginning to think they were making progress.

A little after three, Kevin Dour entered his office. "So, have you found the killer then?"

Felix shook his head.

"I knew you wouldn't have. When have you ever solved a murder without my help?"

"I'm not sure we have – unless you can think of one?" When Dr. Dour was in this sort of mood, attack was the best form of defense.

"Then at least you appreciate my assistance." Kevin's mood improved immediately. He opened his briefcase and took a tin out.

"Here you are: for the tea brigade. Some Rooibos, so that you drink something healthy for once. I might even have a cup with you."

"Should I be worried? You, being healthy – there must be something brewing." Felix surveyed the pathologist, who was enjoying a long draw on his cigarette.

"The only thing brewing is the Rooibos," Kevin laughed. "I'm fine. The last time a doctor saw me was a good fifteen years ago."

The chief inspector refrained from passing comment.

"I just felt like keeping slightly more life-like company today; but don't go getting any ideas. So, should we make our way through to the tea salon?"

Felix called the others straight into the meeting room. Dr. Dour insisted on making the tea for everyone, since it had to be strong enough to have any effect. Meanwhile the Inspector let the team in on his conversations with Mrs. Harris and Kurt Sulzner.

"Gay?" Emilio shook his head. "Perhaps we should look for a motive there?" He gazed around the room.

"Maybe someone was blackmailing him?" Arno said.

"Killing the golden goose? That doesn't make any sense. Was he murdered out of unrequited love? Poisoning suggests a woman to me. Perhaps one of Kaptain's female colleagues fell in love with him and couldn't deal with the rejection?" Frauke looked at the others.

"That's definitely possible. It would fit with finding the same make of wine that poisoned him at his flat," Dr. Dour cut in succinctly.

Felix turned towards the pathologist: "Why are you only telling us this now?"

"The tests were awkward. The wine was chemically altered by the gastric acid; and things weren't made any easier by the presence of the benzodiazepine chloral-hydrate. Still, we've managed to prove that the wine the poison was mixed with was a Romitorio di Santedame. Other than that, I can tell you that there was no match between the hair samples in the car and the sperm traces in the apartment."

Felix already knew the rest. He sipped his tea tentatively. It wasn't bad at all, he thought to himself; he'd have to make a mental note of the brand.

"Then I think I'll pay Kaptain's wine dealer a little visit: I saw the leaflet in his flat. What else do we have?"

Emilio and Arno had a list containing the addresses of all Dr. Zimmer Ltd. company employees. They had already skimmed through the names, but found no-one living in the vicinity of Eppstein.

However, the victim's financial records made for very interesting reading. Frauke had discovered that Kaptain's assets amounted to about 800,000 euros – distributed among fixed rate bonds, time deposits and shares.

"What I find interesting is that his equity portfolio is made up of DAX and MDAX papers, but there's not a single pharmaceutical or chemical company among them." Arno, who enjoyed theorizing about shares, despite never having bought a single one in his life, glanced up from the documents he was reading.

"Don't you think you'd buy shares in the industries you knew most about?" he asked.

"You're the stocks and shares expert – I'm not even sure what they are," Felix responded.

"Could this be a lead?" The chief inspector put the question to the group.

"Probably not," Arno shook his head, "it's just the first thing I noticed."

Emilio glanced towards Frauke. "What about his account records? Are they coming our way too?"

"Yeah, but that'll take until the middle of next week. They need to collate them all first."

"Anything else?" The chief inspector allowed his gaze to pass from one team member to the next. He was just about to adjourn the meeting when Emilio began leafing through his papers again.

"There's one thing I forgot."

The rest waited eagerly.

"Ha, there it is! Didn't I mention our witness had several previous convictions? Well, it seems his victims were all homosexual."

Felix took a long, hard look at his friend.

"Seems like we need to bring him in for some more questioning. If you like, I can subpoena him."

After the meeting, Felix left the building with Kevin Dour.

"As far as I'm concerned you can stop by more often and present your findings in person."

"Maybe I'll do that." Kevin lit another cigarette and made his way down the hall.

The chief inspector climbed into the Focus and drove to Kaptain's wine dealer. Though it looked rather innocuous from the outside, upon entry he found an interior that was both cavernous and tastefully fitted. The proprietor, one Luigi da Conterrossa, was a picture-perfect Italian: elegantly dressed, slicked back salt-and-pepper hair and the stomach of an avowed bon vivant.

He came towards Felix beaming with delight. "Welcome to La dolce vita, the Italian wine store. I am Luigi, the owner. How can I be of service, dottore?"

"I'm looking for a particular red wine: the Romitorio di Santedame," the chief inspector said.

Conterrossa's expression became friendlier still. "A signore with taste and style. I knew it right away. Please follow me."

He led the inspector into a small backroom where the bottles were partially obscured by a thick layer of dust. Felix realized immediately that this was where the most expensive wines were kept.

"Here it is, the Romitorio di Santedame from Tuscany, the city of Pontassieve to be exact. The vintner is a friend of mine. The wine's from 1998 but could easily be stored for another ten or twenty years. It was awarded the highest prize again at a recent tasting."

"It does sound rather tempting."

"It's 72 euros a bottle. If you buy six, I'll give you a special price of 400 euros. How's that for an offer?" Conterrossa beamed from head to toe.

"I don't doubt the wine's worth it, but it's a little expensive for me."

"A pity, but something similar perhaps?" asked the wine dealer.

"In fact, I came to ask you some questions." Felix showed his ID.

"Policia? But I haven't done anything wrong – perhaps we can talk prices again, si?"

"No, it's not about that. I just wanted to know if the name Uwe Kaptain meant anything to you," the inspector reassured him.

"Naturalmente, the dottore is one of my best customers. He buys this wine too, five crates of the stuff each time at least. His boss dottore Zimmer – he buys here as well, the same wine. As a present for his most valued clients, I think."

"Dr. Zimmer buys the same wine? Interesting. And is this wine easy to get hold of?"

"You mean, can you get it in a supermarket?" Luigi da Conterrossa grimaced as if he'd just bitten into a lemon. "I only sell the best wine! This is the only place in Frankfurt you can get the Romitorio di Santedame. I have reps in Munich, Hamburg and Berlin who can each buy for you, otherwise no-one. Basta."

"Would it be possible to get a list of clients who buy from you?"

"Commissario, why do you need such a list? Some of my clients are very well-known: I don't think they'd like it," Luigi replied.

"Because we're in the middle of a murder investigation. Kaptain was poisoned earlier this week."

"The dottore is dead?" The wine dealer grew pale.

"Yes, the poison was dissolved in red wine," Felix explained.

"What? The Romitorio – poisoned? Per l'amor di Dio, what a sacrilege! Commissario, you must believe me, I had nothing to do with it. I am an honest man."

"I believe you, but what about this list?"

"Yes, yes, I can make one for you. I'll send it when it's ready."

The inspector nodded and handed him his business card.

"Please take a bottle of the Romitorio as a gift from me," the wine dealer said.

"You know I can't accept," Felix raised his hands in protest.

"Please, you must. Or buy another bottle, perhaps a Lamaione 1999, it's only nine euros. Then I can give you the Romitorio as a welcome gift. Take the bottle and promise me that you'll catch the killer. The dottore was always so gracious." Luigi was pleading with the inspector now.

"We'll catch him alright – and thank you for your kind offer."

Felix paid for the wine and drove home smiling.

He imagined Luigi da Conterrossa lighting a candle before a statue of the Virgin Mary – not to pray for the soul of Uwe Kaptain; but to atone for crimes committed against the Romitorio di Santedame. He'd take the wine with him when he next visited Emilio's family.

That evening, Felix waited longingly for his cell to ring. When at last it did, he picked up instantly. The conversation resulted in yet another sleepless night.

Chapter 6

Felix was awoken by Django, who was perched on his chest licking his muzzle, which was a clear indication it was breakfast time. Felix yawned, looked at the bedside clock and gave a start. It was almost eleven; he hadn't slept so late in ages.

First he fed Django, then took care of the weekly shop, stacking the trolley up higher than usual. Although he couldn't be sure, he hoped he'd be spending a lot more time with Petra now. She was returning from Berlin that evening. After finishing the household chores the first thing he did was order a pizza.

In the afternoon, he called Emilio's mother and promised to come over for dinner the following Friday – with company. Hopefully he'd be able to convince Petra to join him, otherwise there'd be trouble. Around five, the phone finally rang.

It was her. "I'm back. Do you want to come over at eight?"

Naturally Felix agreed.

After that, time seemed to stand still and he thought about what he should take. A bottle of Primitivo and a rose maybe? In the end he decided on chocolates: there was a specialty confectioners just round the corner. He left Django some food, before letting him out and heading off. Outside Petra's house, he waited another five minutes – he didn't want to be too punctual.

She was wearing a tight fitted jumper and comfy-looking cotton slacks. Felix also noticed her bare feet. She greeted him by wrapping her arms around his neck and kissing him on the lips. Then she took a step back and looked at him, her eyes sparkling. "You're not on stand-by or anything, are you?"

The chief inspector gave a shake of the head.

"Then I'll have your cell, please!" Petra extended her right hand.

He wondered what she could have in mind, but said nothing. A quick push of a button and his work phone was off. Then in a single movement she removed her jumper and forced him up against the front door.

"Finally, I get you all to myself."

She kissed Felix passionately, and impatiently began undressing him. They'd just about made it to the living room before desire overcame them. Soon enough he lay exhausted next to her, his head resting against her soft, warm breasts. He caressed her nipples as she ran her fingers through his hair.

"I haven't been that quick in ages!" He gave Petra a kiss; she just smiled.

"Come on, I'll show you the rest of the flat." She took him by the hand and showed him the different rooms. When they reached the bedroom she threw him onto the bed. The box of pralines remained unopened in the hall.

Felix awoke at nine, stretched and gave a loud yawn. His gaze fell upon Petra, who was still sleeping, nestled tightly up against him. He kissed her and made to get up, but an arm prevented him.

"Where do you think you're going?" she asked in a slightly sulky voice.

"I need to check Django's OK. He's not used to being out this long."

"Right, sorry I'd forgotten… Can't you bring him over?"

"Afraid not – he'd be really anxious here, you know cats and changes of environment."

"Then we'll just have to do it in your apartment!" Petra beamed. "Come on, let's get dressed then head straight over for some breakfast and cat-stroking."

Three minutes later she was ready and grinning at him. "How come you men always take so long?"

Sunday went by in a flash. Felix didn't see anyone except Petra. In the evening they went off to collect toads together. The meaningful glances the group exchanged as Petra emerged from his car didn't bother them in the slightest.

The chief inspector briefly informed them of how things stood with the kamikaze driver from the previous week. Although unable to say much while the investigation was still on-going, he promised to tell them everything once it'd been resolved.

He and Petra began collecting the amphibians together, and on this occasion their time in the field passed without incident. At one point Petra showed Felix a particularly large pair of mating toads. "First we take care of their love life; then we'll see to our own."

On the drive back she showed just how seriously she meant it by refusing to keep her hands away from his pants.

The next morning Felix realized that Django had spent the whole night on Petra's side, which he could only interpret as a good sign. He showered and set the breakfast table. But she didn't want to get up yet.

"I've got today off, in lieu of Saturday. Mind if I stay with Django for a bit?"

"Sure – make yourself at home."

Their morning cup of tea didn't provide any new leads. On Felix's desk was a letter from Luigi da Conterrossa, containing his client list. It read very much like a Who's Who of Frankfurt high society. The only name to catch his eye was that of Dr. Zimmer, who had ordered more than twenty cases of the Romitorio. Uwe Kaptain, meanwhile, had treated himself to five. No wonder Luigi da Conterrossa was so upset.

Felix dialed the number of the consultancy firm and asked whether Dr. Zimmer was in.

"Come on, Emilio. We're going back to Kaptain's office. I think we still need to clear a few things up there."

His colleague went to get the Ford.

"By the way, I read yesterday that in San Francisco they've completed the first milestone of building public charging stations for electric cars, so that people can fill up on electricity for free. Just imagine that!"

Chief Inspector Büschelberger smiled at his friend. "You've become a real fan of our Focus, haven't you? But you're right: it'd be great if they did something like that here. It'd certainly make people more willing to buy electric cars!"

"You'll see a lot more EVs in the next few years, mark my words. Nothing's going to slow this train down!" With that Emilio went back to concentrating on the traffic, and soon they were parked in front of Dr. Heinrich Zimmer Consultancy Ltd.

Again, Felix noted how they were announced the minute they'd crossed the threshold.

"I'm afraid there's no way Dr. Zimmer can see you right now, he has an important meeting," one of the receptionists informed him.

"That's fine. We wanted to speak to his secretary too. If you'd be so kind as to call Ms. Peisker. And if Dr. Zimmer does find the time, then he's more than welcome to join us." The chief inspector gave a friendly nod and turned away.

A little later, Anita Peisker appeared and led them behind the reception to a glazed meeting room on the ground floor. See-through but completely soundproof.

"Thank you for taking the time to speak to us at such short notice. Sometimes we policemen just can't wait – that's why we always forget to make appointments," Felix apologized.

"No problem, if it helps catch the killer, then it's fine by me," the secretary replied.

"Very well. So, what can you tell me about Uwe Kaptain's private life?"

"Not a lot. He was always very courteous and polite. A very nice man; I can't imagine he had any enemies."

"Were there any rumors linking him romantically to his colleagues? Male or female," the inspector probed.

"What do you mean by male?" Anita Peisker was visibly surprised. "Are you implying he was gay?"

Felix nodded. "There are indications he may have been. Was he involved with anyone from the company?"

"I don't know if he was actually involved with anyone, but one or two definitely tried their luck. The fact that he was gay probably explains why none of them ever got anywhere. The office parties can get pretty lively around here, I'm sure you know how it is."

"I'm afraid I don't. Can you tell me what you mean exactly?" He moved a little closer, hoping to create a more intimate atmosphere.

"Our Christmas parties are pretty legendary. Some of the men and women seem to lose all their inhibitions; it can lead to the "The Feast of Love" being taken very literally."

"But Kaptain never showed any interest?"

She shook her head.

71

"Nothing in particular that you remember - a scene involving our victim, anything like that?" Felix wouldn't let go.

Anita Peisker took her time to answer. "Actually, there was someone the year before last – he had to give her the brush-off a good few times."

"What was her name and does she still work for the company?"

"Chief Inspector, do you really think she could have anything to do with the murder after such a long time?" the secretary asked.

"Unrequited love is a powerful emotion and revenge out of wounded pride or vanity a common motive. Plus there's the fact that women are more likely to use poison than men," he explained.

"Her name is Heike Rubin, though it was Kleiber back then. She's since married someone else from the company; they're expecting their first child. But I really don't think she could have had anything to do with it."

Felix nodded. "You're probably right, but best if we check it out anyway. Do you know of any similar incidents?"

Ms. Peisker shook her head.

"Does the name Romitorio di Santedame mean anything to you?" He changed tack.

"That's my favorite label, a very expensive red we often give to our best clients. Why do you ask?" Dr. Heinrich Zimmer's voice sounded from behind. He must have entered the room at some point during the previous few minutes.

Felix turned round. "The poison that killed Uwe Kaptain was dissolved in this wine."

"At least that has some style – don't you think?" Heinrich Zimmer appeared self-assured; there was even a hint of amusement in his voice. "It reminds me of a story from medieval England. There was once a king who drowned his brother - the rightful heir to the throne - in a butt of wine he'd filled with his victim's favorite drink. It's probably where the phrase 'drink oneself to death' comes from."

"That's all very interesting, of course," the inspector interrupted, "but it doesn't help us with our enquiries. Besides, I don't get the joke." His voice was icy.

"No, you're right; it's not the time to be making jokes. I'm sorry." Heinrich Zimmer tried to atone for his faux pas. "As far as I know, Uwe Kaptain also liked this wine very much."

"Yes, he did, but I'm much more interested in finding out who you gave the wine to, especially internally," the inspector said.

"All managers and above receive a bottle on their birthday, a personal gift from me; otherwise only valued clients."

"Is Mr. Rubin a manager?" Felix gazed at Dr. Zimmer with curiosity.

"Yes, he's a divisional director like Dr. Kaptain, though the substances he deals with are far less dangerous."

"And how was their relationship?"

"Friendly and professional, I'd say. Unless you've heard anything different?" Heinrich Zimmer turned to his secretary.

"No, I haven't," she replied.

"Good, in that case there are no further questions. Please remember to inform us if anything else occurs to you, irrespective of how trivial it may seem," Felix ended the conversation.

"Of course, we're happy to help any way we can. Now, if you will please excuse me!" Zimmer disappeared and the two detectives went on their way.

"I wonder if Dr. Zimmer realizes he's just leapfrogged a few places up our list of suspects?" The chief inspector grinned at his partner.

"It's a pretty short list though, and there are still a few strangers on it. Even so, I could have slapped him for that story, what an arrogant bastard," Emilio replied.

"In the meantime we should make an appointment with Mrs. Rubin, if only so we can eliminate her from our enquiries."

They were just getting into the car when Felix received a text.

"Have locked myself out of your flat. Can you come and save me? P x."

"We need to stop by mine quickly," he told his friend.

Petra was sitting on the steps outside his apartment with a book in her lap and two shopping bags beside her. As he bent down to kiss her, he found his gaze met by that of the gorilla on the front cover.

"Hi. I just wanted to take a look at something outside and then the door closed behind me. Thank God I had some money on me, so at least I could do a bit of shopping for us. I want to appeal to all your senses when you come home tonight."

She linked her arm in his while he opened the door. Django began rubbing against his legs as soon as they'd entered the apartment.

"No, my friend, I'm afraid it's not dinner time yet. But I do envy you your company." He stroked him.

"Do you really have to go straightaway? Perhaps we could get a little naughty in the kitchen?"

Felix felt something stirring. "That's a very tempting offer, but Emilio's downstairs in the car. He's bound to come up if I keep him waiting too long."

"Pity!" Petra gave an exaggerated pout, then laughed and grabbed hold of the tom.

"Then off you go, we don't want to see you again until tonight. I can cuddle with Django in the meantime."

After a quick kiss goodbye, Felix was back outside.

"Everything OK?" Emilio gave him a quizzical look.

"Yeah, everything's great. Petra had locked herself out; I just needed to let her back in."

Emilio whistled through his teeth. "You should've said something! Then maybe I could've forgotten I was waiting for you and headed back to the office."

He was rewarded with a pat on the shoulder. "Next time, maybe. You're a good friend."

As they sped away, Felix felt himself transported back to the racetrack.

In the station parking lot, his cell beeped for a second time.

"All your senses, remember!!! And you do always carry a pair of handcuffs, don't you?? P."

The team gathered for a quick meeting.

"So, for now let's focus our efforts on the victim's professional milieu, not forgetting his boss. Zimmer's pretty cynical; plus, he's coping a little too well with Kaptan's death for my liking."

Felix moved towards the whiteboard. "What motives could there be within the company?" he looked at each of them in turn.

"Love and all that jazz." Emilio rolled his eyes, playing the love-struck young girl.

The others laughed in response.

"Always a good motive and we already have our first lead: one Heike Rubin. Said to have been very interested in Kaptain a year ago, only to be sent packing on more than one occasion. Frauke, I want you to have a little talk with her as soon as we've run a background check. Who knows, maybe you'll get something out of her."

"It might also be financially motivated - blackmail for example. Our victim was pretty rich," Arno countered.

Felix nodded. "Also an interesting possibility. Follow it up. See if you can find out where the money came from. There could be a pattern."

"What about illegal waste disposal? Kaptain might've discovered something; or perhaps he was mixed up in it all and angered one of his partners," Frauke piped up.

"Likewise an avenue we ought to pursue. Emilio and I will look at it; that way we'll be able to train our sights a little closer on Dr. Heinrich Zimmer."

When they'd finished there were three motives on the whiteboard, respective names below. Love: Frauke; Money: Arno; Waste: Emilio and Felix.

"Maybe Frauke and I should investigate the waste angle. I mean, you seem to be the expert on love right now." Emilio gave him a knowing look.

"Come on then, put us out of our misery." Frauke's interest was immediately piqued.

Even Arno leaned forward a little so he could hear better.

"There's not much to tell. I have a new girlfriend – Petra from the environmental group. What else can I say? Things are going great."

Frauke beamed at Felix, before embracing him.

"I'll let the DA know where we're at and tell him to expect some political pressure now that we're investigating Dr. Zimmer."

"And you're sure that investigating Heinrich Zimmer is advisable?" the DA asked?

Felix nodded.

"Then we'll be venturing back into Frankfurt's political jungle." Cando sighed. He'd often targeted friends and acquaintances of so-called public personalities – and it hadn't impacted favorably upon his career.

"Are there any other leads we could be pursuing?" he wanted to know.

"Nothing concrete at the moment. Our witness, the one who found the deceased, has previous: GBH, victim's homosexual – and we know that Kaptain was no stranger to the gay scene. Maybe they knew each other. Emilio reckons the witness is hiding something, but I don't think he's the killer," Felix summarized.

"Still, best to bear him in mind; if only to prove that we're investigating all angles. Keep him up your sleeve. If people start throwing their weight around then at least we can say there are other suspects. That should cover our backs." The DA nodded as he spoke.

Although he despised such political maneuvers, Felix found himself agreeing nonetheless. "Emilio's going to bring Grüntal back in as soon as possible."

When he arrived home, Felix was greeted by Petra and a glass of red wine. Django was lying contentedly on the sofa and seemed scarcely interested in his master's presence. He had already been amply provided for.

"Dinner's nearly ready; I made us rocket salad and spaghetti with scallops."

"Sounds delicious; I could get used to this."

"Please don't. My cooking is something of a rarity."

"Then this is a real honor."

"Yes!" Petra's eyes sparkled.

He noticed that the kitchen table had been moved, as well as elegantly laid. The food was fantastic. After the scallops he leaned back, closed his eyes and allowed himself a good, long sip of the wine. He could understand why Django was so blissfully happy.

A moment later he felt Petra sit on his lap and kiss him. Her hands were fumbling around for his trouser zip. He tried to say something but she put a finger to his lips: "Sssshhh…don't talk, just enjoy."

She was kissing his ear now, her tongue gently playing with the lobe. Felix tensed and thrust his hips forward. The rhythmic motion of Petra's body spurred him on. His hands dug into the chair and then it was all over.

"Did my hero have a tough day? Let's just forget all about it and focus on the here and now. OK?" Her forehead was pressed against his.

"OK," he squeezed her tightly.

"Easy does it, we're not finished yet, not by a long shot." Petra got up and cleared the table.

"Do you trust me?" she asked.

"Of course, but why are you asking now?"

She put her finger to his lips once more. "Then I want you to give me your handcuffs and spread yourself out naked on the kitchen table."

The way Petra spoke to him – the whole situation – was turning him on again. He obeyed without fuss. The table top was pleasantly cool. She attached the handcuffs to a heating pipe against the wall and snapped them around his wrists.

"I hope you have the key – otherwise it's going to get pretty embarrassing when your colleagues have to come and free you," she giggled.

"So that's why you moved the table, you planned all this," Felix grinned.

"But of course! Didn't I say I'd find out if you liked these sorts of games?" Her voice was seductive now.

"I'll admit it turns me on; but I never did anything like this with Christine, my ex-wife."

"Not much of a confession, that. I can see it turns you on. The rest we'll talk about later."

Petra started rolling a piece of kitchen towel. "Now I'm going to blindfold you; after that it's just you and your senses."

77

Having left Felix alone on the table, she exited the room. He overheard her making noises in the bedroom, before returning to the kitchen. With only his sense of hearing to guide him, he traced her heels as they click-clacked across the terracotta floor. Petra had reached the fridge. She opened the door and came towards him again.

"So, did you miss me? Then we don't want to keep you waiting any longer, do we?"

She showered his body with kisses and tender caresses. Felix turned this way and that when she came to his sensitive areas. He could hardly bear it any longer. Just then he felt something cold trickle down his inner thigh. He cried out.

"Easy now, there nothing's wrong; it's just ice."

Felix felt the ice cube slide over his lips, briefly licking it as it made its way back down towards his thighs. At which point, he reared up.

"Please don't make me wait any longer!" he groaned.

"Soon. I like it when hard men go all soft." Petra giggled and poured red wine over his chest, allowing it to accumulate down by his navel. Then she licked it all up before they made love for a second time.

"I have to work early tomorrow. Will you be terribly annoyed if I don't stay with you tonight?" she asked finally, after they had been lying silently next to each other for a while.

"Annoyed, no – but it'll break my heart." Felix put on his best puppy dog eyes.

Petra smiled as she pushed him away. "That won't work on me. Besides, I really can't. We'll see each other soon though."

"I can wait, but I miss you already."

"I know!" With that, she leapt to her feet and began to get dressed.

At the door, Felix grabbed her gently by the wrist. "By the way, I'd forgotten to say we're invited to Emilio's mother's house for dinner on Friday."

"Great, I'm sure it'll be fun."

With the clattering of her heels still in his ear, he resolved to finish the bottle of wine.

Chapter 7

Felix was still a little sleepy the next morning when he found a note from Chief Inspector Sulzner. He dialed the number immediately.

"Good morning, Kurt! What've you got for me?"

"We've been asking round a little; a few boys on the street have confirmed your victim was a known client. Seems he paid pretty well. There was one he saw regularly; we can question him together if you like."

"That's great! When can we bring him in?"

"Martin Stritz is his name; he usually starts working the streets about one. If you're here by midday then we can try and pick him up."

"Perfect, see you then."

The meeting room smelt a little strange, though not unpleasantly so. It was the second Tuesday of the month, the day they all drank the same tea: always a new kind, and always selected by a different member of the team. Today was Emilio's turn. Felix was pretty sure he'd have picked one from the Arabic-speaking world, as that's what his friend was into at the moment.

"We've been expecting you. Today we have a Tamr Hindi, made from tamarinds. It's a bit like the Rooibos Dr. Dour brought in for us last week," came the greeting.

The chief inspector found it eminently drinkable. Once again he noticed that despite being a source of ridicule, it was actually his team's penchant for tea that made them such a tight-knit group.

"Good, let's get going! Kurt Sulzner has found one of Kaptain's hustlers - a regular, it seems. Emilio, I want you to come with me when we try and grab him. Anything else?" He gazed round the room.

"The victim's bank records should come today; then I can crosscheck them with his salary and equity portfolio. There could be something there."

Felix nodded at Arno, and looked across to Frauke.

"I'm meeting Mrs. Rubin this afternoon to ask her some questions," she said concisely.

"Sounds good. Emilio and I will try to speak with her husband at the same time. That way, they won't be able to compare notes. Hopefully we'll make it, time-wise."

"I'm sure you'll manage just fine!" Arno joked.

"And what's that supposed to mean?" Emilio snapped. "Just stick to your tractors, why don't you."

"I just meant I thought you'd manage," Arno made a conciliatory gesture with his hands.

"Come on, you two. No fighting, especially over something so trivial. And just so you know, your driving style is pretty notorious," Felix waded in energetically.

"Scusi, Arno – my kids kept me up all night. I'm just a little cranky."

"Anything serious?" Felix asked.

"No, nothing like that," Emilio deflected.

With that, the dispute was resolved and they could continue discussing the case as they breathed in the sweet aroma of their tea.

After Emilio and Felix had picked up their colleague from vice squad, they drove over to the main station in the hope of finding Martin Stritz. Kurt was younger than Felix and regarded within the force as a very good officer. He was in superb physical condition, albeit dressed down in order to avoid being instantly recognized as a policeman.

It'd become pretty pointless these days though, as he himself had commented self-deprecatingly; by now everyone around here knew who he was anyway. Still, he'd gotten used to the grunge style. After they'd been driving through the streets for about an hour, Sulzner pointed out a young man who seemed to be suffering from anorexia – though he did have quite a cute face. The man looked tense and kept peering over his shoulder.

"Emilio, you get out here and stay behind him. Felix and I will approach from the front. He's bound to leg it as soon as he sees us."

Kurt stopped the Focus for Emilio to get out.

Slowly they drove past Martin Stritz and stopped the car at the next crossroads, before jumping out and racing back down the street. They almost collided with him on the corner, whereupon

Martin gave a start, turned on his heels and fled straight in the direction of Emilio. The latter stopped him after thirty feet and pushed his face up against the wall.

"Trying to get away, were we? We've got a few things we'd like to ask you first!" Kurt Sulzner barked.

"Take it easy, Inspector. I just mixed you up with some people I don't want to see right now," Martin defended himself.

"OK, calm down, you know it's us now. Who the hell are you so frightened of anyway?" Sulzner asked mockingly.

"Just a few dealers, that's all," Martin Stritz responded.

Sulzner gave a brief laugh. "Don't give me that shit! Do you owe them money or something? I mean, why else would you be afraid of that rabble all of a sudden?"

"Honestly, Inspector. I've been on methadone for three months now. I'm clean but they keep trying to get me back on drugs. I don't want to, I swear." Martin Stritz voice was almost cracking.

"OK, that's got nothing to do with me. By the way, did I introduce my colleagues Büschelberger and Perfondo from the murder squad? They need to ask you a few questions." Kurt Sulzner spoke in a deliberately composed manner.

In one fell swoop the color was drained from the hustler's face. "But I haven't done anything! Come on man, I swear it wasn't me. Please let me go."

"Just keep calm. No-one's accusing you of anything; it's just that one of your regulars is dead and we wanted to see what you could tell us about him," Felix intervened.

"So I'm not a suspect?" Martin Stritz sounded relieved.

"No, absolutely not. We just wanted to talk." Chief Inspector Büschelberger signaled for his partner to let Martin go.

"Good, OK, I'm calm." Martin put his hands through his greasy, slicked-back hair. "So what's the story?"

"Can we go somewhere to talk? It doesn't have to be headquarters," Felix asked Kurt.

"Hey, there's a good place by the train station; if you give me a little something to put in my coffee I'll tell you everything you need to know," Martin replied before Sulzner could say anything.

The chief inspector nodded, and they made their way to the station across the road. The witness slurped happily away at his coffee, which had been fortified by an entire hip flask of cognac ordered separately by Felix.

"Awesome. So, what do you want to know? Who's this guy that's died?"

"The man's name is Uwe Kaptain; according to our sources you were sometimes with him in his flat."

"That's right. Always up for it, he was; wanted to do the whole bondage thing – but he paid well and usually for the whole night. He's dead? Shit, he didn't mind me sleeping over in winter. Always had a good supply of booze."

Martin mumbled something to himself.

"Speak up please so we can hear what you're saying!" Felix slammed his fist down on the table.

"OK, Chief, take it easy now. I'm just gutted the Doc's dead."

"It's 'Chief Inspector.' Is there anything else you can tell us? How often did you meet? And when did you last see him?"

The junkie quaffed back his coffee. "Can I get another?" he asked.

Emilio ordered him a second.

"I was generally with him once or twice a month; the last time was two weeks ago. I took one of my friends along too. The Doc said he wanted to make a night of it. We did too, had a real orgy, if you know what I mean. Did it a few times, in the living room, the bedroom. Shitloads of booze. We both got five hundred euros out of it too, fucking brilliant." The witness was waxing lyrical by now.

"Your friend – what's his name, and where can we find him?"

"Dieter, he's quite new round here, really into his coke. Big, blond guy. He's almost certainly around here somewhere."

"Kurt, do you know who he's talking about?" Felix asked his colleague.

Sulzner nodded. "Dieter Ballhaupt. Came down from Hamburg two or three months ago. Shouldn't be too hard to find."

"And whose idea was it to bring Dieter? Yours or the Doc's?" Felix turned back to the witness.

"Yeah, well the Doc said he wanted to party real hard, if I knew someone good-looking, not too uptight. So anyway, I'd just seen Dieter. The Doc hadn't met him yet."

"What else can you tell us? Was Mr. Kaptain behaving differently that night or did he say anything? Do you know why he wanted to celebrate?"

"The Doc was in a very good mood, better than usual. Otherwise I didn't notice anything – and he didn't say shit. We just got hammered, fooled around, danced. That was it." Martin was smiling as he spoke.

"Well, give me a call if you think of anything else. And while we're at it, we need to ask for a saliva sample, so we can run it against the DNA from the flat. The same goes for Mr. Ballhaupt, if you find him. Can you take care of that for us, Kurt? We have to head to Kaptain's office."

"No problem. Consider it done; I'll get a lift back from one of my colleagues. See you." Kurt gave them a nod, before disappearing from the café with Martin Stritz in tow.

"So, he was in a good mood, and carrying lots of cash. That's interesting isn't it?" Felix looked at his partner.

"It certainly is," Emilio agreed, as they made their way towards Dr. Zimmer Consultancy Ltd.

"I'm sorry, gentlemen, but Dr. Zimmer is currently away on business. He won't be back until the day after tomorrow." The two detectives hadn't even reached the front desk before being intercepted by one of the receptionists.

"That's OK, we're here to see Mr. Rubin. Is he in?"

"One moment, please. I'll give him a quick call now."

Felix and Emilio waited.

"He'll be with you right away."

"Thanks, but just while we're waiting: where's Dr. Zimmer gone?" The chief inspector asked.

"Nairobi."

Shortly afterwards, they were greeted by a man in his early forties, wearing a dark-blue suit that struggled to conceal his burgeoning waistline.

"Good afternoon, gentlemen, Harald Rubin. What can I do for you? You're the officers in charge of the Kaptain murder enquiry, is that right?"

Felix introduced himself and Emilio. "Yes, that's correct. Is there somewhere we can sit down?"

Mr. Rubin led them to the same meeting room as Anita Peisker the day before.

"How would you describe your relationship with Uwe Kaptain?" Chief Inspector Büschelberger opened proceedings.

"We were colleagues. He was in charge of the really dangerous stuff, while I deal with sewage sludge and the like. Far less hazardous. We saw each other at monthly meetings but otherwise we barely had any contact."

"Any idea who's in line to succeed him?"

"Dr. Zimmer's stepped into the breach for the moment. After that, no-one knows. There are rumors of course, but I don't get involved in stuff like that. It won't be me, that's for sure: I don't have a doctorate in chemistry. But I wouldn't want the job anyway."

A forceful response, but it rang true.

"Why not?"

"I've just got married and we're expecting our first child. My current position only requires me to travel round Germany, occasionally other parts of Europe. If you're responsible for Class III and IV hazardous waste, then you have to go to Asia and Africa the whole time."

Felix leaned back in his chair – another trick he employed when it came to talking about whatever it was that really interested him. It was a way of making his conversation partner think they were just exchanging idle chit-chat.

"My congratulations, Mr. Rubin! How long have you been married?"

"We've been married for five months now; my wife is in her seventh month."

"Our sources say that your wife tried to take up with Mr. Kaptain before marrying you. But he gave her the brush-off."

Mr. Rubin sprang from his chair and began pacing up and down the room.

"Do these stories never end? Everything's been blown way out of proportion! My wife was new to the company and she'd had a little too much to drink – these things happen. I mean she's still very young, after all! I know what people around here say. That she tried it on with one person before simply moving onto the next. Now, I admit there's a practical dimension to our marriage. My wife wanted to be provided for and I wanted kids." He sat down again, though he was still clearly agitated.

"And what's the age difference between you?" Felix asked.

"I'm forty-one and my wife's twenty-five. But we love each other all the same," Mr. Rubin countered.

"I believe you. That's everything for now. Thanks for your help and best wishes again."

They made their way to the car. Back at HQ, Emilio drove straight to the charging station, as their range had sunk below twenty miles.

"So, what do you think? Possible motive?" The chief inspector looked at his partner.

"Hardly. Sure, he was a bit agitated but murder? I mean, they weren't even together when it happened," Emilio summarized, as he connected the cable.

"Yeah, I agree. He's probably just sick of all the innuendo from his colleagues. Let's wait and see what Frauke has got to tell us."

Frauke took an instant dislike to Heike Rubin. Her clothes were expensive but tastelessly put together. Their main selling point was their price tag. She wore her blonde hair up, and there was a box of chocolates open on her lap as she sat facing the detective.

"Thank you for seeing me at such short notice. I'm sure you're well aware that Uwe Kaptain was murdered last week. I'm here to ask you a few questions," Frauke began.

"OK, but make it quick. You can see for yourself what condition I'm in; and I'm not feeling very well today." Another chocolate disappeared into Heike Rubin's mouth.

"I'll do my best. How well did you know the victim?" Frauke tried to continue as objectively as possible.

"Me? Not very well, I only saw him a few times, otherwise we didn't have any contact," came the testy response. By now Heike was gazing out the window, completely bored.

"We heard you were flirting pretty heavily with him at the Christmas party the year before last. Apparently you were quite persistent."

"Who told you that? Bet it was Anna, the old slut. She's just jealous," Heike hissed.

"Why? Was she trying it on with Kaptain too?"

"Her? God, no. She's having it off with the big boss – that's what they say, anyway. She wouldn't mix with people from the lower levels. She's jealous because I'm younger and prettier than her."

Frauke ignored her spiteful remarks. "Back to Mr. Kaptain. So you admit to wanting to start a relationship with him?"

"The idiot knocked me back, can you imagine that? Wait here a moment; I'll get a picture."

Heike Rubin stood up and came back a minute later with a photograph. "Here you are, taken at the Christmas party. I look pretty hot, don't I? No-one had ever turned me down before."

Frauke looked at the photo. It showed the witness in a figure-hugging sweater and tight leather trousers; her hair was much longer than now, parted to one side and almost down to her bottom. Several men in the background could be seen gazing adoringly at her, though the victim remained conspicuous by his absence.

"No, you're right. How could he not want to be with you?"

Heike Rubin seemed not to detect the subtle undertone in her voice. "Do you want one?" Heike waved the box of chocolates in Frauke's face.

"No thanks. Can you tell me anything else about Mr. Kaptain?"

"No, not really; he wasn't involved with any other women from the company, I know that for sure. It's almost as if he was gay."

"He was in fact homosexual."

"Ha, I knew it was nothing to do with me!" The revelation seemed to have restored her world order.

"And shortly after the party, you met your husband?"

"Yeah, it didn't take long. I became pregnant pretty quickly and then we got married."

"Do you love your husband?" Frauke looked at Mrs. Rubin inquisitively.

The latter thought about it for a moment, then replied: "He's very sweet, plus he's rich; that's what it comes down to in the end. But, yes, I think I do love him."

"Then thanks for your help, and all the best with your new family. Please don't hesitate to be in touch if anything else occurs to you."

Frauke handed Heike her card and headed back to the station.

"What did you find out?" Felix was savoring his Arabian tea. He could get used to drinking this.

"The way I see it, Mrs. Rubin is only interested in money and status. She certainly wasn't in love with the victim. I'm not sure she even knows what love is. I don't think she could have done it," Frauke said.

"That matches the impression we got from her husband. Emilio and I don't think there's a connection there either."

Their colleague nodded. "She was relieved when I told her Kaptain was gay. I think it helped her regain her self-esteem. There's no way she was hurt enough to commit murder."

"Good, that's that then. How are things looking in the financial department?" Felix turned to Arno.

"Our victim made a number of cash deposits in the three months before he died, just under 10,000 euros each time – in other words, just under the amount he's obliged to declare. I'm afraid I can't say anything else right now; we need to check if the money could've come from his fixed assets, and that can take a bit of time," Arno explained.

"Any idea how likely that is? I thought dividends and interest payments were always made electronically," Emilio joined in the debate.

"Well, you're right on the whole. But certain deals are conducted under the table, so to speak, and with them you're better off

87

taking cash. Over-the-counter trading isn't as unusual as you might think," Arno replied.

"Sometimes I wonder what you're still doing here. The things you know, you could easily be a millionaire." The inspector laid a hand on Arno's shoulder.

"I'm an idealist: I suppose I want to ensure that good always prevails – even if that's probably just another way of saying I'm a total idiot!"

The others smiled; they knew exactly where he was coming from.

Felix stared at the whiteboard. "I think we can probably rule out love as a motive then, don't you?" he gazed around the room.

Frauke was the first to respond. "I'd say we've got nothing to go on for the moment. But you never know."

"OK, we'll leave it there for the time being, but only in brackets."

After a while they concluded the discussion without having gained any further insights.

Chief Inspector Büschelberger was in his office filing reports when he received a text. Immediately he felt guilty – he hadn't thought about Petra all day long. Hopefully she wasn't mad.

"Hi Felix, I can't make it tonight, will be in the office for another 3 hours at least. See you tomorrow. Kisses to you and Django, P."

That was the last thing he wanted to hear. If he was honest, he'd hoped to see her every night. "Then the 3 of us will be very sad. Pity!!! I can come over if you like."

"No, I don't think I'll be much fun tonight – I'm in a bit of a mood. Why the 3 of you? P."

"Well, Django, me and Felix Jnr ;)"

"Oh, I see! In that case, Petra Snr and Jnr are glad they're being missed. See you tomorrow, I'll call you. P."

A shame; it could have been such a nice evening, Felix thought to himself, as he made his way over to Conny's. Tonight he'd just have to go back to being a typical bachelor.

Chapter 8

For a second time, Kevin Dour graced their morning tea ritual with his presence. On this occasion he tried the green tea favored by Felix and Frauke. He had also brought a coconut with him, though none of the others wanted to try it. As he began his report, the chief inspector was amazed at how one man could drink, smoke and talk all at the same time.

"Kurt Sulzner sent me a saliva sample this morning. I'll check it against the hair from the car. You'll have the results tomorrow."

"What can you tell us about the hair color?"

Kevin looked at Felix. "I was wondering when you'd ask. You seem a little distracted lately."

Laughs all round.

"I understand. Love can drive a man crazy, monopolize his time." The pathologist seemed momentarily lost in thought, before continuing. "Where was I? The hairs are dark blond, about an inch long. We only found two. Going on what we have, I'd say every third person in Frankfurt's a suspect." Dr. Dour inhaled and looked at each member of the team one by one.

"It matches Dr. Zimmer's hair color and length," Emilio chimed in.

"He's right, but we still don't have a motive. We can't just go and take a hair sample from him. If he's our man, then why did he do it? What does he stand to gain? I mean, he's got a lot to lose," Felix added.

"Then whatever he gains through Kaptain's death must be worth the risk. Keep him alive and he loses everything – otherwise none of this makes sense." Arno was first to respond.

"I think Arno's hit the nail on the head. Zimmer would've lost everything if our victim had remained alive; but if we don't catch him, he could still keep it all. It's got to be blackmail. Zimmer was doing something illegal and Kaptain knew about it. Only one way for him to go." Frauke mimed slitting her throat, as if to clarify what she was saying.

The more they discussed it, the more they were convinced they were on the right track. Arno stood up and circled the words 'money' and 'waste' on the board. Then he drew an arrow from both circles leading to another, in which he wrote 'blackmail.'

"If it was Zimmer, then how did he leave the scene? Did he have an accomplice? The central taxi office called yesterday. They've faxed us a list of all the drivers on duty on the evening in question."

"Good, we'll get it checked out. Even though I'm pretty sure Dr. Zimmer wouldn't have made such a basic error. Emilio, get the artist to make a sketch of him. If we start showing photos and it turns out he's innocent, then we could be in trouble. After that, you can question the taxi drivers with Frauke. Kaptain's ex-wife is coming in at lunchtime. Let's see if she can tell us anything we don't know," the chief inspector summarized.

They discussed a few specific details about how to proceed before going their separate ways.

Felix took the coconut into his office, pulled out his cell and began to text.

"Good morning, my darling. How did you sleep? I spent the whole night thinking about you."

The response came immediately: "XOXO, was a little restless, didn't sleep so well. In the office now. P."

"Sorry to hear that. Perhaps you'll sleep better tonight in my arms?"

"That sounds good, I'm pining for you and your body. P."

He couldn't stifle a broad grin. "Good, I've got something for us."

"Tell me more. P."

"A coconut."

"A coconut??? P."

Felix had seen that Petra was reading a book about the intellectual capacity of animals, though his own train of thought was a little harder to follow.

"Let's imagine I'm an ape and you're my partner. What would it mean if I presented you with a coconut?"

"You'd want me to open it, then you'd take it away again. P."

90

"But I'm an ape in love, no: a smitten Felix. What would it mean then?"

"You asked about apes! From you it would be a lover's gift – for erotic games. P."

"Are apes not erotic?"

"No, apes are never erotic; they're completely governed by physical desire! P."

"I think I'm governed by physical desire for you."

"You'll be able to realize all your desires with me. I'm very tolerant. X, P."

"Are you sure you can't stop by now? I'll die if I have to wait until this evening."

"You crazy little love-ball!! I'll be over tonight. P."

Felix fell into a daydream and found it very difficult to refocus on his work.

After a quick pit-stop at Conny's, there was a knock on his door. An officer led Sophie Harris and her husband into the room. Felix offered them a seat and some coffee, briefly surveying them as they sat down.

Mrs. Harris seemed a little nervous; she was obviously ill at ease. Otherwise, she was pleasant and attractive; her holiday tan suited her and matched her sporty, elegant attire. Her light-brown hair was streaked with blonde highlights.

Mr. Harris, on the other hand, looked very calm in his beige polo and blue jeans. He was silently stroking his wife's hand, his eyes fixed on the chief inspector. There was an air of perfect composure about him, the sort that immediately made Felix think of an investment advisor.

"First, I'd like to thank you for coming here today. I hope it wasn't too much trouble," Felix gave an encouraging smile.

"No, it's just I'd hoped to have nothing more to do with Uwe. And now he's dead – murdered, you say – and suddenly all these old wounds have been wrenched open. Somehow it's all very upsetting."

Felix noticed how Mrs. Harris was trying to smile, though her hand clenched and gripped her husband's even tighter.

"That's OK; I'll try and make this as easy as possible for you. But there are still a few things we don't understand about your ex-husband."

She shook her head. "Believe me, Chief Inspector, you're not the only one. I was married to him – and thought I understood him; thought we were happy. But then I discovered I was wrong on both counts. So I know only too well what you mean."

In the meantime, an officer had arrived with their coffee and Felix asked him to get Emilio. While they waited, the three of them discussed the Harris's recent holiday in Kenya. Felix's partner came in and sat down. After ten minutes or so, Mrs. Harris was visibly more relaxed and the inspector was able to steer the conversation back onto Uwe Kaptain.

"Let's talk about your ex-husband. First of all, let me reassure you that you won't have to identify him. But there are still a few questions I'd like to ask."

She nodded and looked him straight in the eye. "I'm ready."

"OK. Now there are indications that Uwe Kaptain had links to the hustler scene here in Frankfurt. You mentioned something similar in our last conversation. How long had he moved in these circles? And what more can you tell us?"

"As I said before, visiting hustlers was the final straw for me. I found out by chance, after I discovered a pack of condoms in his jacket. You can imagine how upset I was. At first I thought he was cheating on me with another woman, which is why I confronted him. He told me straight out that he'd been doing it with these boys because I was no longer able to satisfy him. I screamed at him, lashed out, tried to bite him. I was so mad I could've killed him. Then he said that if I couldn't take it anymore, I should just go. So I did: immediately booked myself into a hotel, only to discover that he'd cancelled all my credit cards on the spot. That was my ex-husband for you." There were tears of rage in her eyes.

Felix was silent for a few moments. "And what did you do next – with no money or roof over your head?"

"I have a close friend here in Frankfurt, who I lived with for two months until I found a job. Her husband's a lawyer; he helped me with the divorce. Do you need their names?"

He shook his head. "If we do, I'll be in touch. So what happened after that? Did your ex-husband pay alimony, and did you see him again?"

"My lawyer made it clear to the court that I had endured an unreasonable hardship and that reconciliation was out of the question. The divorce went through very quickly and Uwe didn't make any trouble. Admittedly, I didn't get a lot of money, but by that stage I wanted as little as possible from him. He disgusted me, I'm sure you can understand that," she said.

"Yes, I can imagine. Though I'd have understood if you'd wanted to fleece him too. People can be pretty vindictive – it's one of the prime motives for murder. Can you think of anyone who hated your ex-husband so much that they might have wanted to kill him?"

"No, in general he was very affable. Not that he was interested in making friends, mind. They were all from my side. No, his work and his career – those were his real friends. I think I was just a kind of trophy he needed to climb the ladder."

"Do you know anything about his work?"

"No, absolutely nothing. We weren't in touch, remember."

"There's just one more thing." Felix leaned in so he could study her reaction more closely.

"Did your ex-husband not enjoy having his picture taken?"

She seemed thoroughly confused. "I don't understand the question. What do you mean?"

"I mean are there photos of you and your ex-husband from your time together?" he probed.

"Yes, of course. Uwe was a good-looking man who spent a lot of money on clothes. He was vain; he loved to be photographed. But I still don't understand your question." There was a note of bewilderment in her voice.

The chief inspector was deep in thought and kept rubbing his nose with his index finger. "There isn't a single photo of your ex-husband in his apartment. We had also noticed how elegant he was and that he must've taken a lot of pride in his appearance. A man like that, we assumed, would enjoy having his photo taken, but there's nothing there. It's just one of the many things we don't understand."

"Uwe always left his photos in the camera bag and kept them in a drawer. It was my job to put them in the albums; he hated doing that," Mrs. Harris recalled. "But the fact that there are none there strikes me as odd too."

"OK, so we know someone broke into his apartment the night he was killed. What we don't know is whether anything was stolen. Would you be prepared to come with us and see if you notice anything? Something that ought to be there, but isn't?"

She grew pale. "I'm not sure I could deal with that." She looked towards her husband for assistance.

"Chief Inspector, do you really think my wife can help you there? The two of them have been divorced for almost five years," Mr. Harris said.

"It's pretty unlikely, but given the lack of alternatives, I don't think we have any other choice."

The couple looked at each other, then she nodded towards the inspector. "OK, then," she sighed.

"Great, my colleague will get the car. You'll be rid of us once we're finished," Felix offered encouragingly.

On the way to the apartment no-one said anything. As Mrs. Harris entered, the pain was clearly etched upon her face. Chief Inspector Büschelberger led the couple through all the rooms, though nothing struck the witness as unusual.

"I'm afraid I can't help you. The only thing I can see is that he still had good taste. Otherwise, the furniture's all new – there's nothing left from our time together."

"Well, it was very good of you to try. We'll take you back to the station now. If you go to reception then someone will cover your costs," said Felix.

"That won't be necessary. We're happy to help the police, but we'd really rather just go. My wife's clearly been exhausted by the whole thing."

Sophie Harris laid her head on her husband's shoulder and hugged him gratefully. The inspector locked up and they drove away.

Felix sat at his desk immersed in thought, only to be interrupted by the shrill ring of the telephone.

"Hello, Felix. Kurt here. I just wanted to say that we've found Dieter Ballhaupt. He's in custody now - had a little too much coke on him. You can question him if you like."

"Thank you. That won't be necessary for the time being. But I will need a saliva sample. If there's anything else, I'll be in touch."

"OK."

"Ciao, Kurt."

Chief Inspector Büschelberger arranged for a saliva sample to be taken and sent to Kevin Dour. Then he called it a day.

Outside his apartment, Petra was waiting for him with a cheeky grin on her face. "So, where's the coconut?"

The next morning, Felix was unexpectedly awoken by Petra. "Hey lazybones, I have to go. I've fed Django already."

"What time is it?" He could barely open his eyes.

"Quarter past six. Last night must've really tired you out. Or maybe you're just older than you say you are."

He reached to grab her but she was too quick for him.

"As if any further proof was needed," she grinned.

Felix threw a pillow at her. "You just wait till I catch you. Then we'll see who's too old."

"That'd be lovely – but I'm afraid I have a flight to catch. To Munich."

"When are you getting back?"

"Tomorrow afternoon."

The disappointment in his voice was audible. "Pity! Just remember we're invited to Emilio's mother for dinner tomorrow night. She'll never forgive me if I show up alone."

"Oh, I don't know. It might be quite fun to drop you in it."

"What?" He was clearly appalled.

A pillow struck him on the head.

"Come on, silly! Of course I'm going. I'm looking forward to it already."

They were interrupted by the sound of the doorbell.

"That'll be the taxi I ordered."

"Oh jeez, how did I miss that? Maybe I am getting old."

Petra laughed and kissed him. "See you tomorrow, old man. You never know, I might have a few rejuvenating cures up my sleeve."

He grunted. "If you tell me what time, I'll pick you up from the airport."

"Let's leave that as another mystery for my Sherlock Holmes to solve…" She blew him a kiss goodbye and left.

Felix fell back into bed. Django used the opportunity to jump up next to him and make himself comfortable.

"At least you never get up at an uncivilized hour," he yawned and closed his eyes once more.

Chapter 9

Already an hour late, Felix arrived at the station out of breath and immediately ran into Emilio.

"Shit, I overslept. Any news?"

"Yeah, there's a Dr. Brax waiting in your office."

"Oh no," Chief Inspector Büschelberger groaned, "not that big-shot lawyer with the Brylcreemed hair?"

Emilio could barely conceal a grin. "Afraid so — and he's already been waiting an hour." He shrugged his shoulders and put on his most innocent face. "Your lie in was worth it then! Old Mr. Important is pissed at having to wait, but it was you he insisted on seeing."

"Well, now that you've had your fun, you're coming with me. I've got no desire to face this shyster alone."

Sitting in his office was a visibly irritated lawyer twiddling his thumbs and dusting the imaginary lint from his Armani suit. He was short - five foot five max - and bald with a big belly. Felix guessed he was wearing an extra-large size, though with the arms and legs shortened. By now he was sweating slightly.

"Good morning, Dr. Brax. They told me you were waiting. I am Chief Inspector Felix Büschelberger." He extended a hand.

"Finally. I'm not accustomed to waiting. Tell me, why am I paying my taxes for police officials to arrive after nine?" He ignored the outstretched hand.

Felix sat down. "And I'm not accustomed to people showing up without an appointment. I'm investigating a murder here; that means I have to get my hands dirty sometimes."

"D'accordo," Emilio murmured audibly.

Dr. Brax's face contorted in anger.

"Fine, let's forget about that. But now to the reason for my visit. Dr. Heinrich Zimmer Consultancy Ltd. has entrusted me with the safeguarding of their rights. You are investigating the murder of Uwe Kaptain and until now Dr. Zimmer has been very accommodating. But you have begun to implicate more and more of his employees — not least Dr. Zimmer himself. As much as my client

97

hopes for a swift resolution to this case, he must also think about the reputation of his company. He has expressed a desire that all future interviews be conducted in my presence and by appointment only. In addition, he has prepared a sworn affidavit in which he confirms that he has told you everything he knows about the case."

He handed over a signed and stamped document, which the chief inspector briefly skimmed before placing it on his desk.

"Here's my card. If you need to question someone then call me first, otherwise there'll be a court order taken against you," Brax raised his voice threateningly.

Felix gave a sickly sweet smile. "You can be sure to hear from me. I know the legal position; and should I fail to reach you or sense that danger is imminent, I will of course notify you as soon as possible after the fact."

Dr. Brax looked him directly in the eye.

The exchange was deadlocked as Kevin Dour burst into the office.

"Morning all, I have the results from the saliva samples here." He threw the papers onto Felix's desk with a loud thud. He took a drag on his cigarette and scowled at the lawyer. As if he wanted to ask what the hell this phony was doing here when he had fresh insights into the case.

The lawyer shook his head and stood up. "I think we understand each other. Good day."

"Goodbye," the chief inspector replied.

Emilio showed Dr. Brax to the door.

"Wasn't that that swish lawyer? You know people, I'll give you that." Dr. Dour stubbed his cigarette out before moving straight onto the next.

"Kevin, Kevin, you never cease to amaze me. That was in fact the most celebrated lawyer in the city. But I had no idea you knew who he was."

"Believe it or not, I also go to the hairdresser," Kevin joked.

Given his unruly mop, this seemed inconceivable.

"Let's see what we have here." Dr. Dour flicked through his papers.

Frauke and Emilio appeared at exactly the same time. "So did our little plan to get rid of that vulture work?" she winked conspiratorially.

"What, Kevin was in on it?"

Frauke was beaming, while Kevin gave a dry laugh.

"I should've been an actor, don't you think?"

Felix and Emilio exchanged surprised glances.

"Here we are." The pathologist didn't even wait for a response.

"We can be 99.9% sure that the two hustlers had sex in the victim's apartment. The sperm traces are either from the victim himself or Dieter Ballhaupt and Martin Stritz."

"Any other traces we haven't been able to identify yet?" Felix was hoping for something that might give them another clue.

"No, nothing like that I'm afraid. There are all kinds of traces, but I don't think they have anything to do with the case," the pathologist replied.

"Shit!" Felix leaned back and thought for a minute. "Then we'll just have to go back over everything and see what we've overlooked."

"I still think Dr. Zimmer's company is our best bet," Frauke said.

"Agreed – but we're skating on pretty thin ice there. Still, realistically what can they do?" he grinned. Suddenly his mood was lifted.

"It's about time I let the tea brigade get back to work. See you later." A quick nod and the pathologist was gone, taking a cloud of smoke with him.

"I can't help but think that's not the Kevin Dour I know. What about you guys?" The chief inspector gazed round the room.

"Absolutely. He's like a changed man: more laidback somehow. Maybe he's become a Buddhist; they're always relaxed aren't they?" Emilio put his hands together and bowed like a monk.

Frauke exploded with laughter. Her boss looked at her questioningly.

"I was just picturing Dr. Dour, The Enlightened One, dressed in yellow and wandering barefoot through his freezing chambers." She hurried outside, still giggling.

"A pretty cool image," Emilio tried to adopt the friendly, detached expression he imagined Buddhist monks wore the whole time. But on him it just looked a bit silly – as his colleague was only too happy to confirm.

"OK, let's reconvene in the meeting room after lunch. Unless you're coming with the rest of us to Conny's?"

Wearing a look of disgust, Emilio promptly made his escape.

Felix tried to gather his thoughts but was forced to admit they were in Munich, with Petra. He was still in a daydream when Arno and Frauke came by to collect him.

"So, boss, finally caught up on your sleep?"

"No secrets here are there?"

"Not really!" Arno grinned.

The chief inspector waited for the inevitable follow-up.

"You should drink more East Frisian tea; I guarantee you wouldn't fall asleep then."

"Fine, but only with rum. Or maybe I should just have a drop of tea with my hot grog?" Felix teased.

His colleague gave him a pat on the shoulder. "OK, but I'm making it. You Bavarians have no idea what real grog is."

For Arno, Bavaria began as soon as you left Hamburg, in the far north.

"We're Hessian, not Bavarian, you bloody northern monkey," Frauke chimed in.

"That's what I'm saying. It's all the same; everyone's Bavarian here."

A tried and tested game. Whenever they hit an impasse and morale was starting to flag, this was a way of relieving the tension. Usually it was Emilio's job, but Arno was pretty good at it too.

The moment Felix was about to go to the meeting room his phone rang. It was DA Cando.

"I've just had an interesting talk with my boss, who wasn't long off the phone to an undersecretary in Wiesbaden. It seems Dr. Zimmer has started to pull a few strings. I indicated that we wouldn't be bothering him again. Unless you have something for me?"

The inspector had to admit he didn't.

"Pity. Then we should give this witness another grilling. The one who found the victim. Plus the two boys from the street," said the DA.

"I still think Dr. Zimmer's the most promising lead," Felix was hoping to leave himself a loophole.

"I thought you didn't have anything concrete there?"

"We don't, but my instinct tells me we'll strike lucky sooner or later."

"Fine, but make sure you proceed discreetly; officially we're pursuing a drugs lead and re-questioning this witness. That ought to keep the suits happy."

The message had got through. Chief Inspector Büschelberger returned to the others disheartened.

"Not only has Dr. Zimmer set his little terrier on us. He's playing the political game too. Cando's got the suits breathing down his neck. We're to keep our distance."

"We're not going to though, are we?" Frauke was incensed and looked at the others belligerently.

They shared her opinion: when people tried to obstruct the police like this, it tended to have the opposite effect. It usually made them even more determined to do some digging around the person in question.

Felix smiled at his team. "I knew I could count on you! But we have to be very careful; Cando's been issued with pretty clear instructions from above. We need to concentrate on the two hustlers and Grüntal, at least officially. Emilio, you have another go at our witness. I'll take care of Stritz and Ballhaupt. Frauke and Arno, you keep an eye on Dr. Zimmer Ltd., but steer clear of questioning people for now. OK so far?"

One question. How tough can I get with Grüntal? Given his previous, he could be a hard nut to crack."

You've got free rein, just try and stick to the rules."

"OK, I'll send a patrol car to pick him up. That's enough to make any ex-con nervous." Emilio rubbed his hands, he loved this part of the job.

"Anything else?" the chief inspector asked.

"Yeah, I've finished looking at Kaptain's bank accounts, but I still can't see a connection between his investments and these cash payments. It's either dirty money or a source of income we know nothing about," Arno replied.

"So it seems blackmail is a good motive, like we said yesterday. Or corruption, that's possible too." Emilio thought out loud and leaned back; his background had made him particularly sensitive to the last topic.

"True, that's something we haven't looked into yet. Arno, do you think you could give it a go?"

The latter scratched his chin, a sign that he was deep in concentration. "I can certainly try, but it's pretty hard to follow the money in a case like this. There's no proof of payment and if they're smart, those involved can camouflage the source with fake receipts. But I'll do my best."

"Good - to work then!"

Emilio arranged for a patrol car to bring Mr. Grüntal in for questioning the next morning. Otherwise, the rest of them were ready to call it a day.

The first thing Felix did in the morning was call the Lufthansa desk. Having duly identified himself, he was obliged to reassure the woman on the other end of the line that Petra posed no risk to cabin crew and passengers.

The last thing he needed was for her to be detained on the ground in Munich. Finally he had his answer: she'd be arriving at quarter to five.

Just that moment Emilio brought in his tea. "Grüntal's been waiting in the interview room for ten minutes. Seems to have lost a little self-confidence. I think I'll let him stew for another ten, that ought to soften him up," he smiled at his boss.

"Sometimes I think you really enjoy this bad-cop routine," Felix replied.

"Sure. Guys like Grüntal need to be taken down a peg or two. They have to know we're not just going to sit back and do nothing when they're up to something. Anyway, unless I'm very much mistaken, you enjoyed clipping Dr. Zimmer's wings a little too."

"No, you're right. But I don't think it'll make any difference with him. Should I come along and play the strong, silent type?" Felix asked.

"Good idea, you can be my foil. By the way, when are you coming over tonight? Mama can hardly contain herself. She's prepared a real party menu."

"I'm picking Petra up at the airport just before five. Then she'll almost certainly want to change and freshen up. I reckon we can be with you about eight."

"Sounds good! So, should we go and keep our guest company then?"

They made their way to the interview room where Felix opened the door to let his colleague go in ahead. Grüntal had been pacing nervously round the table and gave full vent to his anger.

"I don't even know what else you want from me! I have to get to work. And why have you kept me waiting all this time? I'm going to report you!"

In the meantime Emilio had taken his seat at the table. Felix pushed his chair against the wall so he could observe the scene.

"Sit down!" Emilio pointed to the chair opposite.

"I want to know what's going on. I haven't done anything wrong!" The witness continued stubbornly.

Emilio slammed his fist on the table. "I said, sit down. I don't like it when people get testy with me, capisce?"

He had leapt from his seat and was glowering at the witness. Grüntal sat down, still chuntering to himself, but visibly intimidated.

"That wasn't so hard now was it?" The tone was friendlier, though Emilio's gaze remained fixed on the witness.

"You didn't tell us about the GBH charge, did you? What did you think: that we wouldn't find out about the assault?"

"What's that got to do with anything? I'm an honest citizen now." Grüntal's confidence was slowly returning.

"And a gay-hater too?" Emilio's eyes pierced the witness with their stare.

The latter leaned back in his seat. "Yeah! No real man can stand those fags – or maybe you like fairies?"

103

The DI refused to rise to the bait. "As I'm sure you're well aware, the victim was homosexual. Our sources say you knew him from before."

"What?" Grüntal lost his temper. "Hang on, who said that? You gotta believe me, I'd never seen him before; I didn't even know he was a fag."

He turned to Felix, hoping for assistance, but the inspector didn't bat an eyelid.

"I'm talking to you, not my colleague," Emilio hissed.

Grüntal was facing him again. "It's bullshit you know, that I knew him before."

Emilio decided to take a shot in the dark. "We've got CCTV footage from a well known gay bar in the city. It shows you sitting next to him with a drink in your hand."

The witness went pale, his resistance broken. "I really didn't know him. I was only there 'cause my probation officer thought it'd be a way of curbing my aggression towards these fags. Please, you can ask him if you like."

Chief Inspector Büschelberger could hardly conceal his amazement: his partner had a real knack for it, striking lucky like this. Emilio threw his boss a glance, a smile briefly flitting across his face.

"Do you think we're stupid or something? You've been lying to me from the start. Well, it stops now!"

"Please, you gotta believe me, I didn't kill him, I swear. I'm on probation for another two months and it was a real hassle getting a job. Why would I risk it all for a queer?" The witness was whimpering to himself now.

"You're still not telling us everything though, are you? We already know what you did. So why don't you ease your conscience – and we'll see if we can strike a deal."

Grüntal was completely slumped over in his chair. "I thought I'd been so careful but you must've found my fingerprints. OK, I cleaned him out." His head drooped forward and he began to sob. "I just thought he doesn't need it anymore. They pay me peanuts at this job. So I took two hundred from his wallet. But I didn't kill him, you gotta believe me."

"How could you be so stupid, on probation too? I don't get you guys, pretending to be so cool, but acting so dumb!"

Emilio signaled to Felix that he wanted a word in private.

"Wait here, we'll be back shortly."

Outside Felix gave his colleague a pat on the back. "Well, that was a stroke of luck. Kudos to you."

"Nothing to do with luck. It's called having a good nose. But the reason I wanted to speak to you: I don't want to report him, but make him an informant. We've got him where we want him."

"As long as you know we're talking about failure to report an offence here."

"I know, let me handle it – you don't have to be involved."

"Fuck that, we're in this together. If you think it's right then that's good enough for me. You're the one who broke him."

They went back inside.

"We're satisfied you didn't have anything to do with the murder. As for your confession, we've got it on tape. It's all been recorded. But I'm here to offer you a deal. My colleague and I have just suspended the recording. So you have a choice: either, we take it straight to the DA and you go back inside, or we lose the tape and you owe us a favor."

A pregnant pause.

Grüntal nodded. "I get it. You want me to be your snitch."

"I prefer the term informant. Why don't you see it as switching over to the good side?"

Emilio tried to appease him. "Only, if I suspect you're fucking me over again, that tape's going straight to the DA's office. Do we understand each other?"

"Yeah, loud and clear," the witness gave a resigned nod.

"Good, then you can go. Can we give you a lift to work?" Emilio asked.

"No, that's OK. If my boss sees me in a fuzzmobile I'll lose my job there and then."

"Where are you working?" It was the first thing Felix had said.

"In the wholesale warehouse, in Frankfurt."

"Well, all the best, and make sure you behave yourself. We won't always be there to protect you."

The chief inspector accompanied Mr. Grüntal to the main exit. "Bye then, and if you hear anything interesting…"

"Then I'll be in touch. I get it. You can count on me." The witness disappeared through the door.

Felix found his partner sitting at his desk, grinning broadly.

"I knew he wasn't clean," Emilio leaned back contentedly.

"I'm impressed. As a reward you can join me at the prison and help question this Dieter Ballhaupt."

"Lucky me."

"Yeah, you owe me, remember?"

Emilio shook his fist jokingly at Felix, who proceeded to arrange a visit for one o'clock.

"No Conny's for you today then," Emilio teased.

"Given the amount I'll have to eat tonight, probably no bad thing."

Emilio just smiled. "I would've dobbed you in to Mama otherwise, then you'd never have heard the end of it."

They both laughed.

When the two detectives entered the prison visitor center, Dieter Ballhaupt appeared distracted. He was clearly suffering from withdrawal symptoms, but otherwise fairly unassuming.

His appearance could only be described as attractive, with blond, shoulder-length hair and deep-blue eyes that started to keenly focus on his guests. Felix introduced himself and Emilio.

Dieter kept his cool until he realized they were from murder squad. "Murder squad? No shit, what's happened, how I can help?"

He raised a hand in front of his open mouth. His surprise seemed genuine.

"Uwe Kaptain was an acquaintance of yours, wasn't he? He was murdered last week."

Dieter leaned back casually. "No, the name means nothing." Cool as a cucumber, he began playing with his hands.

"According to your friend, Martin Stritz, you knew him pretty well. The three of you had, I quote, 'an orgy' in his apartment."

"You mean the doc? The doc's dead? Fuck me. He was a real specimen, fabulous body, great stamina. Shame, he was generous as well." Dieter fell silent, seemingly lost in thought.

"There's nothing else you can tell us?"

A shake of the head.

"Did you try to see him or meet him again? If you liked him so much, I mean. Maybe he turned you down and you were so furious you decided to poison him." Now it was Felix's turn to take a shot in the dark.

"Chief Inspector, what on earth must you think of me! I barely even knew him. I'm not a violent man, you have to believe me. Now I understand why they had to take a saliva sample; and I thought it was something to do with the coke…"

The detectives exchanged an amused glance; he clearly wasn't the sharpest.

"So, where were you between Sunday night and the early hours of Monday morning?" The chief inspector asked.

"Here," Dieter replied without a moment's thought. "They picked me up at the train station on Saturday. Twenty grams. I'd just stocked up 'cause I wanted to go to the country, then I ran into your guys. It hasn't been easy here, I can tell you. Check it out if you like."

Felix nodded. "We will do. What else can you tell us? Did the doc at least say why he was celebrating?"

"He didn't say anything. Actually no, wait. He did ask for my number. I guess he must've liked me: said we might be seeing more of each other. But he never got in touch after that."

"Have I understood that right? He wanted to see you again, but not Martin?"

"I don't know anything about that. That wasn't my impression."

"Good. Then thanks for your time and best of luck with your hearing. If we need anything else, we'll get back to you," the chief inspector took his leave.

"Don't be shy; hot men are always welcome as far I'm concerned."

Outside the prison, the two detectives couldn't help laughing out loud.

"Mamma mia, they're going to have fun with him in the joint. Hot men…" Emilio smirked. "I think he had an eye on you."

"No, I think it was your Italian charm that impressed him. Bet he goes mad for Mediterranean types, like all women." The chief inspector smiled archly.

"Cut it out, you know I don't like it."

Felix struggled to conceal a grin. That was one of his Italian colleague's weaknesses: calling his masculinity into question was a big no-no.

"What do you think: could Martin Stritz have been jealous? Does that give him a motive?" Emilio tried to steer the discussion back onto the investigation.

"Possibly, but doesn't that mean he should have killed Dieter instead? And how's he supposed to have come by the poison? I doubt he even knows how to pronounce it, let alone get his hands on it. We'll look into it first thing next week. For now let's just go back and talk about the next steps. After that, I need to pick Petra up from the airport."

Despite the rush hour, they were back in a flash, with Emilio enjoying full use of the EV's horsepower at every given opportunity.

Back at the office, they discussed the week ahead with the rest of the team.

Frauke and Arno were to collect as much background information as possible, while the two of them immersed themselves in the Frankfurt prostitution and drug scene.

Chief Inspector Büschelberger said his goodbyes and drove home to feed Django and make himself more presentable. He felt a million dollars in his beige slacks, light-blue zipper shirt and handmade Italian shoes.

Then he reached for the bottle of Romitorio and headed to the airport, stopping at a florist's en route to buy a single red rose.

Chapter 10

Petra's plane was five minutes ahead of schedule, and her bag one of the first off the carousel. She came through security with a big grin on her face and made straight for Felix.

"Weekend at last. Is that for me?" She ran her fingers over the rose as they kissed.

"It's for the woman who's stolen my heart."

Back at her apartment, Petra jumped into the shower, but not before she had tried to persuade Felix to join her – an offer he politely declined. She just about managed to put her make-up on, and then it was time to go. Her insistence that they stop to buy flowers meant they were a little late in the end.

Mama Perfondo opened the door all smiles and gave Felix a big hug. She was a small, stocky woman with her dark hair tied in a bun, and an enormous apron around her waist.

"Felix, there you are. We don't see nearly enough of you at Mama's. Shame on you!"

She pinched his right cheek and then turned towards Petra.

"And you must be his dolcezza, how nice to meet you." Emilio's mother embraced her warmly, and they linked arms as she led Petra into the house. "My name's Luccesa but I'd like you to call me Mama, like everyone in la famiglia."

There was laughter coming from the living room, along with the voices of at least six different people; all of which were overshadowed, however, by the sound of Luciano Pavarotti singing Ed il mio bacio scioglierà il silenzio che to fa mia.

"Puccini's Nessun dorma: that's one of my favorites. Thanks for the invite by the way." Petra finally managed to hand over the bouquet, which Luccesa took into the living room.

Emilio and his wife were sitting on the sofa. Their kids were charging around the huge, festively laid table, where Emilio's two sisters and their fiancés had already taken their seats. While Luccesa was introducing everyone she couldn't resist commenting on the fact that people only got engaged these days; no-one seemed to get married anymore. She gazed quizzically at Felix and his girlfriend.

"Mama, give us a little time, OK?" Felix put an arm round her.

The pair was greeted enthusiastically, though all eyes were fixed on Petra. Emilio's wife was dark-blonde, slender and very elegantly dressed. She surveyed Felix's companion in detail before smilingly extending a hand.

"Hello, I'm Sylvia. You know you really have to be in love when your boyfriend's a policeman – because you'll be sharing him with the job."

"Isn't that true for all women?"

They both laughed and Petra felt at home right away. On TV, an Italian program was broadcasting some football match or other. The men were transfixed by the screen even though it was on mute.

"Sit down, sit down, we'll be eating soon. I'm cooking up a storm for us. First there's a little insalatina al taglio then homemade ravioli di ricotta alla Romana, with roe deer and red wine and cranberry risotto to finish. And afterwards a few dolci. How does that sound?" the hostess asked.

"Irresistible as always, Mama, even if I'm getting so big I soon won't be able to meet any women."

Felix gave Luccesa a squeeze.

"Don't worry! I'll help work that belly of yours into shape, you can be sure of that." Petra gave Emilio's mother a little wink. "I love risotto, though I've never got the hang of it myself."

"Really? But it's so easy! Come with me to the kitchen and I'll show you how it's done."

Signora Perfondo disappeared with Petra in tow.

"Whenever you make risotto, use this recipe. Sauté the rice with a few finely chopped shallots and then add the wine. Normally a bianco but today we're using a vino rosso. Keep pouring whatever stock you're using in little by little until the rice absorbs the liquid. As we're having roe deer, it'll be venison broth this time. Stir gently so that it's all'onda, 'on the wave' as we say in Italian. After half the cooking time, you mix in the rest of the ingredients, the cranberries in this case, then right at the end you add butter and freshly grated parmigiano. And that's it. Come on, why don't you give it a try. Ecco."

Luccesa tied an apron round Petra's waist and helped her prepare the dinner. At the same time she began making the ravioli
filling and searing the roe deer fillet.

"Felix is a good boy, he's been part of the family for ages. But
tell me, how did you two meet?"

"We've known each other for a while. We both help collecting
toads," Petra explained.

"What, so you handle those slippery little things as well?"
Luccesa made a disgusted face.

"Of course – but we wear gloves, as the toads can carry sal-
monella. Anyway, I've always been a little intrigued by him and then
two weeks ago, he saved my life. We've been together ever since."

"Oh!" Luccesa was wide-eyed. "He saved your life?"

Petra nodded gravely and explained what'd happened.

"Yes, Felix is a real hero. You know he saved my Emilio too:
he's been a permanent fixture round here since then. Mess with
him and you mess with the whole family, do you understand? We
take things very personally."

Petra nodded, clearly fascinated. "So what happened back
then?"

"Is Mama telling that old story again?" Felix's voice came from
the kitchen door. "I just wanted to chill the wine I brought."

"Naturalmente, Petra should know what kind of man you really are," Luccesa said defiantly.

"I'm pretty sure she knows that already," he smiled mischievously, beaming at Petra.

"Come on Felix, tell me. I want to know," she urged as she
stirred the risotto enthusiastically.

He sighed. "OK fine, what the hell; otherwise I'll get no peace.
Emilio and I have known each other since we were kids. Our families used to be neighbors, so we grew up together. Then as teenag-
ers we began to go our separate ways. I had decided pretty early on
a police career and Emilio, well, Emilio fell in with a bad crowd.
Somehow he ended up being part of a gang. I remember Luccesa
standing crying outside our door. My training had just finished and
I went to get him out of there."

He gazed into the middle distance before continuing. "It wasn't quite as simple as that: first we had a real good fight. Anyway, he was taken to the hospital and a day later his crew hijacked an armored car. Three people were killed; everyone involved's still inside. Emilio surrendered voluntarily and thanks to my recommendation, got away without a caution. Soon enough he joined the police. That's it, really."

"Mama just can't leave it alone, can she?" Emilio had poked his head round the door and was grinning broadly. "So, now you know: you're looking at a half-Mafioso."

They all laughed.

"You really beat each other so bad that you had to go to hospital?" Petra asked wide-eyed.

Both of them nodded.

"You should see Emilio's left hook; it's quite a weapon, I can tell you. I thought he'd shattered my jaw."

"What about your upper cut, it's not bad either."

The pair of them stood there, arms around each other's shoulders: radiating friendship and solidarity.

"Emilio was lucky it was me he was fighting. If his father had still been alive, I think he'd have been a goner," Felix said.

Luccesa looked towards the heavens. "Dear Franco, God rest his soul. If he'd been alive, he would've killed him, no doubt about it." She crossed herself and shooed the men out of the kitchen.

"Come on, out you go; leave us women alone. Go and have a drink. Avanti."

Felix and Emilio made their exits accordingly.

By the time they'd finished eating and the plates had all been cleared, it was almost eleven. The food had been stunning and the atmosphere was increasingly relaxed. Luccesa leaned back in her big chair.

"Felix, why don't you go and get your wine, and Carlotta, put my CD on."

When Felix re-emerged with the bottle open, José Carreras was already half way through Il lamento di Federico.

"I love this music!" Petra closed her eyes dreamily.

"Si, it's wonderful isn't it? This is real music. I would've loved to see the three of them live but ticket prices were prohibitive. Such a shame Luciano's no longer with us." Luccesa crossed herself again and became lost in the music.

All conversation ceased. The red wine glittered darkly in their glasses as Carreras transported them to faraway lands. The kids were already asleep on the sofa. When the CD was over, everybody began to make the move home.

Felix was held back at the door by Luccesa. "So, what are you doing for your birthday? Do the two of you want to come here?"

"Oh, I'm not sure yet, Mama."

"When's Felix's birthday?" Petra realized she'd never asked.

"In eight days." Luccesa stuck it to her son's best friend. "You should take these things more seriously."

Petra jabbed his ribs. "You jerk! When were you going to tell me? Or did you think you'd keep it a secret?"

"Sorry, it's just my birthday's not that important," he said.

"It is to us," the response was unanimous.

"Well now you know." He tried to put his arm around Petra but she pushed him away.

"You're impossible sometimes, you know that." She embraced Luccesa. "Ciao Mama, and thanks for everything!"

"Ciao, Petra. Promise me we'll see each other again."

"I promise."

Next Luccesa hugged Felix: "Ciao stupido, keep in touch!"

Once Felix had said his goodbyes to the rest of the family, Emilio kissed him on the forehead and teased: "Ciao cupido, see you Monday."

They all laughed and the tension evaporated. Petra linked arms with Felix as they descended the steps. "Do you think Django will be alright on his own tonight?"

Chief Inspector Frog didn't need to think twice.

After they'd both had a good, long sleep, she snuggled up to him. "Do you think you could get next Friday and Monday off?"

"Probably, I've still got some unused holiday. Why?"

"I'd like to take you away for a long weekend, as a birthday present. Surprise location. What do you think?"

"Sounds good to me! My neighbor's daughter likes looking after Django. Let me take care of it on Monday," he said.

That evening they had dinner in a little restaurant before moving on to a cozy cocktail bar. Petra couldn't decide what to have and asked Felix to order for her.

"Do you do custom mixing?"

The barman nodded.

"OK, then give me a double vodka with peach liquor and crushed lime, add a dash of lemon and a shot of Curaçao Blue; and fill it up with passion-fruit juice."

"Sounds interesting!" said the barman.

Felix returned to his seat and five minutes later their cocktails were served. The barman placed a selection of nuts on the table beside them.

"Tastes delicious, I've never had it before. What's it called?"

"That's a Lorenzo Green. I discovered it when I was in Nürnberg recently. In a little bar called Kontiki, right on the Pegnitz. It was the barman's own creation and tasted so good I had to have the recipe."

They ordered a second round and then went back to Felix's, where Django was eagerly awaiting their return.

Sunday went by very peacefully. In the afternoon they discussed animal consciousness. Petra quoted a few examples from the book she was reading. Felix didn't agree with her analysis. He said animals were primarily guided by their instincts. However, in his opinion most people didn't think about their actions either, at least not actively. His main argument was that most murders would never be committed if people took a moment to think about what they were doing.

The discussion ended with Petra ruffling his dark hair and stating that men could never follow women's logic simply because it was a woman stating it. As a result Felix spent the next half hour wagging his finger at her, pretending to be all macho.

Later that evening, Petra made her way home. "Believe me, it's better this way; we don't want you to be late for work again."

Her high-pitched laugh rang in his ears until long after she was gone.

Chapter 11

Sad to see the back of the weekend, Felix turned the shower up to full heat and enveloped himself in its warmth. He left for the office earlier than usual, stopping at the baker's en route. A pile of fresh pastries and steaming hot tea greeted Frauke, Arno and Emilio as they entered the station.

"I could get used to this. But did I miss something? It's not your birthday, is it?" Frauke beamed.

"No, I just felt like it. And by the way, your new hair looks great," he replied.

"I know." Frauke did a little spin so the others could all admire her. "Nice that one of you noticed at least; you're a true gent."

"You know that Emilio only has eyes for his wife. And Arno doesn't have eyes for anyone on Monday mornings."

"Right, I don't think he'd even notice if I came in naked!" she giggled.

"I disagree. There'd be no rustling of bank notes in your purse; our financial whizz wouldn't miss that." Emilio placed a hand on Arno's shoulder.

His colleague mumbled something as he helped himself to his first doughnut. After they had enjoyed a leisurely breakfast, devouring every single last crumb, Felix leaned back in his chair.

"I can't shake the feeling that we're stuck. We're just not making any progress. Is there something we should be doing differently? Or are we wasting our energies on minor details?"

They spent the next two hours discussing the case. Felix took it upon himself to play the role of devil's advocate, forcing them to go back to square one each time and see things from a different perspective. In the end, everyone agreed that their best lead was still the connection between Uwe Kaptain and Dr. Zimmer.

"Right, so we proceed as before: Arno and Frauke dig up as much as they can on Zimmer and company without causing a stir; meanwhile Emilio and I make a bit of noise elsewhere to keep the suits happy."

Then he filled out a request for leave and took it straight to his boss, who glanced at the form briefly before wrinkling his brow.

"I'm afraid there's a problem here. Your request clashes with a one-day conference in Stuttgart held by the German Federal Association for EV Mobility. Since you're the only police unit in Germany currently using an EV, upstairs have decided that you are to take part. I was going to tell you today."

Felix fell silent while his mind searched feverishly for a solution. He had made a promise to Petra, and there was no way he was going to disappoint her. "Wouldn't it make more sense for Emilio to take part? He's the one who drives the EV most of the time and he's a real techno-nerd. I'm sure he'd do a far better job than me."

"That's a good point. We don't want to look stupid after all. Then please tell Inspector Perfondo that he's to hold a presentation on your EV's performance: whether it meets the demands of police service operations; if its acceleration capacity and top speed are sufficient, that sort of thing. He should also focus on how the charge time can be brought into line with shift operations."

Felix took the documents about the conference and promised to inform his colleague accordingly.

"Is this a green light then?"

"Are you not halfway through a rather delicate investigation?" his boss asked.

"Yes, we are, but I've got a great team and I'm sure they'll cope just fine without me for a couple of days; and Emilio would only be away on the Friday."

"Fine, you had a lot of unused holiday anyway."

The chief inspector expressed his thanks, pleased that he hadn't been quizzed on the latest regarding their current case.

He sent a text to Petra: "Holiday OK'd. Very excited."

The response came instantly: "Excellent. Prepare to be surprised! P."

Emilio was in raptures as soon as Felix told him about the forthcoming conference.

"The orders are from up-high; they want us to really shine at this thing. So if there's anything you need that'll make us look good, just let me know. I'm sure it'll be approved right away."

Instantly Emilio's eyes sparkled as he thought about what new gadgets he might need. "My Galaxy has grown old, by today's standards. How about a new tablet? The third generation iPad has amazing graphical resolution. It would be great for showing photos of victims or suspects to potential witnesses. And when we're out and about, we can also take pictures or even videos if need be. Its battery life should be an additional plus, with some ten hours of running time."

"But it won't hold the presentation instead of you, will it?" Felix asked with a hint of irony.

"Well, it won't, but actually it has built-in dictation that can transform whatever I say into notes."

"OK, then why don't you buy one, I'll sign the expense form." The chief inspector admitted defeat, and his colleague pumped his fists before hurrying away to complete the online purchase.

In the afternoon they set off to question Martin Stritz for a second time, and were driving slowly through the railway station area.

Emilio saw him first. "There he is talking to those guys."

The chief inspector looked in the direction his partner was pointing. "That's him. I bet it's a deal going down. If he sees us now, he's bound to make a run for it."

He got out of the car a little further up the street, while Emilio turned and approached from the other side. Felix had been right. As soon as Martin caught sight of the inspector, he and his two companions turned tail and ran in the opposite direction.

Luckily Emilio was there to seize him, though he allowed Martin's friends to escape. "So who did you mix us up with this time?" he enquired mockingly.

"Chief Inspector, it's a natural reflex, just something I've learned. Are we going for coffee again?"

"No, I'm afraid you're coming with us this time. We still have a few questions for you."

"What? But I told you everything I know!" Clearly panic had gained the upper hand.

"Dieter told us that the Doc liked him better than you. Maybe you got jealous and did something stupid?" Emilio said.

117

"Dieter, the fuckwit! He's talking shit, you gotta believe me. Really, there's no need to take me down the station."

"That's where you're wrong. Now let's go."

Felix placed a hand on Martin's shoulder while Emilio forged ahead to get the car. Martin took advantage of the brief moment Felix's mind was elsewhere to push him to one side and make a dash for it.

"What the hell, stay where you are!"

Chief Inspector Büschelberger hated chasing suspects. Now he and his partner were sprinting after Martin, who turned out to be a pretty good runner. Slowly but surely he was opening up a lead over Felix.

Meanwhile Emilio, who was keen on his fitness, was keeping pace. The suspect turned and realized he wouldn't be able to shake off the DI so easily. Then without looking, he started to cross Baseler Strasse, not noticing the heavy vehicle heading straight for him.

The truck caught Martin Stritz head-on before finally grinding to a halt some ten feed down the road. Its driver sprang from the cab horrified, and ran towards the victim lying prone on the street. Emilio was already with Martin, who was bleeding from the mouth. Felix was last to arrive on the scene though by now he had pulled out his cell and notified the ambulance crew. He was just in time to prevent his friend from performing first aid.

"Remember, he's a hustler. He could easily have hepatitis or HIV. Use gloves."

Emilio nodded and rushed to the nearest car, which had come to a standstill right next to them. He flashed his ID. "We need your first-aid box."

The female driver reacted instantly and soon Emilio was donning the gloves. Then he maneuvered Martin into the recovery position.

"Shit, he's losing too much blood. I can't stop it, it must be internal. When's the doctor getting here?" he shouted, more towards the heavens than his colleague.

"Ambulance is on its way."

The truck driver was standing alongside, completely pale. All he could do was stammer: "He just ran into me, I didn't have time to brake." He was clearly in shock.

In the distance they heard a siren approaching fast. Five minutes after the accident, the first patrol car had already arrived directly from HQ on Mainzerstrasse. The chief inspector ran towards the two officers waving his ID.

"Please make sure the emergency route stays clear. I'll fill you in later."

The officers regulated the flow of traffic, advising all rubbernecks to keep moving. All in all it took twelve minutes for the ambulance to arrive and the paramedics to reach Martin Stritz.

The emergency doctor looked concerned as Felix outlined the victim's personal history. "Shit, that doesn't help. Drug addicts usually have poor circulation and weakened immune systems. I'd give him a forty-percent chance."

Chief Inspector Büschelberger wanted to know where they were taking the victim. As he'd suspected, Martin was being admitted straight to the clinic on Theodor-Stern-Kai. In the meantime the paramedics were tending to the truck driver.

Once Felix had ensured there was nothing more he or Emilio could do, they followed their police colleagues back to headquarters to make a statement. Two further witnesses, among them the woman who had helped Emilio with the first-aid box, were also requested to join them.

After the short interview, they drove straight to the clinic's accident and emergency center, where they were informed that the victim was currently in surgery. Felix left his card with the emergency room's senior nurse, who promised to call as soon as there was any news on his progress.

On the way back Chief Inspector Büschelberger was silent.

"Don't get all worked up about it, he's the one who started running. He took his fate into his own hands," Emilio tried to lighten the mood.

But Felix just growled. Despite what Emilio said, he still felt guilty: if he had held onto Martin properly, then maybe the accident would never have happened.

Back at the police station, he disappeared into his office. He wanted to be alone. Half an hour later, he was joined by Frauke.

"Felix, Emilio told me everything. It's not your fault; Martin Stritz chose his own fate." She laid a hand on his shoulder.

"Yeah, I know, but sometimes you just can't control the way you feel. If only I'd held onto him, he'd never have got so far."

"But you wanted to take him in for questioning, not arrest him. You don't use handcuffs for that," she replied.

"Give me another five minutes, then I'll see you all in the meeting room."

Frauke left him to it. He composed himself and tried to organize his thoughts. Just as he was about to join the others he received a message from uniform. It was news from the clinic: Martin Stritz had died fifteen minutes ago.

"Fuck!" Chief Inspector Büschelberger cursed quietly to himself. Next he told the others. There was silence all round as they sipped their tea.

"Does this have any bearing on the case?" Arno addressed the question to the team as a whole.

"We just wanted to question him. Dieter Ballhaupt has made us think the murder could have been linked to jealousy. It's possible Kaptain was hoping to replace Stritz with Ballhaupt."

"And you think Stritz could've got his hands on the poison?" Arno asked.

Felix shook his head. "No, not really. But we need to be careful, in case Dr. Zimmer's friends try and persuade us that Stritz was our man. That'd be pretty convenient for them."

Emilio nodded. "I don't think Martin Stritz did it either, but we need to make sure."

"Then let's go back to the hospital and see if we can get a key to his apartment," the chief inspector sighed.

Felix looked for the senior nurse. "Could you please tell me where I might find Martin Stritz's personal effects? You know, the patient who died today as a result of a car accident."

"I know who you mean. You're the one who left the card – I called your central office. Whenever we admit an emergency case, everything gets stored in a locker, even things we need to cut in two before operating. If you'd be so kind as to follow me," the nurse replied.

Emilio packed everything into a plastic bag. The chief inspector signed the receipt while the nurse took down the number on his ID. Afterwards the two inspectors drove on to Martin Stritz's apartment.

There was an unpleasant smell wafting from the apartment. The victim clearly hadn't attached a great deal of importance to hygiene.

The corridor was so narrow that they were forced to walk in single file. The carpet was hideously stained and there were items of clothing, unopened letters and empty bottles strewn everywhere.

"This is a garbage site, not an apartment!"

In an effort to allay the smell Emilio was holding a handkerchief to his nose.

The chief inspector could only agree. Meanwhile he thanked Mother Nature for providing him with such underdeveloped olfactory nerves. He didn't think the smell was so bad; Emilio, on the other hand, was heavily affected.

The first room on the left-hand side was the kitchen. It was pretty cold inside. A washbasin, piled high with dirty dishes, had been installed to the right, next to a shower, with a dining table alongside. On the far wall was an electric stove and fridge, both covered in a layer of dirt. The fridge contained nothing but a cheap bottle of brandy, two cans of coke and a single bottle of beer. There was still a saucepan of dried ravioli on the stove, the empty can lying on the floor beside an overflowing rubbish bin.

"How can anyone sink so low? The only thing missing is a family of rats."

It didn't look much better in the bedroom either: the sheets couldn't have seen a washing machine for more than a year, and there were clothes and papers scattered in front of the bed. An old, decaying wardrobe rounded things off.

The furniture in the living room consisted solely of two double sofas and a table; the latter adorned by a hash pipe and full ashtray. There were empty beer bottles all over the place, and next to the ashtray they found a little packet wrapped in silver foil.

Felix gave it a sniff, and handed it to his partner. "What do you think it is?"

"Coke!" The reply came quick as a flash.

The chief inspector nodded.

"Looks like we'll have to inform our colleagues from Narcotics. Let's see if we can find anything else. I don't want to stay here any longer than necessary."

The final room was full of cardboard boxes stacked on top of one another. A brief examination revealed items from Martin's previous existence, keepsakes from the time before he had plunged headlong into a world of drug addiction and prostitution. They found old letters, toys, school reports and photos depicting Martin as young - and happy.

At the end of the corridor was the toilet. Like everything else, it was covered in filth.

Relieved to have finally left the apartment, Emilio and Felix waited outside for narcotics to arrive. Again the chief inspector appeared lost in thought. Almost an hour went by before two officers appeared, neither of whom was known to Felix or Emilio.

The four of them identified themselves. Felix took an instant liking to Chief Superintendent Franz Xaver. He seemed calm and considered, his accent betraying the fact he'd been raised in Hesse – despite the Bavarian-sounding name. His colleague, Inspector Stefan Altmühl, looked like he'd come straight from Martin's world. He was wearing a greasy leather jacket, jeans and striking cowboy boots made from pure snakeskin. His hair went down past his shoulders.

Felix noticed Emilio looking at him disapprovingly. As the four of them went through the apartment, Felix explained why they were here.

Franz Xaver took a quick sniff at what they'd found, before confirming their suspicions. "Definitely cocaine. Looks pretty pure to me." He handed the packet to Stefan Altmühl, who placed it in a clear plastic bag.

Emilio could no longer curb his curiosity. "Tell me, is it normal for people like this to live in such disgusting apartments?"

Stefan laughed. "You'd better believe it! This place is actually OK. Come and see a real doss-house sometime, when they're all on heroin and crack. They make tips like this seem the height of cleanliness and hygiene."

Inspector Perfondo shuddered. "Luckily we don't have to see places like that too often. I guess murder's common to all walks of life. I think I'll wait outside." With that he disappeared from the apartment.

Felix waited for Franz Xaver to light up a cigarette before he said his goodbyes. "We'll leave the pair of you to it. Any questions, you know where we are. And if, during the course of your investigations, the name Uwe Kaptain should crop up or the chemical… wait a minute…"

He called his partner back.

"Can you tell our colleagues the name of the substance used to poison Kaptain?"

Emilio looked at his tablet. "It was a mix of benzodiazepine and chloral hydrate."

"How d'you spell the first one?" Stefan Altmühl appeared confused.

Emilio spelt the letters out for him, barely managing to stifle a grin.

"You guys know your stuff, I've never heard of it," Franz shook his head.

"Neither's any of us, except our pathologist; by the way, I couldn't begin to spell it either," the chief inspector assured them, eyeing his partner critically.

"Was it the dour Kevin who discovered it?" Franz asked.

"So you guys work together too?"

"Sometimes. I don't think much gets by him."

"You're right there." Felix had to smile. "Time for us to go, we'll be in touch."

As they were leaving, he gave Emilio a minor ticking-off. "Don't always judge people by the way they look."

"I'd never go around dressed like that Stefan Altmühl."

"And that's why everyone here would instantly have you down as a cop."

"That's why I chase killers, not dealers." Emilio beamed with delight. He was pretty sure he'd won that particular round.

Felix sighed and admitted defeat.

The chief inspector dropped his partner off at police HQ, connected the Focus to the charging station, and drove home in his own car. He'd seen enough for one day.

At the door he was greeted by Django rubbing against his legs. Felix picked him up and stroked the fur on his head. The tom's remaining ear twitched and he purred contentedly. In the kitchen, Felix realized he desperately needed more cat food before going on his long weekend.

While Django was eating, he went to ask if his neighbor's daughter would be willing to look after him. She was enthusiastic, just as Felix had expected. Then before he'd made it back to the apartment, his cell rang.

"Yes," he said curtly.

"Hi, Felix. What's wrong? You sound annoyed."

"Oh Petra, I'm so glad it's you! Sorry, I've just had a really shitty day; I didn't see who was calling."

"That's OK, I just wanted to call quickly to say that I've still got lots to do. I don't think we can see each other tonight."

"Pity, I could've done with you here."

"Why, what's happened?"

"We were just trying to question this witness when he ran off. He was hit by a truck, died in hospital."

"I'm sorry. But if he ran off, then maybe he was guilty?"

"We still can't rule it out, but I don't think he had anything to do with the murder. He was involved in drugs and was probably just worried we were wise to him."

"But Felix, none of this is your fault! If you like, I can try and make it over – but it'll be late."

He forced a smile. "It's fine. We'll see each other tomorrow though?"

"Of course! See you then: just promise me you won't get drunk tonight."

"I won´t. See you."

After the phone call, Felix felt pretty empty. He got his coat, let Django out and went shopping: food for the tom; a few bottles of red for himself.

On the way back he stopped at Burger King and ordered the biggest Whopper they had. But then he couldn't finish it and was forced to leave half on his tray. Back at home, he opened the first bottle and became immersed in his thoughts. He was just onto his second glass when Django reappeared.

Felix smiled. "Your radar still works then! Good that I can count on you."

Django lay down next to him on the sofa and listened as Felix told him what was on his mind. After he had finished the second bottle, Chief Inspector Büschelberger fell asleep on the couch, waking with a start at three in the morning. Swearing to himself, he reached straight for the aspirin and went to bed.

Chapter 12

Despite the aspirin, Felix awoke the next morning with a slight headache. He drove to work without enthusiasm. The day itself brought no progress and he had the feeling they were just going round in circles. His mood got even worse.

Emilio made every effort to cheer him up but it was no use. In the afternoon they looked at everything again from all sides, but it yielded no further insights.

"Dr. Zimmer. It's the same each time. Doesn't matter what leads we follow, we always come back to him. He's our only hope of solving this case – but we don't know anything about him and we can't even ask around without ruffling people's feathers. It's enough to drive you insane!" Felix threw him arms in the air and theatrically buried his face in his hands.

"Don't worry: if he had anything to do with it, we'll get him." Emilio laid a soothing hand on his friend's shoulder.

They discussed the case until work was over, but Chief Inspector Büschelberger couldn't shake the feeling they were going nowhere fast.

Petra was able to raise his spirits when she came round that evening, though she didn't divulge anything about his surprise. The only thing he knew was that she would pack a case for him on Thursday evening and then accompany him to the airport early Friday morning. He was dying to know what was in store; but enjoyed playing her game nevertheless.

The next morning Felix's mood was considerably lighter, and he was certain they'd find a good lead sooner or later. Until, that is, Dr. Brax appeared in his office at ten.

The lawyer came straight to the point: "My client has been informed that you're continuing to investigate him. You seem particularly interested in his finances." Brax leaned back in his chair; he sounded almost exaggeratedly bored.

"I thought I'd made myself abundantly clear last time," he pierced the chief inspector with his gaze. "You will refrain from your investigations immediately or personally face the consequences! Do we understand each other?"

Felix felt his anger rising towards this greasy, no-good shyster, but he just about managed to keep his cool. "Are you threatening me?"

The lawyer laughed. "I would never threaten a police officer. Do you really think I'm that stupid? But please feel free to do a little research; you'll see that I've had an impact on a few promising careers in my time. All I want is for your unit to stop wasting time pursuing useless leads. I hope I've made myself clear. We'll be seeing each other."

With these words, he disappeared from the room.

"Absolutely! And we will; I promise," Felix snarled.

Dr. Brax had just made a new friend. The rest of the day did nothing for Felix's ill temper. Frauke, Arno and Emilio were just as outraged. Arno even took it as a personal affront that his investigation had been blown wide open. If Dr. Brax was wanting to unsettle them or force them into keeping their distance, then he was going about it the wrong way.

In the evening Felix found himself alone with Django once more. Not that it bothered him much, since he had no desire to take out his bad mood on Petra. Instead, he was determined to finish another one of the red wines.

Thursday didn't bring any new insights either. The only thing was a phone call from Franz Xaver.

"Hello, Felix. We've now searched the entire apartment, but found no trace of the poison or anything else. Sorry."

"To be honest, I didn't really think you would. Thanks anyway. It means we can cross Martin Stritz off our list. Have you been able to discover why he was so keen to get away so quickly though?"

"I think he was just about to close a big deal. We found almost fifteen ounces of pure cocaine scattered around his place. Most likely the two people you saw were his delivery men. And based on your description, I've got a fairly good idea of who they were. I'll let you know as soon as we have anything else."

The chief inspector thanked him and hung up.

Then he went over to Conny's with Frauke and Arno. He was astonished to see Dr. Dour walk through the door.

"Kevin! Are you looking for me? Have you found something?"

The pathologist shook his head. "No, I'm here on my own. I've heard the fries are the best in town. Thought I'd try them for myself. Wouldn't've come if I'd known you guys were going to be here though."

Felix smiled. "Come on, you old corpse-hacker, have a seat. I hope you didn't bring your own knife."

Dr. Dour shook his fist gloomily and Frauke shifted to one side to make room for him. Not for the first time, Felix was amazed at the pathologist's ability to smoke without pause – even whilst munching fries. Still, the conversation was entertaining. Kevin told anecdotes about his youth and his former mentor, the latter regarded as even grumpier than Dr. Dour himself. The others struggled to believe him. As they were leaving, Kevin wished the chief inspector all the best for his upcoming holiday.

"How come you know about that?" Felix was clearly confused.

Kevin Dour took his time before answering. "There are no secrets around here, you know that. Besides, I'm Dr. Know-it-all."

They all laughed and Felix didn't give the matter any more thought.

A few hours later, the team gathered for tea and cake in the meeting room: Felix had been to the pastry shop again. Afterwards, he said his goodbyes before leaving for his holiday.

"I'll have my cell on me. If anything important happens, you call straightaway. Is that clear?"

"Yes, boss. We'll be sure to do that!" Frauke tapped the side of her head playfully.

Then she hugged him. "Have fun. I think we'll manage just fine without you for two days."

The chief inspector sighed and was forced to relent. He knew they wouldn't call unless the entire station suddenly went up in flames. Emilio gave him a pat on the shoulder and signaled that everything would be OK. Even Arno managed a smile.

The last thing Felix did was to check if everything was ready for the technology conference.

Emilio nodded and proudly displayed the remote, which had arrived in the mail that morning.

"I'd like to take the Focus to Stuttgart if that's OK with you?"

"Isn't that too far away? It must be at least 120 miles."

"In fact it's 130 miles, but I'd spend tomorrow night with my family near Heidelberg, at a friend's house. I've already checked for gas stations around there offering charging. According to Google Maps, it's about 62 miles to Heidelberg from here, then another 69 miles to the final destination. I could even do a bit of the Bertha Benz Memorial Route on the way. There's a monument dedicated to her at Wiesloch, outside the world's first filling station, where she had to stop for Ligroin. It's something I've always wanted to see."

"OK, but only if you promise to arrive in Stuttgart with blue lights on and sirens flashing," Felix smiled. "What is your family going to do?"

"They're going to take a stroll through Heidelberg and have a look at the castle. I'll join them once the conference is over. But I promise to make your grand entrance – the people will have their show!" Inspector Perfondo grinned from ear to ear.

"Well then, enjoy the Focus – and have a good time at the conference."

A final nod of the head and the chief inspector was gone.

Back at home, he waited eagerly for Petra to arrive. The taxi dropped her off just after eight. She kissed Felix passionately and then turfed him out of the bedroom so she could pack his case undisturbed.

"I hope your kicking me out of the bedroom doesn't become a habit."

"Well, you'll just have to make sure you're nice to me then, won't you?"

"I promise."

She gave him a quick kiss before shooing him away once more. Nonetheless, their night was filled with passion.

The next morning, Felix took Django over to his neighbor's daughter. The tom disappeared into the apartment without giving him so much as a second glance.

"Traitor!" Felix murmured.

Petra just smiled. "Cats and women clearly both have minds of their own. Shall we, then?"

At the airport, Petra made for the Alitalia counter and received an expectant smile from Felix. He'd had an inkling they were going to Italy but he couldn't work out where Lamezia Terme was.

"Calabria, at the very toe-end," his sweetheart explained.

"Ha, right in the Cosa Nostra's backyard. Should be interesting." He put his arm around her.

"Don't you dare get any thoughts. You're on holiday with me, remember."

"You have my word!" he promised.

During the short flight, they ran into turbulence over the Alps and the plane dipped violently. Felix felt his stomach cramping and went pale. But Petra's carefree smile helped to calm him down. The rest of the flight passed without further incident.

Lamezia Terme was a small airport with just one runway and a single terminal. There were a few additional planes stationed along the airstrip. It was pleasantly warm as they stepped outside – at least seventy degrees – and the air was full of spring.

He embraced Petra. "It was a good idea to leave it all behind us."

They took a cab to Pizzo, a town twenty-five miles south of Lamezia Terme, situated right on the Tyrrhenian Sea. Petra had booked them into a little hotel with just ten rooms.

The proprietor doubled as both receptionist and chef; his family now running the hotel in its third generation. The décor merely emphasized the fact that the current owner had invested heart and soul in the business. His wife led Felix and Petra to the room, which she described as the honeymoon suite. Petra could only smile as Felix raised his eyebrows in surprise; though she did a good job of convincing him she hadn't known either.

A little later they were strolling through town. The hotelier had made them promise that they'd eat tartufo at the Piazza della Repubblica, as this was where the desert had been invented and it was still the best in the world. After finding the square without any difficulty, Felix was forced to admit that the owner hadn't been exaggerating. The ice-cream really was fantastic.

They sat outside on the piazza, watching the people amble past and enjoying the dolce far niente. After the tartufo they ordered two caffè corretto with grappa, before visiting the adjoining castle.

This was where Joachim Murat, appointed King of Naples by his brother-in-law Napoleon I, had been put to the firing squad in 1815. His uniform was on display, and the bullet holes were still there for everyone to see.

Felix looked at the coat in fascination and tried to imagine what Kevin Dour would have to say; whether he'd be able to find anything new.

Eventually Petra dragged him away. "Come on, Commissario, this case is closed."

He smiled. "Yeah, you're right. But once a cop, always a cop."

They wandered on through the little shopping street, where Petra bought a wickedly expensive – albeit sexy – new pair of shoes. And she wouldn't stop until Felix had chosen something for himself as well: a light-brown sweater for spring and a stylish silk tie.

"Such a shame you don't have to wear a suit at work. You'd look great in one."

That evening they dined in the hotel's little restaurant, where they were the only non-Italians, before seeing out the day with a bottle of champagne in the tub.

Felix was awoken the next morning by a passionate embrace. When he opened his eyes, Petra wished him a happy birthday and held him for dear life.

Downstairs, there was a candle waiting at the breakfast table. The owner and his wife offered their congratulations, as did their two children; they even sang "happy birthday" in Italian. Felix was touched, though also somewhat embarrassed. Petra meanwhile was beaming away contentedly.

"So, who else did you tell it was my birthday?" He suspected she had something else lined up.

"Only your birthday surprise."

"What, another surprise? But you've already been so generous."

"Just wait and see; we're getting picked up afterwards. They told me you should have a decent breakfast."

Felix knew it would be pointless to ask any more questions, so he kept quiet.

About an hour later they were approached by a thickset man with a huge walrus moustache.

"Hi darling!" He and Petra embraced.

"Hey, Mad Dog! Long time no see." She introduced the two of them.

"Felix, I present your ultimate birthday surprise. This is Mad Dog, I met him three years ago in Hawaii. He's going to do a tandem jump with you."

And turning to Mad Dog: "This is your tandem passenger, my boyfriend Felix."

The men shook hands.

"Tandem jump? Is that what I think it is?" Felix sounded a little unsure.

"Yes, sweetheart. I thought you liked adventures. Mad Dog called to say he was down here for a month and when I heard it was your birthday, I thought it'd be a brilliant surprise. There's no need to be scared: he's done more than 12,000 jumps, and he's a tandem instructor to boot."

Mad Dog put his arm around Petra. "More than 15,000 now, actually. What goes up must come down, as they say. Let's go."

Although Felix could feel the adrenaline pumping through his veins; there was no way he was pulling out now. They drove back to Lamezia Terme, over to a little hangar on the edge of the runway.

"I'll explain everything to you now while Pete takes Petra over to the drop zone, where we'll all meet after," Mad Dog explained.

Petra gave him a hug and kiss. "See you later, my hero. Have fun!" With that she disappeared from the hangar with Pete.

Felix could still hear her laughing outside.

"Good girl our Petra, isn't she?" the sky-diving instructor said.

A silent nod was the only response.

"We were seeing each other in Hawaii. She was doing a tandem course there, but it fizzled out when she went back home. But you know, we stayed in touch. So, let me show you how it's done."

Mad Dog led him over to a light aircraft. "We'll be flying in one like this – before we jump."

They climbed inside. Felix was amazed at how small it was.

"This is where we'll be sitting later, so that we're last to jump. One of the guys will shoot a video. We get you in your gear, give you a helmet and goggles, and then attach your harness. I'll be wearing one too. Then once we're on board I'll fasten us together. At 13,000 feet, we let the others out; in the meantime we slide towards the door on our knees. Next, you put your foot on the step just outside. That's where Eagle, our video-man, will be waiting."

Mad Dog tapped the narrow step: it was about four inches wide and three feet long. Felix couldn't quite believe what he was hearing.

"You want me to stand on this step at 13,000 feet when there's already someone there?" Felix asked nervously.

"Yep, he'll be holding onto this handle here," the instructor pointed to the struts on the side of the plane. "The most important thing is to cross your hands within the harness. In case you instinctively try to grab something. And believe me, that's not something you want to do." He let out a throaty laugh.

"Never happened yet though. Once we're out, you go into the jump position. That is, you extend your arms, curl your legs and arch your back, just like the kids you arrest. But we can practice all that. We start in freefall, until about 5,000 feet, then I'll pull on the line, there'll be a jolt and the parachute will open. If it fails, there's another that opens automatically at 2,500 feet, so don't worry. I'll let you steer for a bit and you can enjoy the view. Just before we land, I'll take over again and make sure we touch ground safely. And that's it."

Felix swallowed audibly. Mad Dog patted him on the shoulder.

"Don't worry. You'll be stoked afterwards, just wait and see."

They practiced all the movements twice, including the slide to the door.

"Everything clear now?" the mustachioed instructor checked.

"Yeah, I think I get it. But later when I'm on the step, I'm still going to wonder why I should jump. The plane's not on fire and I'm safe. So, why?"

Mad Dog smiled again. "Boy, I like you. You've got a sense of humor. Follow me. I'll show you why it's better to jump than stay put."

They went over to a little wooden table, with a folder containing some photographs on top. One of them showed two skydivers in the air, the plane perpendicular to them against a blue sky. The chief inspector turned the photo this way and that, but couldn't work out how to interpret what he saw.

If he held it one way, so that the plane was the right way up, then the two divers were hurtling towards the ground, heads back and feet in front. If he held it the other way, then it was the plane that was now upside down.

Mad Dog laughed. "Now you're holding it right. The pilot gets to have his fun too. Once we're all out, he turns the machine on its head and is down way before us."

Despite his nerves, Felix couldn't help but smile. "A very good argument indeed, especially since I don't see any seat-belts around."

The American slapped him on the back. "Just as I was saying: a good sense of humor. Now, come on, let's practice the jump position one last time, then we'll get changed and be on our way."

Felix practiced the correct maneuvers on the floor until his instructor was satisfied. Then he was led into another room where six more divers were already waiting. One of them stood up and, together with Mad Dog, helped him into his suit.

"This is Eagle, our cameraman."

When they were ready, they sprinted across the runway to a light aircraft whose engine had already been fired up.

"A Pilatus PC-6 Porter - very reliable," Mad Dog explained.

He and Felix were the first to board, followed by Eagle and the others. They took off as soon as the pilot received the all clear.

"Because of all the scheduled flights, there's a very limited window for take-off. That's why we don't jump here, but thirty miles to the south."

The minute the plane left the ground, Felix's heart was in his mouth. Only now did he truly realize what was about to happen. Petra and Mad Dog had been talking so much he hadn't had the chance to think. All of a sudden, it was just him alone with his fear. Mad Dog showed Felix his altimeter: 1,300 feet – a tenth of the height they'd be jumping from. Then the instructor pointed towards a mountain on the right.

"Stromboli, an active volcano that usually only smokes, like now. Tyrrhenian Sea on the right, Ionian Sea on the left. Enjoy the view."

At 3,000 feet he tapped Felix on the shoulder again. "This is roughly where we pull the cord. By now, we'll be travelling at over 125 mph."

It took exactly twenty-eight minutes to reach their desired height and drop zone. Shortly before, Mad Dog had fastened their harnesses together and now there wasn't room for even a hand between them. The door opened and Felix felt pure fear. Meanwhile, the noise from the wind was so extreme that he could no longer make out a single word.

Mad Dog gave Felix an encouraging pat on the shoulder, which was gratefully received. Then the first of the divers was gone, the rest of them following in intervals of thirty seconds. Felix was speechless at how natural it all seemed.

No-one was afraid, quite the opposite. In fact, if anything they looked almost bored. Now it was Eagle's turn: he positioned himself on the step and held on to the strut. Attached to his helmet was a camera, operated by a remote shutter on his wrist.

The American motioned towards the door, and Felix, by now almost in a trance, felt himself being pushed in its direction. When they reached the door, he placed his foot on the step. His hands were folded across the harness, and with a look to the right he saw Eagle grinning back at him. Next he gazed frantically beneath him, and suddenly nothing seemed real anymore.

Mad Dog signaled that it was time and gave him a gentle nudge forward. Then abruptly he increased the pressure and soon they were freefalling together.

For a moment, Felix no longer knew where he was, or which way was up or down. His brain couldn't process what was happening. Two seconds later, he was in the jump position. Directly in front of him Eagle waved and glided towards him. Felix waved back, and all of a sudden burst out laughing.

The feeling was beyond words. He screamed and shouted for joy, his mouth prized so far open by the wind it hurt; and felt all the tension drain from his body. By now he was so excited he could no longer understand his initial fear.

After a while his tandem partner tapped him on the shoulder, a warning sign that the parachute was about to open. A loud noise followed and for a second Felix couldn't breathe. Then everything was completely still. Far below them in the distance, he saw Eagle's parachute opening. Mad Dog handed him the steering toggles.

"Pull to the right, and we fly right. If you want to go left, then pull left."

Felix tried and couldn't believe how easy it was. They spent five minutes gliding through the air before his partner reassumed control and brought them safely to the landing zone. They touched down exactly three feet away from Petra.

"So, my hero. How was it?" she asked.

He was ecstatic. "It was so incredible, it was… it was simply awesome. I want to go again!"

Mad Dog laughed. "Didn't I promise as much? I'll take care of the parachute, then we'll see each other in the shack over there. Petra assures me there's a bottle of champagne waiting." He trudged off.

Felix drew Petra towards him once more. "Thank you. That really was a terrific present. I'm so happy."

Beaming from ear to ear, they made their way over to the shack where the others were having a spot of lunch. After Mad Dog had handed them both a glass; he raised his own. "A toast to our noble sponsor and the birthday boy."

Everyone drank to Felix's health before Mad Dog gave Petra a kiss goodbye, leaving Pete to drive them back to Pizzo.

Chapter 13

On Sunday, the couple drove to Tropea, a little village twelve miles south of Pizzo. It was home to a small, but very famous pilgrimage church named Maria dell'Isola. After the visit, the two of them settled in a cozy-looking café on the central square.

Out of habit Felix was surveying his surroundings, when suddenly he felt his eyes drawn to a convoy of Mercedes limousines. The three vehicles had stopped outside the little restaurant directly opposite.

He was left absolutely dumbfounded when Dr. Zimmer emerged and entered the building with three others; two of them picture-perfect Mafiosi, while the third was a tall black man. Meanwhile three more men had casually positioned themselves in front of the restaurant to keep an eye on things.

The cars disappeared around the corner. Felix couldn't quite believe what he was seeing and anxiously considered his next move. Just at that moment, he spied a little red Alfa Romeo parked at the far corner of the square. The two men inside seemed very interested in the restaurant's latest customers.

"Petra, do you mind if we get the check?"

"Why, what's up?" His girlfriend was just stirring her latte macchiato.

"You won't believe this, but the prime suspect in our murder case has just disappeared into the restaurant opposite with a pretty dubious-looking bunch. I think the pair in the Alfa are police. I need to go over and talk to them."

"Felix, you're not serious are you?"

"Please, Petra, you know you'd do the same."

She shrugged her shoulders, but he could see she understood.

They strolled past the restaurant as inconspicuously as possible, though Petra couldn't help blowing a kiss at the bodyguards: a gesture that drew a broad grin from all sides.

Felix moved towards the Alfa, and slowly pulled out his wallet to identify himself. He knew the Carabinieri could be a little jumpy,

137

especially when tailing the Mafia. The two men in the car didn't seem to have noticed them. Not yet, anyway. He pressed his ID against the passenger window and gave it a gentle tap.

The men reacted quickly but professionally: the passenger throwing himself forward, while the driver drew his weapon and took aim. It all lasted no more than a couple of seconds. As soon as the driver realized there was no immediate danger, the weapon disappeared back inside its holster. Chief Inspector Büschelberger moved slowly away from the vehicle and pointed in the direction he was walking. The driver nodded.

They ambled slowly round the corner and waited. After about a minute, the man from the passenger seat followed and looked at them enquiringly. He was a stocky little fellow wearing a light grey suit with a tasteful tie and well-polished shoes.

Felix guessed he must've been fifty at least: his thin moustache and slicked-back hair were already grey, though he still had sparkling brown eyes. Someone who had seen it all and knew every trick in the book.

"Scusi, but I'm a police officer in Germany and wanted to ask a few questions about the men you're observing." Felix greeted him in Italian, grateful to Emilio's family for having taught him a smattering of the officer's native tongue.

"Commissario, let me extend a warm Italian welcome," came the response in German, emphasized by a gallant kiss on Petra's hand. "Let's take a walk. There's a good restaurant nearby that serves lovely fresh fish. You have to try it."

Without saying another word the Italian inspector led them to a small restaurant two streets further down at the end of a little cul-de-sac. The fish-shaped sign was blowing and creaking in the wind as Felix read the name: Tropea Vecchia.

"May I?" Inside, the Italian ordered for them straightaway. "You have to try the fish soup here, served with a hint of truffle and fresh bread; throw in a good white wine and you know there must be a God."

He clicked his tongue before introducing himself. "I am Commissario Crotone; and you are?"

Felix showed his ID for a second time. He explained briefly why he'd knocked on the Alfa, what his case in Germany was about and how surprised he was at chancing upon a prime suspect like this.

Crotone nodded understandingly. "I think I'd be surprised as well. What a strange coincidence."

In the meantime, bread and wine had arrived.

"Please help yourselves. I just need to call my colleague and tell him to sit tight for a few minutes."

Crotone dialed the number. The conversation grew more animated before quieting down again and finally coming to a close.

"It's a real fluke that you came over to talk to us. We only recognize the two Italians: Don Veschie and his first assistant, both pretty well-known Mafia figures here in the south. The others, we haven't been able to identify yet."

"As I said, it's Dr. Heinrich Zimmer, he's in waste management," Felix replied.

Crotone whistled through his teeth. "That business is like striking oil. And you've no idea who the black guy is?"

"Well, we know Zimmer's just been to Nairobi. I'd start looking there."

"Bene, that's a real help."

The soup arrived and its wonderful smell made Felix suddenly realize how hungry he was. While he and Petra tucked in, Crotone told them amusing stories about Calabria, some of them no doubt exaggerated.

After they'd finished, the Italian noted everything his German colleague had told him, as well as the Frankfurt police station's address. Then he handed Felix his card.

"By the way, how did you learn Italian? You speak quite well."

"Thanks, but I know it's not true. It was my friend and colleague Emilio who taught me. We grew up together. Where did you learn German?"

"I was born in Germany, went to school there. Then my family returned to Italy and I decided to go with them," the Italian explained.

When Felix made a move to pay, Crotone waved him aside.

139

"You're on holiday and here we are talking about work; your wife must be thoroughly bored. The check's on me. Basta."

"Tante Grazie, very kind. But we're not married."

"What? You're only saying that now?" Crotone rolled his eyes. "Signora, why don't you drop this idiot and come with me!" He was smiling all over.

"And what would happen if I agreed?" Petra's eyes were sparkling.

"Then tomorrow I'd be a dead man: my wife would poison me and throw my body into the sea. But it'd be worth it!"

He grinned and kissed her hand for a second time and they all laughed.

On the way back to the Alfa, he asked: "How long are you staying?"

"Leaving tomorrow."

"If you like, I can give you a lift to the airport. Where's your hotel?"

Petra gave him the address.

"Nice, right in the center of Pizzo, I've eaten there before. Bene, then I'll pick you up tomorrow."

Felix thanked him.

"Do you mind checking beforehand if Zimmer's on the same flight? If he finds out I saw him here, we could have a real problem."

"Naturalmente. See you tomorrow."

The Italian climbed into his colleague's car, leaving the pair to enjoy their final evening back at the hotel.

The next morning Crotone met them at reception, as promised.

"I hope you don't mind me joining you for breakfast?"

"Not at all!" Felix showed him to the dining room.

The Commissario laid a few photos and files on the table. "Here you are, from our records. You were a real help to us; I hope we can return the favor."

Felix briefly skimmed through the documents. They were in Italian, of course, but he had Emilio, and the photos were really good.

"Any luck with Zimmer's unidentified companion?"

"Yes, he's the First Secretary to the Kenyan ambassador in Italy. As well as a kind of commercial attaché it seems. Dr. Mugambone hasn't been here too long, and we've never had any dealings with him. One of my cousins works at the national treasury in Rome, he supplied the information." Crotone was beaming with pride.

"I'm impressed. That gives us a clear lead back in Germany," Felix declared, before checking a few more minor details.

When they finally set off for the airport, Crotone said: "Zimmer won't be on board. He's staying in Don Veschie's villa until Wednesday."

On the way to Lamezia Terme, he showed them a few more sights. When they said their goodbyes at the airport, Felix promised to keep his Italian colleague up to speed.

Crotone promised to do likewise.

After a peaceful, uneventful flight, Petra spent the afternoon with Felix, before returning home. Somehow, despite the action-packed weekend, he felt a twinge of loneliness. Or maybe it was because of it.

Chapter 14

On Friday morning, somewhere near Heidelberg, Emilio was walking towards the charging station where he had left the Focus the previous evening. He was looking forward to the day ahead. Despite his initial skepticism, he had become a real fan of the EV, even if he remained well aware of its limitations.

The conference was set to begin at nine; that meant he still had an hour and a half to reach the House of Trade in Stuttgart. He ran his hands almost affectionately along the surface of the car before getting in, still planning to stop briefly en route at Wiesloch.

"Today you and I are going somewhere historic," he smiled, glad that Felix wasn't there to hear him.

The journey passed without a hitch. At Wiesloch, he stopped in front of the world's oldest gas station and used his iPad to take a few pictures of the memorial depicting Bertha Benz and her two sons, which he later mailed to Arno and Frauke.

When Emilio saw the conference center in the distance, he grinned, and flipped the flashing blue light and siren to "on". A promise was a promise. He accelerated and swerved around the corner outside the entrance to the building, leaving the siren at full blast for another moment as he came to a standstill.

After a quick glance at the onlookers – the majority aghast, a few smiles in amongst the rest – he drove onto the row of charging stations, which had been installed by the entrance. He parked in the first space available and connected the lead to the car. Then he headed for the entrance in high spirits, attaching the name badge that identified him as a conference speaker on the way. Cheerily greeting all and sundry, he passed through the stream of participants and searched for the room in which the conference was scheduled to take place.

Appropriately enough, the conference was being held in the Bertha Benz hall. There were already a few briefcases on the tables. Emilio was pleased to note that his VGA adaptor fitted the display cables that were waiting to connect the computers to the projector. He seemed to be the only one who had made the trip with a tablet. The rest of the participants had brought their laptops, while a small minority was using netbooks.

Emilio placed his bag and iPad on the chair provided, and headed towards the back of the room to get a glass of water and some orange juice. He felt the piercing stares of all those who had just witnessed his entrance. Those who hadn't been there were whisperingly informed by others in the know. Emilio didn't care: if anything, he enjoyed playing the role of outlaw in this crowd. Besides, he'd show them he spoke their language. His presentation was the first scheduled after lunch.

When he returned to his seat, an elderly man was gazing at him out of friendly dark-blue eyes. He was about five foot six, the man, with a gray receding hairline.

"Young man, I have to say you made quite an entrance back there. I like that sort of thing."

Emilio examined the outfit of his conversation partner: a blue-and-white check flannel shirt, blue jeans and dark-red - almost black - cowboy boots. As he thanked the man for the compliment, he just about managed to suppress a smile at the contrast with his own appearance: a black bespoke suit, tight white shirt with skinny black tie – back in fashion in Milan – and shiny black brogues that had been polished to the max.

"So you're the first police officer to use an EV as a patrol car! I'm very much looking forward to your presentation!"

Emilio still didn't quite know what to make of the old man, when suddenly the latter began gazing rather quizzically at the nameplate to Emilio's right. That was where the deputy interior minister for Hesse was supposed to be sitting.

"May I?" the man asked, before grabbing the nameplate and heading off with it.

Surprised by what he had seen, Emilio thought to himself: "Wow, this guy really is a cowboy." Although he barely knew the man, he had taken an instant liking to him. He watched him, this guy who still hadn't introduced himself, position the deputy minister's nameplate at the opposite end of the table, only to return seconds later with a replacement.

143

"He'll be better off back there with the industry big shots. I'd only have felt uncomfortable. For me, it's better to be sitting among practical people: people who know what they're talking about!"

There was a twinkle in the old man's eye as he placed his own nameplate next to that of the DI.

"Please excuse me, I realize I haven't introduced myself. My name is Ulrich Held," he extended a hand.

A look at the cowboy's nameplate – in his mind, Emilio had christened him the cowboy – revealed that he was a "Consultant." Although the DI dismissed many so-called consultants as self-important busybodies, he had the feeling there was something understated about Ulrich Held, who had neglected to add any additional titles underneath his name. Emilio's own badge read "Detective Inspector" after all. The two men chatted a while longer, until the conference was officially opened by an assistant of the environment minister.

There was something old-fashioned about the assistant, who was standing in front of his chair, reading a pre-prepared speech straight from his notes. He began with a message of greeting on behalf of the chancellor, and emphasized how important alternative energy and energy-saving measures were to the current federal government. Next he went on to say that the annual report recently submitted by the German National Electric Mobility Platform had met with great favor from the chancellor.

By this stage, Emilio had switched off: experience told him that nothing of great significance would follow. A quick glance at the agenda revealed that the opening speech was set to last fifteen minutes. He surveyed the other participants, who seemed to be hanging on the speaker's every word. While the majority were nodding in agreement or even taking notes, the cowboy was leaning casually back in his chair. His pen lay unused on the notepad whose white lettering Emilio was now reading: White Stallion Ranch. No doubt about it, his neighbor had chutzpah and he didn't seem in the least bit bothered by other people's opinions. Emilio was beginning to like him more and more.

Straight afterwards, it was the turn of the first specialist speaker, a member of the German Federal Association for EV Mobility, who had traveled down from Berlin. The slide he projected on the wall contained only a single phrase: "The nine advantages of electric vehicles."

After officially greeting everyone, the marketing man gazed expectantly into the throng of participants. "Ladies and gentlemen, I would like to outline the nine advantages of electric vehicles together with your assistance. Because if we experts don't know the arguments inside out, then how can we convey them effectively to the greater public?"

The speaker stopped next to the interactive whiteboard and took a magic pen in his hand.

"A SMART Board!" Emilio murmured quietly, genuinely impressed by this kind of technology.

"Ladies and gentlemen, there is no need to take notes. Everything I write up here will be automatically saved and emailed to you at the end of the conference. If as many speakers as possible make use of this board, then we can collect all the information and make it available to you in its entirety."

Emilio grinned. He doubted any of the politicians present would know how to operate it.

"So, my esteemed colleagues, who would like to name the first advantage that an EV undoubtedly offers?"

The speaker gazed around the room. Emilio felt a nudge in his side. It was the cowboy, nodding encouragingly.

"Come on, be brave, it'll be a point in your favor!"

Emilio didn't have to think for long. "I think the biggest advantage is that they protect the environment. There's no internal combustion engine, which means there are no CO_2 emissions!"

"Excellent, thank you," said the marketing man. "The argument is spot-on. Although opponents of EVs would object that there are CO_2 emissions from electricity generation as well; or worse, that energy generated by nuclear power results in the production of radioactive waste. How would you counter this claim?" He focused directly on Emilio.

The Italian thought for a minute and replied: "If the electricity was generated from renewable sources, such as wind power or solar energy, then there'd be no CO_2 emitted."

"Exactly! If you had mentioned water power too, that would've been everything. Now, you could conceivably object that by building wind turbines, hydropower or solar-power plants, you'd also be generating CO_2 – but since that's true of every production, it's a rather spurious argument. The fact is that sustainable practices improve the energy balance across the entire production chain. Now, onto the second point. Ideas anybody?"

When nobody reacted, he turned once more to Emilio: "I don't want to have to call on you again, maybe someone else would like to make a contribution?" He looked encouragingly at his audience.

"Since we're on the subject of environmental damage, what about the extremely low levels of noise pollution? It's a natural follow-on from the first argument," a woman from a large European automobile club said.

"Is the right answer! The topic has been discussed at the UN, who subsequently decreed that EVs are required to make noise. Though it shouldn't exceed that of a car with an internal combustion engine travelling at twelve mph. So yes, they're a lot quieter. Nevertheless, several companies have started to develop their own sound," the speaker said.

While he wrote the point up on the SMART Board, Emilio whispered to his neighbor. „Audi seems to be the frontrunner here. They've developed a system that actually generates sound in real-time. From what I've seen in a video, it's pretty sophisticated: the system takes values from the electric motors and mixes them on the fly with stuff like the current vehicle speed. Sounds like an artificial DJ built into the car, a 'play as you drive,' so to speak. And each different model will have its own tune."

Before the speaker had the chance to ask about a possible third advantage, there was a voice from a woman working for a utility company.

"Lower travel costs are a further advantage. If you compare the cost of a gallon of super unleaded or diesel to a kilowatt hour of electricity, it quickly becomes clear that you can run an EV at a much lower cost than a conventional car. The calculated fuel economy of EVs today is around 100 miles per gallon. Most likely the price of fuel will keep increasing far quicker than the price of electricity, even taking extra costs incurred through the use of alternative energies into account."

The speaker nodded in agreement as he noted down the new argument. "Yes, so travel itself finally makes an appearance. I like it. What else?"

The next to make his point was a representative from IBM.

"In future, EVs should be used to offset peak demand – to function as short-term storage systems – since this will lead to improved grid stability. Maintaining a stable grid is important as sources of electricity become more and more diverse - with the increased number of alternative energies available. Within our Smarter Planet platform, we're developing an information technology infrastructure to enable the seamless integration of electric vehicles. We'll hear more about that later this afternoon from my colleague here!"

The man from the Federal Association added the point to the list without further comment.

Emilio, who was enjoying the discussion more and more, and who found his respect for the various conference participants growing, said the next thing that came into his head.

"I've noticed that our Focus has pretty good acceleration. When it comes to hill starts especially, a number of so-called 'normal' cars just can't keep up! That really wowed me at the start of our tests. But more on that later in my presentation on the everyday use of electric vehicles."

He couldn't resist the little dig, even if he was pretty sure no-one had noticed. To his right, the cowboy smiled.

No sooner had the marketing man finished noting down Emilio's point than Ulrich Held began to speak.

"The efficiency of EV engines is what marks them out from their competitors. It comes in at around 95%. An internal combustion engine operating on super unleaded runs at 35% maximum, while a diesel engine using direct injection can reach 45%, but no more. A high-end fuel cell is capable of running at 60%, but only when it's stationary. What's more, an EV engine can recuperate energy during braking, and then store it for acceleration. Recently, the Electric RaceAbout, an EV developed at the Helsinki Metropolia

University, even set a new world record by reaching a top speed of 160 mph on a frozen Finnish lake – talk about harsh test conditions."

Nods of agreement all round.

The speaker named the next point himself after adding "efficiency" to the list.

"Even if charging stations have been optimized to charge an EV's battery up to 80% of its capacity in only thirty minutes, we must nevertheless let the consumers know that they can also charge their vehicles at home. With some utility companies charging off-peak rates, it could even be a cheaper alternative."

No-one contradicted him.

"Another huge advantage of EVs is that there is very little mechanical wear and tear. Unlike an internal combustion engine, an electric engine only has a rotating axis. No oil change necessary, and maintenance costs are kept to the bare minimum. Only very occasionally will an EV have to come in for a service – and that's a big saving right there," said an engineer from a motor manufacturer.

This advantage was also duly noted.

After a longish pause, during which participants chewed over any points yet to be mentioned, Ulrich Held chimed in once more.

"An additional point in favor of EVs is that they can have a completely different design from conventional cars. They don't need a tank, exhaust pipe or gearbox. That makes it possible to come up with something truly futuristic that stays very low to the ground. A lower body means less drag and less weight, thus resulting in reduced energy consumption."

"Very good," the speaker said, delighted. "That's all the advantages."

He ended his presentation with a brief summary, emphasizing once more the urgent need to use alternative energy sources, and to develop a solution for anticipated problems regarding grid stability.

Finally, he reminded his audience that if EVs were to be successful, it was essential that all those present committed each argument to memory.

Next up was a sales manager from GM, who spoke without referring to his notes. After greeting the participants and reporting on the number of their vehicles already out on the road, he listed the points that, in his opinion, required special attention: changing public perception of EVs; improving engines; batteries and problems associated with them; charging stations and their efficiency; examples of applications; and reports from practical experience.

On mentioning the last point, he regarded Emilio with a smile.

"In particular I am looking forward to hearing about the Frankfurt police department's experiences with our competitor's vehicle; I understand it's already created something of a stir."

A number of participants laughed and looked over towards Emilio.

After that, a young woman from the Fraunhofer Institute for Systems and Innovation Research presented her report on the potential buyers of electric vehicles. The institute's findings suggested that the typical first-time buyer was an upper middle-class male in his early forties with a technical background. With a glint in her eye, the woman pointed out that this „male" notion could not be entirely trusted, as only one of the 180 females who had filled in the original online questionnaire had actually volunteered for a personal in-depth interview. However, she concluded that all buyers shared an affinity for new technical toys, a passion for driving and a high level of individuality.

During the short coffee break that followed, Emilio took the chance to speak to the cowboy.

"How come EVs don't need gearboxes anymore? I don't understand. There are still plenty that have them."

"It's very simple. Let's go grab a coffee and I'll explain it to you."

Emilio helped himself to a tea, although as far as its quality went, he remained unconvinced. Back at their seats, Ulrich Held took his pen and began to draw two power curves: one for an internal combustion engine, the other for its electric counterpart.

"Emilio – may I call you Emilio?"

The DI nodded.

"Good, please call me Ulrich. If you look at the electric motor's curve, you'll see that it gives you an immediate full torque response, even at zero rpm, so no more stalling. The same cannot be said of an internal combustion engine, however. Take a look."

Ulrich pointed to the second curve. Emilio nodded. He could remember stalling his dad's car when he was still learning to drive, either because he had set off too fast or, in his excitement, engaged the wrong gear.

"Why do EVs still have a gearbox then?" he asked.

"That's because a number of designs were based on models that were initially conceived as conventional cars with internal combustion engines. You convert the engine and leave the rest as it is. Besides, a differential increases the synchronization of the wheels when driving in a straight line. In such a case, equal torque has to be applied to each wheel; if not you veer off course when you stop steering. If there's no differential, you have to steady the wheel the whole time and that affects your comfort. When you take a turn, the differential is equally crucial, as the inner wheel needs to travel a shorter distance than the outer wheel; otherwise you spin. Now, you can easily build EVs without a differential or clutch, because you can mount several smaller motors directly onto the axle next to the wheels. That way the torque is electronically synchronized instead of being controlled mechanically by the differential. Generally you use a current or voltage limiter. However, since the control algorithm is difficult to calculate, development costs remain high, increasing the overall price tag of an EV. And since the majority of people are unwilling to pay extra just for the sake of improved driving comfort, most EVs are still fitted with mechanical differentials. As soon as sales go up, prices can go down and we'll start seeing more pure EVs, that is to say: ones without clutches, gearboxes or differentials. It's what we call economy of sale."

In the face of all this information, the DI could only shake his head.

"So I think I understand, basically. But how does an EV go backwards? I'm still not clear on that. If there's no gearbox, then there's no reverse, is there?"

"Again, very simple. We physicists refer to something called the right-hand rule. Do you know it?"

Emilio said he didn't.

"OK," Ulrich said, "just copy me. First, clench your fist and stretch your arm out in front of you. Your thumb should be on top. Now point your thumb upwards while keeping your first clenched. Your thumb indicates the direction in which the current is flowing. Next extend your index finger, making sure the others remain clenched. Since Maxwell, we know that a magnetic field arises when a current changes its direction or alters its strength. Your index finger is now pointing in the direction of the newly created magnetic field. As you can see, your index finger is perpendicular to your thumb. Lastly, extend your middle finger as if you were about to give someone the bird. Your ring finger and pinkie are still clenched. The newly created magnetic field exerts a force in the direction indicated by your swearing finger. Now let's assume this force represents the direction of travel and that you're going forwards. Next step is to turn your hand through 180 degrees. You can see how your thumb is now pointing in exactly the opposite direction. The same is true for the current. Magnetic field and direction of force have also been reversed and you are now driving backwards. So, an electric motor achieves reverse motion simply by changing the polarity of the current. That's all!"

Emilio continued to play with his fingers and hands for a short time afterwards, still murmuring the words "direction of current, magnetic field, force."

Gradually, a broad grin spread across his features."Man, Ulrich, you're quite something you know that? I wish we'd had a physics teacher like you in school. Then we might have learned something!"

"Thanks, but I doubt your teacher never tried to explain it. Probably you were just more interested in girls and sport at the time." There was a conspiratorial glint in Ulrich's eye.

Emilio couldn't help but acknowledge the truth, even if he didn't admit it out loud.

After the break, it was the turn of the business development chief of a major market research company. He began his presentation with a brief introduction to the history of batteries and accumulators.

One statement in particular took Emilio by surprise:

"The sad truth is we've taken things about as far as they can go with lithium-ion technology. Yes, we can make them higher performance but nowadays that means more weight, and more weight means less range for an EV. A vicious circle that cannot be prevented if we continue to use the old technology. That's why we're pursuing new avenues and working together with international research institutes. As you all know, batteries currently rely on anodes made from graphite. But it would be much better to make them from silicon. The problem with silicon is that the anodes begin to decompose during the charging/discharging process and can break shortly thereafter. On that note, there's an interesting product by Prieto batteries, who are affiliated with the University of Colorado. They've developed a new architecture for Li-ion batteries that overcomes the slow diffusion of ions into and between the anode and cathode, which is basically responsible for long charging cycles. Their three-dimensional architecture, which uses nano-wires and a substrate of copper foam, results in higher energy densities, leading to reduced charging times."

The speaker cleared his throat and reached for his water.

"As far as heat dissipation goes, there's a concept based on a folding technique using aluminum tubes. Just like Japanese origami, where a simple piece of paper can take on entirely new characteristics, folding aluminum drastically changes the metal's cooling properties."

The presentation now became so detailed that Emilio could barely follow it any longer, no matter how hard he tried. Nevertheless, he found the topic absolutely fascinating. And indeed, the next point mentioned seemed even more incredible.

"The KIT Institute for Nanotechnology in Karlsruhe has developed a concept for battery systems of enhanced energy density based on a certain type of nano-material. Using metal-fluoride instead of lithium-ion batteries, they've already managed to significantly increase the current battery capacity, with the potential to reach a ratio of plus ten."

Emilio's imagination was running away with him: nano-materials; it sounded like something from a sci-fi novel. He was absolutely thrilled to be learning so many new things.

"Finally, I'm sure you're all aware of the simple solution for increasing the range, or shortening the charge time that Better Place has been working on: battery switch. Here, you go to a battery switch station and have your empty battery exchanged for a full one. The company has been conducting trials in Israel and other countries for some time already together with Renault and Nissan, two of their major OEM partners. For example, they opened up a switch station at Amsterdam airport to serve Fluence Z.E. taxis."

A thought-provoking note on which to finish.

The last speaker before lunch was the sales manager of Qualcomm Halo, whose subject was wireless electric-vehicle charging. His presentation centered on Europe's largest WEVC project, partially conducted in East London Tech City with the backing of the British prime minister. The initiative had followed a bold announcement made by the city a few years back to make London the „electric car capital of Europe." Partnerships with several companies had been established to form a consortium whose aim was to drive the implementation of this technology in a mega city and find out what consumer expectations needed to be fulfilled.

In his opinion, WEVC was a pre-requisite if EVs were to become established on the mass market, despite the fact that several leading car manufacturers had just announced their intention to standardize a combined, cable-based charging system. Inductive charging, he continued, involved installing a pad in the parking lot and connecting it to a power-feeding device, while a module in the underbody of the vehicle assumed the role of receiver.

"The energy is transmitted inductively, that is ‚wirelessly,' up to a distance of seven inches between the ground and vehicle via a magnetic field. Energy transfer occurs when an EV arrives, activating the power-feeding device via near-field communication and switching it from standby to operating mode. Once the battery is fully-charged the device returns to standby," the speaker explained, before highlighting further details.

„The technology can be integrated into company parking lots, multi-storey car parks, filling stations; or even installed at traffic lights, on the motorway or at home."

The thought appealed to Emilio and he nodded approvingly. Anything that was done automatically and made your life easier was good enough for him. But somehow it worried him too: the fact that the current could flow undetected like this.

What would happen if something came between the vehicle and the charging pad? All of a sudden he felt the hairs on the back of his neck stand up as he thought of Django. What if his colleague's feline friend unsuspectingly crawled under a vehicle at night hoping to make himself comfortable?

Ulrich Held leant over towards Emilio and whispered the response in his ear: "Electromagnetic fields are all around us, there's even one in the atmosphere produced by rays from outer space. It's significantly stronger during storms; and the electrical discharge results in lightning. But these fields can also be found at home. If, for example, you're using an induction hob to cook pasta, the electromagnetic field could in some cases be stronger than that occurring in the charging technology just mentioned."

During the lunch break, Emilio was joined by an engineer employed by an Asian manufacturer of charging stations, who was only too happy to discuss his work. In summary, the message was that, depending on battery size and capacity, the next generation would see the charging time reduced to half an hour.

But, ultimately it was a little note aside that amused and fascinated Emilio in equal measure. There was a Japanese consortium called CHAdeMO, which was involved in the international standardization of charging stations. The thing that intrigued Emilio was the name. In English it stood for "change and move", but the original Japanese phrase from which it was derived was "Ocha demo ikaga desuka," meaning "let's have a cup of tea while the car's charging." That appealed enormously to the DI. This rapid Japanese charging technology had already won him over.

He used the rest of the lunch break to relax and mentally prepare himself for his presentation. Normally he wasn't shy about speaking in public, but this audience was important to him and he wanted to make a good impression.

Just before the end of the break, he went to the bathroom a second time to check his tie in the mirror. When he re-entered the conference room, the other participants were already gathered. The chairman gave him a friendly nod.

Emilio connected his iPad to the digital projector and moved towards the front, as he had his remote pointer with him. His gaze rested on the other participants and he remained silent for another half minute, a trick he also employed in police questioning: a way of ensuring that people remained eager to hear what he had to say.

"Good afternoon, ladies and gentlemen. First I'd like to thank you for inviting me to this conference; I've learned a lot of new and exciting things already. Today I'm going to talk to you about the practical experiences we've gained in the last four months using an EV as a police vehicle. My name is Detective Inspector Perfondo from murder squad and the Focus you see in the courtyard is our patrol car. I must admit that as a native Italian, I was initially skeptical when my boss informed me that he, together with the mayoress, had agreed to test the EV's suitability for public service functions. Yes, as an Italian, you learn the words Ferrari, Maserati and Lamborghini before you can say 'Mama.' Indeed, there are many people who say it is not blood, but petrol, that flows through our veins."

Delighted laughter interrupted his presentation at this point.

He waited for it to die down before continuing. All eyes were focused on him.

"But I have changed my opinion. Today I stand before you a genuine EV fan. It was an argument from my superior that first stirred my curiosity: the EV, he said, had better acceleration than a car with internal combustion engine. A point we discussed this morning – and I can confirm it's true. The acceleration is first class and it's so much fun to drive. I was concerned that my reputation as the force's number one racing driver might be at risk, but you'll be pleased to know I have succeeded in defending it."

Emilio smiled when he saw how well his presentation was being received. He was just about to resume when Ulrich Held interrupted.

"Emilio, just so you know: the FIA is planning a racing series exclusively for EVs. The races are scheduled for 2012 and will take place on inner-city circuits, with Montreal currently the frontrunner; their aim is to sway public perception on EV performance. They are still discussing the actual field – but I can well imagine they'll let experienced amateurs take part alongside the pros. Maybe that'd be something for you!"

Before the DI could find his tongue again, Ulrich Held had turned towards the deputy minister: "What do you think? Should I speak to your boss about it?"

Flabbergasted, the minister replied: "Of course, Dr. Held, we always appreciate hearing your view. And, yes, I think it's a wonderful idea; I'd be more than happy to lend my support."

The cowboy winked at Emilio.

"Oh…wow! I'd be delighted," the latter stuttered, a little taken aback. It seemed he had completely underestimated the minister. Then he took two deep breaths, refocused on his presentation, and pointed to the graphs displaying their daily vehicle mileage. In four months, Emilio and his team had been required to switch to a car with diesel engine a mere six times, their destination having lain outside the EV's range on each occasion.

Next he presented the figures for electricity consumption when the blue light was on and the sirens flashing. These, he explained, were passed on to various companies each month. The discussion that followed concluded with the decision that further testing ought to be conducted in the near future on the Nürburgring racing circuit. Initiator of this idea? Ulrich Held once more.

"As already mentioned, all data presented indicates that EVs have a 96% suitability rating for daily use in public service functions. Part of that, I'm sure, is because we instinctively adapt our driving style to the reality, as well as proceeding in a more energy-conscious and forward-thinking manner. We're not involved in high-speed chases every day after all."

Emilio gazed at his audience, and for a moment it seemed like he might add the word "unfortunately."

"Nevertheless, I have no desire to overlook some of the difficulties encountered over the course of the past four months. And it begins with the language: I still talk about stepping on the gas, even when I'm driving the Focus. Likewise, I haven't got used to saying 'charge' instead of 'fill up.' If you really want to make EVs popular, they need to be cool and hip rather than simply earnest. Perhaps the marketing experts should consider how to make them sexy and heartfelt as well as masculine. You wouldn't believe how much stick I still have to put up with from my colleagues, let alone the criminals themselves, when we arrive at the scene of a crime. In Frankfurt alone, there are more four wheel drives than there is wild countryside in the whole of Germany. That's going to be a huge obstacle to success. I don't think any of you have worked out how to get the people on your side. Most know that the era of the internal combustion engine is drawing to a close, but their hearts still beat in time to the sound of diesel and super unleaded. That's why I'm intrigued to see how the manufacturers respond to the potential for innovative design that this new wave of EVs so undoubtedly provides."

His final comment was greeted with warm applause.

"And on two things I think we are all agreed: first, irrespective of whether it's for public or for private use, the EV range needs to be extended. Second, the purchase price needs to be lowered. Only then does it have a realistic chance of achieving mass-market success and being seen as a genuine alternative, rather than just a city – or a second – car."

Before he took his seat, he wrote his conclusion on the interactive board, a move which earned him a favorable glance from the conference leader.

"You're absolutely right. If we don't manage to reduce the price of EVs and make everyone aware of the potential cost benefits, then we're going to have an equally hard time of it in the future. Lots of managers from the traditional automotive industry still view it as a niche product, which they have no need or desire to exploit. The high costs are connected to the batteries. That's one of the reasons I'm so keen to be kept up-to-date on the latest research."

The next speaker worked in management for a leading utility company, and had already played an active role in the discussion about the advantages of EVs. Emilio was therefore eager to hear what she had to say.

"Good afternoon, ladies and gentlemen. I hope you all still have the energy for another technical presentation. First of all, I'd like to begin with a few remarks about some of the challenges energy companies are facing today. Energy providers in Europe are required to maintain a 50 Hertz standard with a tolerance of 100 millihertz for the entire European power grid. In the past, this was achieved thanks to forecasts taking place at fifteen-minute intervals. Following the passing of the German Renewable Energy Act, however, more and more private energy producers are feeding electricity into the grid – regardless of whether it's needed at that moment or not. Wind or photovoltaic power stations generate electricity when the wind blows or the sun shines. Wind power in particular often generates electricity in the middle of the night when consumption in Europe is minimal. That can lead to over-currents in local areas. When that happens, supply lines are disconnected and removed from the grid in order to prevent any damage to the infrastructure. Unfortunately it is precisely these shutdowns that lead to electricity 'cascades' and blackouts. That means there are unwanted voltage peaks flowing through the entire European power grid, causing transformers to fail. A shutdown in Denmark, therefore, can result in a large-scale power cut in Austria or vice-versa. The stability of the European power grid is at risk and I, for one, am convinced we will see Europe-wide power cuts in the future, with all the attendant problems that might bring. Not least the potential for rioting."

The speaker allowed her last sentence to hang in the air.

"Billions are required in order to maintain grid stability, especially for new power lines, transformers and electric-energy storage systems. You are all no doubt aware of the difficulties in building power lines: everyone wants electricity, but as soon as a new overhead line is proposed, there are countless protests from citizens' action groups. One experiment currently underway in LA is to install overhead electric lines along the highway for electric trucks, thus reducing CO_2 emissions: a real problem due to all the cargo freight arriving at the city's sea ports. But I'm still a little skeptical about this since, like many projects involving renewable energies, the initial costs are so high – in this case about several million dollars for each mile of wiring. A good option in my opinion would be to use EV batteries as storage systems. There are plans to allow EV owners to charge their vehicles at home overnight, and in this way reduce the overflow of electricity. Software fitted in the car enables owners to see whether they require the energy stored in the battery for driving, or if they can sell it back to the electricity companies. The profit for owners would be the difference in price between night and day rate electricity, of which the latter is far more expensive."

She followed this up with a range of formulae calculating how many EVs were needed for each amount of stored or surplus energy. Emilio had switched off by this stage, even if he was fascinated that besides everything else, an EV could also earn you money.

The conference ended with an open discussion, though Emilio barely participated as his head was spinning with so much new information.

"Perhaps we'll see each other again at the EV conferences and trade shows in Frankfurt or Munich?" Ulrich Held said by way of goodbye.

"Just two of the many interesting events on the subject in Germany, not to mention international events like the EVS. I'm sure you'd have a good time and not just because they showcase and discuss the latest vehicles and technology; you can even test drive them at the trade show."

"Sounds good, I'll have to tell my boss as soon as I get back," Emilio resolved, as he extended a hand towards the consultant.

With his vehicle fully charged, he made his way back to Heidelberg to collect his family and from there it was on to Frankfurt.

Chapter 15

Monday brought no further progress for the team, but that evening Felix called his partner to tell him the latest from Calabria.

Clearly impressed, Emilio dropped by straightaway and after briefly studying the files on Don Veschie, he decided to take them home, promising to have them translated by the next morning.

On Tuesday, Felix was warmly greeted when he arrived at the station. Frauke had bought a bottle of champagne and Arno had taken care of the cake. The chief inspector spent the first half hour telling the team about his mini-break, and understandably it was the description of his tandem experience that fascinated them most. When he came to share details of his meeting with Crotone and the circumstances leading up to it, there was silence all round.

"That's unbelievable," was Frauke's only comment.

Felix nodded. "Exactly what I thought. Emilio stopped by yesterday to have a look at the documents Crotone gave me. How's the translation going?"

"Finished, as promised." Inspector Perfondo distributed the documents he had printed out before his boss arrived at the station.

"I just hope you didn't spend the whole night working, otherwise I'll have Sylvia on my back."

"Yeah, well, she wasn't exactly thrilled but she let go in the end."

"I think I'll have to put you on involuntary leave when we're done. Don't want you to be our next case."

Emilio rolled his eyes but didn't contradict him. He had a lot of unused vacation like the rest of them; in fact, in that regard, he was top of the list and more than ready for a break.

"Good, now that's sorted, let's see what we have here."

For the next few minutes all that could be heard was the rustling of paper. Arno was the first to finish reading.

"A real hard-case, this Don Veschie. And he's the kind of person Zimmer meets with. I wonder what his friends would say if they knew?"

Felix couldn't help but agree. It seemed the Mafia boss had reached the top by killing his predecessor, as well as the latter's most trusted advisor.

He had dealt with all other resistance in the most brutal fashion. Still, nothing could ever be proven as the law of omerta applied even for internal struggles. The only thing for certain was that a number of old-school Mafiosi had disappeared without trace since Don Veschie had appeared on the scene.

There had been fires, a few accidents and lots of rumors; but never any proof. What's more, Italian police suspected that Don Veschie was involved in people smuggling, drug trafficking, and even illegal waste disposal. On one occasion, the police had been investigating him for trafficking plutonium, only for all the witnesses to suddenly disappear, forcing the case to be dropped.

"Mafia, waste, Dr. Zimmer; and the Kenyan embassy's first secretary and cultural attaché. If that doesn't stink to high heaven, I don't know what does," Emilio summarized.

The chief inspector concurred. "But does it give us a new lead? Or is it just a coincidence?"

"Is poisoning typical for the Mafia? And if they are behind it, how come we found Kaptain's body? I thought Don Veschie's victims always disappeared?" Frauke objected.

"Frauke's right. What if Kaptain was trying to oust Zimmer, only for Zimmer to find out and kill him in order to protect himself? If I'm reading this correct, Don Veschie is not the kind of man you want to mess with."

Arno scratched his head. "But that shouldn't stop us. I'll see what I can find out about him."

"Yes, you do that. Frauke can help. And ask Europol if they know anything about this Mugambone while you're at it. I'll go to Cando and tell him the latest developments. Maybe now he'll give us permission to dig a little deeper into Zimmer and company."

The chief inspector was just about to get up, when Frauke started giggling.

"I've just thought of something! Dr. Zimmer's pretty arrogant and complacent isn't he? Why don't we break him down a little and see how he reacts?"

"What do you have in mind?" Now Felix was curious.

"You said he's coming back tomorrow, right? What if we just happen to be waiting in arrivals when he touches down? Only we ignore him and act all calm. Make him think we're still shadowing him. Maybe his reaction will give him away."

Frauke's eyes were sparkling impishly. Her colleagues, meanwhile, had burst out laughing.

"Good lord, Frauke, you women really are better than us men. It's genius, I wouldn't want to be up against you."

Her boss gave her a peck on the forehead, which made her blush slightly, while both Emilio and Arno responded with an appreciative whistle.

Felix was sitting across from Cando, as the latter glanced over Emilio's translation and examined pictures of Heinrich Zimmer, the Kenyan and their Mafia entourage. The DA leaned back, placed his forefinger to his lips and gazed at the chief inspector in silence. Felix waited until he was addressed.

"An interesting turn of events. You should have been resting in Italy. But I suppose if you had been, we wouldn't be sitting here now." Cando shook his head in disbelief and continued with a smile.

"I'm sure this will help persuade the odd judge or two I know to lift certain sanctions. What were you thinking?"

"We still haven't been able to assign various cash payments received by Kaptain; and we'd like to know whether they match withdrawals made by Zimmer over the same period. In addition, I'd like to take a closer look at his company. I need to check their records for similarities between business trips made by Kaptain and Zimmer. Zimmer told me the first time we met that the substances used to poison Kaptain could be ordered through the company. Maybe we'll get lucky and find an order signed by Zimmer," the chief inspector outlined his thoughts.

"Do you really think he's that stupid; that he'll lead you straight to it on top of everything else?"

"No, of course not. But he's arrogant. He might come unstuck somewhere because he thinks we're too stupid."

"I can see he's really rubbed you up the wrong way. But fine, I think the signatures will be there in two days tops. Then you can launch your attack with full judicial approval."

Felix thanked him and got up to leave, only to be held back at the door.

"It might be a good idea to involve Financial Crimes."

"Whose case would that make it?"

The DA smiled. "Murder's still the most serious offence: it takes priority over everything else. You'll remain in charge."

"Good, then I'll call Hans Werners. We've already discussed the case anyway."

Back in the office, Felix dialed the number of his old colleague.

"Hans, can you talk? It's about the murder at the east port and its possible connection to Zimmer Consultancy Ltd. We've found something interesting and need your help."

Werners was immediately wide-awake.

The chief inspector outlined the latest developments, before explaining the plan. Inspector Werners was grinning from ear to ear.

"So we finally get our hands on one of these financial big-shots. It sounds almost too good to be true."

"We still don't have anything concrete, but with the help of the judges we should be able to find something. Maybe we'll strike lucky and notice something we previously overlooked. If you could explore the waste connection along with the financial angle, I'd be very grateful."

Hans agreed and they arranged to meet outside the entrance to Dr. Zimmer Consultancy Ltd. on Thursday at ten. Felix hoped the search warrant would be ready by then.

Deep in thought, he was ambling his way down the hall with a cup of tea when he heard Arno shout: "Wow, that's interesting!"

Immediately Felix went to look over his shoulder at his screen. Frauke shot him a curious glance.

"I've found Dr. Mugambone's CV online. He studied here in Germany, in Hannover. Given his age, he could have easily known our victim – if Kaptain also studied in Hannover, that is. You can do chemistry there, I've already checked."

Felix felt electrified: suddenly the pieces were starting to fall into place. He signaled to Frauke, whose hands were already by the receiver.

"I'll call Frau Harris right away."

The conversation was brief and by the time it was over, she too had caught the scent.

"She says her ex-husband studied in Hannover, from 1982 to 1990. Lived in a dorm the whole time, right by the university library, afraid she couldn't remember the name," Frauke revealed.

Felix took another look at the CV. Mugambone had studied in Hannover from 1985 to 1991, albeit business management, but it was still a lead they couldn't afford to ignore.

"I'll speak with our colleagues in Hannover, they should be able to make some enquiries."

With that he disappeared into his office, only to return twenty minutes later.

"Hannover are going to look into it first thing tomorrow, so maybe soon we'll have a result. I've faxed over the photos of Kaptain and Mugambone."

The four of them spent the rest of the afternoon discussing various theories and planning the next steps. At the end of the day, Felix invited his three colleagues for a quick beer. Though Frauke didn't stay long and Emilio excused himself after the second round, Felix and Arno decided to take a tour through Sachsenhausen, the south bank's own little drinking quarter.

When the chief inspector finally made it home, all he got from Django was a look of contempt. Having accidentally left his cell in the office, it wasn't until the next morning that Felix discovered four texts from Petra. With a guilty conscience, he reached for the phone. The response was cool: she didn't want to see him before the weekend. Felix sighed – but he knew it served him right.

The team's morning tea ritual was a little more subdued than usual, with Felix deep in thought and Arno looking slightly the worse for wear, as Emilio was quick to point out. Chief Inspector Büschelberger decided that Frauke should accompany him to the airport, thus surprising his female colleague. Felix, however, found it only right; it had been her idea, after all.

The two detectives positioned themselves directly in front of the exit from where Dr. Zimmer would shortly emerge. They were impossible to ignore. Felix saw how happy Frauke was that her idea was being put into action.

Unfortunately, his own enjoyment was marred by the fact that Petra was still pissed at him. He thought about their time together in Calabria, where Zimmer's plane had taken off that morning.

Suddenly his daydreaming was interrupted by a sharp nudge in the ribs.

"Hey, wake up! That's him at the back."

Dr. Zimmer was wheeling his trolley behind him, and seemed to be talking to someone on his cell phone. He was heading right in their direction. When he got to within thirty feet he saw them and was barely capable of concealing his dismay. The detectives couldn't help indulging in a little Schadenfreude.

The businessman stood still for a moment, turned his back and abruptly ended the phone conversation. Then he was facing the two of them once more, glowering as he headed straight for Felix.

"Are you still on my heels? You're really going to regret this, do you understand?" His voice was loud and lacking all control.

The chief inspector gave his most charming smile. "Dr. Zimmer, what an amazing coincidence. No, we don't want anything from you; we're just waiting for a colleague."

Felix turned away but kept looking at Zimmer out of the corner of his eye, at great pains not to grin. Dr. Zimmer was clearly unsettled and didn't know quite what to say. He was just about to go when the chief inspector spoke to him once more: "And say hello to Dr. Brax from me, I'm sure we'll be hearing from him soon."

With that he pointed ahead and said to Frauke: "Look, there he is!"

They moved towards a hesitant-looking man clearly waiting to be collected. Felix addressed him briefly, taking the time to look back at Dr. Zimmer, who was hurrying away.

The chief inspector made his apologies to the stranger and beamed at his female colleague.

"So, should we try and find a café?"

They discussed what had just happened as they sat slurping their tea.

"I'd say that's a pretty major stone cast, now let's wait and see if there are any ripples," Felix said.

"You were pretty convincing back there. And that stuff with the colleague from Italy: that'll give him something to think about."

"Not too much I hope. I just couldn't resist having a little dig at that shyster of his."

The two detectives laughed and Felix's mood lifted considerably. He leaned back and gazed at Frauke, who was stirring her tea absent-mindedly.

There was something different about her, she seemed happy, more together somehow; she was a good-looking woman. The chief inspector was surprised it had only just dawned on him. He was so deep in thought that he didn't realize Frauke was staring straight at him.

"What are you thinking about? You look miles away."

"You're different somehow," he said, smiling. "It's like you're glowing from the inside, if you know what I mean?"

She blushed slightly and fixed her gaze outside. "Thanks, I'm feeling really good too."

"Could it have something to do with a man?"

She just grinned. "Could do."

Felix waited to see if she'd say anything more. But since she didn't, he decided not to press the matter.

Back at the station, Arno and Emilio were impatiently awaiting their return. All four agreed it had been a successful mission. Emilio regretted that they still didn't have permission to bug Dr. Zimmer's calls: it would've been interesting to see who he told about their little airport meeting.

Just before they were about to call it a night, Felix received a message from Hannover. It was a young officer, fresh from Police College, who had taken care of their enquiry. He confirmed that both men had lived in the same dormitory, on the same floor too as it happened. In addition, he had managed to locate two photos taken at a party, which showed Kaptain and Mugambone together.

On one, they had their arms around each other and were smiling drunkenly for the camera.

Impressed by the hard work of his Hannover colleague, Felix faxed him a note of thanks before turning his attention back to the images of the young Kaptain. The first pictures they had of the victim alive. He took them over to Arno and Emilio. Frauke had already left. They hung the photos next to the pictures of Kaptain's corpse, alongside all those of Zimmer, Mugambone and Don Veschie taken in Italy.

"Until tomorrow; looking forward to seeing your reaction," Felix was addressing the image of Dr. Zimmer.

Then he turned towards Emilio and Arno. "Make sure you get an early night. Tomorrow's going to be a long day. Come on, off you go."

Felix himself had no desire to go home. Somehow it felt lonely there. When he finally got back, it was too late to go shopping. He grabbed hold of Django, put him on his lead – purchased for rare occasions like this – and drove over to Conny's. The smell of deep-fried food didn't seem to bother Django, particularly maybe because the owner always gave him a little bowl of raw meat that had just been through the mincer. While Felix sat poking listlessly at his food, his tom was perched on the table enjoying every mouthful.

A disenchanted yet thoroughly attractive-looking woman was giving Felix the eye. For about five seconds he was tempted to start something, only to abruptly reconsider. Clearly insulted, the woman retired to the far end of the restaurant. Felix immediately regretted snubbing her so rudely and went over briefly to apologize.

"I'm sorry, I've got a lot on my plate right now – bad timing that's all. I hope you don't take it personally."

But the woman simply turned away. With a shrug of his shoulders Chief Inspector Büschelberger made his way home. There, he decided on half a bottle of red before sending Petra a text.

"Good night, sweet dreams. I miss you, Felix x."

Her response was brief: "Sleep well, P."

Felix climbed into bed, feeling depressed.

Chapter 16

The next morning everyone arrived at work a little earlier than usual, the tension writ large on their faces. They were convinced that today was the day they'd finally make the breakthrough.

Shortly after eight, DA Cando entered with a signed search warrant and power of attorney to access Dr. Zimmer's private and business accounts. He even accepted the offer of a cup of tea.

"I'd like you to keep me updated on a daily basis from now on. My argument that the case could be linked to organized crime, along with my naming of Dr. Zimmer's contacts, has caused a minor earthquake. Likewise, my boss wishes to be kept regularly informed."

"The senior district attorney knows about today's operation?"

"Yes, why? Is there a problem? What are you trying to insinuate?"

"No, no, absolutely nothing. I'm just surprised, that's all."

"Even if I don't always share your opinion, we're still on the same side. You know that, don't you?"

"Sure, for a lawyer you're a pretty decent guy," the chief inspector teased.

Cando laughed and chatted for a while about the latest office gossip. As he left, he wished them all good luck. Shortly afterwards, Felix's cell phone rang.

"Felix, Hans here. I just wanted to check we had all the necessary documents."

"Yeah, the DA's just delivered them personally. So let's get going."

"Great, then let's meet as planned. At ten outside the entrance. I'll have a couple of officers from my team with me."

"Good, then we'll be seven in total; that should be enough for the time being."

The chief inspector requested two extra patrol cars, since he found that uniformed police always left more of an impression than their plainclothes colleagues.

Emilio drove the Focus round and the whole team made their way to the meeting point together. Hans Werners and his unit were already discussing matters with the patrol officers. The financial crimes detective couldn't help but smile when he saw the car.

"Next thing we know, your eco-troop will be arriving on bicycles. Just a shame the bad guys will always have the bigger engines."

Emilio's response was pretty frosty. "I'd have expected a little more expertise from the financial crime boys. Zero Motorcycles, a California-based company whose experts used to work for manufacturers like Triumph and Buell, produce high-performance electric motorcycles with a special line in police bikes. Their bikes don't just have a lightweight aluminum frame but also instant torque and no shifting. Top speed is 80 mph and as they don't produce any exhaust gases, you can even go indoors with them. Also, they're barely audible, which is handy for hunting villains. Another example is the TGM in Vienna. The school for engineering has even developed an electric motorcycle that took part in this year's 'Tourist Trophy' on the Isle of Man, the toughest motorcycle race in the world, they say; top speed 145 mph. Talk about big engines, eh?"

„Well, there have always been exotics in the car business, but they never made it mainstream," came the doubtful response from Werners.

"Exotics? All major car manufacturers worldwide are working on EVs, be it pure electric cars or hybrid versions. Yes, there are exotic and pricy sports cars like the Audi R8 e-tron Spyder, which goes from zero to one hundred in under five seconds. But there are also family vehicles out on the road already, like the Tesla S. It's a spacious sedan that can run up to 300 miles on a single charge, depending on the battery pack you choose and your driving behavior, of course. Convenience and safety are state-of-the-Art. Hell, I could fit my wife and kids in and still have space for you two."

Emilio paused briefly to catch his breath, before continuing, still agitated.

"And just for your information, the Bertha Benz Challenge will take place again this year in September, in honor of Bertha Benz and her historic 1888 trip from Mannheim to Pforzheim. Very few people know that no-one wanted to buy the first automobile, patented by Dr. Carl Benz. That is, not until Dr. Benz's wife proved it was suitable for longer distances by making the trip just described. A few years ago, a couple near Heidelberg agreed that Bertha Benz, without whom her husband's life's work would never have been achieved, deserved greater credit for her role. So they decided to build a memorial to her pioneering spirit. The result was the Memorial Route, a dynamic tribute that is the destination of countless drivers each year. Only the most modern vehicles running on alternative fuel are allowed to take part, EVs of course among them. Back then, people laughed at Bertha and her two sons, and now look around you. The world is full of cars. Wake up, the future has a new name – and it's EV mobility." He glared belligerently at the officers from the financial crimes department.

"News to me," Hans Werners said with a rueful shake of the head. "But hey, if I offended you, then sorry. It was only meant to be a stupid joke."

"Come on Emilio, let it go. And behave yourselves from now on!" Felix ended the quarrel and both detectives shook hands.

"Just you wait: some day you'll be jealous of our EV here!" Inspector Perfondo couldn't resist the retort.

"Okay, let's get going" the chief inspector said as he led the way into the building.

Their appearance had the desired effect. The women at reception were so shocked by the heightened police presence that they didn't even inform their boss. The chief inspector used the opportunity to produce the search warrant.

"Good morning, we need to inspect your accounting, personnel and purchasing departments. Please take us to them immediately."

The woman, who had been all smiles with Felix on his previous visits, could only stutter now: "Um…I'm not sure if that's possible. Let me call Dr. Zimmer first."

"I'm afraid that won't be necessary. This is a legal document granting us instant access to the departments just mentioned. You can inform Dr. Zimmer later." He had placed his hand on her phone to prevent her making the call.

Visibly taken aback, she did as she was told. Felix instructed one of the uniformed officers to remain at reception.

"Please ensure this lady doesn't call her boss while we're en route. And if Dr. Zimmer attempts to leave the building with a suitcase or portfolio, stop him. She will point him out to you."

He motioned towards the second receptionist. "Right? You'll be so kind as to help out my colleague here?"

There was a nod in response.

"Good, and should he come here, please take him straight to us. He may, of course, inform his lawyer."

With these words, the squad began to disperse. The chief inspector was more than happy with the way things had gone so far.

First they came to the purchasing department, where Arno, Frauke, a uniformed officer and a colleague from finance broke off from the rest. Personnel and accounts were housed in the same open-plan office just a floor above, which struck Felix as very convenient. He was just showing his ID when Dr. Zimmer suddenly burst in, his face bright red. Since the officer back at reception wasn't with him, Felix assumed Zimmer had taken the direct route.

"What the hell do you think you're doing? I'll have you sued for defamation!" The company owner could barely conceal his anger.

Felix silently showed him the warrant and waited for his reaction. Dr. Zimmer's hands were shaking as he read.

"Perhaps you should consult your lawyer," Felix said.

"No doubt I will, and I can assure you that he'll put an immediate stop to your disgraceful behavior."

"I think that's unlikely, as you've already seen yourself." The chief inspector waved one of the uniformed officers over.

"This officer will accompany you."

"You're arresting me?" Dr. Zimmer was losing all control.

"No, just making sure you don't destroy any sensitive documents. Now please feel free to call Dr. Brax, or whoever you like."

The company owner left the office without another word, accompanied by the uniformed policeman.

Felix looked around. All employees of Zimmer Consultancy Ltd were staring at him with gaping mouths. They had obviously

171

never seen anyone speak to their boss like that. Any resistance they might have planned crumbled instantly and their cooperation was ensured.

Chief Inspector Büschelberger smiled to himself. If he was honest, this was the part he loved most about the job: being able to draw on the raw power of the state. He leaned back and contentedly observed the others going about their work. He wouldn't be needed again until Dr. Zimmer turned up with his lawyer, or lawyers; not that it would take too long, he thought to himself.

Exactly thirty seven minutes later, the company owner appeared in tow with Dr. Brax and another man, presumably one of the lawyer's assistants. Felix was pleased to note that Brax looked pretty exhausted. Probably hadn't had time to construct a decent defense.

The lawyer came straight to the point. "Chief Inspector, could you please show me the search warrant?"

Felix handed it over silently for Dr. Brax to read. The latter did so carefully.

"A pretty weighty document you have here. Not very specific, but everything seems to be in order."

Dr. Brax sounded disappointed. Did he really think the police could be so sloppy?

"I'm afraid we'll have to let them continue for the time being," the lawyer turned towards Zimmer.

"But I would like to know what basis you have for this warrant." He looked Felix straight in the eye, challenging him to a round of verbal boxing.

The chief inspector savored the opportunity to put this puffed-up phony back in his place.

"By all means, shall we get down to brass tacks then?" He pointed towards the table next to them, knowing full well that the majority of employees were only too keen to listen in.

Now it was Dr. Brax's turn to smile. "I think it's better to discuss it in private. Perhaps in my client's office?"

Felix nodded and signaled to the officer who had stayed with Zimmer all this time to stand down. Then the four disappeared into Zimmer's office, the chief inspector for the first time. If the building as a whole and its décor were impressive, then this office was even more so. A huge desk stood right in front of a big glass façade; while behind it a heavy-duty leather armchair stood in solitary splendor.

Three telephones and two flat screens adorned the desk. In addition, there was a large corner seating unit with English lounge chairs made from expensive leather and a big, round wooden table in the middle. On the walls above the unit were two modern paintings that didn't look like copies.

Felix thought one of them was a Dali, but decided not to ask. After all, he didn't want Dr. Zimmer, who by now was pouring himself a Cognac from a crystal decanter, to regain his self-assurance. He offered both Dr. Brax and his assistant a drink, deliberately ignoring the chief inspector. Not that it bothered Felix.

Heinrich Zimmer was the only one drinking in the end. He downed the first cognac in a single gulp and poured himself another. The chief inspector thought it was a good sign that Zimmer was nervous.

"Now, you were telling me about the accusations being leveled at my client." The lawyer smiled at Zimmer, who was gradually beginning to settle down.

"As you know, we are still investigating the murder of Uwe Kaptain. Our enquiries have yielded grounds for suspicion that there may be links to organized crime. And that the links extend to this company." The chief inspector paused and waited eagerly for a response.

The room was completely still until Heinrich Zimmer leapt to his feet and started talking feverishly, only to be immediately cut short by his lawyer.

"Please, let me do the talking."

He forced Zimmer to sit back down, and smiled at Felix.

"Those are very serious allegations. I'm looking forward to hearing your proof, which I'm sure is completely unfounded."

"You know yourself that you can earn a lot of money through illegal waste disposal. We found a number of cash payments made to Uwe Kaptain that we're unable to account for. That naturally aroused our suspicion," Felix said.

"But surely that doesn't mean anything?" Dr. Brax asked.

"No, of course it doesn't, but we have further grounds. While still a student, Kaptain lived in the same dorm as a Kenyan man who now holds a very high position in his country's government. Mugambone is his name, and as you can see, he has contacts in the Italian mafia."

Felix placed the photo showing Mugambone and Don Veschie outside the latter's house on the table. He was delighted to note that Zimmer had grown visibly paler; he was on the right track here.

"And what does that prove? Have the two of them had any further contact?" the lawyer probed.

"We're still looking into that. But we do know that your client met with both of these men in Calabria last weekend. See for yourself." Felix placed another image on the table in front of him.

Zimmer was now white as a sheet. Dr. Brax took the photo in his hand and was silent for a long time. "And this Italian is a known member of the Mafia?"

"Well, he's never been convicted."

"So, nothing's proven then. Then I'd say what you have is pretty thin."

"And that's precisely why we're here: to see if we can find further evidence of these links."

The lawyer turned to face his client. "Don't worry, as far as I'm concerned this warrant isn't sustainable. I'll call the judge who signed it right away and request a meeting. We'll get this quashed and all your records returned in no time, believe me. And now, Chief Inspector, if you don't mind, I'd like to consult with my client in private."

"But of course. I would like to go and see if my colleagues have found anything anyway."

Felix left Dr. Zimmer's office in high spirits, certain he had put up a good show. He asked both groups if they'd found anything, but the answer was no in each case.

They had, however, collected a number of files that they wanted to take a closer look at. Among them were travel expenses from Kaptain and Zimmer; invoices detailing chemical purchases; and documents dealing with consultancy contracts for foreign waste disposal and the like. The files were stacking up pretty fast.

The chief inspector was chatting to Frauke, when all of a sudden Dr. Brax marched angrily towards him.

"Well played, just don't go thinking you can get around me with a stunt like that." The lawyer was waving a pen furiously in Felix's face.

"I'm sorry; I don't know what you're talking about. Care to explain?"

"I've just tried to secure a meeting with this judge, only to discover he's gone for a long weekend somewhere. He's not back until Tuesday. Cheap trick, but rest assured I'll find a different judge." Dr. Brax swept out of the room.

"What was all that about?" Frauke said in amazement as she followed the lawyer with her gaze.

Felix smiled quietly to himself. "I had no idea how clever our friend Cando could be. No judge is going to revoke a search warrant issued by another colleague without being in full possession of the facts. It's a kind of code of honor, an unwritten rule amongst judges. Means we've got free rein until at least Tuesday – and there's nothing Dr. Brax or any of Zimmer's other friends can do about it."

Frauke giggled. "The DA's a real fox!"

Her boss rubbed his hands in glee. "Exactly. And now let's make sure we use our time wisely."

At around four o'clock, the officers left the grounds of Dr. Heinrich Zimmer Consultancy Ltd. But not without Dr. Brax making sure Felix had signed a written acknowledgement of receipt for the files. The chief inspector thanked the officers from uniform. In total they had collected eight boxes, all of which were to be taken back to the station.

Hans Werners and his team accompanied them back to HQ. Things got a bit tight in the meeting room, but the zeal with which everyone went about the task at hand more than compensated for any lack of space. The files were sorted into three different piles: business trips and hospitality; purchasing orders; and hazardous waste.

By eight o'clock they were finished with the sorting. Next, Felix allocated different officers to each separate pile: Emilio and he would look after Zimmer and Kaptain's travel expenses and trips abroad; Frauke and Peter Rauchnagel from Financial Crimes were responsible for all purchasing orders; while Arno, Hans Werners, and Günther Vogel were to sift through all consultancy contracts and hazardous waste transactions.

Once that was done Felix sent them all home, under instructions that they should return at eight thirty sharp the following morning.

Back at home, he realized he only had a single tin of cat food for Django, who was rubbing against his legs ravenously. For Felix himself, there was nothing. He decided to order takeaway: sweet-and-sour duck and a bottle of red.

As expected, the wine didn't taste good. Still, he managed to finish the whole bottle while going over the case in his head. Briefly he considered calling Petra, but decided to leave it since she was probably still pissed. Seeing how desperately he needed to go shopping, he set his morning alarm clock for half an hour earlier than usual.

Chapter 17

Despite the precaution, he was still ten minutes late for work the next morning. There had been a woman of at least eighty at the supermarket, engaged in an interminable conversation with the female cashier about whether the groceries were actually fresh.

The chief inspector had just rolled his eyes. He could never understand why all senior citizens seemed to go shopping either first thing in the morning or last thing at night. What did they do the rest of the day? Somehow he suspected that when he got to their age, he'd know the answer – even if by that stage he'd have forgotten the question.

There was already a bustle of activity in the meeting room, and an unfamiliar smell wafting towards him. It took him a while to realize what it was: coffee. But of course, there were now three people in the office who didn't drink tea. He grinned. Even if their reputation hadn't spread as far as Financial Crimes, things would soon change.

Frauke guessed what he was thinking and pointed towards the gurgling coffee machine. "Borrowed it from our janitor; even bought the coffee myself this morning."

Hans Werners shook his head. "I've never heard anything like it. A unit that only drinks tea."

Emilio and Felix compiled a comprehensive list detailing Zimmer and Kaptain's trips abroad, leaving several columns on the paper free for Arno and his team to add their summarized findings.

During a short break to stretch their legs, Emilio conveyed his disappointment. "Shame that we can't get these details for Mugambone too. It'd be interesting to see if there was any overlap."

Arno took a quick breath. "Do you have any idea how much that would cost? First we'd have to make an official and watertight request to the Kenyan embassy in Berlin to avoid being rejected there. Then Berlin would have to ask the government back in Kenya, who would crosscheck, in turn, with their embassy in Rome. That is, if they want to. The info has to come back the same way, and we're left waiting at least half a year. Worst case, they say it's none of our business what their embassies are up to – immunity and all that stuff."

Inspector Perfondo grumbled: "I know, you're right. I'm just saying it would be nice if they finally let us get on with things without all these obstacles in our way."

Felix was listening to the conversation with increasing interest. "I might know a way we can avoid the red tape and still get our hands on the information."

He fished Commissario Crotone's card out of his wallet.

"Here, this man's got a cousin at the national treasury in Rome. I'll check if he can help us through the backdoor."

Emilio gave his boss an approving pat on the shoulder. "Mama always said we'd make a real Italian out of you."

The chief inspector went into his office and dialed Crotone's number. The phone rang three times before it was picked up.

"Pronto."

"Commissario Crotone, Chief Inspector Büschelberger from Germany."

"Ah yes, and how are you and your charming companion?"

"We're both very well, thank you, with fond memories of Calabria."

"Wonderful. I hope we'll meet again soon. Now what can I do for you?"

"I just wanted to let you know that we've made real progress since our meeting in Tropea. We're currently trying to establish a profile of Dr. Zimmer and our victim's movements. It would be great to have a similar profile for Mugambone, but it seems pointless going through official channels. Do you think your cousin might be able to help us?"

Felix heard laughter at the other end of the line.

"Commissario, are you sure you're not related to your Italian colleague? You're already thinking like one of us; I like that."

"Emilio said the same thing: that he'd make a real Italian out of me yet."

Laughter again.

"I have to say this is all incredibly amusing. Listen, I'll get back to you – say hello to your colleague from me."

Crotone had hung up before Felix could even say thanks.

Immensely satisfied, the chief inspector returned to his partner. "Looks like you can kiss goodbye to the red tape, and I'm to say hello from Calabria."

They all went to Conny's for lunch, including Emilio, to the amazement of his colleagues.

"If everyone's going, then I don't want to be left out. Just don't get used to it," he muttered in response to Frauke's teasing. All he ordered was two beef rissoles and coleslaw. After a slightly longer lunch break than usual, the chief inspector picked up the check for everyone.

In the afternoon they continued to work at a brisk clip, and soon Felix and Emilio were finished with their profile.

While his colleagues were still poring over various files, Felix withdrew to his office to call Petra.

"Hello Felix." If anything, she sounded frosty.

"Hey Petra. I hope you're not still mad at me. I'm sorry. I miss you."

"You've made yourself pretty scarce lately. I thought you'd call or at least send me a rose. But no, nothing from the chief inspector."

He could hear the bitterness in her voice.

"I wanted to call you. But I thought you didn't want to speak to me, so I left it."

"I didn't want to speak to you!"

"Then why are you pissed I didn't call?"

He was baffled. Petra always managed to confuse him with her mixed signals.

"You could've at least tried. It would've shown what I mean to you, which isn't much apparently."

"Petra, you know that's not true. You mean the world to me!"

Felix realized the conversation was slipping away from him. It was definitely not going according to plan.

Silence at the other end.

"Can we see each other later? Then we can talk about it in our own time. OK?"

179

"No, I'm going on a bar crawl with a girlfriend tonight. Not sure when I'll be back. So, no need to wait up. Do you understand?" Petra dismissed the suggestion brusquely.

"Yes."

There was a hint of sadness in his voice. He could see that he was losing her, but he didn't know what to say. Both of them waited for the silence to be broken.

"Felix?"

"Yes?"

"If you like, you can come over for breakfast tomorrow at eleven. Bring Django with you; at least he knows how to behave."

"I'll be there. Looking forward to it. I love you."

"We'll see about that. Until tomorrow then."

"OK, and have fun tonight."

The line was dead: Petra had already hung up.

Head down, he returned to the meeting room.

The rest of the day really dragged and Felix was happy when he could finally call it a night and head home. He spent the evening in front of the TV with Django and a bottle of mineral water.

There was a whodunnit on, but instead of getting all worked up by the stupid script – normally one of his favorite pastimes – he just followed the story absent-mindedly. His thoughts were somewhere else entirely.

He woke up early the next morning, and bought a bottle of Petra's favorite champagne, along with three dozen red roses. Back at home, he combed Django's fur until it was silky and smooth, before putting on his best shirt and the tie they had purchased together in Pizzo. He waited nervously until it was time to go, and was outside Petra's apartment block almost fifteen minutes early.

Still agitated, he remained in the car until eleven sharp, and just as the clock chimed for a final time he knocked on her door. Django was mewing and gazing curiously at his new surroundings.

Felix held the roses in his hand, with the champagne tucked under his arm. Petra opened the door, took Django in her arms and kissed the tom on the forehead.

"Hello, sweetie," she turned back inside with the animal. "Shut the door behind you if you're coming in."

Felix followed her, uncertain what to make of her performance, and handed over the flowers.

"How nice. But you men never seem to get it right, do you? A single rose would have been enough for now, and the bouquet after we've made up. Still, thanks anyway!"

She placed the roses in a vase.

"Have a seat."

Petra pointed towards the dining table, which was decorated with candles and champagne glasses. In the middle were fresh rolls, croissants, jam, sausages, cheese and salmon.

"Well, that's handy – I brought us something to drink."

"I knew you would." Petra's voice came from the kitchen where she was filling the vase with water.

"Should I open the bottle?"

"No, let's talk first." She placed the vase on a table in the hall and sat down opposite Felix.

"You should know that I'm a strong person and I don't need a partner to be happy, OK? I'm not one of these women who can only function properly in a stable relationship. If I need intimacy, then I look for a man - sometimes a woman even - and have my fun – no ties, no complications. With you, I have the feeling this could be something different, but there's no way I'm making the mistake of putting someone else's needs before my own again. I don't need you. Do you understand what I'm saying?"

Felix just nodded, and remained awkwardly silent.

Petra gazed at him for a long time, and then smiled. "No need to be upset, it wasn't that bad. I only wanted to make a few things clear. Now you can open it."

And for Petra, the whole thing did actually seem to be forgotten; though Felix couldn't shake the feeling that something had been lost. In the evening, they went to a drag show. She enjoyed herself enormously, while he continued to struggle with doubts and feelings of guilt.

Monday brought further progress in their investigation. At exactly fourteen minutes past ten, Frauke clapped her hands together.

"I don't believe it, we've got him!" She leapt to her feet with an invoice in her hand. "Felix you have to take a look at this."

All the officers in the room stopped what they were doing and stared at Frauke, who was waving a sheet of paper around excitedly. Chief Inspector Büschelberger took it and glanced over it briefly.

Since it was an invoice of several thousand euros with more than thirty different items, he didn't immediately find it. Frauke pointed to one of the lines: one hundred grams of purest benzodiazepine charged at twelve euros and five cents. He passed the sheet of paper around without saying a word.

Arno clenched his fist. "Now we've got him, the dirty bastard!"

Emilio simply nodded while the rest of the officers congratulated Frauke on her find.

"Still doesn't mean Dr. Zimmer's our man. Only that we're on the right track. I'll inform Cando right away – I forgot to give him my daily report on Friday anyway." Felix left the room.

Even if, as head of team, he ought to have maintained a degree of professionalism, he couldn't resist letting out a little cry of joy in the corridor.

"Well look at this, Chief Inspector Büschelberger is here to grace me with his presence. Unless I'm very much mistaken, we agreed on a daily report. No matter how brief," Cando greeted him frostily.

"We did, you're right. Somehow I didn't get round to it on Friday. But we've just discovered something and I wanted to inform you straightaway."

"Let's hear it."

"We found an invoice from the week of the murder containing the substance we're looking for."

The DA leaned back, his anger all but evaporated, and whistled through his teeth. "Good work! So, we're on the right track then. What are you going to do next? Bring Zimmer in for questioning?"

"I think I'll leave him to stew a while. It'd be good if he made the next move. Plus, we don't have the purchase order, so we don't know who signed it. We're currently drawing up a profile of Zimmer and Kaptain's movements. Hans Werners and his team are refocusing their efforts on illegal waste disposal. Maybe there'll be something there. We're also trying to get more information on this Kenyan."

"Doesn't he work for their embassy in Rome?"

The chief inspector nodded.

"I don't recall you applying for permission to question an employee from a foreign embassy. Maybe I don't want to know," Cando said.

"I think you don't want to know. Let's just say I'm making use of my pan-European network."

"Okay, let's not mention it again. Make sure you keep me in the loop. Email is fine."

Felix promised he would and left.

After the lunch break, he wanted an overview of all the latest findings. The most important of these was still the invoice discovered by Frauke. Despite an intensive search, they hadn't been able to locate the purchase order yet.

"That has priority. If Zimmer's the one who signed it, then we've got him nailed. No matter what his lawyers do," Chief Inspector Büschelberger growled.

Their profile was rounded off by Hans Werners and his team. It clearly showed that Uwe Kaptain had made the most trips abroad. He had been a pretty frequent visitor to Africa, travelling to Nairobi, among other places, eleven times during the previous year.

Three months ago, his trips to Kenya had ceased; since then he had been in Rome twice. Everyone was convinced that Kaptain had been meeting with Mugambone.

Zimmer had accompanied him once to Kenya and once to Rome. Otherwise there was nothing unusual about his movements: he had been to the USA, India, China, South Africa and Japan. There were no clusters like the victim.

"So, what does this tell us? If it's illegal waste disposal, then we know Kaptain was involved at any rate. The payments weren't made by Zimmer to keep him quiet." Felix gazed round the room.

"But even if Kaptain was blackmailing his boss, wouldn't it have been far easier for Zimmer to disguise the money as salary payments? True, both would've had to pay taxes, but Zimmer could have written off the increased wages by squeezing profits. I can't imagine the payments were made by Zimmer either," Hans Werners said.

The logic behind his argument was undeniable.

"Have we found any withdrawals in the company accounts?" the chief inspector asked.

"No, but we haven't been looking either," Frauke shook her head.

"OK, get on it straightaway. Peter can check the purchase orders on his own; we have the invoice already. Emilio, go to Zimmer's bank and examine his private accounts."

"What I don't understand is: if Zimmer's our man, then why did he mention that his company could order the substances the first time we met? And why did he say there'd be a written purchase order?" Emilio asked.

"Maybe there's no purchase order because he got rid of it, only to forget about the invoice. Perhaps he was too arrogant," his boss replied.

"Still," Inspector Perfondo countered, "something's not right. I guess time will tell."

Chief Inspector Büschelberger turned to his colleagues from financial crimes:

"Anything on illegal waste disposal?"

"No and I'm afraid I don't think there will be for some time. They're clearly all very careful. I'd be surprised if we found anything." Hans Werners sounded a little disheartened.

"It's always the same. You don't catch the big guns this way. We need to start digging a lot deeper. I suggest we take all the consultancy contracts back to our office and compare them with the rest of our information. There's nothing more we can do here."

"If you think you can work better over at Financial Crimes, then that's what we'll do. Arno you take care of the purchase orders from now on. And Hans, let us know as soon as you find anything."

Hans promised he would.

While Emilio headed to the bank, the others sorted all the documents for Werners and his team.

Emilio returned just before the end of the shift. "They haven't found anything yet, but they'll keep looking until they do."

184

Chapter 18

Felix's phone rang early the next morning. It was Cando.

"Dr. Brax is meeting with the judge at two this afternoon to try and have the search warrant revoked and all documents immediately surrendered. It would be helpful if you were there with your latest findings. If it comes down to it, we'll have to show the invoice. Then we can prove that the substances used to poison the victim were ordered from Zimmer's company. That should be enough for us to continue investigating them. But I might still be able to convince the judge without playing our trump card," said the DA.

"Of course, if it helps I'll be there. I saw that Kortz had signed the papers. Is the meeting in his office?" Felix asked.

"Yes, room 340 in the district court building. See you there — unless you have anything else for me?"

Felix didn't. Instead he put all the documents in order and tried to build a causal chain so that he could present a logical argument to Judge Kortz. He had to admit there were still lots of gaps that could be exploited by a skillful lawyer — and Dr. Brax was certainly that. Just before lunch, a fax from Italy came through.

Crotone had sent them the results of his investigation. A brief comparison with Zimmer and Kaptain's data had yielded significant overlap: Mugambone had been in Nairobi at the same time as Zimmer the week before last; and they had met again in Calabria the following week. That was no coincidence. What's more, they now had confirmation that the Kenyan had relocated to Rome three months ago, exactly the same amount of time since the victim's last trip to Nairobi.

"It seems like Kaptain did the dirty work for his boss; only now that he's dead, Zimmer himself has stepped into the breach. He probably couldn't trust anyone else," Emilio summarized the fax.

"But how does that fit with our theory that Kaptain had to die because he was blackmailing Zimmer?" Frauke looked at each individual team member in turn. "It doesn't make sense to me."

"Maybe the money has nothing to do with the murder? I guess we'll know soon enough. The fact is that someone from Dr. Zimmer's company ordered the poison and it's our job to find out why," her boss replied.

After lunch, Felix drove to the district court and met the DA outside the entrance. Together they made their way to Judge Kortz's office, where Zimmer's lawyer was already waiting. As soon as they had sat down at the judge's table, Dr. Brax went on the offensive:

"My client is a highly respected member of society with many friends and a clean record. It is our view that police obtained their search warrant using evidence that doesn't hold water. Your Honor, if the police or DA cannot provide tangible grounds for charging my client, then I hereby request that the court order be withdrawn. I have prepared some information for you about Dr. Heinrich Zimmer's career; the organizations he is part of; the charitable associations he supports; and other ways in which he is engaged in the community."

He handed the judge a selection of press clippings and membership cards, which were supposed to prove what a public-spirited person Dr. Zimmer was. Many of the photos showed high-ranking officials; on one he was even shaking hands with the interior minister for Hesse while both were smiling into the camera.

The chief inspector was a little concerned that the judge might be swayed by this. He looked over to Cando, who was still sitting there, calmness personified. Judge Kortz placed the documents to one side.

"That's a nice selection. But even public-spirited people with friends in high places commit crimes. Plus, I seem to recall a certain photo that shows your client alongside alleged Mafia members. Can you explain that?" asked the judge.

"But that's just it. This Italian businessman is merely suspected of Mafia involvement; nothing has ever been proven. In dubio pro reo. Furthermore, my client had never seen him before and was only introduced to him through Dr. Mugambone. Mugambone is a middleman who worked together with the murder victim. He was responsible for facilitating contracts between Dr. Heinrich Zimmer Consultancy Ltd. and the Kenyan government, as well as other companies from Kenya and surrounding countries. Here is a sworn affidavit stating not only that Dr. Zimmer had never had any previous contact with the Italian; but that he never would've gone to meet him if he'd known about his questionable reputation."

Dr. Brax handed over a further document. While the judge was glancing over it, Felix's cell phone vibrated. He looked at the screen and saw that Frauke was trying to reach him. He pressed "ignore." But the cell phone immediately sounded again. Just as the chief inspector was about to turn it off, Judge Kortz nodded towards him:

"If someone is desperately trying to reach you, then you should pick up. It doesn't bother me."

"Thanks. Yes, hello Frauke. What is it? You know where I am, right?" Felix said before listening attentively.

He nodded a few times and looked towards Cando meaningfully.

"Thank you! You did the right thing calling."

He turned his gaze to the judge. "Your Honor, I would like to ask for a deferral. Important information has just come to light, which could help solve the case."

"You can't ask for anything here!" Dr. Brax waved his hands threateningly in front of Felix's face.

"Let's calm down now. What sort of information?" Judge Kortz invited the chief inspector to continue.

"It seems like our uniformed colleagues have just caught a burglar red-handed. The man has a pretty long rap sheet and has informed arresting officers that he knows something about the murder. In doing so, he mentioned a detail not previously released to the press, as well as hinting at the involvement of Dr. Brax's client. He was unwilling to elaborate any further until he had spoken with the DA. Most likely, he wants to cut a deal."

"What do you mean hinting? What kind of detail?" Dr. Brax had clearly been thrown off guard.

"I'm afraid I can't say anything more at this point. Do I have permission to leave, Your Honor?"

Judge Kortz nodded. "Fine. The search warrant stands, as for the time being there is no cause to have it withdrawn. I suggest that you inform me of the latest developments on Friday; and that Dr. Brax re-submits his application at the same time."

With these words, the discussion was closed.

"Felix, wait for me. I want to listen to this as well," said Cando, as they left the room.

"I'm coming too, you're not the only ones who'd like to question this witness," a voice sounded from behind.

A wolfish grin spread across the features of the DA. "Dr. Brax, you are more than entitled to cross-examine our witness if it comes to trial, as you well know. Before that, however, all we can offer is access to our records – nothing more."

Brax was forced to admit defeat.

"Our lawyer friend looked pretty crestfallen. Not so self-important anymore," Felix grinned at his companion triumphantly.

He had a feeling that today was about to get even better.

Back at headquarters, there was an air of nervous anticipation.

"The witness should be here any minute. They're just bringing him in now," Frauke informed them.

"Do you know anything more?" Felix asked.

"No, but I think this could be our breakthrough," she replied.

"Sure, especially with the discovery of the invoice, which Zimmer and his lawyer still know nothing about," he turned contentedly towards the DA.

"That'll be even more of a headache for Brax," Cando smiled.

They moved into Felix's office, taking a few extra chairs so that the whole team could hear what this dubious witness had to say. Cando sat down by the chief inspector, while the others took their places along the wall. Opposite Felix was a seat reserved for the witness.

Emilio had his tablet-PC in front of him, fingers on the keyboard ready to take down the statement. He was the fastest typer among them. For that reason, Arno had dubbed him "Fingers" a few months before and said he could appear in Spaghetti-Westerns. The resulting verbal exchange had been extremely entertaining.

Two uniformed officers led the witness in, before removing his handcuffs and handing Felix a file containing some information. The chief inspector signaled for them to take a break in the cafeteria; Emilio would call them as soon as they had finished questioning the witness. Then he glanced over the documents.

The witness, an old friend of the German justice system, was only forty-one but had already spent more than fifteen years in various prisons across the country.

Either a serial offender or just plain stupid, or possibly a mixture of the two, Felix thought to himself.

For a moment he surveyed Angelos Zapas, who was now sitting in front of him, superficially calm. Then he passed the documents on to the DA and waited for Cando to finish reading. Meanwhile he offered the prisoner coffee, freshly brewed by Frauke, who had invested in a small supply for visitors and witnesses.

Angelos Zapas was a tiny wisp of a man, about five foot six with thin, black hair arranged in a comb-over. He had an olive-brown complexion and a slim, V-shaped face. His dark-brown eyes gazed attentively around the room but displayed no sign of fear or panic. Cando cleared his throat before Felix got the questioning under way.

"Good afternoon, Mr. Zapas, my name is Chief Inspector Büschelberger and next to me is District Attorney Cando. You said to our colleagues in uniform that you had information in connection with the east port murder. Would you please care to elaborate?"

"That's correct. I know who ordered the hit, perhaps even who carried it out."

The witness took a sip of coffee and avoided direct eye contact.

A deathly silence descended upon the room, with everyone holding their breath and waiting for the next statement. But Zapas was saying nothing. He was most likely a good orator and knew all the tricks used by police during interrogations. It wouldn't be easy to drag him out of his shell.

"That is, of course, very important information for us. Therefore please continue."

The felon smiled. "But Chief Inspector, you must know that nothing comes free in this life. I can help you, but only if you help me in return – that's just the way it goes."

He looked the DA straight in the eye. "What do you think about that?"

Cando waited almost an entire minute before answering. "I hear what you're saying. But what kind of help are you expecting?"

"Well," Zapas scratched his chin. "You've read my file. I've been in jail too often. If I get sent down again, it'll be for a long time, an extended term for persistent reoffending. You know the law better than me. As I'm sure you can well imagine, I have no particular desire to go back inside. I want you to make sure I get probation or day release at worst."

"You know I can't promise anything. But I will put in a word for you and see what I can do."

"Bullshit! If you can't offer me anything concrete, then maybe I'll have a sudden bout of amnesia!" The career criminal leaned back, folded his arms, and fell silent.

Felix and Cando briefly exchanged glances, with the DA rolling his eyes before focusing back on the witness.

"Okay, I hereby promise in front of witnesses, that I will convince the judge to make you a day-release prisoner. Probation's not an option because you've already violated the terms of your agreement. There's nothing more I can do. Either you accept my offer or you stop wasting my time."

Slowly but deliberately, he stood up and offered Zapas a hand by way of goodbye.

The witness hesitated. "I'd like that in writing, please."

Looking over towards Emilio, the DA asked: "Do you mind taking this down?"

Emilio nodded, hands poised over the keyboard as Cando dictated his statement.

"District Attorney Cando hereby assures the witness present, Mr. Angelos Zapas, that he will assist him in his forthcoming trial. He will ensure that Zapas' help in solving the Kaptain murder case will be accordingly acknowledged in court. Furthermore, he will see to it that Zapas be classified as a day-release prisoner on two conditions: one, that the latter shows proof of gainful employment; and two that his assistance leads to the arrest of the perpetrator and the murder's resolution. Date, location, witnesses and signature."

It took less than a minute for Emilio to have the printed text in the DA's hands. Cando scanned it, and gave a satisfied nod before signing. Then he passed it on for Felix to countersign, and finally handed the statement to Zapas.

"Happy now?"

The witness read it, nodded and tried to put it in his pocket.

"Unfortunately that's not how it works. We'll keep the document in your file – that's the safest place for it. It will then become operative during your trial."

Angelos Zapas was about to protest, but he was sharply rebuked by Cando.

"You should have a little faith in the German justice system. If you won't, or can't, then the deal's off."

Having recovered the document, Cando glowered at the witness, before filing everything away with the rest of Zapas' papers.

"Afterwards our colleagues in uniform will take your file and restore everything to its rightful place. But now it's up to you to fulfill your part of the agreement."

"OK, fine. I received instruction from a certain person to break into the apartment of Uwe Kaptain and abstract documents, as well as a particular photo."

"Time to stop talking in riddles. Who gave you the instruction? What did you 'abstract'? And when? This isn't a guessing game, is that clear?"

"Right, I get it. It was the Doc, I mean the head of Zimmer Consultancy Ltd., who hired me. I worked as a porter there for six months, before I was given the boot for dipping into the till. He knew me from back then."

"When you say the Doc, you mean Dr. Heinrich Zimmer, is that correct?" Chief Inspector Büschelberger asked.

"Yeah, that's right. I call him the Doc. He was always friendly to me, used to come and chat to me when I was on nights, sometimes even gave me something to eat or drink."

Felix noticed the dumbfounded expression on his colleagues' faces. He assumed he was looked similarly disbelieving.

"And you didn't find this behavior strange for the CEO of a major company?" he asked.

"Well, now that you mention it, I've never had a boss like him, before or since."

In the meantime, the DA had been leafing through the files again. "But you weren't reported for the theft? No conviction either."

"No, the Doc was very generous and turned a blind eye. Said he couldn't keep me on, of course, but he didn't want to report me."

Felix exchanged meaningful glances with Cando, then nodded towards Angelos, and signaled for him to continue.

"So, almost five weeks ago I get a call from the Doc. He asks me how I'm doing and whether I'm free. Course, I said yes right away."

"When did the call come exactly? As District Attorney Cando said, we need hard facts." The chief inspector reprimanded the witness a second time.

"Sure, I get it. The call came on Sunday morning, exactly a week before this Kaptain was murdered. I had been sleeping late, when suddenly the phone rang. It was the Doc. We arranged to meet the next morning, in a restaurant called Le Mirage. There, he explained exactly what he wanted. I was to break into an apartment at 16 Beethovenstraße, into Kaptain's apartment to be exact, and look for a photo showing Kaptain, the Doc, some Mediterranean type and a few black guys. The Doc knew exactly how many copies there were and said I should get them all. He offered me ten grand if I did it without asking any questions. I said: 'twenty thousand and I'll do.' We negotiated a little and agreed on seventeen. That was it. Then we went our separate ways and I began staking out the apartment, waiting for the right opportunity."

"Were you paid straightaway, or what was the deal?" DA Cando interrupted the thief.

"I see you know your stuff. I got three thousand as a down payment, the rest on delivery. He also gave me a picture so I could recognize the guy. The deal was to get it done as quickly as possible but take no risks. On no account was Kaptain to realize he was being tailed; the Doc was very clear on that. So I started watching the apartment. Knew pretty soon it was a no-go during the day. One of the neighbors – she seemed pretty sharp, and the house was too busy otherwise. Besides, the entrance was so secure there was no way for me to get in unnoticed when it was light. Kaptain wasn't away long enough in the evening for me to manage either. Whenever he left the house I followed him to see if he might spend the night somewhere, but he was never gone for long."

"So exactly five weeks ago you were following Kaptain as well?" Felix asked.

"Bingo," the witness grinned. "I saw him pick up a couple of hustlers from the railway station. They didn't leave until the following morning. Otherwise there was nothing the whole time. I was there every night. Then on the Sunday, he got into his car and drove off. I followed him to the outskirts before turning back round, thinking it was now or never. But there was too much going on in the house, so I had to wait a while until I was certain no-one would bother me."

"When exactly did Uwe Kaptain leave his apartment? And what direction was he driving in?" Felix wanted to know.

"He must have left about half nine, driving towards Taunus. Had a travel bag with him, so I reckoned he wouldn't be coming back. I'd never have guessed just how right I was."

Felix was thinking the victim must have driven straight towards them; time and route matched anyway.

"About half twelve I went into the apartment and started searching. I put all the photos I found into a big bag. There weren't very many – and I couldn't find the one I was after. So I turned the whole apartment upside down, trying to leave as few traces as possible. It got pretty late and I was becoming nervous: that's why I pulled one of the drawers out. Luckily for me, because that's where the photo and the negatives were. I straightened everything back up and cleared off as fast as I could. Then when I got home, I sent the Doc a text as promised. He called about eight the next morning and wanted to meet right away. We agreed on eleven in the outdoor mall, where he gave me an envelope of money and I handed over the photos. After that I went to bed and had a long sleep. And that was that. Until I read the report the next day in the papers and realized there must have been more to it. My first thought was whether the Doc was trying to frame me. But I couldn't believe he would, so I decided to stay put here in the city."

"And you're prepared to swear to this statement in court?" the DA asked.

Angelos Zapas nodded. "If it helps me, absolutely! Charity begins at home; and I'm pretty sure the Doc has a good lawyer. I can't afford people like that."

"You're probably right there," said Chief Inspector Büschelberger.

He printed the statement, gave it the once over and then passed it on for the witness to sign. Zapas read it very carefully before adding his name hesitantly underneath. "I'm not too keen on this, especially seeing as I'm admitting further offences."

DA Cando just smiled. "Don't you worry about that. If you've helped us solve this, it will not be to your disadvantage. That I can assure you."

Angelos Zapas lit a cigarette and fell silent. In the meantime Emilio had gone to get the officers from the canteen. They took the witness back into custody and led him away.

Felix leaned back and gazed around the room.

"Your impressions of the witness?"

Cando was the first to speak: "If we can prove everything he says, it'll be a real breakthrough."

"Then we can finally nail Zimmer. I think we've got him," Emilio agreed.

"Just a shame his asshole lawyer isn't involved as well; I'd be only too happy to take him down," Arno sided with his colleague.

Frauke was the only one to advise caution. "It's still only circumstantial. We need proof and we don't have a motive yet."

Felix scratched his head, a gesture he very rarely made. Anyone who knew him would tell you he only did it when he was painfully embarrassed – or when he had been caught jumping to conclusions.

"I have to agree with Frauke there. We have to prove his statement is credible and collect more facts. Right now, all we've got is circumstantial evidence, and we need a little more than the word of a career criminal. Brax will make short work of him if we don't have any proof. Or how do you see it, Cando?"

"Before I can bring any charges, I need more ammunition. Brax is a pretty wily opponent. I can well imagine he's working out countermeasures with his client even as we speak. And if our prime suspect really did hire Zapas, then he'll know straightaway who we've been talking to, and has probably already started destroying evidence and coming up with new lines of defense."

"Then shouldn't we just subpoena him and start searching his apartment?" Emilio was thirsty for action.

All eyes rested on DA Cando, who was thinking through the possibilities and what they might mean for the investigation as a whole. It seemed an age before he replied.

"Although I can see the risk it poses for suppression of evidence, I still think we should wait before issuing a subpoena. Zimmer's almost certainly shrewd enough to have destroyed the photos on receipt. But even if he isn't, his lawyer will have told him to do so long ago, and he's had all the time in the world since. Let's keep him stewing, make it seem like we're not doing anything: it's sure to make him nervous. And that's when he'll start making mistakes we can use. Uncertainty is a weapon we shouldn't underestimate."

"Good, then let's focus on the restaurant and see if anyone there can help us. Emilio and Frauke, take pictures of Zapas and Zimmer down there and check if anyone saw them together. Arno, you take another look in Zimmer's accounts and scan for a payment, or part-payment, of fourteen thousand anywhere. It must have been made on the Monday we found the victim, or shortly before," Felix summarized the next steps.

While everyone got down to work, Felix walked Cando out to say goodbye. There, he thought about what he should do next. Since he was convinced the case was as good as closed, he decided to head home and make himself look more presentable.

He planned to surprise Petra: to pick her up from work and cook dinner for her. A homemade pizza was what he had in mind, with brown mushrooms, rocket, bacon and a little buffalo mozzarella; all washed down with a good red. It promised to be an enjoyable evening.

Barely two hours later, he was standing outside Petra's office, wearing a suit and tie in the best of spirits. Maybe that was the reason he marched so briskly towards reception and showed his ID.

"Good evening, my name is Felix Büschelberger and I'm in charge of the murder squad. Please take me to Petra Marshall straightaway. I don't want her to be given any advance warning, do you understand?"

The man behind the counter grew visibly paler and avoided making direct eye contact. His dark-blue uniform, which normally would have afforded him a degree of authority, appeared shabby in comparison with Felix's suit. He showed the chief inspector to the elevator and pressed the button for the twelfth floor.

"Straight on when you leave the elevator, her office is the third door on your right. You can't miss it."

The doors closed, leaving behind a somewhat frightened and confused porter. Felix, meanwhile, was delighting in his own mischief, thinking to himself that it wouldn't be such a bad idea to wear a suit more often.

Petra had been right: wearing a suit made you seem more respectable somehow; and people definitely took you more seriously. Still, he abandoned the idea before the elevator had reached its destination – he was too fond of going to work in jeans.

Petra's office was just like the one in Zimmer Consultancy Ltd: very modern with glass partition walls. She was alone, looking fixedly at her PC screen. Felix waited to see if she would notice him. After a while, he entered without knocking and gave her a cheeky grin.

"Sorry, Ms. Marshall! I'm afraid you're under arrest. You are charged with stealing men's hearts and occasionally breaking them."

He pulled out the handcuffs from his jacket pocket.

"Felix, you're crazy!" Petra squealed, staring at the handcuffs with a twinkle in her eye and then looking him up and down in his suit.

"I guess with such a good-looking inspector, I don't have much of a choice."

Felix winked at the porter, as he and Petra made their way arm in arm through the corridor and out towards the exit.

Chapter 19

Wednesday began quietly. Frauke and Emilio had only managed to get the name of the waitress who had been working that day: Maike Behnke, a student who wasn't on roster again until Thursday.

During their morning tea break, the team considered whether to try and find the witness today, before eventually discarding the idea. Although it was an important detail, it could definitely wait until tomorrow.

Next, Felix had a long telephone conversation with Hans Werners to discuss what Financial Crimes had uncovered in the interim. The answer was nothing. Hans explained that the books were clean: almost too clean to be true. And he couldn't promise they'd find anything else.

Chief Inspector Büschelberger thought long and hard after this exchange without reaching any tangible conclusions. At lunch, Arno swung by and they went to Conny's. Frauke had another commitment and Emilio didn't want to come.

Most of the afternoon was spent writing memos, mainly to organize his thoughts, though Felix also sent a few texts to Petra. Her responses were brief, as she had to catch up on her unfinished work from the previous day. However, she made it perfectly clear that she had nothing against further arrests, followed by questioning and solitary confinement.

The working day ended without further incident. That evening Felix treated himself to a hot bath and a nice glass of whisky, all to the backdrop of Carl Orff's Carmina Burana playing at full blast. Django, on the other hand, preferred to seek his pleasure elsewhere.

DA Cando was in the best of moods the next morning when he called on the team during their tea break.

"I think we should tell Dr. Zimmer that we want to speak with him pretty soon – before we pay Judge Kortz another visit, at any rate. Let him wait until early tomorrow morning; that should soften him up a little."

Felix offered him a mug of green tea and tried his best to sound outraged. "If I didn't know any better, I'd say you enjoyed tormenting our suspects."

Cando just sighed and rolled his eyes, before gazing at the mug critically. "I don't know; you're a strange bunch. How do you live without coffee? Sometimes I think you're from a different planet."

Joking over, Cando made his excuses. "I have to be in court. See you tomorrow; I want all witness statements collated by then, as well as a plausible chain of events."

The chief inspector nodded. "You can count on it."

Then he looked at each individual member of his team: "Who wants to give Zimmer the good news?"

Emilio volunteered right away.

"OK, then on you go. Best to tell him in private, and don't answer any questions," Felix instructed.

"Got it. I won't let them grill me or fob me off. You know I'm not a probationer anymore, boss." Emilio set off immediately.

"So, Frauke, you and I will try to find Maike. Arno, you get the files sorted. We'll go through them all together this afternoon, so that we're ready for tomorrow's meeting."

Le Mirage was a modern bar, whose music was too loud and décor too hip for Felix's liking. Still, it was compact and there were only a few people eating.

His gaze fell on the female waitress: Maike Behnke, he assumed. He had to admit she was extremely cute – dark-blonde hair with highlights and a center-parting, a hairstyle that, for want of a better description, Felix termed a "Prince Valiant."

Her azure eyes sparkled as he sat down with Frauke at the counter.

"Hello, I'll be right with you," she said and handed them a menu.

Felix leafed through it out of pure curiosity, finding a tea he had never come across before: Hilba, made from fenugreek. He decided to order it. Just as the waitress was about to come over, there was a shout from another table.

"Hey Maike, can I have the check?"

"What's up with you today, Jochen? Are you leaving me already? It's not like you – I hope you're not being unfaithful."

She received a throaty laugh in response. "How could anyone be unfaithful to you? I've got an interview. Cross your fingers for me."

"I will, Jochen, I'm sure it'll work out this time."

Maike radiated genuine sympathy and understanding. While she went over to cash up, Felix grabbed the chance to take a closer look at her. She had a very feminine build and her open manner had surely won her many admirers among customers.

Frauke nudged him in the side. "Make sure you don't forget why we're here, while you're sitting there drooling open-mouthed."

"Certainly not, but there's no harm mixing business with pleasure, and that's why I'm buying you a cup of tea. They've got one I've never tried before. Or maybe you know Hilba?"

Frauke shook her head, so Felix ordered two cups once Maike had returned.

"Well, you've got excellent taste. We don't get many orders for that, only from Turks, Arabs and old eco-warriors still trying to save the world. But you're not any of those groups," the waitress said.

"So which group are we?" The chief inspector was enjoying the conversation already.

"You look like police officers, or something like that."

He was truly surprised. "Correct. But how did you realize so quickly? We're not usually identified as police."

Felix glanced at Frauke in amazement, but she seemed equally bemused.

Maike grinned broadly and motioned towards Frauke. "Pretty easy, really. My colleague, the one you came to see yesterday, is also my roommate; she described you pretty well."

Then she looked at Felix. "But she was completely wrong about you."

"You shouldn't be too hard on her, it was one of my colleagues. It seems like you have a real talent for observation. I hope you'll be able to help us."

He placed the photos of Zapas and Zimmer on the counter.

"Have you seen either of these two men before - alone, together or with someone else?"

Maike served the tea in two tall glasses and took a close look at the pictures.

"Yeah, they were here on a Monday morning, must have been about five weeks ago."

"How come you remember it so well?" Frauke chimed in.

"Well, it was my first day back after my last exam – exactly six weeks ago. I went to France for the weekend with some friends, then on Monday I was working here again. I remember this one because he was so arrogant." She pointed to Dr. Zimmer's photo.

"The two of them were sitting talking at a table back there. When it came to settling the bill, one of them only had a five hundred, and I didn't have enough change. The other one got his American Express Platinum out and asked if we took it. He was pretty condescending. Most of our customers pay cash; they don't have such flashy cards."

Felix focused on the picture of Zapas. "So this one here only had five hundreds on him, and the other paid by credit card?"

Maike nodded and the chief inspector could hardly believe their luck.

"And do you still have the receipt from his check?"

"Almost certainly. My boss is pretty meticulous when it comes to stuff like that."

The two detectives looked at each other speechlessly.

"Do you mind trying to find it? It could be really important," Chief Inspector Büschelberger explained.

"Sure."

The waitress checked to see if anyone was waiting, before disappearing through a door into the office.

"I'd never have thought Zimmer would be stupid enough to pay with credit card when he's here planning a break-in," Felix shook his head.

"But you know they always slip up in the end," his colleague smiled. "Though I must say, this one's particularly satisfying."

About five minutes passed, then Maike was standing in front of them again, placing a photocopy on the counter.

"Here, I've made you a copy. It's yours to keep."

The Chief Inspector was impressed.

"Many thanks, you've been a great help. Would you be willing to make a formal statement? Just drop by anytime, OK?" He handed her his card.

"Sure, you can count on it," Maike smiled.

Felix paid for the tea, left a very generous tip and headed back with his colleague.

"I think you quite liked Maike, didn't you?" Frauke teased.

But she couldn't get a rise out of him. He was too excited to hear what Emilio had to say.

The Italian was beaming from ear to ear.

"I'm telling you, it was a real pleasure putting the fear into that puffed-up imbecile." He took a sip of tea and waited until his colleagues, who were hanging on his every word, invited him to continue.

Arno was first to crack. "Hey Emilio, this isn't some family secret you're banned from telling. There's no omerta here; we're your famiglia, capisce?" He shook his fists at Inspector Perfondo in mock agitation.

Emilio just smiled. "Arno, you need more practice at impersonating Italians. But don't worry; we'll get it right before you retire. Alright then, I won't keep you in suspense any longer. So, I burst into the building, past the receptionist, just shouting: 'I need to see the Big Boss' and then I was in the elevator. Dr. Zimmer was standing directly in front of what's her name's desk. Anita Peisker, that's it. Anyway, he looked pretty dumbfounded when he saw me. No-one from reception had warned him, but he was quick to get on his high horse, told his secretary to call Dr. Brax right away. Then I handed him the summons and told him he'd better instruct his lawyer to cancel all his appointments for the next day; he'd be needed at Dr. Zimmer's hearing at ten. The stuck-up asshole was absolutely stunned. With that, I turned around and headed towards the elevator. Just before I got there, I looked back and shouted to Zimmer that he ought to pack a toothbrush and some pajamas. It could last a while this time. You should have seen him, gesticulating all over the place: his eyes almost popped out of his head. He came hurtling towards me, waving the summons around furiously, asking what was the meaning of all this. I just mumbled and apologized from inside the elevator that I couldn't say any more without his lawyer present. Then the doors closed and I was gone as soon as I'd arrived, laughing my ass off when I got back to the car. God, sometimes I love my job."

The Italian leaned back and grinned at his colleagues.

They'd found it all extremely entertaining, and there wasn't a single one who didn't wish they could've been there. Dr. Zimmer really hadn't made any friends in this unit.

"Right, let's examine all the evidence we have and arrange it so that we can tighten the noose tomorrow morning. I want this case closed!" Felix instructed his colleagues.

After almost two hours of discussion, they were pretty sure they'd built a solid chain of evidence.

"There's still one thing I don't understand. If Zimmer wanted to kill the victim, then why did he hire a pro to look for the photos? Had he not planned the murder yet? Or did he not want to risk being seen near the apartment?" Frauke's gaze was met by silence.

"I don't understand either, but we're not about to go pointing out flaws in our argument to Zimmer now, are we? Maybe he'll break down and confess everything when he sees the evidence we've got." Felix scratched his head.

"What the hell, we'll see tomorrow; I've got a good feeling about this." He was radiating optimism.

Finally he called the DA and told him that everything was pre-pared for the interrogation tomorrow at ten. Cando promised to be there on time; this he just had to see.

Afterwards, Felix sent Petra a text.

"Fancy Greek tonight?"

It didn't take long for her to reply.

"Do you mean food or love? P."

He shook his head: he'd never met a woman like her.

"I meant food, but feel free to persuade me otherwise."

"Good, I'll be round at eight. P."

Felix was in the best of spirits. He would take her to the local Greek restaurant not far from his apartment.

Its biggest plus was that he could bring Django. The owner was crazy about cats and always gave him a little plate of raw fish or meat, whatever he had left over.

What's more, the knowledge that he would be sitting opposite Dr. Zimmer the next morning with garlic breath amused him no end. True, his colleagues might also be affected but Emilio was already immune. Now he just needed to make sure Petra ate some too.

Chapter 20

DA Cando arrived at half past nine and was immediately halted in his tracks.

"Good God! It reeks of garlic in here!"

"My fault, sorry. Couldn't control myself at the Greek last night," came Felix's response.

"And not only there I see," Cando pointed to a scratch on the chief inspector's neck. Arno, Emilio and Frauke snorted with laughter.

"If Brax really is as good as people say, he'll have us for violating the Geneva Convention. Torture by bad breath," added the DA.

"Take a herbal tea from Emilio and make sure you hold it in front of your face when you're not speaking. That helps!" Frauke passed him a steaming mug.

"It does actually," the DA thanked her. "Though I assume you won't be informing Drs Zimmer and Brax?"

"They're getting coffee, it's already waiting in the interview room," she replied.

"Emilio, can you take everything down again while Felix leads?" Cando asked.

The Italian nodded.

"Good, then I'll stay in the background and just listen for the time being. I'm very excited about today."

Dr. Brax was first to enter the interview room, closely followed by Zimmer, who pulled a disgusted face as he detected the pungent smell of garlic. He was just about to say something when his lawyer prevented it with a shake of the head. Brax himself carried on as normal, ever the consummate professional.

Felix couldn't resist a smile when he saw how closely the DA was holding the mug to his face. Even so, there was still the faintest of twinkles in his eye.

The chief inspector greeted the new arrivals, before offering them a seat and some coffee.

"So, Chief Inspector," Dr. Brax wasted no time. "Your little games are becoming tiresome. I intend to put a stop to them once and for all this afternoon with Judge Kortz. You have no proof against my client and he wants you to leave him in peace. In addition, we will be lodging a malpractice complaint against you and your colleagues for harassment of my highly respected client. Your conduct against him has quite clearly been injurious both to the interests of his company and his reputation."

Felix listened to the preamble without paying any particular attention. He knew only too well how conversations like this could go, and had no desire to present Brax with a target; instead he prepared for his own little introduction.

"I can well believe it, Dr. Brax, and of course you are legally entitled to do so. But believe me when I say there is no way we would be investigating Dr. Zimmer without good cause. If you allow me to outline briefly the case as we see it, then we can proceed directly to questioning your client."

He didn't take his eyes off Brax for one minute, allowing Cando and Emilio to take in the scene and draw their own conclusions.

Then without any further ado, he decided to take the bull by the horns.

"Dr. Zimmer, we know that you and your company are involved in illegal waste disposal. The connection with the Italian Mafia and Kenyan government officials is plain for all to see; we also know that the victim, Dr. Uwe Kaptain, was caught up in the affair. Now, we assume that one of two things happened: either he got greedy, or wanted out. At any rate, he was pressuring you. Your response was to kill him using a mix of benzodiazepine and choral hydrate, administered in his favorite wine: Romitorio di Santedame. Then you drove Kaptain to the east port and proceeded to fake his suicide before leaving the scene."

Dr. Zimmer snorted in derision. "That's completely ridiculous! Do I have to listen to this? You have no proof whatsoever."

Dr. Brax laid a hand on the CEO's arm to prevent him from continuing. "I agree with my client. You have no proof. And for the record, from now on Dr. Zimmer will be exercising his right to remain silent."

Pity, Felix thought to himself. He was pretty sure he'd just made a sizeable dent in Dr. Zimmer's self-confidence.

"Fine, let's talk about the evidence you are justifiably demanding. As Dr. Zimmer is already aware, I saw him in Calabria meeting with Dr. Mugambone, an employee of the Kenyan embassy in Rome, and a well-known Mafia boss. Dr. Mugambone is also a friend of the victim from student days, as you can see here."

Felix placed the photos from Italy and Hannover on the table. He was pleased to see the suspect grow pale once more.

"And so we have the first link in the chain. Now, let's look at my claim that the relationship between Dr. Zimmer and the murder victim was no longer as trusting as you might expect from a CEO and his leading employee. Here we have a signed testimony by Angelos Zapas, in which he confesses to having broken into the victim's apartment at the behest of Dr. Zimmer. There he stole photos showing Dr. Zimmer, the victim and other accomplices involved in illegal waste trafficking together."

By now, Zimmer was becoming increasingly nervous. Indeed, he seemed almost to wince internally whenever Felix placed any emphasis on his name – as if being slapped. The chief inspector, meanwhile, was beginning to enjoy himself; the interview was going exactly according to plan.

"I hope you have more than just the statement of an attention-seeking career criminal out to sully the good name of my client?" Dr. Brax tried to sound as objective as possible.

"We certainly do!" Felix leaned back contentedly.

"This is the waitress's statement from the restaurant where Dr. Zimmer and Angelos Zapas met. It confirms the two were together. The waitress also saw Dr. Zimmer handing money to Mr. Zapas; and we have a receipt from the credit card your client used to pay the check."

Felix smiled and fell silent in order to allow this final remark to sink in. He was doing a good job; and the fact he'd just lied seemed to have escaped both Dr. Brax and his client.

Maike Behnke hadn't seen any money exchanged: she had only noticed the big bucks Zapas was carrying. But they didn't need to know that. If this was a boxing match, then Dr. Zimmer was already on the ropes, and it wouldn't be long before the ref started giving the count.

"May I continue?" Felix gazed at Dr. Brax, innocence personified.

The lawyer nodded silently and seemed unsure about how to react. That suited Felix just fine.

"Now, to my claim that Dr. Zimmer was responsible for the murder. In its purest form, the poison is difficult to locate. You can't dissolve sleeping pills in water to achieve the concentration required. Instead, you have to either synthesize it yourself or order it from somewhere else."

He paused for dramatic effect.

"And what did we find contained in the books of Dr. Zimmer Consultancy Ltd? An order for one hundred grams of benzodiazepine chloral hydrate. Can you explain what you needed this substance for? What kind of analysis you conducted with it? Because our chemists couldn't think of any."

While Felix looked the CEO straight in the eye, the latter was gazing at the purchase order in disbelief.

"I don't understand, this doesn't make any sense. It has nothing to do with me," Dr. Zimmer stammered.

Dr. Brax was finding it increasingly difficult to prevent his client from speaking. "Please be quiet, Dr. Zimmer. I'm sure we can sort this out. There must be other reasons for such a purchase order, don't you think, Chief Inspector?"

"Possibly, but then there's also the fact that the poison was administered to the victim through a pretty expensive red wine. And there's only one dealer in the whole of Frankfurt who can get it for you. We have his client list here. Take a guess who's top of the list!"

Felix fixed his gaze on the lawyer. "What do you say to the mounting evidence against your client?"

"I must admit there are some unusual coincidences here. If I may, I should like to consult with Dr. Zimmer," Brax replied.

"As you are entitled to; nevertheless based on these facts and the danger that further evidence may be suppressed, I am suspending this interview in order to apply for an arrest warrant," DA Cando made his first contribution.

"Chief Inspector Büschelberger, please take the suspect into custody. I will see to it that formalities are completed. And you, Dr. Brax, may consult with your client for as long as you wish. We will continue the questioning on Monday morning."

Dr. Zimmer was keen to protest but his lawyer advised him to bow to the inevitable, and the two were led out. Felix sent for two officers from uniform to escort them to the detention center, before turning to Cando in disappointment.

"Why are you giving him the chance to launch a counterattack? I almost had him. One more little push and he'd have fallen straight into our hands!"

"You were very good, but Dr. Brax is too clever. We couldn't prevent the interruption and he made no objection to Zimmer being taken into custody. It's give and take. Besides, I get the impression that Dr. Zimmer still hasn't told his lawyer absolutely everything. A guy like Brax may not know what justice means, but he still takes it personally if you lie to him. That might just come in handy. Let's give them both a little more time. A weekend in jail will wear Zimmer down even further, you mark my words."

Cando left the room and made his way to Judge Kortz in order to request an arrest warrant.

"Sometimes even I'm afraid of you. You were great today; the pair of them were really on the ropes. We had the upper hand. And for what it's worth, I wouldn't have let them go either," Emilio remarked.

Felix looked at him gratefully. "I think we scored well, too. Now let's wait until Monday and just hope we've got him. What d'you think: should we go for a team meal in honor of the occasion?" he asked the rest of the unit.

"As long as it isn't Conny's. There's a good Italian close by; come on, it's on me this time," said Emilio.

"Sounds good!"

They stretched the lunch break out into an official meeting, sharing a bottle of wine too many, and were eventually forced to walk back to the office.

After a hearty breakfast on Saturday morning, Petra persuaded Felix to join her on a shopping tour of Mainz. The evening was spent at a private view. Petra's company had been promoting the artist who was exhibiting his work, and she had received two VIP tickets in return.

It was a mixed crowd and an extremely daring exhibition, which the two of them quite enjoyed nevertheless. Felix had a lot of fun with the art lovers and critics who tried to talk shop with him. He just said whatever came into his head, and received high praise for his expert knowledge. At one point his female companion had to box him in the ribs to prevent him from completely losing his grip on reality.

"Sometimes you're just impossible," she said with a grimace. Felix took it as a compliment.

The next morning, he was awoken by the sun shining on his face. Petra had snuggled up to him, and Django was lying purring on the covers; for a moment Felix suddenly felt totally at ease. He kissed Petra on the forehead, and she beamed with delight in response.

"It could always be like this. You, me, and Django; leave the rest of the world behind us."

"Oh, Felix, you are, and always will be, a hopeless romantic. I'm just not made for long-term relationships. Once I was with a man who'd have done anything for me; and even he didn't last more than seven years. So please, do me a favor and stop dreaming impossible dreams. I mean, maybe it'll work out with us, but I can't give you any guarantees."

"So, this guy, what did he do wrong?"

Petra propped herself up on her elbows and gazed deeply into his eyes before answering.

"Nothing. I was just scared of missing out on something - losing my freedom maybe. Sometimes I think I'm incapable of commitment, but what do I know? Anyway, I hate conversations like this. Right now, I'm much more interested in your body than your intellect." With that, she flung herself onto him and they made passionate love. Django, meanwhile, had left the room: he wanted a little peace.

Later Petra snuggled up to him again and began nibbling his ear. "Everything OK?"

"Yeah, of course; everything's great." He avoided Petra's gaze.

"Hey, don't take everything I say so seriously. Things might work out with us. So come on, let's try and have a nice Sunday together."

He smiled. "Sure."

But that was the moment Felix realized they had no future together. The thought hurt. Still, he decided to make the most of the here and now and be happy with her for as long as possible – even if he knew that someday it would come to an end.

"Let's take a shower together. You can lather me up, and rub me down; then I'll do the same for you. How does that sound?" she beamed.

"Last person under the shower makes breakfast."

With these words, Felix jumped out of bed and ran towards the bathroom, closely followed by a giggling Petra.

Chapter 21

At nine o'clock sharp the following Monday, Brax and Zimmer were back in the interview room, sitting opposite DA Cando, Felix and Emilio for a second time. It was Brax who opened proceedings.

"Mr. District Attorney, my client and I have been consulting all weekend and we would like to offer you a deal."

Cando winked at Felix, as if to say: Told you, didn't I?

"Let's hear it, then."

"My client is willing to confess to certain things; in return he would like to be granted leniency."

"You know we can't do that for murder, only for those involved in terrorism or organized crime. So what's going on here?"

"May I explain something briefly off the record?" the star lawyer asked.

The DA exchanged a look of astonishment with the chief inspector, but nodded.

"Fine, off the record. Inspector Perfondo, please stop typing," came the instruction.

Emilio's fingers remained poised motionless over the keyboard.

"Let's assume for a minute that my client was caught up in illegal waste disposal, but would be prepared to say which companies were involved and where the waste was brought to, as well as naming players on the Italian, Kenyan and even German side of things. Let's also say he can prove he had nothing to do with the murder. Would you drop any outstanding charges and allow him to be accepted in the witness protection program? He'd only require a new identity, as he already has the financial means to retire."

Bombshell dropped, Dr. Brax fell silent and allowed his words to sink in.

Chief Inspector Büschelberger was speechless. This was the last thing he had expected. One look at his colleagues was enough to know that they were just as surprised.

DA Cando was the first to recover his composure. "And your client would be prepared to make his statement immediately?"

"As soon as he has confirmation that he will be granted leniency," Dr. Brax nodded.

"Can he prove once and for all that he had nothing to do with the murder?" Felix sounded skeptical.

"I can well understand your disappointment, but I've no doubt we can convince you of his innocence. Of course it means you'll have to start all over again, but I'm sure you can cope with that," the lawyer stared mockingly at the chief inspector.

"Fine, just let me consult with these officers; and we'll be back as soon as we've reached a decision. Now if you would excuse us," the DA said.

"Of course, we'll be waiting right here," the star lawyer replied.

Cando exited the room with the detectives in tow, both of them still pretty stunned by it all.

They sat down in the chief inspector's office.

"Do you believe them?"

The DA shrugged his shoulders. "I don't know. But if what he's offering's true, then we can't afford to turn him down. Plus we're not certain he's actually responsible."

"You're right, we don't have irrefutable evidence. But if it wasn't him, why is he trying to cut a deal?" Felix sounded agitated.

"I don't know that either, but I'm not about to ask. Maybe he did do it, and Dr. Brax is well aware that suspects are untouchable once they're granted leniency and taken into witness protection. Zimmer could slip through the net; that's a risk. On the other hand, we get to nab a whole bunch of crooks, as well as a couple of corrupt officials and an Italian Mafia boss. Think about it. If he did commit the murder and also testifies, then he's a Mafia target. He might have money, but from now on he's living in fear. One day he wakes up and there's a hitman by his bed, who lets him live just long enough for him to know it's all over. In my eyes, that's not a bad swap."

The chief inspector mumbled, "What do you think, Emilio?"

"We get to reel in a few big fish for letting one pompous asshole off the hook. Who probably doesn't know what he's letting himself in for. And besides, maybe he isn't responsible. I think we should make the deal."

Felix knew when to admit defeat. "Then that's what we'll do."

Back in the interview room, the DA gave them the news.

"OK, we accept your offer. I'll contact Senior District Attorney Schürfel and Judge Kortz right away. As soon as they agree, you'll have the necessary documentation. It could take a while though. If you would care to wait in the canteen?"

"We'd prefer to wait somewhere else. Would it be possible to take breakfast at the Hilton? As long as these two officers accompany us, of course," the lawyer pointed towards Felix and Emilio.

Cando thought it over for a moment. "If this is some kind of cheap trick, then you'll have a real problem, do I make myself clear?"

Turning to Felix he added, "Would you be prepared to escort them?"

The two officers looked at each other silently in agreement. They were both incensed by the breathtaking arrogance of these men, but this was the path they had chosen, and now they needed to see it through to the end. Felix signaled his approval.

"If your client should try to escape, then the deal's off and he won't get a single phone call. He speaks to you only and the two officers are close by at all times," the DA instructed.

Chief Inspector Büschelberger moved towards Zimmer to place him in handcuffs.

"I really don't think that's necessary. Mr. District Attorney?"

Cando motioned to Felix to put the handcuffs away. "Fine, but there'll be two uniformed officers stationed directly outside the Hilton. Just in case."

Dr. Brax nodded. "Quid pro quo, as it were."

DA Cando promised to be quick.

The six men set off towards the hotel to wait and see what would happen. It rubbed Felix the wrong way to see how Zimmer and Dr. Brax made straight for the buffet, complacency personified. Though the food on offer did provide some consolation: he realized he had hit the jackpot compared with the two officers forced to wait outside. The buffet itself was spread across two large tables and contained seafood and shellfish, salmon, trout, and a wide selection of cold meats; crab salad, homemade jam, every kind of roll and pastry; not to mention fried eggs with bacon; sausage, cheese, fruit, freshly squeezed orange juice, champagne and a huge range of teas.

The two detectives took full advantage, before taking their seats not far from Dr. Brax and Zimmer.

"Say what you like, at least we get a decent breakfast out of it. I've certainly never dined in the Hilton before," Emilio said.

"True, but the two of them seem pretty well-known. The waiters treat them like royalty, while all we get are pitying stares."

"Doesn't bother me. When they need our help, we'll be good enough again. In the meantime, I'm going to help myself."

That was what the chief inspector liked about Emilio: he always made the best of every situation. Finally after four hours, Felix's cell phone rang.

It was Cando, telling him that the deal was on. They were to bring Zimmer and his lawyer back to headquarters, where he would be waiting with the necessary papers.

"The DA's ready for us. Time to get going," the chief inspector prompted the two men under surveillance.

"Couldn't we continue the interview somewhere more agreeable? Here, for instance?" Dr. Zimmer asked. It seemed he had regained his self-assurance.

"Don't push your luck; there's still a warrant out for your arrest. So what's it to be?" Felix made his irritation known.

"Right – I was only thinking of you. You obviously like it here."

Ignoring the CEO's meek reply, the chief inspector motioned towards the door.

"The papers are all here, signed by the senior district attorney and relevant judge. As soon as your client signs, he becomes a protected key witness and is granted immunity from prosecution," the DA greeted them back at the station.

Dr. Brax read the documents very carefully before passing them over for Zimmer to sign.

"Congratulations, you're a free man again," the lawyer shook his client by the hand.

"Now it's over to you to keep your part of the deal," Felix interrupted their celebrations.

"But of course, Chief Inspector." Dr. Zimmer sounded poised and in control once again.

"As you're no doubt aware, the company was in danger of going under a few years back. That's when Uwe Kaptain came to me with this Kenyan contact, Dr. Mugambone. They had studied together. Anyway, this guy had offered him the chance to store hazardous waste cheaply in abandoned Kenyan mines. Even back then, we had already had a few enquiries from European companies, nothing direct of course, but phrased in such a way it was clear what they wanted. My colleague made the initial contact and then half a year on, we'd carried out our first commission. The Italians were responsible for the transport, and they collected the toxic waste directly from us. How they got it out of the country, I'm not absolutely sure, but the containers arrived by boat in Kilifi; Dr. Mugambone's cousin is their head of harbor police. From there, the cargo was taken inland by truck before being deposited in the Ndoto Mountains."

After a brief pause, the CEO continued. "We received three million for the first delivery: a million for the Kenyans and a million each for us and the Italians. After that, the pressure to continue grew from all sides. The Italians and Kenyans were interested in profit, and there were other companies who wanted rid of their waste; it was money that persuaded me too in the end. So we made contact with a city councilor in Frankfurt and an official in the Hessian environment ministry. Don Veschie's organization gave us the names; they must have done business with them in the past."

"Who are these men?" Cando interrupted Zimmer mid-flow.

"The councilor on our pay roll is Wolfgang Stumpf; the ministry official is Günther Krulle from Wiesbaden," Zimmer replied candidly.

"A pretty big fish, the last name. He's directly reporting to the Minister for the Environment. Can you prove all this?" the DA asked.

"I can give you dates and amounts, who received how much and when. Should make it easy to prove they were on the take."

"When?"

"Give me a little time. I have copies of the documents in a safety-deposit box in Luxembourg, which I can have sent over."

Cando nodded approvingly. "What did you need the German officials for?" he probed.

"They warned us about checks, or provided forms and stamps when we needed a NOC."

"And how much have you earned through illegal waste disposal so far?"

"Around 250 million in total."

"In total?" the DA couldn't quite believe what he was hearing.

"Well, for each of the three parties."

Cando and Felix gazed at each other completely dumbfounded. Neither of them had had any idea about the scale of the operation.

"What was Uwe Kaptain's share?"

"He has a Swiss numbered account with about fifty million euros in it."

The chief inspector was speechless. He just couldn't understand how a person could make so much money in such a short space of time.

"And why did you hire Angelos Zapas to break into his apartment?" he joined in the questioning.

"Ah yes, Angelos Zapas, that's an old story. He applied for a job as porter but lied about his previous convictions. Well, I have every new employee checked by a P.I., so we discovered pretty soon what kind of record he had. He even managed to fake a certificate issued by police stating he had no criminal record. It wasn't a bad job either. Anyway, I always gave him shifts when the waste was being collected or deposited, since I was pretty sure he wouldn't be paying attention too closely. On top of that, I used to stop by every so often with something to eat or drink; to keep him talking in those critical moments when a really big shipment was coming in. He never suspected anything. But then the idiot got caught with his hand in the till and I had to let him go."

As no-one looked like they were about to interrupt, Zimmer carried on.

216

"But back to your question, Chief Inspector. The thing is, Kaptain got greedy, lost sight of where he came from. He wanted to become my partner, and demanded fifty percent of the company. But the biggest joke was that he was unwilling to make a down-payment. When I just laughed at him, he tried to blackmail me, to blow my cover. I told him he'd end up in jail too, but he just said he'd apply for leniency. Actually, that's what gave me the idea. Anyways, he was threatening to send certain pictures of me, Don Veschie, and Dr. Mugambone to journalists. That was about two weeks before he died. So I called Zapas and hired him to steal the photos. It was also meant as a warning to Kaptain: that it was about time he came to his senses. Whether it would've worked or not, I'm afraid we'll never know," Dr. Zimmer concluded

Felix drummed his fingers on the table, seemingly lost in thought. "Dr. Zimmer, you realize you've just given us a perfect motive for the murder of Uwe Kaptain."

"Yes, and the fact alone that I'm saying it on record should be enough to convince you I had nothing to do with it," the witness replied.

"Then how do you explain the purchase order?"

"With the best will in the world, I can't. With such a small amount, there's usually no signature needed. You might be able to find out who picked it up from the warehouse but even that's not guaranteed. We don't keep a record of non-security related chemicals when there's no legal requirement to do so. Plus, the system has a few loopholes – otherwise we'd have to let too many people in on our scheme," Zimmer explained.

"You have to admit that's pretty shaky," Felix was still unconvinced.

"True, Chief Inspector, but I have an alibi for the night in question; and it ought to be of interest to you, since Krulle and Stumpf were also present."

"OK, so where were you?"

"Do you know the Waldschlösschen here in Frankfurt?"

Neither Felix nor Cando knew it.

"I'd have been surprised if you did. It's the most expensive establishment in the city. A very exclusive night spot that doesn't advertise but instead relies strictly on word of mouth. The only way to get in is by naming a sponsor who's already a regular. And if you step out of line, it's not just you but your sponsor who gets barred. Sounds crazy, but believe me, they make so much money it doesn't matter how they treat their guests. Anyway, I was there from ten until four the next morning, as a guest of our German friends. By the way, they have CCTV there. If you stop by, you'll find further evidence of just how corrupt they are. Money's fine, but they're quite happy to make use of any other services on offer as well. Myself, I was with Celine the whole night. She'll confirm my story," Zimmer concluded his statement.

"We'll get it checked out," said Felix.

"I think that's enough for the time being. But we'll be questioning you in more detail soon. Right now you need to get a few things packed. You won't be able to go back to your office or apartment," Cando rejoined the conversation.

Dr. Zimmer looked at him in disbelief.

"Think about it: you've just given a deposition on organized crime, against a man who's well known for making witnesses disappear. We'll provide protection of course, but only if you trust us and do as we say. You can come out of hiding as soon as Don Veschie's behind bars," the DA explained.

It was clear from the look on Zimmer's face that he hadn't thought about this aspect of leniency until now. But it was far too late to retract his statement.

"And how do I know he hasn't bought the officers protecting me?" the witness asked in some dismay.

"Don't worry. In order to prevent that from happening, key witnesses from Hesse are never protected by local officers. There's a rotational system in place, whereby a new team takes charge every week. This week, it's our colleagues from Bavaria who'll be looking after you until the trial. Just them, no swaps. Their chief was in counter-terrorism and they're hard as nails down there. This rotation policy ensures that officers can't be bought. Because otherwise you'd have to buy them all; and believe me, that'd be pretty unlikely."

The DA placed a reassuring hand on the key witness's shoulder.

"You'll spend tonight in a regular hotel, under police protection. Then tomorrow, you'll be handed over to a special task force," he added.

Dr. Zimmer accepted his fate and left the room with his lawyer.

"Who'd have thought we'd get so much information out of him. Unbelievable!" Cando was rubbing his hands with glee.

"Granted, that was pretty surprising, but I'm still not sure I buy it - I mean that he's not our man. Emilio and I will get this Celine checked out. And if she confirms what he says, then we'll just have to start over from scratch," Felix sighed.

"You and your team have a lot of work ahead of you – including helping us verify Zimmer's statement in detail. I think this case is going to look pretty good on your record."

"I'd like to give Commissario Crotone the latest; we'll be needing his help anyway. The quicker he hears about it, the sooner he'll be able to respond."

The DA expressed his approval and left. He wanted to inform his superiors about this explosive development as soon as possible.

"Emilio, tell Arno and Frauke about the interview. I'll call Italy. We'll meet afterwards to discuss what happens next."

Crotone picked up after the fourth ring.

"Pronto."

"Hello, Commissario Crotone. It's Chief Inspector Büschelberger from Frankfurt."

"Ah, Commissario! How are you and your charming girlfriend?"

"Both very well, thank you. What about you?"

"Va bene; same old, same old. You know what it's like here in southern Italy; very little changes."

"That's why I'm calling. I have information that could really shake things up."

"Uno momento, Commissario. Is it about our recent meeting in Tropea?"

"Exactly, I've just--"

"Commissario, it's a very bad line. Can I call you back in half an hour?" the Italian interrupted.

"Sure, but I can hear just fine."

"Other people too, believe me. Are you in your office?"

"Yes."

"Good, I'll get back to you." Crotone had hung up.

A strange exchange. If he had understood correctly, then Crotone was worried the line was being tapped. Something like that was inconceivable to Felix. After eighteen minutes, his phone rang.

"Chief Inspector Büschelberger."

"Commissario, I'm sorry, but we recently had a case where our calls were being bugged. Anything sensitive and I go to the restaurant or a friend now."

"No problem, I understand. Anyway, I'm calling because the chief suspect in our murder enquiry has just turned state's witness. And he's implicated Don Veschie pretty heavily. I thought you'd like to know."

"Naturalmente! What else can you tell me?"

The chief inspector gave a brief outline of Zimmer's confession while the Italian listened in silence.

"If we can prove it, then we've got him nailed. Sounds too good to be true. Mind if I come over to Germany?"

"No, quite the opposite. Then I can pay you back for Italy."

"Good, I'll let you know when I'm landing."

"Perfect. I'll come and pick you up."

"Grazie. See you."

Felix returned to his colleagues, who were chatting quietly over a cup of tea.

"We'll have a visitor from Italy shortly. It's the inspector I met over in Calabria. He's interested in our findings. If we want to break down these syndicates, then we have to move fast," he informed his team.

"Emilio told us everything. Unbelievable, isn't it?" Frauke looked at her boss in amazement.

"I know, I still can't believe it either, but it probably means we're back to square one in terms of our investigation. Well, I'm going to call it a night. Tomorrow Emilio and I will go to this club and check out Zimmer's alibi," Felix said on his way out.

On the way home, he felt a headache coming on, and his mood, which had been so optimistic in the morning, darkened considerably.

That evening, Crotone called to say he'd be getting in to Frankfurt at one thirty on Wednesday afternoon. Felix promised to pick him up, before heading off to bed, still bemoaning his fate.

Chapter 22

Felix still had a headache when he awoke the next morning. Cursing under his breath, he shambled into the bathroom and took an aspirin.

At least if he'd had too much to drink, he'd have been able to understand the pain. Must have been all the damn stress. He felt somewhat better after a shower and decided to spin breakfast out, as he didn't have the slightest desire to go to work. Eventually, however, he was ready to leave – though not before he had enviously stroked the fur on Django's head.

"You've got it made: no work, no stress, and when a mouse escapes, you don't take it personally."

The tom purred contentedly as if in agreement.

"I'm glad we're on the same wavelength; though sometimes I wish you'd tell me I had it made too."

Django's ear twitched to the rhythm of his voice.

In the car, the chief inspector decided to try and be more like his cat. He wouldn't take it personally that Dr. Zimmer had slipped through his fingers. Besides, maybe he really wasn't the right mouse.

Likewise, his team seemed to have recovered their equilibrium. They were sitting over their morning tea, gazing at him with confidence and resolve.

He clapped his hands. "OK, it seems we were investigating the wrong man, but the result is still fantastic. We've uncovered a mafia-style syndicate and we'll be hearing a lot more about it in future. But now it's time to take a step back and pursue other leads. Saying that, Emilio and I still need to check Zimmer's alibi. So let's hold off until we know for sure he's innocent."

"What if he didn't do it but hired someone else to carry out the hit?" Arno asked.

"I don't think that's likely. We know the victim's wine was poisoned. The fact it was his favorite kind, and also extremely expensive, means we can rule out strangers. No, the killer must have known Kaptain well enough for them to drink a good wine together. You don't just do that with anyone. We need to focus on his immediate circle again," Felix said.

"What I don't understand is: how come we've found so little of the money he's supposed to have stashed away somewhere?"

Felix had to suppress a smile. He knew Arno was taking this point personally: he should have found the money by now. Normally he was unbeatable in that respect.

"He must've been extremely clever; but that's something for the task force, which I'm sure is being formed even as we speak."

"Took the words right out of my mouth. There's a first meeting taking place in an hour. I'd like you to be there. After all, it was your team that got the ball rolling on this," Cando had just emerged through the door.

"I'm happy to provide a report, but I'm not sure I want to be in full-time. After all, we still have a murder to solve. Hans Werners and his team are much better suited to something like this. He's got most of the documents already, anyway," Felix replied.

"That's why the new task force will be based at Financial Crimes – Werners is definitely on board. Anyway, have a think about it. See you at the meeting," said the DA.

"Sure. By the way, before I forget. Our Italian colleague is flying out tomorrow. He's been after Don Veschie for a long time and should be a real help."

"Great, that's a good start." For Cando, results were more important than playing things strictly by the book. He gave his blessing and disappeared.

"OK folks, that means I'll be spending the rest of the day disputing areas of responsibility. Emilio, I want you to take the afternoon off, because tonight we'll be taking a trip to Waldschlösschen."

With that, he drained the contents of his mug and left.

The temporary meeting room set up for the new task force, "Hazardous Waste Kenya Connection" – or "Kenco" for short – was packed. There were open laptops everywhere, and officers Felix had never seen before typing away assiduously. Heaven alone knew what all these identikit youngsters could possibly be writing.

Hans Werners came towards him. "Decent catch you made there. I'm part of this team now – finally we get a foot in the door."

"Yeah, seems like we stumbled on something pretty big. But who are all these people?" The chief inspector gestured around the room.

"From Wiesbaden. Mostly State Police Office, but also a few from other departments like Tax and Environment. They've had to be very careful with the last, so that nothing gets back to Krulle. Seems they're in the process of tapping his phone. The same thing's happening here in Frankfurt; Councilor Stumpf has been under surveillance since early this morning."

"I have to say, we can be pretty efficient when it comes down to it. Impressive, really."

"True; worth remembering when you're feeling disillusioned. See you later." The financial crimes investigator went on his way.

The next to pat him on the back was the senior district attorney. "Good morning, Chief Inspector. My congratulations on a spectacular success! I'm afraid they're all too rare."

Before Felix could respond, Schürfel had already moved on.

His gaze fell upon a group of six men standing together in the corner, likewise casting a critical eye on proceedings. They all looked fairly toned and were casually dressed. Felix wondered whether it was the surveillance unit responsible for Dr. Zimmer.

As he examined their sneakers, with their noiseless rubber soles, and the obligatory sunglasses perched casually on their jackets, he became convinced his hunch was correct. One of the men came forward and extended a hand.

"Allow me to introduce myself: Police Superintendent Baron von Weinhammer. Head of the surveillance team. I assume you're the one responsible for all this."

Chief Inspector Büschelberger noticed he hadn't phrased it as a question. He shook the outstretched hand and grinned. "I'm afraid you're right there."

"I can see you loathe this sort of thing; all the brouhaha!" the Police Superintendent remarked.

Felix surveyed his interlocutor. "What makes you say that?"

"It's your eyes that give you away."

"I'm impressed: you must have a real talent for surveillance."

"It's my job – sometimes it's the difference between life and death for me and my client. This Dr. Zimmer, guilty or innocent? Of murder, I mean."

The chief inspector considered the question for a moment. "That's a difficult one. If you'd asked me a week ago, I'd have been willing to bet he was the killer. But now I think it's unlikely. We're checking his alibi tonight. Is it important to you?"

"Doesn't matter if he's a murderer, eco-criminal or tax dodger, we'll protect him as best we can. For me personally, though, it's important. For my sense of justice if you know what I mean."

Felix nodded; he had taken a real shine to this guy.

"Anyway, I very much hope you're going to be part of this team!" von Weinhammer interrupted his thoughts.

"I'm not sure I understand." By now Chief Inspector Büschelberger was truly surprised. Could the Police Super read minds as well?

"As I said, you seem pretty skeptical about the whole thing, but that's exactly what makes you the perfect foil. The officers from State Police can be a little too corporate at times. See you around."

While the chief inspector was still chewing things over, Senior District Attorney Schürfel got proceedings underway.

"Good morning and a warm welcome to the first meeting of the newly formed task force, Kenco. Please take your seats."

There followed the usual spiel, as all participants were formally introduced. After DA Cando had presented a brief overview of the facts, Felix was invited to provide a more detailed description, including a summary of his team's latest findings. When it came to the Mafia connection, he found himself interrupted by Police Superintendent von Weinhammer.

"What's the risk factor here?"

Felix shrugged his shoulders. "I'm afraid I can't say exactly. Don Veschie has a reputation for not messing around with witnesses. But there'll be more news on that score tomorrow from my Italian colleague, Commissario Crotone, who's arriving mid-afternoon in Frankfurt. I thought he'd make a good addition to the team."

After a brief discussion about areas of jurisdiction and who authorized an Italian inspector to come over to Germany in the first place, Felix's suggestion was accepted. When he had finished his two-hour presentation, the different roles were assigned, and he was offered the chance to head up the task force.

He turned to the senior district attorney. "I am of course honored. Nevertheless, I still have a murder to solve and the activities of this task force have nothing to do with my investigation. I'm afraid to say, I don't think I can accept."

He looked over towards Police Superintendent von Weinhammer, who was sitting there piercing him with his gaze.

"But naturally I am loath to refuse completely and will attend meetings as often as possible, as well as keeping everyone up-to-date on the latest from our case. Maybe we'll be able to do some useful cross-referencing."

He saw the Police Super nod approvingly. The supervising role was eventually offered to Hans Werners, with an official from the State Police his second-in-command. The task force decided to bring Dr. Zimmer in for more questioning that afternoon; and to meet each morning at eight to discuss where they stood.

"There goes your morning tea ritual. But I'm sure we'll be able to offer you something here. In fact, I'll see to it personally," DA Cando teased Felix as he passed.

Back at the station, the chief inspector told the others about the meeting. Frauke was the only one who thought he should have accepted the senior district attorney's offer. Afterwards, Felix ordered his Italian colleague to go home at last, an instruction the latter was only prepared to follow if the chief inspector himself did the same.

Thus he was able to take care of the shopping he'd been putting off for ages, as well as making a long call to Petra. She agreed with Frauke. In order to change the subject, Felix mentioned that he would be spending the evening in a high-class brothel.

She teased him a little, before saying she didn't mind him getting a bit hot under the collar – so long as she was the one who got to cool him down.

About half past eight that evening, Emilio picked him up in the Focus. Having arrived at Waldschlösschen, they rang the bell.

The villa, which was part of a large estate, looked very well maintained from the outside and there were three expensive-looking cars parked in the drive.

"Yes, how can I help?" a pleasant-sounding woman's voice came from the intercom.

"Good evening, we're here on the recommendation of Dr. Zimmer. We'd like to see Celine, please."

The chief inspector winked at his colleague as they were buzzed in. They were received by a good-looking, well-proportioned blonde wearing a black wraparound blouse, tight black flared leather jeans and elegant pumps. Her smile seemed genuine and friendly as she offered an outstretched hand to the two detectives.

"Good evening and welcome to Waldschlösschen. You will see that the satisfaction of clients is our number-one priority. My name is Nina and I'm in charge of this modest establishment."

She led the detectives into a club lounge dominated by a dark mahogany counter surrounded by leather bar stools. The drinks selection, resting neatly on the shelves against the wall, compared favorably with any cocktail bar in Frankfurt. A very elegant and expensively dressed man was chatting away to a young woman wearing only a bikini and high heels. They were drinking and laughing together.

There were several three-piece suites that looked like they had been imported straight from an old-school English gentlemen's club. Candles were burning on the tables, and a few women, all of whom were very cute, were sitting on the leather seats smiling at the two detectives. Apart from their bikinis, which were more revealing than concealing, the only thing any of them had on were high-heeled shoes.

Built into the wall were two private booths, both of which were currently unoccupied. On a table in the corner was an appetizing-looking finger buffet. Felix saw that there was also a swimming pool in the adjoining room from where a man's voice could be heard, alongside his female companion. The detectives took their seats at the bar.

"What would you like to drink? Beer and all non-alcoholic beverages are free; cocktails are twenty five euros; a small sparkling wine for the ladies costs fifty; the house champagne is eighty; a bottle of Metternich comes in at two hundred; and the champagne starts at five hundred euros." Nina smiled at the pair of them.

"I think we'll have two beers in that case. What do you say?" Felix looked at his companion, who shrugged his shoulders.

"Sure, why not?"

As she served the beer, Nina pointed towards a woman in an ochre-colored bikini. Her long black hair came down past her shoulders and she had dark-brown eyes.

"That's Celine there. Should I send her over?"

The chief inspector took a good look at her and guessed Celine was about twenty-one, maybe a size four. There was something vaguely Lolita-like about her, as she flashed Felix her best smile and looked at him all sweetness and light.

"No, hang on a minute. We need to clarify something first." He flashed his ID. "We're not clients, but police investigating a murder. And we're here to ask Celine a few questions. Sorry."

Nina's expression darkened. "You're cops? But you said Heinrich was your sponsor. He's got some serious explaining to do."

"We'll try to be as discreet as possible, since I can imagine our presence here is somewhat undesired. Still, you'd better help us – otherwise we can make this all official and send in the cavalry."

She tried her best to conceal her irritation. "Fine. But what's happened? You said something about a murder. Is Heinrich OK?"

"Yeah, he's alive and well. We just have to check his alibi."

She motioned towards an empty booth. "Take a seat in there. I'll get your drinks, and then send Celine over."

While the two detectives waited in the booth, Nina brought them a bottle of Veuve Clicquot and glasses.

"We didn't order that, and we won't be paying for it." The chief inspector tried to send the bottle straight back.

"You don't have to pay for it, or even drink it if you don't want to. But believe me, it's the easiest way to blend in. I'll get the money back on the other guests, so don't worry about it." Nina waved Celine over and poured the champagne into three glasses, before heading back behind the bar.

"Hi, I'm Celine. Nice to see you here." She extended a hand.

The detectives also gave their names. Then as soon as Celine sat down, Felix showed his ID. He wanted to be up front from the start.

Celine displayed no outward show of emotion. "Does that mean you didn't buy the champagne?" she pointed towards the bottle.

Felix shook his head. "But does it make a difference?"

"Financially, yes. Girls get fifty percent of the money made on drinks consumed with their guests. But what the hell? It tastes just as good."

She took a glass and clinked it against the other two. "Don't be a drag, one glass won't hurt, or else I won't say a thing," she teased.

It didn't really matter anymore, Felix was thinking to himself, so he raised his glass and nodded at his colleague: after all, he was only half on duty. They took a large gulp, though in Emilio's case it was more of a nip.

"Shame you're pigs, I mean police. You're really sweet, especially you." Celine looked at Emilio coquettishly. "But I'm sure you'd be a lot of fun too."

Her gaze wandered to the chief inspector, as she took another deep sip of champagne.

Felix was beginning to feel increasingly uncomfortable. "I can tell you now; it's not going to happen. We're here to ask a few questions about Dr. Zimmer."

The hostess threw her hands dramatically over her forehead. "Heinrich! I shudder at thee!"

Felix looked at her in astonishment, but she just smiled mockingly.

"Yes, Chief Inspector, there are well-educated working girls too. I majored in German literature and was part of the drama society at school: we used to perform Faust all the time."

"I am impressed. So how come you ended up here?" he asked with some interest.

"Why not? You can earn shitloads of money and there aren't as many anti-socials as on the street. At least, that's what I thought. Turns out they're just better dressed."

After a moment's silence, Celine looked him straight in the eye. "So, what is it that you'd like to know?"

Felix noticed straightaway the change in register. More official, somehow. He explained why they were here, before enquiring whether Dr. Zimmer had been there on the Sunday in question.

"Sounds about right. The last time he was here was a Sunday night about five weeks ago. He brought two guests along and they all stayed until we closed at four on Monday morning," she said.

"Did you know the men with him?"

"No, I'd never seen them before, but my boss will know who they are. We also have CCTV at reception; the tapes are kept for a long time. You never know what you might need them for."

She couldn't help noticing Felix's prying eyes. "Trust me; it's not what you think. We don't have CCTV to blackmail our clients. Certainly not, there's no way we could afford it."

With that, she leaned back and took another sip of champagne. Her gaze wandered around the room, before eventually falling on a new arrival, who greeted her warmly. She waved back.

"Listen, Chief Inspector, one of my regulars has just arrived. He's always very generous and books me for the entire night. He's in love with me and I don't like to keep him waiting. So, if we're finished here..."

Felix surveyed the new arrival, a well-dressed man in his late forties. "And are you in love with him?"

"Are you joking?" The hostess gave a snort of laughter. "Take a look at him. He's completely unattractive and a lousy lover at that. It's his money that turns me on."

"Yes, you may go, but could you send your boss over again?"

She left to give her client a kiss on both cheeks, before snuggling up to him while he ordered a Grande Cuvée Krug. Felix didn't even want to think about how much it must've cost.

After Nina had served them she came over to their table, still disgruntled. "Is there something else you want?"

"We'd like the CCTV footage from the Sunday Dr. Zimmer was last here. It was five weeks ago," he replied.

"You realize I'm not obliged to give you the DVD without a court order."

"That's correct, but we would greatly appreciate your cooperation."

"Fine, but after that you'll be gone?" she asked hopefully.

The chief inspector nodded.

Half an hour later, they were leaving the brothel with DVD in hand.

Emilio was shaking his head. "I'll never understand why men pay to be with such cold women. They're all failures in my eyes."

"On a psychological level, you're probably right. Maybe they do view themselves as failures deep down, but what do I know? Still, I agree with you, it's not my thing either. All they do's fleece you – and people like us don't have the money."

Felix had set himself thinking with his answer.

They made their way to the car in silence and Emilio drove his boss home.

When he got back, Felix found a message from Petra on his answer phone telling him to come over; she was waiting patiently.

Chapter 23

After what had happened last night, it was no surprise that Felix emerged ten minutes late for the task force's daily briefing.

Hans Werners indicated a free seat next to him. "Morning, I thought for a moment you might have changed your mind, but you haven't missed much."

The chief inspector just nodded briefly, before listening to the speaker from Environmental Crimes, who was providing the latest info on Krulle. In the meantime, the ministry official had been placed under round-the-clock surveillance and his finances were being monitored.

Felix interrupted, placing the DVD on the table. "Please excuse me, but I think this might be of interest. It's supposed to contain footage of Dr. Zimmer together with Krulle and Stumpf at Waldschlösschen, a high-class brothel. I haven't looked at it too closely yet, but it should prove the pair of them were in cahoots with Zimmer."

Hans Werners signaled his approval. He was next, and informed the others about the bogus companies Zimmer had set up abroad in order to effect the illegal payments and disguise his income. There were seven in total, all belonging to the key witness.

The financial crimes investigator used bookkeeping receipts to show how skillfully the money was being laundered. Chief Inspector Büschelberger was fascinated. Zimmer must have told them a great deal since agreeing to cooperate.

The third speaker was Police Superintendent von Weinhammer, who explained how he aimed to guarantee the witness's safety. Only the surveillance team would know where Zimmer was staying and they'd be alternating between five safe houses to avoid following a pattern. If anyone wished to submit the witness to further questioning, they'd have to make an appointment in advance. The surveillance team would then decide upon the time and location of the interview.

Felix interrupted again. "I'm pretty sure our Italian colleague, Commissario Crotone, will want to speak with Dr. Zimmer."

Baron von Weinhammer nodded. "Then I'll call you on your cell later and tell you the location. Early tomorrow morning should be fine."

Chief Inspector Büschelberger briefed them on what he had learned at Waldschlösschen, and drew their attention to the DVD once more, before returning to the station so that he and Emilio could pick up Crotone from the airport.

Crotone was genuinely delighted to see him again and extended a warm greeting to Emilio as well.

In the car, he turned to Felix. "You won't believe it, but not even Alitalia seems to offer decent food anymore. Should we find somewhere to eat? Chinese would be good."

Over lunch, Felix provided a detailed summary of the investigation. The Italian interrupted only seldom: he was a good listener.

"What do you want to do this afternoon? Should we head straight to the task force so you can introduce yourself, or would you like to look for a hotel first? We won't be able to question Dr. Zimmer until early tomorrow morning," Felix asked as their guest ordered espresso.

Crotone turned to Emilio. "You must know a good hotel run by Italians?"

Emilio considered for a moment. "Villa Roma's the only one I can think of, but it's a great setting and not far from Police HQ."

"Bene. Relatives of yours?"

Inspector Perfondo shook his head.

"Oh well, can't have everything I suppose. If you don't mind, I'd like to check in first, then we can go to this – what's it called again?"

"Kenco, that's the name of the task force. Fine, let's get you to your hotel then," Felix said.

The three officers were just in time for the afternoon briefing. Felix introduced his two companions. The initial period was devoted to financial considerations, something that neither the chief inspector nor Emilio found especially interesting. Crotone, on the other hand, listened very carefully. After an hour, the Italian detective was asked to provide a little background information on Don Veschie.

He cleared his throat. "Dear colleagues, thank you for giving me the opportunity to take part in your investigation. First of all, I would like to apologize for my poor German. I hope you can understand me nevertheless."

Whereupon he was assured from all sides that his German was excellent. Police Superintendent von Weinhammer, in particular, seemed intrigued by what he had to say.

"Don Veschie was born in Sicily on a remote mountain farm just north of the village of Caltabellotta. His father was a simple shepherd whom Don Veschie helped from an early age, only spending six years in school. He was eleven when his father died after falling down a ravine. The boy had carried his seriously wounded father over four miles to the nearest city, but there was nothing anyone could do. From then on, the family lived in total poverty. The boy was now head of the family and forced to provide for his mother and three siblings. There are rumors that that's when he started running errands for the Mozarras – the reigning Mafia family in the region back then. It's also around then that his mother began to attract the attentions of a neighbor, whose advances she rejected out of hand. Apparently this neighbor was one of the Mozarra's button men. Whether that's true or not, in the eyes of the young Don Veschie, he's dishonoring both his mother and family. So the boy gets hold of a Lupara, a sawn-off shotgun, and kills him. He was thirteen years old." Crotone sighed.

"Although they had nothing to go on, local police initially assumed it was the work of a rival family. Only ten years later did the finger begin to point at Don Veschie. But like I said, there was no evidence against him. The Mozarras didn't punish him either; instead, impressed by his cold-bloodedness they ended up offering him a place in their organization. A few years later, the era of gang warfare began in Sicily. Families were jostling for control of the drug trade. There were 137 deaths in total on all sides. Don Veschie, meanwhile, used the time to murder his way to the top. We estimate that he killed about ten people himself during this period. For the next eight years, the Mozarras were the most powerful family in the whole of Sicily. Don Veschie was living in Palermo and was now third in charge. When he was twenty-eight, the head of the Mozarra family was killed in an explosion on his yacht, along with his two sons. Officially, the police were investigating a Kurdish gang trying to gain a foothold in Sicily. But I wouldn't be too surprised if Don Veschie had orchestrated the whole thing. Even so, he took a bloody revenge and the Kurds disappeared without trace. Although none of them were ever found, after three weeks our man had been installed as head of the family. No-one else dared to oppose him. Excuse me."

Crotone coughed a few times, before clearing his throat and reaching for a glass of water, which he emptied in a single gulp.

"That's better. Now where was I? Ah yes, Don Veschie was now head of the most powerful Mafia family in Sicily. His influence spread to Calabria, and he began working in tandem with the Camorra further to the north. He moved to the mainland, where he flitted between seven different properties. On three occasions we received details about informants prepared to give evidence against his organization. However, they all disappeared before we could interview them and provide protection. The first was killed in a car accident, the second drowned and the third died in his car as a result of carbon monoxide poisoning."

Felix cut Crotone short. "You're aware that our victim also died as a result of carbon monoxide poisoning. But the suicide was staged; we know now that he was murdered. Do you think the Italians could've been involved?"

Crotone shrugged his shoulders. "I'm afraid I can't answer that, but personally I don't think so. Don Veschie is normally pretty bloodthirsty; it's only witnesses who are dealt with so clinically. Was your victim about to testify? As far as I know, our current witness flew to Italy immediately after Uwe Kaptain's sudden death to ensure his contacts that business wouldn't suffer because of it. Of course, we could always ask Dr. Zimmer if he thinks it's possible. For me, though, it's sheer coincidence," he replied.

"How many murders do you hold Veschie directly responsible for? Can you give me a rough idea?"

Von Weinhammer drummed his fingers nervously on the tabletop, while the Italian was busy calculating.

"I think he himself has killed at least eighteen people. These days, he usually leaves it to his button men, but don't underestimate his determination. If necessary, he would kill again without hesitation. What's more, he has links to the police in our region, and politically, his influence can be felt as far north as Rome. That's also the reason I'm here unofficially. No-one from Italy knows about this; they all think I'm on holiday." Crotone leaned back casually, more than satisfied with his work.

Next up was an official who spoke about the insights gleaned from the DVD. Krulle and Stumpf were clearly recognizable on it. The icing on the cake, however, was the scene in which Zimmer had passed Krulle a suspicious-looking envelope as they were leaving the club.

Felix wondered whether that wasn't Zimmer's way of hedging his bets. Either way, he was only backing the one horse now. The task force decided that the two public servants should be brought in for questioning on Monday; and that a search of their respective apartments and offices should be conducted at the same time. With that, the official part of the meeting was over.

Police Superintendent von Weinhammer asked to speak to Crotone for ten minutes in another office. He wanted to discuss security measures with him, get the Italian's opinion on them. Meanwhile, Felix and Emilio waited in the now-deserted room.

"Things are really gaining momentum. Just a shame our own investigation is stalling right now," Felix said.

Emilio nodded in agreement. "Maybe something'll come up. The link to Don Veschie's not a bad angle; something we hadn't looked into yet."

He didn't say any more, but Felix knew his friend too well not to realize there was something else on his mind.

"Come on, spit it out. What's eating you?"

The response was hesitant. "I don't know how to say this – but are you sure we can trust Crotone completely? What if he belongs to Don Veschie? We'd be digging our own grave, not to mention Zimmer's. I know as an Italian myself I should be the last to say this, but, particularly in the south, it can be difficult for police to stay on the right side of the law."

He looked his boss straight in the eye.

The chief inspector considered what he'd said a long time before answering:

"That's a very worrying idea, of course. And I don't think we should disregard it entirely. But my instinct tells me he's OK, and nothing he's done up till now suggests any different. You should have seen how he reacted in Tropea when I rapped on his window. I'm sure he'd have been much calmer if he belonged to Don Veschie. They probably thought I was one of them at first. Plus, he's helped us avoid a whole lot of red tape. Add it all together and I'm certain he's one of the good guys. Don't forget that this von Weinhammer's supposed to be one of the best – maybe he's sounding Crotone out right now. But I really don't think we have anything to worry about on that score." Felix grinned at his partner and patted him on the shoulder.

Moments later, Crotone reappeared in the room.

"Mamma mia, he's a cunning old dog, that Baron. Got a good few tricks up his sleeve. Next time we're protecting a witness, I could do with having him on side. He's going bring Zimmer to us early tomorrow morning so I can question him. Now, it'd be great if you could drive me to my hotel."

During the journey, Crotone asked his German colleagues if they could drive through the city with the siren on for a bit. What with all the traffic, it would be much more fun than the country lanes he was used to. Emilio looked over towards Felix, who, after a quick glance at the on-board computer, nodded his assent. Emilio sped away like lightning; Crotone should have something to tell his friends when he got home.

Crotone pointed at the display on the on-board computer. "What do these figures mean?"

"This one shows how much battery we've got left: we're currently running at fifty-percent capacity. And the figure here tells us we can keep going for another forty miles."

"And how do the blue light and siren affect the range?" Crotone asked, genuinely interested.

"That we're still not sure, but we're planning a test drive on the Nürburgring with the car manufacturer, battery producer, and the company responsible for the charging stations. The idea is to see how far the Focus can go fully charged. Once with blue light and siren and once just on its own. Then we'll know for certain," Emilio replied.

"First I've heard of it. When was that decided?" the chief inspector asked in astonishment.

"Oh, just at the conference, you know the one you sent me to," his partner countered mischievously.

When they nearly became involved in an accident close to the hotel, Felix decided they'd had enough for one day. Commissario Crotone had clearly enjoyed being driven by Emilio.

"Please allow me to take you for dinner tomorrow night. Felix, bring that charming girlfriend of yours; your wife would be most welcome too, Emilio. Do you think you could find a good Italian? We'll have plenty to celebrate."

The detectives accepted the invitation.

Felix promised to pick Crotone up at half eight the following morning, then he and Emilio returned to the station.

"Should we take him to the Da Claudia?"

Inspector Perfondo smiled. "Why not? Bet you he claims it back on expenses once he's nailed this Don Veschie character. And I'm sure the Italians will allow him that much."

"OK, then I'll ask Petra if she can make the reservation. She's friends with the owner."

Half an hour later, she called to say everything had been arranged. That was all, however, so Felix spent the evening in front of the TV mulling things over. Eventually he fell asleep on the sofa, with Django curled up beside him.

Felix awoke at five, stiff as anything. After he had tossed and turned in his bed for another hour, he decided to get up. As he stepped underneath the hot shower, he knew something had to give.

If things continued like this, he'd either end up an alcoholic or a senile old codger, neither of which sounded particularly appealing. He decided to talk to Petra about it as soon as possible – maybe they did have more of a future together after all.

On the way to the hotel, he received a call from Police Superintendent von Weinhammer informing him that Dr. Zimmer would be at the station for questioning at nine. Having arrived, he introduced Crotone to Arno and Frauke. They had tea, while their guest drank an espresso Frauke had managed to scrounge from a neighboring department. Crotone, who was a gifted story-teller, entertained them with a series of anecdotes from Calabria and everybody enjoyed the momentary source of distraction.

At nine sharp, Dr. Zimmer arrived with his escort and was led into the room where he had been previously interviewed. The key witness was joined by Felix, Crotone and Emilio.

"Good morning, Dr. Zimmer. This is Commissario Crotone, a colleague from Italy. He's been investigating Don Veschie and his organization for a long time and would like to ask you a few questions. We hope you will be happy to cooperate with us in this regard," the chief inspector began.

Dr. Zimmer shrugged his shoulders. "I've already told you everything I know. I'm not sure I can be any more use to you."

"Good morning, dottore. We'll see about that, won't we? I'm certain you can still be of use to us – after all, it's in your own interests. The more efficiently we can crush Don Veschie's organization, the safer you'll be in future. If we succeed in destroying it completely, then perhaps you'll even be able to stay here and keep your identity." The Italian allowed his words to sink in.

When the witness eventually nodded, it was clear they'd had the desired effect. "That would be nice. I must say, I probably didn't think this leniency program through completely. And that's why I'm prepared to tell you everything I know."

For the first two hours, Zimmer merely repeated the statement he'd given on Monday. Commissario Crotone interrupted very rarely, only when he was trying to get to the bottom of one remark or another. He was particularly interested in the route the waste took once it had left Frankfurt.

"As I've already explained to your German colleagues, I don't know what happens after Frankfurt. I only know the destination in Kenya."

"I understand that, dottore, but maybe something'll occur to you. Did Don Veschie ever name any harbor towns? Livorno, Pescara, Molfetta or Bari? Naples is also pretty popular with the Mafia. Perhaps he mentioned one of these?" the Italian probed.

The key witness took his time to consider the question. "If I remember rightly, he did mention Bari a couple of times. Yes, exactly, I remember now. Previously I only knew it as the ferry port to Greece."

Crotone nodded contentedly and asked Felix to get him a map. Five minutes later, the pair of them were hunched over an atlas.

"That would mean they're using the E55. The only question now is whether they're coming via Milan and Switzerland or taking the Brenner pass up through Verona. Ultimately it doesn't matter, since we now know where they're shipping from. After Bari, it's probably on through the Suez canal towards the Horn of Africa, then straight to Kilifi."

Crotone shot a glance at Dr. Zimmer. "When's the next load scheduled?"

"We've got another three requests but our price negotiations have been put on ice. Don Veschie, Dr. Mugambone, and I were all agreed that we should wait until the murder investigation was concluded. I wanted to keep the company out of it as far as possible, so as not to endanger our little operation," Zimmer replied.

"Didn't do a very good job there," Felix could barely conceal a smirk.

"And you know the best thing about it, Chief Inspector? I'm actually grateful for the way things have turned out. Now I can finally be an honest citizen again. Whether you believe it or not, I used to be a man of principle," the key witness countered.

"Did Don Veschie say anything about Kaptain's death or seem particularly interested in it?" Crotone steered the conversation back on track.

"No, not really. He just said he didn't think it'd affect our business relationship. Still, he wasn't exactly over the moon when I told him we should wait until after the investigation. Luckily, Mugambone agreed with me, so he was eventually forced to admit defeat. But no, Kaptain's death didn't affect him personally in any way. Mugambone, on the other hand, well the two of them had known each other a long time."

"They were friends from student days, we know that already," the chief inspector said.

Crotone winked at him. He seemed to be enjoying the way they were complementing one another. The conversation might've appeared relaxed but they both had a definite goal in mind.

"Should we take a break there, have something to drink, maybe even a little snack?" he asked.

Dr. Zimmer accepted gratefully and Felix organized a few sandwiches, as well as tea and coffee. During the break, no-one said anything.

When they were finished, the chief inspector turned to face the witness once more. "How long do you think you can be off the scene before Don Veschie and others start getting worried?"

"Not sure, but since I can give instructions from my company by phone, I doubt they suspect anything yet. Let another week go by, though…"

"I think with your help, we can arrest Don Veschie early next week. But I'm also interested to know how you made contact with him after Kaptain's death. Did he initiate it? Or was it you who got the ball rolling?" Crotone asked.

"Actually it was Mugambone. Shortly after Kaptain was murdered, he called me at my office and suggested we meet as soon as possible to discuss how best to proceed. He contacted Don Veschie and set up the meeting. The whole thing began in the concourse at Lamezia Terme, before we were picked up by a driver and taken to Don Veschie's villa near Briatico."

"Did you see what security measures were in place? People carrying weapons? Was there a boat just outside the villa? Bulletproof windows? Anything you can think of will help to ensure Don Veschie's safe arrest."

Dr. Zimmer smiled. "I'm sorry, I feel increasingly like I'm appearing in some cheap imitation of The Godfather. The only thing I noticed was that his bodyguards wore sunglasses the whole time, even when they were inside. But I'm certain they were armed – and that there's a pretty decent arsenal in the house. I didn't see any boats or getaway cars, just the obligatory Mercedes 500-Series, as well as an SLK."

"How many security guards were there?" Crotone enquired.

"He was constantly surrounded by four people. Some of them seemed more like assistants or secretaries though. In total, there were about ten people on the estate."

Crotone seemed satisfied. "Well, to be honest, I don't have any further questions." He hesitated before continuing. "But I do have a request."

"You want something else?" By now, Dr. Zimmer looked pretty exhausted.

"They've just returned a landmark verdict in Italy, according to which, witnesses testifying against the Mafia no longer have to appear in court. Instead, those in potential danger can give video testimony without their evidence being affected in any way. I think it would be safer for you if we recorded your statement this afternoon and had it signed by a district attorney. Then you wouldn't have to go to Italy."

The witness seemed agitated. "You could've mentioned it sooner!"

"Scusi, sometimes I'm a little forgetful," the Italian apologized. "But would you be willing to give your statement again and have it filmed this time?"

"I suppose if I must. But I'd like to be left in peace tomorrow in return," Dr. Zimmer said.

While Felix made the necessary preparations for the video recording, Frauke organized lunch. The surveillance team didn't want to take any risks, and so they were unable to go to a local restaurant, as Crotone had hoped. Luckily, however, Emilio's mother had once again provided ample supplies – and Crotone was only too happy to share in her munificence.

In the afternoon, the key witness was interviewed for a third time. They had agreed that DA Cando would read the questions from the statement and Dr. Zimmer would simply reply as before. Then Crotone, Emilio and Felix also appeared on film until finally, after three hours, a worn out Dr. Zimmer was ready to leave the building in the company of his surveillance team.

Commissario Crotone was beside himself with joy. "Well, that was productive! I'd never have dreamed he'd be such a good witness. Thank you."

He patted Felix on the shoulder. "My name's Sante Maria by the way, but my friends call me Sante."

The chief inspector struggled to conceal a grin as he shook Crotone's outstretched hand.

The Italian couldn't help laughing either. "I know, it's hilarious here in Germany. Believe me, it was hell in school; I spent a lot of time cursing my parents. But once we moved to Italy, no-one found it amusing anymore – it's one of the many reasons I stayed."

"I've never heard of video evidence being accorded the same weight as testimony in court. Is that how it is in Italy?" Felix asked on the way to the hotel.

"No, it's pretty exceptional – but I don't want to take any risks. Although the team in charge of Zimmer seems highly capable, I want to have something in case anything should happen. That's why I want you to keep an additional copy. So we can make sure that Don Veschie goes down once and for all."

The chief inspector nodded and agreed to pick him up at half past seven.

Back at home, he took a shower and put on his best shirt, before heading to collect a ravishing-looking Petra en route to the hotel. Her Italian outfit was by a designer he'd never even heard of.

Crotone, on the other hand, recognized it straightaway as he greeted Petra with the obligatory peck on both cheeks. Then he held the car door open for her and took his place in the passenger seat next to his German colleague.

Emilio and Sylvia were already waiting at the table they'd reserved with a glass of prosecco. The owner was equally delighted to see Petra again and extended the whole group a very warm welcome. When he heard that one of his guests was actually from Calabria, he became friendlier still: his wife also hailed from the area.

Crotone and the owner spent five minutes chatting very quickly and animatedly in Italian. Felix could only understand about half of it, but they were speaking about relatives, possible mutual acquaintances, and gossip from Calabria.

In the end it transpired that Crotone didn't know anyone from the owner's family. However, it didn't stop the latter calling a waiter over to bring them more glasses of prosecco.

"A little welcome present, on the house. If you'll allow me, I'd very much like to put together a menu for you. So, do you trust me?"

It didn't take long for all five to answer in the affirmative.

The owner clapped his hands in delight.

"Va bene! You won't be disappointed."

And he wasn't wrong.

The meal began with a melon soup, served with crayfish, clams and scampi. Next up was a cold bean salad with gorgonzola sauce and home-made pasta mixed with fresh chopped tomatoes and buffalo mozzarella. After that, it was swordfish served on a bed of eggplant. Petra tried to protest and skip the next course, lamb, but Sante and the owner persuaded her it was a delicacy not to be missed. For dessert, there was a golden kiwi fruit sorbet, followed by espresso and grappa.

After such a fantastic meal, everyone felt thoroughly sated and leaned back contentedly – if a little tired – in their chairs. The feast had lasted almost three hours and Felix noticed that the profile of the other customers had changed in the meantime. If it had been predominantly Germans eating when they had arrived, by now the vast majority were Italian. When the owner, who had spent the evening catering to his various guests, finally returned to their table, he was beaming all over.

"Did I not promise you as much?"

Everyone was full of praise. But when Crotone started to hug him and pronounce him a master of Italian cuisine, the owner was beside himself with laughter.

"Please stay: we're having a little celebration in half an hour."

Felix's objection that they all had to work the next morning was quickly brushed aside.

"Don't be silly. It's time for a pick-me-up, a real Calabrian cocktail. Made exclusively from ingredients produced in the region: limoncello, a dash of pepper and lots more besides. An ancient family secret that'll get you going again. But probably better to take a taxi afterwards."

Seeing that all resistance was futile, the five had no choice but to accept. The cocktail was strong and fruity and did in fact pep them up considerably. At half past eleven, a number of tables were pushed to one side.

The last remaining German customers had already left when the owner suddenly produced a guitar and began to sing, while his wife and Crotone performed an age-old Calabrian folk dance. Petra danced alternately with Crotone, the owner and two of the waiting staff; and the rest savored the atmosphere, full of gusto and joie de vivre.

Three hours later, the group were ready to take their leave. In the taxi on the way back, Felix was mad at Petra for not having danced with him.

"Oh, my Chief Inspector's jealous! Isn't that sweet?"

But he became more and more tetchy in response to her teasing, and in the end both parties slept alone.

Chapter 24

Felix wasn't the only one to turn up late for work the next morning nursing a hangover. Emilio had found it equally difficult to get out of bed, and Frauke had appeared even later. She just murmured a brief apology and said she didn't want to talk about it.

After an unusually quiet cup of tea, Arno drove Felix over to the Da Claudia so he could pick up the Focus and drive on to the hotel to collect Crotone. The Commissario was just having breakfast.

"Felix, won't you join me? I must say, yesterday evening was wonderful, but this morning I realize I'm getting old. It's becoming more and more difficult to get out of bed after nights like that."

The chief inspector sat down, more than happy to escape the office and task force briefing for a little while yet.

"Would you like some coffee or a roll?"

Felix shook his head.

"There's tea too."

Crotone beckoned the waiter over. "Bring my friend here a cup of tea, and make it short and strong so he wakes up."

Then he looked at his colleague. "Trouble with your girlfriend?"

Felix nodded. "We had a fight last night in the taxi on the way home. I think I was just jealous, anyway I behaved like a total idiot."

Crotone gave him a fatherly pat on the shoulder. "Women, my friend, are difficult to understand. But if I know Petra, she's not the type to be constrained. In Italy we have a saying: Put a nightingale in a cage and it will stop singing and die of grief."

Felix thought about the proverb for a long time, and they spent the rest of their breakfast in silence. After Crotone had paid the check, they set off for the task force, where the Italian wanted to say his goodbyes. He thanked everyone for their unbureaucratic help and promised to keep them posted on his progress.

Back at Felix's office, Crotone was handed the recording of his interview with Dr. Zimmer. Emilio gave him the original footage, as well as a copy on DVD. He had also made two additional copies:

one would go to DA Cando for safekeeping; while the other would be kept in the station.

"I think we should be safe now," Emilio said.

Crotone thanked him once more, along with the rest of the team. Then Felix drove him to the airport, where they shook hands for a final time.

"Sante, all the best to you, and I hope Don Veschie doesn't get away this time."

Crotone drew Felix towards him for an embrace. "Thank you, our meeting in Tropea was a real stroke of luck. I hope you can come and visit me again sometime."

He began making his way through security, only to turn round once more at the gate. "Amico – remember the nightingale and the cage."

Felix sat thinking in the departure lounge until after take-off, before slowly heading back to the office.

On his desk he found a message from the Kenco team; it looked like it had been written by Arno. It said that Councilor Stumpf and Ministry Official Krulle would be arrested at six o'clock on Monday morning; and that a press conference would follow at one, at which Felix was expected to appear.

The chief inspector called the team together. "I'm afraid that's me for the day; I'm going home. You're all to take the rest of the afternoon off. We'll see if we can hit the ground running on Monday. I don't want to hear any whining, especially not from you, Emilio. Off you go."

The group went their separate ways and half an hour later the office was deserted. Back at home, Felix thought about calling Petra, only to decide against it and head for a nap. With Django purring away on his stomach, he fell asleep instantly. After he'd awoken, he showered and spruced himself up. Then he combed Django's fur until it was silky smooth and placed the lead around his neck. His plan was to turn up at Petra's without warning and beg for forgiveness.

Django was meant to be the ice-breaker. Felix purchased a single red rose en route and waited in the stairwell outside her apartment.

Petra arrived back home just before seven, took Django under her arm and gave him a kiss on the forehead.

"Hello sweetie, what are you doing here? And who's that on your lead?"

She shot Felix a quizzical glance, making him feel pretty stupid. Finally, she opened the door. "I suppose you'd better come in. Then we can talk properly," she said.

Felix sat down at her dining table while Django scouted out the kitchen, earning a saucer of milk for his troubles. Then Petra placed two glasses on the table, gave Felix a bottle of wine to open and headed for the shower. A short while later she returned, free of make-up and dressed in casual clothes. She took a swig of wine without clinking glasses, and then looked Felix straight in the eye before beginning to speak.

"I don't know, maybe it just isn't meant to be. All I can say is that right now I'm pretty unhappy with our relationship."

He didn't know how to react and could only stammer in response. "Yeah, I'm really sorry. I don't know what came over me last night, but you weren't paying me any attention and that bothered me."

"Listen, I can't be with a man who doesn't trust me. Who doesn't let me have my freedom. I need evenings like last night. Sometimes I just have to dance and let myself go."

"I said I'm sorry – what more do you want me to do? It'll never happen again, OK?" He gazed in embarrassment at the rose Petra had placed in an empty bottle.

"It isn't just about last night, Felix. Sometimes you're so sweet and attentive, but then suddenly it feels like you couldn't care less. What kind of relationship is that?"

"I'm sorry, I don't get it. On the one hand, I'm to give you your freedom because you're a strong, independent woman; but at the same time you're accusing me of not looking after you properly? From where I'm standing, that's a pretty clear contradiction!"

She took a sip of wine. "I hope this isn't going to turn into an interrogation, Chief Inspector. You're right, I am full of contradictions, and maybe I do expect the impossible – but it's just the way I'm wired. My best friend thinks I'm incapable of maintaining a relationship and perhaps she's right. As soon as things start getting complicated, I'm gone. I thought it'd be different with you, but once again I've reached the point where I want to back out; where I need to back out."

She stared helplessly at Felix, who was just sitting there as if rooted to the spot. The conversation had taken an unwanted turn, but one that, deep down, he had feared was always coming.

"Damn it, Petra, I love you! I want to be with you! What are we supposed to do now?"

"I'm afraid I don't know either."

He knelt down before her and took her in his arms, while she stroked his hair. Both of them were silent a long time.

"I just need a little time to think things through on my own. Who knows, maybe I never even loved you in the first place."

At that moment Felix felt something inside him shatter. He stood up and drained his glass in one gulp. "I think I should go now," he said bitterly.

"No, that's not what I want either. Stay. But you'll have to sleep on the sofa. I can't be with you tonight – but maybe tomorrow it'll be different."

He gave a dry laugh. "No, thanks, I'm done playing the fool."

Then he attached Django's lead and left without saying good-bye, not even pausing to turn round.

Back at home he opened a bottle of whisky from the year he was born: a fortieth birthday present from colleagues, which until now he'd been keeping for special occasions.

He downed two large glasses before falling into a dreamless, fitful sleep. About eleven the next morning, he was awoken by Django asking for food and so he went shopping, surprised to discover that people were looking at him strangely. It must have been his drawn, unshaven appearance. His purchases were limited to cat food, two TV dinners and a healthy supply of Chilean red wine. He felt like a hobo.

It was only after returning to his apartment that he realized he was wearing odd shoes: one brown and one black. Now he understood why he'd been getting strange looks. He promised not to let himself go like this again.

Petra and the pain of their broken relationship wouldn't get him down. A text message informed him that he had voicemail. Petra, as expected.

"I'm sorry if I hurt you. Now that I've thought about it, I realize I don't have any feelings left for you. Believe me, it's better this way. Maybe you're just too good for me. Still, I'd like to ask one more favor: please don't get in touch, I need to deal with this alone. Good luck."

In his rage, Felix nearly smashed his cell phone against the wall, but just about managed to control himself. He listened to the message fourteen times in all – until he could bear it no longer. Then he deleted it and opened a bottle of wine. The rest of the weekend was a total blur.

On Monday morning, Felix felt like death warmed up. He took a long shower and shaved, noticing that his hands were shaking. He cursed himself and the fact that he'd let things get this far.

Over breakfast, his stomach revolted. Still completely hungover, he headed for the station, though not before he had seriously contemplated staying home. It was time to get his life back on track. His colleagues looked at him in horror, Kevin Dour in particular gazing into the chief inspector's bloodshot eyes and shaking his head.

"Believe me, too much alcohol is a pretty effective form of poison. Take care: I've only just got used to you – I don't want you to become one of my assignments."

Felix waved him aside in irritation. "If I need medical advice, I'll go to a doctor, not some body-stripper like you."

Kevin took a deep breath and looked at him with contempt. "Fine, drink yourself to death. See if I care!"

Chief Inspector Büschelberger realized he had taken his anger out on the wrong person.

"Sorry, but my girlfriend broke up with me unexpectedly on Friday. My weekend was completely ruined and I don't feel well. I never meant to insult you."

Kevin shook the chief inspector's outstretched hand.

"Forgotten. But you should take an aspirin and balance out your mineral levels, then you'll feel fine. My mother always prescribed plain rye bread with salt and a cup of stock. Sounds disgusting, but believe me it works," the pathologist said.

Frauke stood up to prepare the ingredients. In the meantime, Kevin had gone back to forensics. Half an hour later, Felix was forced to take his hangover cure under the watchful eye of his colleagues. It really did taste disgusting, though he felt a little better afterwards.

"What was Kevin doing here? Do we have a new case?"

Arno shook his head. "He just said how much he liked having tea with us in the mornings and that he wanted to stop by again."

"Strange… But why shouldn't he, I guess; he can be a really nice guy sometimes."

"But should we get back to work on our case?" Emilio reminded them of the task at hand.

For the first time since Friday, Felix forced a smile. He could count on his partner. When the time was right, he'd be there to console him and offer advice, but for now he knew work was the only way to distract the chief inspector from his emotional turmoil.

"Not now, I'm afraid: I have to attend this press conference. Since I'm not sure how long it'll take, I think we should get stuck back in tomorrow morning. It won't be long until we're assigned a new case; then we'll have to shelve this one. And we all know how much that would suck. So, get everything ready and start discussions without me. We'll decide how best to proceed tomorrow."

Felix went into his office to have a little rest, but he was interrupted by the ringing of a telephone.

"Bon giorno, Sante here. I just wanted to say that we're about to pick up our mutual friend. It's a huge operation with over a hundred officers involved. We've been planning it the whole weekend and will strike at five different locations simultaneously. I'll let you know as soon as we have him."

"Good news. Best of luck! Our press conference is taking place in just under two hours."

"Si, it's time. Talk to you later."

Before Crotone hung up, Felix could hear orders being issued in the background, and then it was still. He closed his eyes and leaned back. At least this side of the case seemed to be going well.

He thought about that last evening with Sante. But then he was overcome by the pain of his loss. He wanted to make it known to the whole world, but instead he just dug his fingers into his desk. After two minutes, he had regained control.

Chin up and concentrate on your case, he exhorted himself.

As kids, he and Emilio had always played Star Wars. Felix had taken the role of Yoda, and now he mimicked the old Jedi once more:

"Chin up you must keep, provide comfort and help the future will."

Suddenly he laughed and it felt good. While speaking he had raised an admonitory finger, which made him look more like a cheap imitation of ET than Yoda. Still, it was also the moment he realized he would get over the split: his work, colleagues and friends would see him through. Emboldened by this realization, he stood up and made himself a cup of tea.

An hour later, he was heading over to Cando's office, feeling like a new man. They briefly discussed the order of the press conference, and Felix informed the DA that the Italians were about to make their move on Don Veschie.

The room in Police HQ could hold about fifty people, with forty-odd reporters having appeared by the time Senior District Attorney Schürfel opened proceedings.

"Good afternoon, ladies and gentlemen. I'm delighted you're all here today and I can assure you we have information that is more than worthy of the front pages. It concerns large-scale illegal waste disposal and links to organized crime. Without any further ado then, I pass you over to Chief Inspector Felix Büschelberger, whose investigation of the east port murder was what got the ball rolling."

He made an inviting gesture towards Felix, who cleared his throat and paused for effect before beginning to speak. All eyes and camera lenses were focused on him.

"Good afternoon. I am also delighted that we can reveal the successful outcome of an investigation spanning a number of weeks."

He briefly outlined the starting position, before coming on to the matter of illegal waste disposal. In addition, he highlighted the good cooperation with the Italian police, provided a vivid account of the danger presented by Don Veschie, and announced that an operation to arrest him was currently underway. Following these revelations, he was bombarded with questions, which he tried to answer precisely and in the correct sequence.

"Has Dr. Heinrich Zimmer been implicated in the murder?"

"Absolutely not. In this regard, he is completely innocent."

"Where is he now?"

Felix looked across to the senior district attorney, who briefly took the floor.

"Dr. Zimmer has chosen to side with the DA's office and is currently in witness protection. That is all I'm prepared to say on the matter." He motioned back towards the chief inspector.

"Do you have any more suspects in the east port murder?"

"No, we're back to square one on that."

"Could the Mafia be behind it?"

"There's no evidence to suggest it, but we still can't rule it out. Our Italian colleagues will be searching for leads following the arrest of Don Veschie."

Felix didn't mention that the poison administered to Uwe Kaptain had been purchased through Dr. Zimmer's company. He still hoped this knowledge might ultimately lead them to the killer.

"And to what extent are you cooperating with the Kenyan police?"

It was the senior district attorney who responded here too. "Our ambassador in Kenya was notified of the case and is currently meeting with the Kenyan government. As far as I'm aware, the federal government is prepared to assist in the removal of waste stemming from German companies. In addition, our ambassador is providing photocopies of all evidence obtained. How things proceed from there is the responsibility of the Kenyan authorities."

"Are there any German officials involved?"

Felix motioned towards his colleague sitting next to him. "Inspector Hans Werners from Financial Crimes will handle that question. He's in charge of the task force investigating this case." He was happy to escape the mob of reporters.

"Good afternoon. Yes, there are two German officials involved. A city councilor from Frankfurt and a ministry official from the Hessian Office for the Environment were both arrested earlier this morning. They are currently being questioned," the financial crimes detective explained.

"Can you reveal names?"

"At this stage in the investigation, I'm afraid I can't give you any names. Sorry."

The reporters' questions became increasingly probing. Inspector Werners' responses were very down-to-earth, even if they weren't detailed enough for the majority of those present. Still, he refused to be drawn into making sensationalist comments. After an hour, the press conference ended and Felix, the DA, and Werners all went for a bite to eat. Upon returning to the station, Felix found a note on his desk.

Commissario Crotone had tried to reach him.

Felix called back straightaway. "Sante, how did it go?"

"We've got him! I can hardly believe it, but we've got him!"

The excitement at the other end of the line was almost tangible.

"Don Veschie was foolish enough to resist arrest. We had surrounded his villa with more than twenty heavily armed Carabinieri and as we drove the car up, he opened fire. Can you believe it; he had those idiots fire on us! My driver immediately put the car into reverse to get us out of the firing line. Then we really gave it to them. All my men fired on the villa, and after twenty minutes there was no more resistance forthcoming. We stormed the house and found four dead, as well as seven injured. Don Veschie himself had hidden and at first we couldn't find him. Turns out he had a kind of panic room. It took us a whole hour to get in. There he was just sitting there, injured and no longer so arrogant. Incidentally, it looked like he was making preparations to go underground. Must have had a warning from somewhere, but clearly didn't have enough time to disappear. Since his men injured two of my officers, all the contacts and lawyers in the world will be no use to him now. "

Felix could almost feel the adrenaline through the receiver.

"Sante, it sounds like you've done a brilliant job. Congratulations!"

"Si, after all these years we've finally got him. I need to get back to our questioning. I'll be in touch as soon as I have all the results. Say hello to your colleagues, and Petra in particular."

"Of course, will do."

The chief inspector hung up with a sigh, told the team about Crotone's success, and headed home.

That evening, Felix caught sight of himself on the regional news, a report that lasted almost seven minutes.

The national news, on the other hand, only showed a photo of Dr. Zimmer's company and a short statement read by Senior District Attorney Schürfel. After that, there was a clip from Italian TV showing a bullet-ridden villa surrounded by a number of burning vehicles.

Felix stroked Django's fur. "Well, my old friend, at least justice has prevailed this once."

He felt the desire to open a bottle of wine, but was able to resist the urge. Until the case was solved, he wouldn't touch another drop. With that, he released the tom into the night and headed for an early bed.

Chapter 25

For the first time in ages, Felix arrived at the office before his colleagues and prepared everything for their morning tea and subsequent meeting. A little later, Emilio gave him an encouraging pat on the shoulder and a sly wink; while Frauke grinned; and Arno couldn't resist making a comment.

"The captain's back at the helm: everything's going to be just fine."

Kevin Dour also swung by, a turn of events anticipated by the chief inspector, who had placed an ashtray and extra cup on the table.

"Morning, nice to see you here again," he said to the specialist.

"I can't help it; somehow I've developed quite a crush on Team Frog. That's why I've brought you something to eat." The pathologist waved a bag full of pastries.

"I hope it isn't flies." Frauke's remark had made everyone laugh: even Dour could scarcely contain himself.

When they were all sitting down, Arno stared at the pathologist for a long time in silence, until the latter finally registered his gaze.

"What's up, something wrong? Why are you looking at me like that?"

"I'm just wondering what's happened to the real Kevin Dour, the bogey man from the morgue. You've changed, you're no longer such a sour old bastard," said Arno.

"Sour old bastard? Maybe the bogey man should give our East Frisian fogey something to purge his foggy brain?"

"I have to agree with Arno here, Kevin. You're far more relaxed than usual," Felix said.

Emilio clutched his chest and said: "Has to be a woman: only the feminine touch can lend a man culture."

Dr. Dour drummed his fingers on the table. "So this is the reward I get for bringing pastries. Sometimes I think I get more love from my cold clients. Besides, what woman would have me?"

Arno smiled. "Our professor's right there: it can only be one of his dead bodies. We ought to check if he hasn't secretly prepared a corpse for himself and replaced her with a sack of potatoes."

The pathologist tapped his fingers against Arno's forehead. "That's the sort of thing only someone from a region plagued by centuries of incest could come up with. Is there a single intelligent thought going on in there?"

The rest of them had a great time following the verbal exchange and the room resounded with laughter. Suddenly DA Cando emerged.

"Happy campers all around, I see. Have you found Uwe Kaptain's killer?"

"Morning, District Attorney. No, we're just cheering ourselves up a bit," Chief Inspector Büschelberger explained.

"That's the way it should be. We're surrounded by enough suffering, it's important to keep a sense of humor. I just wanted to inform you that our corrupt officials made a full confession last night. The case is moving onto the next stage. We need to search the companies named by Dr. Zimmer. Since that's no longer your responsibility, you don't have to attend the task force meetings anymore – unless you have an express desire to do so," Cando explained to the chief inspector.

Felix shook his head. "No thanks, I've seen enough. I want to refocus on our original case."

"Be honest, now: how highly do you rate your chances of catching the killer?" the DA asked.

"I'm sure we'll get him. We must've just overlooked something right at the start. But we'll find it."

"Fine, as long as you know there are other cases needing to be solved. I'll give you another week, but after that I'll have to start reassigning members of your team."

"Make it two. If we still don't have anything concrete, then we can talk about what happens to my team," the chief inspector tried to negotiate.

"The maximum I can give you is ten days. Make sure you have something tangible. See it as a bonus after your success with the illegal waste disposal. Ten days and I want to be looking at the killer."

With that, the DA disappeared before Felix could raise any further objections.

"Looks like you guys are under a lot of pressure. So that's why you're always giving me the hurry-up." Kevin Dour scratched his chin.

"And yet, you give us hell every time."

"And that's the way it's going to stay; you can be sure of that," the pathologist growled.

"I thought as much." Felix fell silent a moment, before continuing with a sigh. "You know, sometimes I really doubt we're ever going to crack this."

"Don't be so pessimistic. We'll stick at it. It's only human to have doubts: that's what marks us out!"

Felix smiled gratefully at Arno.

Kevin cleared his throat. "At the risk of being called a smart-ass, I have to contradict you there, Arno. Nearly all highly evolved primates experience self-doubt. It's been proven with some species of ape. I've just read an article about it."

"Just my luck, Kevin, that's typical of you. Recently I had an argument with someone about whether animals could think or not. Please don't tell me they can," the chief inspector responded.

"Maybe not in the way we'd imagine, but there does seem to be such a thing as animal consciousness. Whatever, I'd love to stay and chat, but there are a few interesting cases waiting for me down in the basement." The pathologist stubbed out his cigarette and made his way to the door.

After a few moments, during which each team member seemed temporarily lost in thought, the chief inspector steered discussion back onto the case.

"Okay folks, you all heard the DA, we've got ten days. Any ideas, suggestions?"

Frauke took the floor. "We spoke for a long time yesterday and only came up with two possible lines of enquiry. The first – and probably the best – lead remains the purchase order from Dr. Zimmer's company. If he didn't do it himself, then the killer either has to work for the company or have an accomplice on the inside. We should take a closer look at the victim's colleagues again."

"A crime of passion. Who's your money on, then? Heike and Harald Rubin?" the chief inspector asked the team.

"Could be. Maybe it's another man's child and the husband found out?" Frauke continued.

"Certainly a possibility. Let's get it checked out. But I don't want to focus solely on the Rubins. We need to dig a little deeper, see if there are any more stories about Kaptain doing the rounds. Plus, there must be a way of finding out who put that order through the system. What's the other line of enquiry?"

"What was Kaptain doing that night? Why was he in such a hurry? That's something we never established."

Felix nodded approvingly at her. "My thoughts exactly. It seems there are no other possibilities. Well done, guys: good job. Now, let's go! Arno, get some printouts of Kaptain and his BMW. Make sure they're distributed in Eppstein and neighboring locations. Anyone who knows or has seen the victim, particularly on the night in question, is to contact us immediately. Frauke and Emilio, I want you to head back to Zimmer's company. First you grill Harald Rubin, and then pay a visit to the IT department. Emilio, have someone explain to you why it's impossible to find out who ordered the poison. Talk to the system administrator and check if there might be a way to trace the data after all. In the meantime, I'll have another look at the company's personal files, maybe something will come up," the chief inspector issued his instructions.

The three detectives got down to work straightaway.

"Just a moment," Felix held Arno back a minute. "I've been wondering what's happened to the rest of Kaptain's money. Is there any way of finding out?"

"I doubt it, I'm afraid. Not if he paid it into a numbered account in a tax haven like Switzerland. You see it suits the bank just fine if no-one lays claim to the money. They can sit tight until Judgment Day and earn a shitload on the interest. I'm pretty sure that money's lost for good."

The chief inspector grimaced: it was just as he'd expected.

Frauke and Emilio discussed their plan of action on the way to Zimmer Consultancy Ltd. They agreed to take the bull by the horns: to use a bluff in order to gauge the reaction of Harald Rubin and try and bring him out of his shell. Frauke was to lead the questioning.

The women at reception made no secret of their antipathy towards the pair, greeting them coolly and with exaggerated formality. On the instructions of Dr. Zimmer, Harald Rubin had since taken over the role of CEO and found himself short on time. He received them nevertheless, albeit with the same reserve as the receptionists before him.

"Good afternoon, please take a seat."

He pointed towards a three-piece suite next to his desk. Now that his responsibilities had increased, Rubin had also been given a bigger office. When all three had sat down, he continued, still visibly irritated.

"What do you want from me now? The police have caused this company enough damage already."

"Good afternoon, Mr. Rubin, and first of all, congratulations on your promotion. It wasn't the police that caused this damage, but Zimmer and Kaptain with their illegal machinations," Frauke countered.

"My apologies, detective, you're right of course. I don't know whether I'm coming or going at the moment. A number of clients have cancelled their contracts for fear of losing their reputation. And then there's the companies involved in the waste disposal itself, who naturally want nothing more to do with us. While I can sympathize, I'm afraid it means that everyone's job here is on the line. People are scared and they blame you for it, at least in part. But I'm sure you don't want to sit there listening to my problems. What can I do for you?"

Frauke hesitated. She liked Rubin – and respected his attempts to save the company, and its employees' jobs. "Mr. Rubin, there are a number of points which suggest that Uwe Kaptain's killer came from this company."

"What do you mean? I don't believe that for a second, the people here are all honest. That's impossible," Rubin snapped.

"I'm afraid not. We found a purchase order for the poison administered to the victim."

"Are you trying to tell me that someone from this company was responsible?" The acting CEO was clearly shaken.

"That's right, and what's more, the quantity ordered was just enough to poison Kaptain. There's nothing else it could've been used for; at least nothing our chemists could think of, anyway."

Rubin fell silent and waited for Frauke to resume.

"We've also heard rumors that your wife was having an affair with the victim. Are you sure the baby's yours?"

The interviewee went pale and sat with his mouth wide open, speechless. He just stared at Frauke, dumfounded. It took a whole minute before he managed to splutter a response.

"What are you trying to insinuate? I don't understand what you want from me."

Frauke looked helplessly towards her colleague: she felt sorry for Rubin. Emilio avoided her gaze, and instead faced their interlocutor directly.

"Mr. Rubin, we're still looking for a motive and if the rumors are true, then…" he left the sentence unfinished.

The CEO still didn't understand. "Who's spreading such nasty rumors? I've never heard anything like it. Why can't you just leave me and my family alone?"

Frauke and Emilio fell silent, and all of a sudden Rubin realized what they were up to.

His face went bright red and he started yelling. "You dare to come here with these outrageous lies! Just back off! What the hell are you thinking? Kaptain's death has nothing to do with me and as for these rumors…"

Frauke tried to make her voice as calm and soothing as possible. "We don't think they're true either, but we had to ask; for what it's worth we only heard the rumor about your paternity once, and the source wasn't exactly reliable. So how about we just forget it?"

Rubin glowered at the two detectives, but gradually calmed back down. "I don't believe it anyway. Fine, let's forget about it. However, I would still like to ask you to leave, as I have a lot of work to do."

Frauke and Emilio stood up.

"If you hear anything about the purchase order, please get in touch. Now, if we may, we'd like to speak with someone from purchasing, as well as your IT specialist."

Rubin nodded. "That's fine. Just go now, please."

Once they had left the office, Frauke turned to Emilio. "Hope we haven't ruined his marriage. I felt so sorry for him. I don't think he has anything to do with it."

Her colleague could only agree. "I don't think it was him either. And you're right; we probably were too hard on him. At least we know now that in all probability he wasn't the culprit. As for his wife, you did say yourself she was a snake. Maybe we've opened his eyes."

Their trip to purchasing was a quick one: nobody had any idea who'd placed the order and their hopes of finding out were receding rapidly. So they went on to the company network administrator and data protection officer. Emilio explained what they were after, and the IT specialist thought long and hard before answering.

"If there's no record from purchasing then I don't think we stand much of a chance. Especially given the order value and the fact that it's a non-hazardous chemical. The company doesn't keep a log of stuff like that."

"But don't you keep a log of remote access connections? Surely that's possible if you know the IP address?" Emilio probed.

"In theory, yes, but our IP addresses are allocated dynamically, meaning that they change. New ones are assigned every Monday morning, making it more difficult for hackers to tunnel through our firewall."

Emilio considered whether there was another way of tracing the order back to its origin. "Does your software send a confirmation to the buyer that his order has been correctly processed? If so, maybe the file can still be found?"

The IT guy scratched his head. "There is an automatic response, containing the details of the order in plain text. But it's only saved in a temporary file, which is deleted at the end of each month. If the order was placed last month, then it's already gone. Sorry."

Inspector Perfondo cursed quietly to himself, even if it was the answer he'd been expecting.

Back at the station, they filled the others in on their findings while Arno showed them the appeal he had printed and sent to local police stations for distribution. Then the team discussed what could still be done. Two frustrating hours later, and with no discernible progress made, they were ready to call it a night.

Wednesday seemed to drag on interminably, with the four detectives spending hours discussing the case and going over the files. They cross-referenced all the names in the vain hope that one of them would mean something.

But no matter how hard they tried, there was no breakthrough, no new ideas forthcoming. Finally, after what felt like an eternity, Emilio, Arno and Frauke went home none the wiser. Felix, meanwhile, decided to stay an extra two hours, which he spent grimly sifting through the files once more.

Thursday's only news was that the police appeal had been launched in Eppstein, with photos of the victim now displayed in public. Felix, who had become increasingly exasperated by their faltering investigation, had pinned all his hopes on the successful outcome of this campaign.

Privately, he was beginning to admit to himself that this particular murder would remain unsolved. Professional, rather than personal, failure was the thing he hated most. And his bad mood was contagious: his colleagues clearly doubted they'd find the solution either. They'd even stopped trying to motivate each other and all joking had ceased. Thus the day ended on an even more bitter note than before.

That evening, Felix went to the local Greek with Django, but managed to prevent himself from drowning his sorrows in alcohol. Even the free ouzo remained untouched.

By Friday, motivation was at an all-time low. As they sat drinking their morning tea, Arno was the first to say he didn't think they had much hope of cracking the case. No-one contradicted him, and Felix knew that DA Cando had been right when he had only given them ten days.

Around lunchtime, a courier parcel arrived from Italy. Commissario Crotone had sent them his findings, as well as further evidence for the task force. More in the hope of distracting himself than uncovering something interesting for their case, Felix decided to leaf through them. Just before he was about to make his way to Hans Werners with the documents, Emilio took him to one side.

"Mama's inviting you for lunch on Saturday, we'll be there too. It'd be good if you could make it, then we can talk in private."

Felix agreed to the invitation and wished them all a good weekend. After handing over the files, he wanted to go straight home and get his apartment into shape, but first he had to do some shopping. Django was very fussy when it came to the household, and always mewed angrily if Felix let things get out of hand. The chief inspector laughed at the thoughts going through his mind: with a cat like that, who needs a woman?

In contrast with his own department, members of the task force were extremely satisfied, as their assignment was already drawing to a close. The documents from Italy were gratefully received. In response to Inspector Werners' question about the state of the murder investigation, Felix explained that things had stalled, before outlining the most recent steps they had taken.

Hans placed a hand on his shoulder.

"Sorry to hear that, but sometimes you can do everything right and still not get a result. Only thing you can do is wait and see if old Inspector Chance gives you a helping hand. Maybe another witness will turn up."

"Yeah, that's my last hope. I hate it when a killer slips through the net," Felix muttered.

"Don't give up. Yesterday I heard about a murder in Munich they finally solved after nineteen years. We catch them all in the end."

Chapter 26

Having spent the previous evening shopping and cleaning his apartment like mad, Felix was going stir-crazy by Saturday morning. Phone already in hand, he had even thought about calling his ex-wife for a split second.

Then, at the last moment, he had forced himself to reconsider and headed to the office with Django instead. Once there, he leafed through the files again half-heartedly and stared at the photos of Uwe Kaptain's corpse taken at the crime scene.

"What have I been overlooking? How did you spend your final hours?" he spoke out loud to himself and smashed his fist against the wall in frustration.

Now he was pacing up and down gazing at the photos, but no inspiration was forthcoming. Ultimately, only the sound of his cell phone snapped him out of it.

"Yes," he said.

"Mama's been waiting with the food for half an hour. Where are you? What's wrong?" his friend asked.

The chief inspector slapped himself on the forehead. "Shit, I'm really sorry Emilio! I'm at the office and completely lost track of time. I'll be there in twenty minutes. Ciao!"

With Django tucked under his arm, he hurried out to the car. Fourteen minutes later he was sprinting up the steps. Luccesa embraced and scolded him at the same time.

"Nobody keeps me waiting this long! The pasta's ruined and the fish'll soon be dry."

Then she pretended to give him a slap, before taking him in her arms once more. Felix moved into the dining room, where Emilio was already sitting with Sylvia and the kids.

The little ones made straight for Django, wanting to play with him, but Sylvia ordered them back to the table. As ever, the food was outstanding and Felix forgot everything that was going on around him. Here, it was as if nothing had changed.

Luccesa pinched him on the cheek. "You should've married Carmelita back when she was head over heels in love with you. She'd never have made you so unhappy."

He rolled his eyes. It was true: Emilio's sister had once had a huge crush on him, but that was a long time ago.

"Thanks for keeping it quiet! Maybe it's a good thing you're on the right side of the law these days, otherwise you'd have had a pretty short career," he joked to his friend.

"With you around, for sure." Emilio boxed him playfully in the ribs.

They went out to Luccesa's balcony and were standing in the sun, while Felix told his partner everything.

"If Petra really is incapable of committing to a relationship, then you should be happy it ended when it did, and not years down the line."

"Maybe she just didn't want to hurt my feelings," Felix sighed.

"Whatever, just suck it up! You know you always have friends here, and there'll be other women. Right now, it's spring and that's no time to be moping around." Emilio pointed to the street, where two young women were walking past.

Felix understood. "You're right. Now come on, let's talk about something else. What's happening with you? Got any new gadgets to play with?"

"Not a new gadget exactly, but I saw something in a renewable energy magazine recently that's really cool. It wouldn't only be a way of replacing current electric charging stations; but something that was aesthetically pleasing at the same time. It would help give the headquarters a real makeover, as well as generating tons of publicity and securing our status once and for all as ecological trail-blazers," his friend began, eyes sparkling.

"I'm in agony here – what is it?"

"I think it's awesome – it's called 'Point.One' and it's a so-lar charging station with totally futuristic architecture," Emilio beamed. "It already won a major competition. The design's a trib-ute to the gas stations of the 1950s, which made such an important contribution to the success of the motor car when they became places where young people could hang out at night. You know,

266

like in the James Dean films. It was all the rage back then. The people from Eight – the company that's developed this technology – believe that we need to create similar excitement among today's generation Y in order for EVs to enjoy the same level of success. Charging stations that are effective but just plain square won't make the grade any longer."

To emphasize his point, Emilio went to get the magazine, which carried a full-page spread complete with photo.

"I have to say it does look pretty good. But I very much doubt we'll be able to persuade the powers that be to go along with it. After all, it's a police station, not an entertainment center," Felix countered.

"But that's exactly what might help us get rid of our stuffy reputation," his friend argued. "It could do those old farts upstairs a real favor. Any leftover solar energy can be fed back into the power grid or buffered in an integrated battery storage system – at least, that's the plan. Throw inductive charging technology into the mix and…"

Emilio's enthusiasm for his latest discovery helped Felix forget all about his problems; and it wasn't until after dinner that he finally headed back to his apartment to watch TV with Django.

Felix spent the entire Sunday morning in bed contemplating life. He thought about Christine, his ex-wife, and Petra, and realized that the pain of their split was already abating.

That was a good sign, so he got up and took a hot shower, singing at the top of his lungs. He considered heading to the office again, before deciding to go to the victim's apartment instead. It would soon be declassified and cleared accordingly. But maybe it could still provide a moment's inspiration.

Around half three, he opened the door, sat down on the victim's sofa and let his gaze wander through the apartment.

"Who are you and what's your secret? We both want to bring your killer to justice, so come on; throw me a bone here!" Felix said what he was thinking out loud.

For half an hour he remained sitting there, allowing the apartment to wash over him. Then he went from room to room, observing their interior: the furniture, the layout. He opened various cupboards but still the dead man remained a mystery to him. Just as he was leaving the apartment, pulling the door behind him as he went, he was confronted by a man on the stairwell gazing at him in surprise.

"May I ask what business you have here?"

Felix flashed his ID and introduced himself. "And who are you? I've never seen you before either."

"I am the janitor, Rosen."

"Yes, I remember, Mrs. Schumm mentioned you right at the start of our investigation. You were on vacation."

"That's right. And you're investigating the murder of Uwe Kaptain? Know anything about this appeal?" Rosen produced a folded piece of paper from his trouser pocket. It was the notice they had ordered to be distributed around Eppstein.

"Where did you get this from?" Felix felt his hunting instincts being stirred. Was this the lead they'd been chasing for so long?

"My sister lives in Eppstein with her family and I visit her once a month, just like today. Then I saw this notice. I was going to call you first thing tomorrow morning, but since you're already here, I can tell you now."

"If I remember correctly, you live here in the building? Why don't we go to your apartment?"

The janitor nodded and pressed on ahead. His apartment was quite a lot smaller than the others in the complex and, for a bachelor flat – Felix couldn't see any sign of female habitation –, almost pedantically tidy. In truth, it lacked a little life, a little charm.

"Would you like something to drink?" Rosen showed the inspector to the kitchen table.

"A cup of tea, if you have it."

"I'm afraid I can only offer you fruit tea."

"That's fine."

While the janitor boiled the kettle, the chief inspector waited to hear what he had to say with bated breath.

Finally he sat down next to Felix and slurped his coffee.

"So, I was going to call you because I saw Kaptain in Eppstein about a year ago. No, that's not quite true. What actually happened is I saw his BMW sitting in an open garage in the street parallel to my sister's. A man, who I hadn't seen before, closed the garage and disappeared into the house. But I was pretty sure it was Kaptain's car. I talked to him about it the next time I saw him, but he denied it flat out, said he'd never been to Eppstein, didn't know anyone there. Still, like I said, I was sure. In the end Kaptain was so firm, so annoyed even, that I said I must have been mistaken. We never spoke about it again and I never saw him in Eppstein after that. However, I thought it might interest you."

Chief Inspector Büschelberger had listened in stunned silence.

"Can you give me the address?"

"Of course, 9 Taunusgasse."

"And do you know who lives there?"

"No, but my sister said the man's a bit strange. He lives on his own; no-one's ever seen a woman there. In banking somehow, my sister says, but she doesn't know anything else."

In Felix's mind's eye, the puzzle was beginning to fall into place. A banker and the kickbacks they hadn't been able to find. The journey to Eppstein on the night of the murder. That was their lead, no doubt about it. He leapt to his feet, feeling completely reinvigorated.

"Thank you so much, you've been a real help! If you'd be so kind as to drop by in the next few days so we can take a statement? I'm afraid I have to go now!"

He left his card and stormed down the steps, his cell phone already in hand, fingers speed-dialing Emilio's number. But then he thought better of it and broke off the connection: the last thing he wanted was to ruin his partner's weekend. If Felix knew Emilio, he'd have been in Eppstein like a shot. Still, this couldn't wait until tomorrow. He'd have to go alone.

The house at 9 Taunusgasse was extremely well looked after. There was a fashionable Japanese rock garden out front, which took Felix up to the main door.

Constantin Levin, read the name on the panel. The chief inspector pushed the buzzer, a Big Ben style chime sounded from within, and the door was opened by a casually dressed man in his late thirties.

He had short, blond hair and his brown eyes surveyed Felix critically. "I assume you're from the police. Please come in, I've been expecting you."

Astonished, Felix followed the man through a large entrance hall into a very tastefully arranged living room, which looked as if it had been imported straight from a Spanish finca.

Levin sat down in a light brown leather sofa and motioned for the chief inspector to do the same. "Would you like something to drink? I need a strong cognac before we get started."

Felix politely declined, but could scarcely contain his curiosity any longer. "Mr. Levin, how did you know the police would be paying you a visit?"

"I saw the notice and knew it wouldn't be long until someone came here asking about Uwe."

"You were a friend of his, then?" The fact that Levin had called the victim by his first name had not escaped the chief inspector.

Levin knocked back his cognac and, poured himself another right away. "We were lovers. You know Uwe was gay, don't you?"

"Yes. But why didn't you call us? If my significant other was murdered, I'd go straight to the police and give them all the help I could!"

"Two reasons. First, it wasn't murder and second, Uwe died here in this room," Levin replied.

"What do you mean, it wasn't murder? Of course he was murdered. Someone put poison in his red wine," Felix said.

"Not someone: he bought the poison himself, then put it in the wine and drank it."

"You're trying to tell me it was suicide? Then surely you should have come to us right away?"

"No," Levin shook his head sadly and took another swig of cognac. "I'm not saying it was suicide. Someone was supposed to be killed that night. Not him, though: me. I was the intended victim."

Felix's head was spinning. He had no idea what was going on. "Sorry, I don't understand what you're trying to say. Perhaps we should continue this conversation down at the station!" he said forcefully.

"Please, Inspector. Just let me explain. Then you can decide what to do with me. I've already written and signed a statement. It's in the brown envelope there in front of you." Levin pointed towards the table.

The chief inspector reached for the envelope and opened it. It contained five sides of typed script, dated and signed by Constantin Levin. It had been written the same day Kaptain died.

"You've been keeping your statement here since your lover died, without a single word to the police? This I can't wait to hear!"

"OK, Inspector, but before I begin: are you sure you don't want a cognac after all? Something else perhaps?"

Felix considered for a minute. How dangerous was this Levin? Would he try to poison him as well? Felix rejected the notion as ridiculous. "Why not, I'll have a cognac, but only a little one. And by the way, it's Chief Inspector." He showed his ID.

Levin got a second glass and poured a small measure. At once, Felix realized he was drinking an expensive cognac, one that he couldn't afford.

"Why don't you start again from the beginning? Tell me how you knew each other, about your relationship, whether there was even a professional dimension to it; then I want to hear exactly how Kaptain died."

Felix nodded towards Levin, leaning back casually as the witness began to tell his story.

"I met Uwe in the Blue Boy, a high-end gay club in the city, much classier than all those other joints. That was about two and a half years ago, and we hit it off right away. It wasn't long before we were together."

"So you were in a steady relationship with Kaptain for over two years? You do know he was a regular on the Frankfurt hustler scene, don't you?" Felix interjected.

"Yes, I know. Uwe could be pretty insatiable, and since I loved him, and didn't want to lose him, I put up with it. Anyway, he promised he'd look after himself, use condoms."

Levin fell silent, deep in contemplation. Chief Inspector Büschelberger motioned for him to continue.

"After we'd been together for about three months, Uwe asked if I could help him: he needed to divert some funds abroad, by-pass the tax system. That's my job, you see – I transfer client funds abroad. I don't ask whether it's money made illegally; I just give clients the necessary papers so they can fill out their tax returns. And if they don't, well then it's not my problem."

"How much money did you divert, for Kaptain I mean?" the chief inspector probed.

"About twenty million euros in total, half of it to Switzerland. They still have the safest banks in the world, you should know that."

"I'll bear it in mind."

"You really must, Chief Inspector, there's nowhere safer for your money! But, back to your question, I also transferred five mil-lion to Luxemburg and another five to Bermuda. Diversification - minimizes the risk of loss if you get busted," Levin explained.

"Dr. Zimmer claimed that Kaptain received fifty million for his part in the illegal waste disposal. So what happened to the rest?"

"I don't think Uwe earned that much. This guy Zimmer is probably lying to you, hoping to keep the other thirty million for himself."

"That wouldn't be out of character. Did you know where the money came from?"

"Not at first, no. But when there was more and more, I asked and eventually Uwe told me. He was pretty drunk at the time – and I'm sure he regretted it afterwards. Anyway, things were sort of cooling off between us, not from my side, but from his. That's when he started visiting hustlers again. But, like I said, I didn't want to lose him. Exactly two months ago we had a huge fight. He want-ed to break up for good, and in my despair I threatened to blow the whistle on him if he left me. After that he scarpered, though he called me later to say we shouldn't jump the gun, he still loved me, and all that. He promised he'd move heaven and earth for me, and suggested that we met the following Sunday - then everything would be back to normal. I asked why we needed to wait a week, but he just said he had to go abroad, it just wasn't possible before. Then on the Sunday night he came round between nine and ten.

We talked for a long time; he'd brought a very expensive bottle of wine. It was his favorite: a Romitorio di Santedame."

Levin sipped his cognac thoughtfully before continuing.

"Uwe wanted to have it straightaway but I wasn't in the mood, so we made love first. Afterwards I got up to cut a few slices of salmon. In the meantime, Uwe had opened the wine and poured it into two glasses. When I came back into the living room, he was sitting here, where I'm sitting now, with glass in hand. Mine was over by you. We were just about to toast, when I realized I'd forgotten the horseradish. Uwe would only eat a particular brand. I stood up to get it but then Uwe said he'd go instead. While I was waiting, I noticed that the rim of his glass was chipped. And as Uwe was always really sensitive about stuff like that I swapped them over. I didn't think anything of it."

He shrugged his shoulders, as if to lend weight to what he'd just said.

"When he returned, he just said we should drink to our second chance, which we did. Afterwards he was looking at me really intently. Delighted that we were together again, I made another toast and we drained our glasses. Uwe sat back in this chair; he looked so happy. But then all of a sudden, he started acting strangely, slurring his words. Not that he was drunk, just miles away somehow. I thought he was kidding around. He pointed at me, all weird now, and asked if I'd switched the glasses. I just said yes, that the rim of his was chipped. Then he just gave a brief laugh and said: 'You stupid asshole!' before collapsing into his chair."

Levin paused for a moment, clearly struggling.

"What happened next?" Felix asked.

"At first I didn't understand what was going on. What did he mean? Why was he behaving so strangely? It wasn't funny anymore. So I had a bit of a go at him, told him enough was enough. But then I saw that he wasn't moving anymore and went over to give him a good shake, but he didn't react. I tried to get him on the floor, raise his legs in order to stabilize circulation. Suddenly a little bottle rolled out of his jacket; there was a long chemical name with a skull and crossbones under it. At that moment I understood. So there I was just sitting next him, my boyfriend who's dying, just crying my eyes out. When I'd pulled myself together, I checked his pulse but there was nothing. Then I held a pocket mirror under his nose, no steam either. A wave of panic came over me and I ran for my phone in order to call an ambulance – and the police. However, once I had the cell in my hand, I asked myself who'd believe me. I spent about two hours just sitting here, thinking about what to do. Then I carried him out to his car, grabbed the garden hose and drove to the east port in Frankfurt, where I staged his suicide. I had my rollerblades with me and skated to the train station, before taking a bus back to Eppstein."

Levin fell silent and waited for Felix to say something. But there was nothing forthcoming. The chief inspector simply couldn't believe what he'd just heard – even if his instincts told him it was the truth. Instead, he was wondering what his colleagues would think.

He shook his head. "Mr. Levin, you are aware that your story is quite simply unbelievable. In fact, it's so bizarre I doubt you could make it up. That's why I'd like another cognac before I ask you anything else."

"Of course!" Levin poured them both another drink. "I still don't understand it myself, seven weeks later. What was he thinking? Did he really want to kill me just so he could continue with his illegal deals?" he asked, still bemused.

"Let's just say people are not always good by nature. I've encountered a lot of evil in my time." The chief inspector paused. "And I won't deny that you're still in the frame. You could easily have killed your boyfriend in order to get at his money. After all, you're the only one who knows where it is. However, it's also a fact that the poison was ordered through the victim's company, which would point to you having an accomplice."

Levin swirled the cognac in his glass and looked the chief inspector straight in the eye. "If you truly believed that, then you'd never have said it. What I don't understand is why you came here alone. Pretty dangerous move, if you had me down as the killer."

"You're probably right. I might have bent a few rules, but I never expected to hear all these revelations. Everything you told me, it's written here?" Felix held the envelope aloft.

"Yes, it's exactly the same. I wrote and signed it on the Monday evening, straight after Uwe's death. It's a kind of confession: I studied law before moving into finance, you know," Levin replied.

"Fine. I won't arrest you but you need to come to the station tomorrow morning and talk to the district attorney. He'll decide whether you're guilty of any crime, and if you have to go to jail or not."

"Is tomorrow afternoon OK? I've got an important client meeting in the morning."

Felix nodded. "I think I can allow that. Come around three. Now I just need to check your personal details for form's sake."

He took down the number on Levin's ID and started on his way, but the witness held him back at the door.

"There's something else that proves I didn't do it. I don't have any power of attorney on his bank accounts. So I couldn't access the money even if I wanted to."

"If that's true, then you're in a strong position," Felix said as he left, still dumbfounded by the unexpected resolution of the case.

Chapter 27

The next morning, Felix bought a cake on his way to the office: a chocolate pear tart. After all, the team had reason to celebrate. Emilio, Frauke, Arno, and Kevin were already there, sipping their tea.

"Morning. Great that you're all here. I have some good news, and a tart to make it taste even sweeter."

"Did you win the lottery? Or make up with Petra?" Frauke beamed.

"Neither, unfortunately. But I did solve the case. I know who has Uwe Kaptain's death on their conscience," he said.

In the silence that followed, you could have heard a pin drop.

"Come on, don't keep us in suspense; who was it?" Kevin was the first to rediscover his voice.

"The person behind Uwe Kaptain's death was – Uwe Kaptain."

"You never listen to me, do you? We talked about this right at the start, it couldn't have been suicide," the pathologist countered.

"I never said it was suicide. Kaptain wasn't trying to kill himself, but his boyfriend – who he thought was about to blow his cover. By a twist of fate, maybe even a higher form of justice, he consumed the poison himself."

Suddenly everyone was talking over one another.

"I don't believe it!"

"How did you come up with that?"

"Who's this dubious boyfriend?"

Once the storm had died down, the chief inspector smiled quietly to himself and produced Constantin Levin's confession from his pocket. "It's all here."

With that, he began to replay the events of the previous day. Although initially irritated that he'd gone to Eppstein alone, by the end his colleagues were hanging on his every word.

An hour later, Felix started cutting the tart. "Come on then, I didn't buy this for nothing."

Even Kevin Dour, who had been due in Forensics a long time ago, couldn't tear himself away. "If that's true, it's the best joke I've heard all year."

"I admit it's a strange story. But not nearly as strange as the fact that you haven't lit up a single time since you've been here," came the retort.

"Well, I'm trying to give up."

All eyes turned on the pathologist.

"You've stopped smoking?" Emilio uttered in disbelief.

"It's like Mark Twain said: 'Giving up smoking is the easiest thing in the world. I know, because I've done it thousands of times.' I promised myself I'd have another go, even if I miss the nicotine already. Luckily there are more than enough ways to compensate." Kevin stuffed his mouth full of tart. "Maybe I should try an electronic cigarette – to go with your EV!"

"What's an electronic cigarette? Is there anything that isn't going to be electronic in the future?" Arno looked around the room, shaking his head.

"There are in fact certain parallels. Before the EV, cars used internal combustion engines, and of course, our old friend the cigarette involves combustion too. But while we all know it's nicotine that provides the kick, smoking a tobacco cigarette also exposes you to a number of dangerous substances. In contrast, an e-cigarette is a plastic tube that looks like a filter and houses a heating element, battery, control electronics and a cartridge of liquid containing nicotine. When the smoker inhales, the liquid is vaporized and the smoker receives a nicotine hit. An LED simulates the effect of burning. However, since I'm still unconvinced, besides deciding on a flavor, I'm using patches for the moment." Kevin rolled up his sleeve to show the patch he had stuck to his arm.

"Funny old world!" Felix was astonished. "Soon you'll be one of us!"

"Gotta' go – before you ask any more stupid questions," the pathologist made his exit.

"If anyone else wants to come out with something outlandish, then now's the time. Today, nothing can surprise me anymore," Emilio made no secret of his astonishment.

"I wouldn't have believed it either," the chief inspector agreed.

"Is there some way of checking Levin's story? If it's true, then Kaptain must've ordered the poison himself. Only there's no proof," DI Perfondo tried to steer the conversation back onto the case.

Suddenly he leapt to his feet and shouted: "I've got it!" before sprinting out of the room.

Felix looked at him in amazement, while Arno could only shake his head.

"What the hell is going on today? Did I miss a solar eclipse or something? Why is everyone acting so weird?"

Felix could sympathize all too readily: he had no idea what Emilio was up to.

Ten minutes later, their colleague returned looking very pleased.

"I know how we can prove it. I've just spoken to the IT special-ist at Zimmer Consultancy Ltd. He said Kaptain's PC hasn't been used since his death. That means the purchase order confirmation should still be on his computer. All he needs to do is disconnect it from the company network and turn it back on. He's going to print the order off and fax it through when he finds it. Then he'll mail us the original file."

"Emilio, sometimes you are just brilliant," Felix gave him a quick hug.

It took about twenty minutes for the fax to arrive – and there it was: confirmation that Uwe Kaptain had ordered over one hun-dred grams of benzodiazepine chloral hydrate.

The chief inspector called the DA to inform him of the latest developments; and tell him that Levin would be in at three. Cando was just as surprised as everyone else but promised, nevertheless, to be there for the questioning.

"What a strange little story you've managed to uncover," the DA said, as he appeared at two o'clock. "I could scarcely believe what you were telling me on the phone."

"You're not the only one. But we have a written statement from Levin, as well as proof of the order confirmation on Kap-tain's computer. I think the case is closed."

The chief inspector handed him the statement and the fax, while the DA read them, shaking his head.

"Incredible! Imagine if Kaptain had succeeded. We'd have never known anything about the illegal waste disposal. But instead he lost everything trying to protect himself – and his illegal enterprise," Cando smiled.

"What I'm interested in is whether Levin himself committed a crime?" Felix asked.

"That's a good question; I can't give you a categorical reply. We need to check if there was denial of assistance. Or aiding and abetting after the fact. But in all likelihood, he'll escape without a caution."

After Constantin Levin had been brought in at three, Felix asked whether he had any objections to his colleagues listening in. He didn't, and soon everyone had taken their place in the interview room.

It wasn't necessary for Emilio to take notes, as the statement was already there in writing. The DA simply allowed the witness to repeat what he had said the previous day, without interruption. They all listened spellbound – the chief inspector as fascinated as before – and when Levin had finished, there was silence all around.

"I still have one question, Mr. Levin. Why did you drive Kaptain to the east port and stage his suicide?" Felix asked.

Levin gazed absent-mindedly out of the window, while answering the question. "You know, Chief Inspector, it was a kind of epiphany. As I sat there completely exhausted next to his corpse, and realized that Uwe had meant to kill me, I thought to myself: I'm going to make it look like suicide. I suppose that's what it was in a way – and the view from the east port is so romantic. It was a final farewell to my lost love. Somehow, it just felt right."

After pausing briefly, he continued. "So what happens now? Am I going to jail?"

"No, you can go home. But you should place yourself at our disposal. And before you go, how about naming the accounts you transferred the money into. The Kenyan government will need the funds to help repair the damage to the environment caused by the toxic waste," Cando said, as he handed Levin his card and dismissed him.

Then he turned back towards Felix.

"Finally, two things I thought would be of special interest. First, the area Zimmer and company used to dump the waste is home to an incredibly rare species of toad. The species was already threatened with extinction, and has suffered further losses owing to this episode. Thanks to your work, there's still a chance they could be saved. So we've come full circle. I had a good laugh when I heard about it this morning. Second, your team has been selected for a new pilot project. The days of notice boards and blackboards are drawing to a close. An interactive whiteboard has been purchased for testing purposes. It enables you to collate all data for the case you're working on without the use of paper. All electronic: everything can be saved or sent at the touch of a button. And you'll be the first unit in the whole of Hesse to have one."

"Wow!" Emilio's eyes sparkled. "Do you know which model we're getting?"

"If I remember correctly, it's the interactive whiteboard system from Smart Technology – the premium version at that. The company's products are used in Canada and the US by various investigation authorities, the FBI among them. See it as a kind of reward, for generating such good publicity with the Don Veschie case. Besides, I'm pretty sure Emilio here already knows how to operate it. If it makes investigations run more efficiently, then we'll be introducing it in several other departments."

While Cando was still speaking, Inspector Perfondo had googled the model on his tablet and couldn't resist a little cry of joy.

"Awesome, what this thing can do! We can create a network, send data to every PC. It's even got digital ink and--"

"What in God's name is digital ink?" the chief inspector looked towards his colleague, completely bewildered.

"You can be so old-fashioned sometimes! Imagine we receive photos or reports connected to a case. As soon as they're available electronically and appear on the board, you can use your fingers to add stuff, draw circles; you can even make notes and save everything so that the changes you've made are still there the next day. It's like using a permanent marker to write on the photos we'd usually have pinned to the board. Because of the network, we no longer have to make copies, since everyone's got them on their computer. That's what really sets it apart: the network. If we're out and about, I can use my tablet to take photos and highlight certain aspects. Then because the board's online, the others back at the station can look at the images and start investigating straightaway. Along with the Cloud, it's what I call state-of-the-art crime fighting!"

"This board can do all this? Do we need pens or anything?" Felix asked.

"No, you can just use your fingers to write, or draw arrows if you're trying to make a link."

"And you can erase stuff digitally as well?"

"Of course, you do it with a pen. The system knows what it is, even if it makes no difference to you."

Emilio turned towards Cando. "One question: who else is connected? Is it just us? Because otherwise we wouldn't be maximizing the system's potential."

"Good point. No, the plan is for me to have access to the data as well, so that I can connect to the electronic board via the intranet. That way, I'll be able to ask for progress reports online, and save us all this toing and froing."

The excitement was clearly etched on Emilio's face.

"Way I see it, you've got everything under control here – and Emilio, I'm sure you'll have a lot of fun with it. Gentlemen," Cando left the room.

"After all these years, you've finally got your wish: we're all eco-warriors and techno-freaks now," Frauke's remark was greeted by laughter all around.

After Felix and his team had written their final report, they called it a night and left the station together. The chief inspector was just about to invite everyone for a drink, when he saw Kevin Dour hovering by the door.

"Well hello, are you hoping to switch departments or something? How come you're here again?" he teased.

"Oh no, I'm just picking up Frauke."

Kevin took Frauke in his arms and kissed her, before the two of them made their way laughing and joking out into the evening air. Felix, Emilio and Arno just stood there open-mouthed.

"Frauke and Kevin: I don't believe it. How long's it been going on? And why didn't we notice anything? Felix turned to face his two colleagues but all they could do was shrug.

"So, what do you say we end this day of surprises accordingly? Who's in for some wine and cheese at a local bar?"

Together the trio headed out in their Focus towards Sachsenhausen, safe in the knowledge that their next case would be upon them soon enough.

ALSO BY CAPSCOVIL

MATTHEW HART
The Last Iteration of Dexter Maxwell
*

Publication in December 2012

Available in print (ISBN 978-3-942358-30-9, perfect paperback) and as electronic edition for various reading devices and platforms.

Adventurous Science Fiction Seasoned with Sustainability

Dex knows first hand that living on the edge of civilization in Grenver, Colorado is tough. But it also has its perks. With his small league of rebels, he has pulled off some of the most brazen acts of the 22nd Century to snarl the system. Not bad for an orphan sewer rat, another un-nationalized civilian that can´t afford to get a citizen chip implanted.

Dex doesn´t care about his missing memory of early childhood before the orphanage or about most likely ending up on ice like all the other crims. No past, no future: no problem. As long as he has his friends and his mischief, he's going to be alright.

But after a botched stunt, Dex wakes up to find himself in a brutal, foreign underground city—blind, with a sword strapped to his back, and an old man telling him he's the final ingredient for a revolution.

Dex can barely start to take it all in before he's on the run, hunted by deadly assassins, looking for answers, and somehow imbued with skills he shouldn't have. Before he knows it, he finds himself in the center of a plot a millennium in the making, with the fate of two worlds at stake.

Start an exciting and adventurous journey with THE LAST ITERATION OF DEXTER MAXWELL to find out who Dexter Maxwell really is.

Connect with the author: http://about.me/hartmatthew

Alice N. York
GAME
FAINT SIGNALS

Published in May 2011, available in print (ISBN 978-3-942358-08-8, perfect paperback) and as electronic edition for various reading devices and platforms.

Delicate Career Novel With Smart Solar Ideas

Alex leads a thoroughly contented life. In Sandro she has found the right man, and the new consultancy job at a leading solar company seems tailor-made for her.

In no time, she familiarises herself with the technology and establishes a complex network incorporating both external partners and prospective clients, as well as various departments within the intricate company organisational structure. Developing long-term strategies and innovational product ideas is just as inspiring for her as implementing them practically. In addition, business trips to globally operating clients offer Alex an insight into different cultures, taking her to fascinating cities along the way. Winning new projects with innovative, successful solutions quickly enables her to gain the respect of her superiors.

As time goes by, however, her existence begins to resemble a rollercoaster ride. Grave events in her private life result in Alex throwing herself ever deeper into work. Yet slowly but surely menacing clouds are gathering there too. Alex does everything in her power to retain control. But like a game of poker, she is constantly being dealt a new hand; and no-one quite knows who holds the aces.

***

„Alice N. York portrays life in the workplace with extraordinary accuracy"
Ebersberger Zeitung

***

Follow Alex how she plays the game to win. Until the rules change and the world turns ruthless...

Chapter 1

//

January

Before Alex entered the PsoraCom building through the automatic double doors, she turned once more to Sandro. He sat in his slightly dented, red Hyundai and blew her a good luck kiss.

"In bocca al lupo!" he cried in Italian, wishing her luck in the would-be lion's den. "Crepi!" came the obligatory, smiling response – although of course she didn't seriously hope he would die.

She squared her shoulders and made her way confidently to the reception, asking politely for Thomas. For her first day at work she had decided on a plain black suit with a white blouse and flat, black patent leather lace-ups. She always felt good in this outfit because it was classic: not too feminine, but rather business-like and professional. Besides, black contrasted nicely with her copper-red hair, and Alex had never been that into skirts. Even as a child she had loved lederhosen and jeans because whenever she cycled, climbed trees or played football, dresses had just got in the way.

In her professional life she had encountered some women who displayed their feminine charms provocatively in order to achieve their goals. Alex had never understood the logic behind this. Despite being only five foot five she almost never wore heels, even though she thought they looked really good with suits. Unfortunately she couldn't walk in them for very long.

While she attached her visitor badge and waited, she marvelled once more at the imposing, modern lobby, which seemed to be made completely of glass. Actually the exterior consisted entirely of solar modules, the electricity generated from which was fed into the company's own energy network. "Building-integrated photovoltaics" was the name of this concept, she remembered. The solar modules were part of the building itself. The reception area was oval shaped, a good 1000 square feet, with a counter in the centre underneath a dome-like cupola. PsoraCom's fir-green company colours stood in direct contrast to the breezy transparency of the glass. Three women dressed elegantly in green uniforms attended to visitors. Some distance to the right of the counter, surrounded by an oasis of palms, were a few dark-green wing chairs and small plain chrome tables. Behind the counter, in front of the passage through to the building, there was a biometric scanner similar to those at airport security. To the left stood high bistro tables, amply spaced. Only these weren't just tables, but highly developed pieces of computer furniture whose entire surfaces doubled as touch-sensitive screens. Visitors could surf the net while they waited, or watch the latest updates from PsoraCom as they hovered in holographic 3D above the tables.

Thomas, her new boss, picked her up from reception. He was a good head taller than her and looked as though he had sprung straight from the glossy catalogue of a luxury gentlemen's outfitter. She guessed that he was probably in his mid-forties although there was not a single strand of grey in his black hair. He was sportily elegant and dressed in a classic double-breasted suit with a white shirt and grey pullover. Calmly, he came towards her.

"Good morning. I trust you had a good journey."

Despite the polite greeting, she found him just as impenetrable as she had at her interview a few months before. He was the type of person who was difficult to read. Not that he looked at her in an unfriendly way, just seriously and without any discernible emotion.

"Good morning. Yes, thanks. I didn't have far to go."

The biometric scanner briefly flashed green as Thomas led her through into the hallway, which forked a little further on into two double-storey corridors. Just as in the lobby, everything was solar-glazed and very bright. They took the left-hand corridor past the bright meeting rooms that Alex already knew from her first visit.

At the end of the corridor, past the glass elevator to the upper storey, they reached an enormous open-plan office. All the outer walls were made of pale-coloured solar modules and the approximately 25-foot-high ceiling furnished the room with sufficient air. A good hundred workstations had been set up in a circular arrangement, like a honeycomb in a hive, separated only by head-high walls of tinted glass that offered a little privacy from one's neighbour. While Thomas took Alex to his cubicle, she noticed that there was an outer and an inner circle, both of which were broken in four places by a gangway, dividing the room into eight segments in total. At each crossing there was a sign with the names of the people who sat in that particular segment. In the middle of the inner circle there was a colossal sculpture that looked like the pointed apex of a cone.

"Inside are encapsulated rooms for secret strategy meetings," explained her boss as they walked past.

There was a free space opposite his cubicle which she could use for the time being. Alex wouldn't be allocated a desk in the office; she would work from home. This was not at all unusual: indeed many companies saw cost benefits in staff working from home. Field managers were with clients most of the time anyway – at least, that's what was expected of them. All the members of her team worked from home; only Thomas, as group leader, preferred a designated desk in the office building.

Alex put her bag down and Thomas led her back to a small room next to the elevator. There were coffee and drinks machines, as well as a few tables with ashtrays on them. It was highly unusual for an American company to have a smokers' room. Nevertheless, the tables were equipped with mushroom-shaped suction units, which ensured that there was no lingering smell of cold smoke. Coffee of all kinds, from espresso to latte macchiato, as well as tea and non-alcoholic drinks, were available to employees free of cost. The company probably hoped this would encourage them to work longer hours. After both of them had taken what they wanted, he accompanied her to the IT department.

"This is where new employees get their laptop and an IT systems briefing," he said. "Everyone is on first name terms here by the way," he added. "Come back to me when you're finished and I'll give you a tour of the office."

He turned round abruptly and seemed almost happy to be rid of her for a while.

After an hour she went back to Thomas. He led her through the entire office on the ground floor and explained where Sales and Marketing and New Businesses were located. Whenever they met a colleague, he introduced Alex immediately. As time went on, she found it increasingly difficult to remember all the names, let alone their positions. On the first floor they found the design and development, book-keeping and legal departments. After the tour there was still enough time for Alex to collect her company car and home office equipment.

"Let's meet in the canteen for lunch," said Thomas, after he had left her with the relevant colleague.

The facility manager was in her early fifties and told Alex that she had previously worked as a self-employed office clerk.

"I always took care of whatever my clients asked of me and became the go-to girl for everything, so to speak. PsoraCom was one of my first clients and after the company's explosive growth they made me a very generous takeover offer. The good thing about the job is that I can afford to work just half days."

That explained the state of her desk, perhaps: it was overflowing with all sorts of different papers, and she seemed to be a genius in chaos.

"Do you need a mobile?" she asked.

"Yes," replied Alex. "But I'd like a Zeus68. Since I work in New Businesses, I should have the latest kind of netphone."

"No problem," said the facility manager. "I'll order you one. It should be here by tomorrow."

Alex loved new gadgets and would have bought one for herself anyway. Currently the Zeus68 was the only netphone with integrated thin-film solar cells.

Next they put together Alex's employee ID. Unlike the temporary visitor badges, this wasn't just a piece of plastic. PsoraCom highly valued the use of the latest technology and new employees were given a corporate accessory pack comprising a watch, bracelet, necklace and earrings. Each of these objects was a combination of plain but high-grade leather with beaded gold or silver, and included an integrated microchip containing all personal and biometric details. If lost, the items could not be misused. The microchip generated its electricity using body heat, or rather by using a thermo-generator, which exploited the differences between ambient and body temperature. If you took your watch off, the chip was deactivated; it could only be reactivated by an integrated voice sensor. If you lost it, it would be of no use to anybody else, other than as a nice piece of jewellery.

In order to programme the sensor, they needed to record Alex's voice. Being somewhat vain, it took her three attempts. But that was nothing compared with some of her other colleagues, the facility manager smiled kindly.

Afterwards it was time for lunch and together they made their way back to the reception area, taking the right-hand corridor at the V-shaped fork, which also led into a big, round room. The canteen took up the front quarter, with the research department in a cordoned section further back. Work there was top secret and only certain people were allowed access to this area.

"Hey, listen, I know your surname from somewhere," began her colleague unexpectedly. "You're not related to Franz Ruby are you? I worked for him before I became self-employed."

"Yes, Franz is my father," replied Alex, astounded. "Do you still remember him?"

"Of course I do, we worked together for a few years in an office by the station."

"I can still remember that office," Alex smiled. "My dad used to take me there occasionally during the school holidays. I must have been eleven or twelve. The thing I remember most is the big fridge with lots of coke cans. They were for clients, of course, but you could always take a few, and since we didn't have coke at home I didn't hold back."

"I wish I had such fond memories," laughed her colleague. "I remember one time when a colleague of Franz's had a rip in his trouser seam just before a client meeting. Very unprofessionally, we used a stapler to mend it. After the meeting he came and told us that the whole time he had felt like a fakir."

Thomas came into the canteen shortly afterwards and explained that the food was subsidised. There were various round counters with wooden roofs located on the left-hand side. Each counter offered different dishes, ranging from Asian, Italian and American, right through to vegetarian and traditional fare or just fresh salad.

There was no fixed seating plan so they sat down at a long table. Several people had already taken their place. All of them worked in Sales and Marketing. However, none of them were from Alex's team. They greeted her pleasantly and some of them asked what she was responsible for at PsoraCom.

"I've been hired as part of the new Vabilmo team to work as a consultant for a select group of solar plant manufacturers. I've been in the power plant and energy sector for a long time and I'm really looking forward to viewing everything from the perspective of the solar industry."

Her colleagues nodded appreciatively.

"That sounds very exciting – best of luck," said one of them.

PsoraCom were the market leader for solar cells. Originally their photovoltaic cells were made from pure silicon. In company factories, solar cells were still made from big silicon chips, also known as wafers, and then used by PsoraCom's customers to build larger solar modules. In turn, plant manufacturers combined many electrically connected solar modules to build power plants.

However, the manufacture of crystalline silicon solar cells was expensive and used up too much energy; alternative products were therefore being sought. Alongside thin-film, concentrator and dye-sensitised solar cells, there was now Vabilmo: a new sector that aimed to be more cost effective and energy efficient when it came to mass production. Here, solar cells were processed using organic solutions. The cells were razor-thin and as flexible as film, enabling the assembly of completely new configurations, which, together with the reduction in weight, would result in considerable savings.

In the first instance, PsoraCom saw two principal markets for these polymer cells. There were the traditional solar plant manufacturers, who built both grid-connected plants and off-grid systems; and then there were the companies who made robots. These robots ranged from complex machines in the production industry to machines built for specific tasks, and even simple household robots that could cook, iron or mow the lawn.

Based on these twin approaches, their basic aims were to increase the efficiency of solar power plants and to reduce robot energy requirements, thus lowering cost. Once the polymer cells were market-ready, contracts needed to be won from suitable clients because the implementation stage would take one to three years, depending on the size and nature of the project. Only if the new solar cells were widely used in the industry could appreciable savings be made.

For this kind of product launch, PsoraCom adopted a two-fold strategy. First there was direct sales – the classic approach, which allowed the company to speak to solar module manufacturers. In order to generate revenue, they had to be steered away from the currently employed solar cells and convinced to use the polymer cells (internally code-named "Vabilmo"). Second, PsoraCom also had an indirect sales unit made up of consultants whose objective it was to influence new market trends. The consultants worked together with end customers - that is, plant and robot manufacturers -, analysed processes, delivered strategy recommendations and assisted in the transfer of knowledge.

Their job was to make sure end customers would buy from module manufacturers who used PsoraCom's polymer cells.

In the past few years Alex had learned everything there was to know about power stations. It was her long-standing knowledge and experience that had got her the job. At least that's what Thomas had said.

The task of the Vabilmo team was to concentrate exclusively on the potential market for polymer-based solar cells. Aside from Alex, the team consisted of an additional consultant, a colleague from direct sales and a developer who worked on new concepts for the configuration of the solar modules. As yet, Alex had only met Brian – the other consultant – at the interview. She was scheduled to have a joint strategy meeting with him and Thomas in the afternoon. The meeting would also serve as a training session on existing activities of the Vabilmo team.

Lunch went by in a flash. Alex was delighted by the warm welcome and the keen interest her new colleagues had shown in her. Somehow, she immediately felt as if she belonged. After lunch she accompanied Thomas to one of the conference rooms on the ground floor, which was elegantly furnished with black gloss marble tiles, a large, round polished wood table and high-backed, fir-green leather chairs. Everything in the room could be controlled by a touch screen device which stood on the table. Besides the obligatory air-conditioning, telephone system and Bonsai data projector, the device also boasted the controls for a large plasma screen with an integrated webcam for video conferences.

Brian followed closely behind and greeted them both with a jovial "Hello". At five foot nine, he was not only smaller than Thomas; his whole appearance stood in stark contrast to him...

***

Connect with the author: http://about.me/yorkalice

www.ingramcontent.com/pod-product-compliance
Lightning Source LLC
Chambersburg PA
CBHW030350020726
47493CB00003B/760